He looked even better now at thirty-four than he had at seventeen.

And yep, right on cue, as she took in the two-day stubble on his square jaw, the fine laugh lines around his mesmerizing eyes and the effortlessly charming smile, she melted like a glob of butter on a stack of pancakes.

"What?" he asked.

She studied his big, wet, gorgeous self and slowly shook her head. "Why couldn't you have gone bald or gotten fat? The least you can do is burp or scratch an impolite body part, or something equally unattractive."

His smile came slow and sure.

"*What?*" Tara asked.

"You want to jump me."

God, yes. "Look, I have bigger problems than this, okay?"

Ford looked at her for a beat, then stepped into her space, crowding her up against the wall of the marina building. "I can give you something to take your mind off your other problems," he said in a silky promise.

There was no doubt in her mind.

Sensing capitulation, he pressed his mouth to the underside of her jaw. "Just say the word."

Praise for
Jill Shalvis
and Simply Irresistible

"Shalvis writes with humor, heart, and sizzling heat!"
**—Carly Phillips, *New York Times*
bestselling author**

"Heartwarming and sexy…an abundance of chemistry, smoldering romance, and hilarious sisterly antics."
—*Publishers Weekly*

"A Jill Shalvis hero is the stuff naughty dreams are made of."
**—Vicki Lewis Thompson, *New York Times*
bestselling author of *Chick with a Charm***

"Jill Shalvis has the incredible talent for creating characters who are intelligent, quick-witted, and gorgeously sexy, all the while giving them just the right amount of weakness to keep them from being unrealistically perfect."
—RomanceJunkies.com

"Witty, fun, and sexy—the perfect romance!"
**—Lori Foster, *New York Times*
bestselling author of *Back in Black***

"Ms. Shalvis's characters leap off the page."
—*RT Book Reviews*

"Fast-paced and deliciously fun. Jill Shalvis sweeps you away!"
**—Cherry Adair, *New York Times*
bestselling author of *Black Magic***

"Shalvis's writing is a perfect trifecta of win: hilarious dialogue, evocative and real characters, and settings that are as much a part of the story as the hero and heroine. I've never been disappointed by a Shalvis book."
—SmartBitchesTrashyBooks.com

"Five Stars!...A talented writer. *Simply Irresistible* is fun, full of humor, and simply delightful in every way."

—HuntressReviews.com

"Riveting suspense laced with humor and heart is her hallmark and Jill Shalvis always delivers."

—Donna Kauffman, *USA Today* bestselling author of *Some Like It Scot*

"A fun, energetic read...this series is going to be one to watch as Jill Shalvis combines her quirky writing with a small-town America setting, while adding in some sizzling heat to make *Simply Irresistible*...simply irresistible!"

—RomRevToday.com

"A beautiful start to this new series. The characters are as charming as the town itself. A pleasure to read."

—FreshFiction.com

"A fun, hot, sexy story of the redemptive powers of love. Jill Shalvis sizzles."

—JoAnn Ross, *New York Times* bestselling author of *The Homecoming*

"Great leads and a stand-out romance...I laughed outright after a few pages. Soon after that, I had to gulp back my tears...what a range of drawn emotions."

—LikesBooks.com

"The very talented Jill Shalvis delivers up a delicious romance...hilarious...sparkling...one of her best books so far. I, for one, cannot wait to read the next two books in the series."

—TheRomanceReadersConnection.com

"One of those books that totally and absolutely encapsulates its title...utterly irresistible. The romance instantly jumps off the page...Jill Shalvis seems to have a golden touch with her books. Each one is better than the previous story."

—RomanceJunkiesReviews.com

Also by Jill Shalvis

Simply Irresistible

The Sweetest Thing

♥

Jill Shalvis

FOREVER

NEW YORK   BOSTON

This book is a work of fiction. Names, characters, places, and incidents are the product of the author's imagination or are used fictitiously. Any resemblance to actual events, locales, or persons, living or dead, is coincidental.

Copyright © 2011 by Jill Shalvis
Excerpt from *Head Over Heels* copyright © 2011 by Jill Shalvis
All rights reserved. Except as permitted under the U.S. Copyright Act of 1976, no part of this publication may be reproduced, distributed, or transmitted in any form or by any means, or stored in a database or retrieval system, without the prior written permission of the publisher.

Forever
Hachette Book Group
237 Park Avenue
New York, NY 10017
Visit our website at www.HachetteBookGroup.com.

Forever is an imprint of Grand Central Publishing. The Forever name and logo is a trademark of Hachette Book Group, Inc.

The publisher is not responsible for websites (or their content) that are not owned by the publisher.

Printed in the United States of America

First Printing: April 2011

10   9   8   7   6   5

*To another oldest sister, Kelsey, who always knows
what to do and how to make us feel better.
Love you forever.*

The Sweetest Thing

Chapter 1

"There is no snooze button on life."
TARA DANIELS

Muffin?" Tara asked as she walked along the long line of people waiting on the pier to enter Lucky Harbor's summer festival. "Have a free Life's-a-Peach Muffin?"

The large basket was heavier than she'd anticipated, and the late afternoon June sun beat down on her head in tune to the Pacific's thrashing waves beating the shore. Perspiration beaded on her skin, which really chapped her hide. It was the steel magnolia in her. Perspiring wasn't just undignified, it contradicted her *never let 'em see you sweat* motto.

Telling herself that she was merely glistening, and hopefully looking luminous while she was at it, Tara amped up her smile and kept going. At least her sundress was lightweight, the material gauzy and playful against her skin. She'd bought it to look sophisticated and elegant. And to boost her confidence.

This was a tall order for a dress.

"Muffin?" she asked the next woman in line.

Mrs. Taylor, the owner of the local craft and supply shop, looked the basket over carefully. "Are they low-fat?"

Before coming to Washington state, Tara had spent most of her life just outside of Houston on her grandparents' ranch, where holding back the use of butter and lard was considered sacrilegious. Low-fat? Not exactly. She gave a brief thought to lying, but she didn't want to be struck dead by lightning—it would ruin her good hair day. "Definitely not, sorry."

"Do you know the calorie count?"

Tara looked down at her beautiful muffins, fat and soft and gently browned, each perfectly baked and undoubtedly overflowing with calories. "A gazillion," she said. "Per bite."

"I'm surprised at you," Mrs. Taylor said disappointedly, "promoting cholesterol consumption like this."

Tara had read somewhere that it took less effort to be nice than bitchy. And since she was all for energy conservation, she let her mouth curve into a smile. "Actually, what I'm promoting is the renovation of the inn my sisters and I are opening in two weeks—" She broke off when Mrs. Taylor held up a polite finger and pulled out her vibrating phone.

Tara had a finger of her own to hold up, but since it wasn't a polite one, she refrained. She moved on, assuring herself that the continuous swallowing of her pride since coming to Lucky Harbor only *felt* like it was going to kill her, but surely it wouldn't.

Probably.

"Muffin?" Tara asked a new section of the line, handing them out as people expressed interest. "Y'all want a free Life's-a-Peach muffin?"

Each had been painstakingly wrapped in cellophane with a folded flyer for the Lucky Harbor Beach Inn tucked into a ribbon. It was part of Tara's mission, and that mission was different than it'd been last year. Last year, she'd wanted peace on earth and a manicure that lasted a full two weeks. This year, things were more basic. She wanted to be able to pay her bills at the end of the month without robbing Peter to pay Paul, and maybe to feel like she was in control of her own life.

That was all.

Just a single month in which her ends met her means. Thirty days during which she wasn't constantly in angst over the arrival of a paycheck.

Or lack thereof.

The sun continued to beat down on Tara as she walked the length of the pier. Behind her, the sharp, craggy cliffs were cast in shadow. Out in front, the surf continued to pound the beach, shuddering the pier beneath her feet. She passed the beauty shop, the Eat Me Diner where she worked four nights a week, and then the arcade, ice cream parlor, and the five-story-high Ferris wheel.

The crowd grew around her, seeming to surge in closer. It was as if the entire state of Washington had showed up for the Summer Arts and Musical Fest, but that wasn't a surprise to Tara. The only thing the people of Lucky Harbor liked more than their gossip was a social gathering, and there would be plenty of both to be had tonight. A warm night, good music, dancing, drinking…a recipe for a good time, no doubt.

"I'll most definitely take a muffin," Chloe said, appearing at Tara's side.

At twenty-four, Tara's sister was the baby of the family, and as such had inherited all the free-spiritedness—aka wildness—of their mother, Phoebe Traeger. Chloe wore snug hip-hugging cargo shorts and a sunshine yellow tank top that required sunglasses to look at. Her glossy dark red hair was streaked with twin hot-pink highlights, one down each temple, the rest cascading down her back in a perfect disarray of waves to give her a just-out-of-bed look.

She could have been a cover model.

Well, except for the fact that she was five foot three in her high-tops and had absolutely no discipline nor inclination to follow instructions. Chloe was freshly back from a two-month trip traveling through Miami Beach's high-end hotel spas, where she'd put her aesthetician license to good use while fine-tuning her own natural skincare line. And probably also finding trouble, as was Chloe's habit.

Tara was just glad to have her back in Lucky Harbor. She'd worried the entire time Chloe had been gone. It was a lifelong thing for Tara, worrying about her troubled baby sister.

Chloe, looking tan and happy and sporting a new Chinese symbol tat on the inside of her wrist that she'd refused to translate, bit into a muffin and let out a heartfelt moan. "Damn, Tara, these rock. Can you tell me something?"

"If you're going to ask me if the muffins are low fat," Tara said, "you should know I'm running out of places to hide all the dead bodies."

Chloe laughed. "No, I can feel my arteries clogging even as I swallow, and I'm good with that." She licked the crumbs off her fingers. "Just wanted to know if you noticed Ford making his way toward you."

Tara turned to follow Chloe's gaze and felt her breath catch. Ford Walker was indeed headed her way, moving sure and easy, his long-legged stride in no hurry. Which was a good thing, as he was stopped by nearly everyone that he passed. He didn't appear to mind, which made it damn hard to dislike him—although Tara still gave it her all.

"You ever going to tell me what's the deal with you two?" Chloe was digging into a second muffin as if she hadn't eaten in a week. And maybe she hadn't. The perpetually broke Chloe never seemed to worry about her next meal.

"There's no deal with me and Ford."

Chloe's low laugh rang in Tara's ears, calling her out for the liar she was. "You know what you need?"

Tara slid her a look. "A trip to some South Pacific island with no sisters named Chloe?"

"Hmm. Maybe for Christmas. For now, you need to relax. More yoga, less stress."

"I'm plenty relaxed." Or she had been until she'd looked at Ford. He'd gotten stopped again and was talking to someone in the line behind her, but as if he felt her appraisal, he turned his head and met her gaze. An odd tension hummed through her veins. Her pulse kicked up as well, not quite into heart-attack territory, but close enough. "Totally, completely relaxed," she murmured.

"Uh-huh," Chloe said, sounding amused. "Is that why

you're hugging the basket so tight you're squishing the muffins? Or why you compulsively cleaned the cottage from top to bottom last night?"

"Hey," Tara said in her own defense. "There was a lot of dust, which would have aggravated your asthma. *And*, if you remember, it's only been two weeks since you've landed in the hospital unable to breathe thanks to nothing more than a pollen storm. So you're welcome."

Chloe rolled her eyes and turned to the woman behind her in line. Lucille owned an art gallery in town and was somewhere between seventy and two hundred years old. She wore white-on-white Nikes and her favorite track suit in hot, Day-Glo pink. She took a muffin, bit into it, and sighed in pleasure. "Tara, darling, you're as amazing as you are uptight."

"I'm not—" *Oh, forget it.*

Lucille looked her over from eyes lined thickly with blue eye shadow. "Pretty dress. You always dress so nice. Ross? Wal-Mart?"

Actually, Nordstrom's, Tara thought, back from her old life when she'd had a viable credit card. "It's several years old, so—"

"We have a question," Chloe said to Lucille, interrupting. "Tell me, does my sister look relaxed to you?"

"Relaxed?" Taking the question very seriously, Lucille studied Tara closely. "Actually, she looks a little constipated." She turned to the person who came up behind her, but Tara didn't have to look to see who it was because her nipples got hard.

At six-feet-three inches, Ford was pure testosterone and sinew. His build suggested one of those lean extreme fighters but Ford was too laid-back to ever bother being a fighter of any kind.

He wore low-slung, button-fly Levi's and a white button-down shoved up to his elbows, yet somehow he managed to look as dressed up as Tara. His brown hair was sun-kissed, his green eyes sharp, his smile ready. Everything about him said *ready*, from his tough build to the air of confidence he wore like other men wore cologne. Half the people in Lucky Harbor were in love with him.

The other half were men and didn't count.

Tara was the odd person out, of course. Not only was she *not* in love with him, he tended to step on her last nerve.

There was a very good reason for that.

Several, in fact. But she'd long ago given herself permission to pretend that the thing that had happened between them *hadn't* happened.

"We're trying to figure out what's wrong with Tara, dear," Lucille told him, having to tilt her blue-haired head way up to meet his eyes. "I'm thinking constipation."

Chloe laughed.

Ford looked as if he wanted to laugh.

Tara ground her teeth. "I'm not—"

"It's okay," Lucille said. "It happens to the best of us. All you need are some plums and a blender, and you—"

"*I'm not constipated!*" Great. Now everyone within a thirty-foot radius was privy to the knowledge.

"Well, good," Lucille said. "Because tonight's Bingo Night at the Rec Center."

Extremely aware of Ford standing *way* too close, Tara

shifted on her wedged sandals. "Bingo's not really my thing."

"Well, mine either, honey," Lucille said. "But there are men there and lots of 'em. A man could unwind you real nice. Isn't that right, Ford?"

"Yes, ma'am," Ford said with an utterly straight face. "Real nice."

"See?" Lucille said to Tara. "Sure, you're a little young for our crowd, but you could probably snag a real live wire, maybe two."

Tara had seen the Bingo Crowd. The "live wires" were the mobile ones, and using a walker qualified as mobile. "I don't really need a live wire." Much less two.

"Oh my dear," Lucille said. "*Every* woman needs a man. Why even your momma—God rest her soul—used to say it was a shame you couldn't buy sex on eBay."

Beside her, Ford laughed softly. Tara very carefully didn't look at him, the man she'd once needed with her whole being. These days she didn't do "need."

Chloe wisely and gently slipped her arm in Lucille's. "I have friends in high places and can get around this line," she told the older woman. "Come tell me all about all these live wires." She shot Tara a you-owe-me smile over her shoulder as she led Lucille away.

Not that Tara could think about that because now she was alone with Ford. Or as alone as one could be while surrounded by hundreds of people. This was not how she'd envisioned the day going when she got up this morning and made that bargain with God, the one where she promised to be a better person if he gave her a whole day where she didn't have to face anything from her past.

But God had just reneged on the deal. Which meant she didn't have to be a better person...

Ford was looking at her. She could feel the weight of his gaze. She kept hers resolutely out on the water. Maybe she should take up knitting like her other sister, Maddie. Knitting was supposedly very cathartic, and Tara could use cathartic. The late afternoon sun sank lower on the ocean as if it was just dipping its toes in to cool off. She stared at it until long fingers brushed hers.

"Tara."

That was it, just her name from Ford's lips, and just like that she... softened. She had no other word for what happened inside her body whenever he spoke to her. She softened, and her entire being went on full alert for him.

Just like old times.

Ford stood there, patient and steady, all day-old scruff and straight white teeth and sparkling gorgeous eyes, bringing out feelings she wasn't prepared for.

"Aren't you going to offer me a muffin?" he asked.

Since a part of her wanted to offer far more, she held her tongue and silently offered the basket. Ford perused his choices as if he was contemplating his life's path.

"They're all the same," Tara finally said.

At that he flashed a grin, and her knees wobbled. Sweet baby Jesus, that smile should come with a label: WARNING: *Prolonged exposure will cause yearning, lust, and stupidity.* "Don't you have a bar to run?" she asked.

"Jax is there, handling things for now."

Ford was a world-class sailing expert. When he wasn't on the water competing, or listed in *Cosmo* as one of the year's "Fun Fearless Males," of all things, he lived here in Lucky Harbor. Here, with his best friend, Jax, he co-owned and ran The Love Shack, the town's most popular watering hole. He did so mostly because, near as Tara could tell, he'd majored in shooting the breeze— which he did plenty of when he was behind the bar mixing drinks and enjoying life.

She enjoyed life, too. Or enjoyed the *idea* of life.

Okay, so she was *working* on the enjoying part. The problem was that her enjoyment kept getting held up by her reality. "Are you going to take a muffin or what?"

Ford cocked his head and ran his gaze over her like a caress. "I'll take whatever crumb you're offering."

That brought a genuine smile from her. "Like you'd settle for a crumb."

"I did once." He was still smiling, but his eyes were serious now, and something pinged low in her belly.

Memories. Unwelcome ones. "Ford—"

"Ah," he said very softly. "So you *do* remember my name. That's a start."

She gave a push to his solid chest. Not that she could move him if she tried, the big, sexy lout.

And she'd forgotten nothing about him—*nothing*. "What do you want?"

"I thought after all this time," he said lightly, "we could be friends."

"Friends," she repeated.

"Yes. Make polite conversation, occasionally see each other socially. Maybe even go out on a date."

She stared at him. "That would make us more than friends."

"You always were smart as hell."

Her stomach tightened again. He wanted to sleep with her. Or not sleep, as the case might be. Her body reacted hopefully to the mere thought. "We don't—" She closed her eyes to hide the lie. "We don't like each other like that anymore."

"No?" In the next beat, she felt the air shift as he moved closer. She opened her eyes just as he lifted his hand and tucked a strand of her hair behind her ear, making her shiver.

He noticed—of course he did; he noticed *everything*—and his mouth curved. But his eyes remained serious, so very serious as he leaned in.

To anyone watching, it would look as if he was whispering something in her ear.

But he wasn't.

No, he was up to something far more devastatingly sneaky. His lips brushed against her throat, and then her jaw, and while she fought with a moan and lost, he whispered, "I like you just fine."

Her body quivered, assuring herself she returned the favor whether she liked it or not.

"Think about it, Tara."

And then he was gone, leaving her unable to do anything *but* think of it.

Of him.

Chapter 2

"Good judgment comes from bad experience.
Unfortunately, most of that comes
from bad judgment."
TARA DANIELS

A week later, the heat had amped up to nearly one hundred degrees. The beach shimmered, the ocean stilled, and Ford came back into Lucky Harbor after a sailing event he'd competed in down in Baja.

He wasn't on the world circuit anymore, but sometimes he couldn't help himself. He liked the thrill of the race.

The sense of being alive.

He'd like to say that he'd worked his ass off most of his life to be the best of the best, but he hadn't. Sailing had come relatively easily, as if he'd been born with the knack to read the waters and handle the controls of a boat, outguessing and outmaneuvering the wind as he pleased. He'd lived and breathed racing for as long as it'd been fun, in the process leaving blood and sweat and little pieces of his soul in every ocean on the planet.

These past few days had been no different. And as it had been just last month in Perth, his time had been well spent, paying off big. Ford had placed in the top ten, pocketing a very lucrative purse for the honor.

Once upon a time, it'd been all about the money. Back when he'd been so poor he couldn't even pay attention.

Now it was about something else. Something... elusive.

The win should have left him feeling flush and happy, and yeah, for a brief moment, the adrenaline and thrill had coursed through his body, fooling him with the elusive, fleeting sense of having it all.

But it'd faded quickly, leaving... nothing.

He felt nothing at all.

And damn if he wasn't getting tired of that. He'd gotten back late last night, docking at the Lucky Harbor marina. He'd spent the morning cleaning up his Finn, the strict, simple design solo boat he raced in. Then he'd done a maintenance check on his thirty-two-foot 10R Beneteau, which he'd slept on last night rather than drive up the hill to his house on the bluffs.

Moving on from his boats, he worked on the Cape Dory Cruiser docked next to his Beneteau as a favor to Maddie Moore.

The favor had been a no-brainer. Maddie was one of Tara's two sisters, and together with Chloe, they ran and operated the marina and inn. And when a pretty lady like Maddie asked Ford for help getting her boat to run, he did his best to solve her problem. Even if said pretty lady was sleeping with his best friend Jax.

The problem with the Cape Dory had been a relatively easy fix. It hadn't been properly winterized, and condensation had formed on the inside of the fuel tanks.

The repair, along with some other things, had taken several hours in the unbearable heat, but Ford hadn't cared. It'd occupied his brain and kept him from thinking too much—always a good thing.

As a bonus, getting his hands dirty had done more for his mental health than the racing had. He loved wrenching. It was something else that came easy to him and gave him great pleasure.

When he'd finished, he pulled off his trashed shirt and washed up the best he could in the marina building. Then he headed across the property to the inn, looking for a big, tall glass of ice water.

Sure, he could have just gone home, but Tara's car was out front, and he...hell. She tended to look right through him, and in return, he liked to drive her crazy. Home was a short drive on the best of days, and a vast improvement from being ignored by her. He toyed with coming right out and asking what her problem was, but he realized that if she said, "You, Ford, *you're* my problem," he'd still have to see her daily for the duration of her stay here in Lucky Harbor. And that would suck.

This was at least the hundredth day he'd come to this "realization," and he was no closer to figuring out what to do than when she'd first come back to town six months ago. So mostly, he'd steered clear. It'd seemed the easiest route, and he was all about the easy.

But today he had a gift to deliver. Lucille had cornered him when he'd stopped by his bar last night to check in after his trip, handing him a wooden box with the word RECIPES written across it.

"Can you give this to Tara for me?" she'd asked. "Don't peek."

So, of course, he'd peeked. There'd been nothing inside but plain—and blank—3×5 index cards. "For her recipes?"

Lucille snapped the box shut, narrowly missing his fingers. "No."

Ford recognized the spark of trouble in Lucille's rheumy eyes. There was no bigger gossip or meddler in town, and since Lucky Harbor was chock-full of gossips and meddlers, this was saying a lot. Lucille and her cronies had recently started a Facebook page for Lucky Harbor residents, bringing the gossip mill to even new heights.

"Okay, spill," Ford said, pinning her with a hard look that wouldn't slow her down—she was unstoppable *and* unflappable. "What are you up to?"

She'd cackled and patted him again. "No good. I'm up to no good. Just see that Tara gets the box."

So that's what he was doing.

Delivering the box to Tara.

She wouldn't be happy to see him, that was for damn sure. Her eyes would chill and so would her voice. She'd pretend they were virtually strangers.

And in a way, they were. It'd been a damn long time since they'd known each other, and the past was the past. He wasn't a guy to spend much time looking back. Nope, he liked to live with both feet firmly in the present, thank you very much. He didn't do regrets, or any other useless emotions for that matter. If he made a mistake, he learned

from it and moved on. If he wanted something, he went
about getting it. Or learned to live without it.

Period.

Of course, as it pertained to Tara, he'd made plenty of
mistakes, and he wasn't all that sure he'd learned much
except maybe how to bury the pain.

He'd gotten damn good at that.

But lately, whenever he caught a glimpse of Tara in
those look-but-don't-touch clothes and that hoity-toity
'tude she wore like Gucci, he had the most insane urge to
ruffle her up. Get her dirty. Make her squirm.

Preferably while naked and beneath him.

Ford swiped the sweat off his forehead with his arm
and strode up the steps to the inn. A two-story Victorian,
it'd been freshly rebuilt and renovated after a bad fire six
months ago. There was still a lot to do before the grand
opening: painting and landscaping, as well as interior
touches, and the kitchen appliances hadn't yet been delivered. Still, character dripped from the place. All it needed
were guests to come and fill it up, and Tara, Maddie, and
Chloe could make a success of it.

As a family.

To the best of Ford's knowledge, the whole family
thing was new to the sisters. Very new. And also to the
best of his knowledge, they weren't very good at it. He just
hoped they managed without bloodshed. Probably they
should put that into their business plan and get everyone
to sign it: *Murder Not Allowed*. Especially Tara.

Bloodthirsty wench, he thought fondly, and walked
across the wraparound porch. There were seedlings laid
out to be planted along the new railings. Someone had

a green thumb. Not Chloe, he'd bet. The youngest sister didn't have the patience.

Not Maddie either, since she was currently spending every spare second in Jax's bed, the lucky bastard.

Tara then?

Ford tried to picture her pretty hands in the dirt... and then his mind went to other places, like her being dirty with him.

Shaking his head at himself, he stepped inside. Before the devastating fire, the interior decorating had been *Little House on the Prairie* meets the Roseanne Conner household. Things had changed once Tara had gotten hold of the place. Gone were the chicken, rooster, and cow motifs; replaced by a softer, warmer beachy look of soothing earth tones mixed with pale blues and greens.

Not a cow in sight.

As Ford walked inside on the brand-new wood floors, he could hear female laughter coming from the deck off the living room. Heading down the hall, he opened the slider door and found the party.

Seated around a table were four women of varying ages, shapes, and sizes. At the head of the table stood Tara. She had eyes the color of perfectly aged whiskey, outlined by long black lashes. Her mouth could be soft and warm—when she was feeling soft and warm, that is. Today it was glossed and giving off one of her professional smiles. She'd let her short, brunette layers grow out a little these past months so that the silky strands just brushed her shoulders, framing the face that haunted his dreams. As always, she was dressed as if she was speeding down the road to success. Today she wore an elegant

fitted dress with a row of buttons running down her deliciously long, willowy body.

Ford fantasized about undoing those buttons—one at
a time.

With his teeth.

She held a tray, and on that tray—be still his heart—was
a huge pitcher of iced tea, complete with a bucket of ice and
lemon wedges, and condensation on the pitcher itself, assuring him it would quench his thirst. He must have made a
sound because all eyes swiveled in his direction. Including
Tara's. In fact, hers dropped down over his body, and then
jerked back up to his eyes. Her gaze was gratifyingly wide.

There were a couple of gasps from the others, and
several *"oh my's"* mixed in with a single, heartfelt *"good
Lord,"* prompting him to look down at himself.

Nope, he wasn't having the naked-in-public dream
again. He was awake and wearing his favorite basketball
shorts—admittedly slung a little low on the hips but cov-
ering the essentials—and running shoes, no socks.

No shirt, either. He'd forgotten to replace the one he'd
stripped off. "Hey," he said in greeting.

"What are you doing?" Tara asked, her voice soft and
Southern and dialed to Not Happy to See Him.

And yet interestingly enough, she was looking at him
like maybe he was a twelve-course meal and she hadn't
eaten in a week.

He'd take that, Ford decided, and he'd especially take
the way her breathing had quickened. "I have a gift for
you from Lucille."

At the sight of the small wood box, Tara went still,
then came around the table to take it.

"It looks just like the one we lost," she murmured, opening it. When she looked inside, a flash of disappointment came and went in her eyes, so fast Ford nearly missed it.

"What?" he asked, ignoring everyone else on the deck as he took a step toward her. "What's wrong?"

"Nothing." Tara clutched the box to her chest and shook her head. "It's just that we lost the original in the fire. It was filled with Phoebe-isms."

"Phoebe-isms?"

"My mom. She'd written these little...tidbits of advice, I guess you'd call them, for me and my sisters over the years. Things like 'A glass of wine is always the solution, even if you aren't sure of the problem.'"

The four women at the table, each of whom had known and loved Phoebe, laughed softly, fondly.

Ford had a soft spot for Phoebe as well. She'd been in Lucille's "gang" and one of Ford's best customers at the bar. As he smiled at the memory, Tara did that pretend-not-to-look-at-his-bare-chest thing again, then quickly turned away.

Interesting reaction for someone who'd exerted a lot of energy and time over the past months *not* noticing him.

"Get him a chair, honey," one of the women said— Rani, the town librarian.

Tara turned to Ford, panic growing in her eyes at the thought of him hanging around.

Yet another interesting reaction. "Ford can't stay," she said, eyes locked on his. "He's...busy. Very busy. I'm sure he doesn't have time to bother with our little meeting."

"I'm not that busy," Ford said, looking around the

table. Each woman had an assortment of plates in front of her, filled with what looked like delicious desserts that Tara must have baked at the diner since the inn's kitchen wasn't yet functioning.

They looked good, real good.

There was also wine, mostly gone now, and everyone but Tara was looking pretty darn relaxed for a *meeting*. "Besides," he said, "this looks more like a party."

"It's the Garden Society." Tara was still blocking his way from moving farther onto the deck. "The ladies here were gracious enough to come and sample some snacks that I hope to have available for our inn guests upon request."

His belly stirred, reminding him he'd skipped lunch. "I'm an excellent taster," he said with his most charming smile.

"But you're *so* busy," Tara said, with *her* most charming smile, although her eyes were saying *Don't You Dare*.

"Aw, but I'm never too busy for you." Ford had no idea why he was baiting her. Maybe because she'd spent so much time pretending he didn't exist, and this was much more fun. Plus there was the added benefit that he knew her Southern manners wouldn't allow her to say what she *really* wanted to, not in front of company, anyway. *Heaven forbid we be rude in front of guests.*

Tara was now giving him the look that assured him that she was indeed imagining wrapping her fingers around his neck. He smiled wider. He couldn't help it. For the first time in too damn long, he was feeling alive. Very alive.

Admitting defeat with her usual good grace, Tara never let her smile falter as she shifted to the railing, where she had supplies stacked up. She grabbed a spare plate and loaded it with her goodies before wrapping it in foil.

Ford was getting the to-go version.

"He looks thirsty, too, Tara," Rani said.

Ford loved Rani.

"Yes, dear," another of the women said. "Pour the poor, overworked man a glass of tea. You don't let a man of this caliber drink from a garden hose."

"Thank you, Ethel," Ford murmured, and since he was watching Tara's arresting face, he saw the flicker of surprise cross her features. Yes, he knew Ethel, too. She ran the Rec Center. She'd been there when, twenty years ago now, he'd hit a baseball through her office window, nearly decapitating her. Good times.

"Please stay," Ethel said to Ford, and patted an empty chair right next to hers.

"But he's not dressed for this," Tara said, once again eyeing Ford's bare chest. Her pupils dilated. "There are health codes, and—"

"We won't tell." This from Sandy, the town clerk and city manager of Lucky Harbor. "Besides, we're outside. He's dressed just *perfect*."

Sandy had gone to school with Ford. She'd been class president, head cheerleader, and a lot of fun. Ford smiled at her.

She returned it with a saucy wink. "My sister's husband is looking into buying a boat," she told him. "A fixer-upper. I told her that I'd ask your opinion."

"It's a good time," Ford told her. "The market's down so you could get a deal. If he wants my help working on it, have him call me."

"A man who can wield a set of tools *and* read the market," Rani said on a dreamy sigh.

"Yes," Tara said, grinding her back teeth together as she looked at Ford. "Bless your heart."

She didn't mean it, of course, which only made him smile again. Sure, her voice was all gentle and soft, but her real feelings were visible if you knew her.

And whether she wanted to believe it or not, Ford knew her. He knew she wanted to knock him into next week.

"A moment?" Tara requested sweetly.

"Sure," he said just as sweetly as he leaned back against the railing and got comfy.

"*Alone.*"

And then, without waiting for an answer, she dropped his foiled to-go goodies into a pretty bag, poured one of the glasses full of iced tea, and walked right past him, hips swinging with attitude, inside the inn.

Clearly assuming he'd follow.

He watched her go, enjoying the view, but he didn't move. He wasn't much into being bossed around, even by an incredibly beautiful woman who was anal retentive and a bit of a control freak.

Well, unless they were in bed. He didn't mind then, not as long as he got to return the favor.

But there was something about Tara that drew him in spite of himself, that snagged him by the throat and held tight. Maybe it was the tough-girl exterior, which he knew barely covered a bruised and tender heart. He'd seen that heart once, and truth be told he wasn't all that interested in going back there. But he wouldn't mind seeing her other parts.

He couldn't help it. She had really great parts.

And he wanted that cold iced tea, bad. Almost as much as he wanted...

Her, he realized grimly. Against all caution and sanity, he wanted her. So he followed her inside the inn.

Chapter 3

"Change is good but dollars are better."
TARA DANIELS

Tara waited in the freshly painted hallway off the inn's large, open living room with what she felt was admirable calm until *finally*, a half-naked Ford slowly strode inside.

Not hurrying.

Of course not. Ford never hurried when he could saunter. He never rushed a damn thing in his life. The big, sexy lug moved when and where he wanted.

She knew she was just damn lucky he'd decided to move at all. He was unpredictable.

Spontaneous.

Not to be confused with uncontrolled. Because Ford, for all his sense of humor and smart-ass-ness, was one of the most controlled people Tara had ever met. It was one of the few things they had in common. She did her best to keep her eyes on his, but she couldn't seem to help herself. She'd seen him without a shirt before, of course. But it'd been a while.

Watching her watch him, he reached out and played with the lace on her collarbone. "Why are you always dressed like you're going to a business meeting?"

"I *am* at a business meeting. Sort of." She paused and admitted the truth. "But mostly I wear dresses or skirts because I don't have a good butt in jeans."

With a laugh, Ford stepped close, so close that she could smell the ocean on him. He was salty and tangy, and so indelibly male that Tara almost closed the last inch between them simply so that she could lick him like a lollipop. Just one lick, she told herself, from sternum to the very low waistband of the basketball shorts...

His eyes lit with wickedness, as if he knew her secret longings, but he said nothing as he leaned over her shoulder to view her backside.

Ford Walker, Resident Butt Inspector.

"Looks fine from here," he assured her in a low, husky voice that scraped at every single erogenous zone she owned. "Damned fine." He paused. "Maybe I should give it a hand test to be sure." Before she could say a word, he slid a hand down her spine, heading south with wicked and nefarious intent.

With a shocked laugh, she shoved him away. "I'll take your word for it."

"So," he said, recovering far faster than she. "Still constipated?"

Tara choked. "What?"

Ford lifted a broad shoulder and unsuccessfully bit

back a smile. "After the other day, it got around town that you were having troubles."

" 'Got around town,' " she repeated faintly and closed her eyes to count to ten. For peace and Zen.

Neither made an appearance.

"I think Lucille tweeted it, and it ended up on Facebook," he said, amusement heavy in his voice. "She took the opportunity to put up a recipe to fix the problem. You take a few plums, pit them, get a blender and—"

"I'm not—" Tara broke off, glancing through the inn to the sliding glass door before purposely lowering her voice. "*Constipated!*"

"You sure?"

"Very!"

He grinned, and she felt conflicting reactions—her brain melting, and steam coming out her ears.

How could this be? How could he drive her so insane and make her want him with equal intensity? She didn't understand, she really didn't. "Here," she said and thrust the glass of iced tea and the bag of desserts at him. "And you should know, regarding your *friend* request the other day at the music fest, I've thought about it. Us." Fact was, she'd done nothing *but* think about it. But they'd failed once. More like crashed and burned, spectacularly, and she shook her head. "I can't go there again, Ford." The last time had nearly destroyed her. Only he seemed to have the power to do that, and she wouldn't, *couldn't*, let it happen again.

"I didn't ask you to go there again," he said.

She met his gaze, his giving nothing away, and she flushed because he was right. He hadn't asked her to fall in young, crazy love; he'd only suggested they have sex. *Very* different. "That's an equally bad idea. You know it, and I know it. Now please go."

"You're big on that word," he noted. " 'Go.' "

His was a not-so-subtle rebuke, and an unpleasant reminder of their past. And she resented like hell that he was throwing it in her face. By leaving as she had, she'd done him the biggest favor of his life. And not for one minute did she believe he hadn't been thrilled to see the last of her, given how she'd turned his life upside down. He certainly hadn't chased after her. He'd just let her go. The painful memories reared up and bit her, making her voice tight. "We are not doing this now, Ford."

"Fine. Later then."

"Never."

"Never is a long time," he said evenly, calmly, and since she couldn't find her *even* or *calm* to save her life, it pissed her off. That he could be so relaxed through this conversation made her fingers itch to pour the tea right over his damn sexy head. Two things stopped her. One, he'd be half-naked *and* wet, and watching the iced tea drip down that bronzed chest, with its barely there spattering of sun-kissed hair and six-pack abs, might just be too much for her to take. And that was just his upper half. Lord almighty, if his basketball shorts got wet, they'd cling to all his glory.

And there was a lot of glory.

The second problem, the *real* problem, was that dumping the tea over his head would show her hand to him, because she could make no mistake with Ford. He might look and act like a frat boy with no concerns beyond the next good time, but she knew better. Behind that lazy smile was a mind as sharp as a tack. She thrust the goodie bag and the glass at him.

Ford accepted both. Their hands brushed together, his tanned and big against her much smaller one. "Thanks," he said. "I'm sure it's perfect, as well as the desserts."

"Are you buttering me up?"

"Trying." He smiled. "Is it working?"

"No." *Yes.* Dammit.

Through the sliding glass door, she could still hear the ladies chattering amongst themselves, and she kept her voice as low as possible. "Just drink up. You looked parched, and I don't want you passing out."

"Aw. You care."

Yes. But caring wasn't the problem, for either of them. Longevity was. His. She was no longer seventeen and looking for a good time. She wanted more. Certainly more than Ford was looking to give. She knew him, or at least she was pretty sure she did. She'd read about him over the years and followed his career. For the six months she'd been in Lucky Harbor, she'd paid attention to his current life as well.

He'd grown up, there was no doubt. Once upon a time, he'd been headed for trouble but he'd gotten it together. He was a good man who was doing exactly as he wanted for a living and making it work for himself. But he was still content to live his life *c'est la vie*, to let the cards fall where they might, not all that interested in keeping anything, or anyone, long term.

And then there was her real stumbling block. They'd already had their chance and had missed it. End of story.

"I don't want to make Lucky Harbor's Facebook page again," she said. "We don't need that kind of publicity."

"You care," he repeated softly.

She paused, but there was no reason not to admit it when he'd always been able to read both her heart and her soul like a book. Once, he'd seen everything she was, and he'd made her feel like the most beautiful, love-worthy woman on the planet—at least as much as a seventeen-year-old could feel. "Yes," she said softly. "I care."

He looked at her for a long moment, clearly surprised at the admission. Then he broke eye contact and downed the iced tea she'd given him in approximately two huge swallows. Letting out a heartfelt sigh of appreciation, he smiled down at her from his towering height as he handed back the glass.

Which was another thing. She wasn't petite. She was five-seven in her bare feet, but today she was wearing three inch heels, and she *still* felt small next to Ford.

Small and…feminine. "Okay, then." Tara set the glass aside and turned him toward the front door, ignoring the way her hands tingled at the feel of his biceps beneath her fingers, hard and warm. "This has been fun," she said. "But buh-bye now."

"What's your hurry? Afraid you'll be unable to keep from having your merry way with me?"

Since that was far too close to the truth for comfort, she nudged him again, a little harder now. "*Shh!* If the women hear you talk like that, I'm going to blame you."

"Not my fault. You're the one who can't keep her hands off me."

She looked down and realized her fingers were indeed

still on him, practically stroking him. *Crap*. She snatched her hands back and searched for her dignity, but there was little to be found. "I didn't say it would be your fault. I said I'd blame you."

He laughed. "Since when do you care what anyone thinks of you?"

"Since I want to impress these women—all of whom have connections and will hopefully send their family and friends here to the inn. So please. *Please*, Ford, you have to go. You can mess with my head another time, I swear."

From outside on the deck, the women were still talking and their voices drifted in. "Lord alive," someone said, possibly Ethel. "I'm *still* having a hot flash. If this inn comes with that man walking around like that, I'll shout recommendations for this place from the rooftops."

Ford's gaze met Tara's, and he slowly raised a brow.

"Oh, for God's sake." She gave up trying to push him out. "It's your damn body, that's all!"

"I have charm, too," he cajoled. "Let me back out there, Tara. It'll help, you'll see."

And here was the thing she knew about Ford. He never made pie-crust promises. His word was as good as money in the bank. If he said he'd help, he would.

She could trust him.

Problem was, she couldn't trust herself.

Not even a little bit. Leaning back against the wall, she covered her eyes, thinking that *not* looking at him might help clear her thoughts.

Except that he planted a hand on the wall next to her head and leaned in.

"Stop that," she said weakly when he leaned close. "You're all…" *Delicious.* "Sweaty."

He sidled up even closer, so that their bodies were brushing against each other. "You used to love it when I got all sweaty."

Oh yeah. Yeah, she had. She'd loved the way their bodies had heated and clung together. She'd loved how they'd moved together, she'd loved…"That was a damn long time ago," she said, ruthlessly reminding herself how it'd ended.

Badly.

Eyes holding hers prisoner, Ford remained against her for an interminable beat before finally taking a slow step back, still far too close for comfort.

She busied herself by grabbing the empty glass and striding back out onto the deck to refill it. She smiled at her guests and said, "I'll just be one more moment."

"Take your time, honey," someone replied. "I certainly would."

Doing her best not to grimace, Tara once again entered the cool interior of the inn.

Ford was almost at the front door, but he turned when she said his name. She watched the surprise cross his face when he took in the refilled tea. He moved back toward her and never took his gaze off her face as he accepted the glass.

"Why?" he asked.

"Because you looked like you're still thirsty."

His mouth quirked. "Thanks. But that's not what I meant."

Tara exhaled in an attempt to hold it together. No, she knew that. "You make me forget my manners. I hate that."

"Can't have you without your manners." He ran his fingers over her jaw, his eyes at half-mast as he took in her expression. "You ever remember it, Tara? Us?"

She'd done little but remember. Her emotions had long ago been shoved deep down, but being back in Lucky Harbor had cracked her self-made brick walls, and all those messy, devastating emotions came tumbling down every single time she looked at him.

She'd first arrived in town, a pissed-off-at-the-world seventeen-year-old, banished here by her father and her paternal grandparents for the summer, and she'd resented everything about Lucky Harbor.

Until her second night.

She'd had a simple but particularly nasty fight with her mother. Tara hadn't known Phoebe well, which hadn't helped. The fight had sent Tara sulking off to the marina, where she'd run smack into another seventeen-year-old. A tall, laid-back, easygoing, sexy-as-hell Ford Walker.

He'd been sprawled out on one of his boats, hands behind his head, watching the stars as if he didn't have a care in the world. One slow, lazy smile and an offer of a soda had pretty much been all it'd taken for her to fall, and fall hard.

He hadn't been like the guys back home. He hadn't been a rancher's kid or a cowboy. Not an intellectual or the typical jock, either.

Ford had been the bad boy and the good-time guy all in one, and effortlessly sexy. He'd drawn her right in, making her laugh when she hadn't had much to laugh at. His eyes had sparkled with wicked wit and a great deal of promised trouble, and yet he'd also been shockingly kind.

They'd gone out sailing by the light of the stars and swam beneath the moon's glow.

She'd escaped to his boat every night after that.

As unbelievable as it seemed, they'd truly been just friends. She'd come from a broken home and had all the emotional baggage that went with that, including anger and confusion and restlessness.

She'd felt...alone.

Ford had known what that was like. His parents had split up when he was young, too, and his father had taken off. His mom had remarried a few times, so he also knew how tenuous "family" was.

But he'd been far more optimistic than she, possessing a make-your-family-where-you-can mentality. And actually, she'd loved that about him. She'd loved a lot about him, including the fact that he'd been a bit of a troublemaker and had encouraged her to step outside her comfort zone.

It hadn't taken much encouragement. That's when they'd become more than friends.

They'd gone for a long sail, dropped anchor...and their clothes. They'd made love—her first time.

Not his.

Ford had showed her just how good it could be, how amazing it could feel, and for that one long, glorious month of July, Tara had found herself hopelessly and thoroughly addicted to his body.

He'd felt the same about her; she'd seen it, felt it. There'd been no spoken vows of love between them, but it'd been there. They'd been lovers in every sense of the word.

A very grown-up word, *lovers*. And given that Tara had ended up pregnant and giving the baby up for adoption before hightailing it back to Texas, she hadn't been ready for all that went with being grown up.

No matter what Ford thought, neither of them had been.

Tara hadn't come back to Lucky Harbor after she'd had the baby, not once in all these years. She'd moved on. She'd gone to college. Traveled. Sown some wild oats. She'd even fallen in love. Logan Perrish had been charming, funny, and accepting, and a huge NASCAR star. Tara had married him, and, determined to get things right, she'd done everything in her power to fit into Logan's world of whirlwind travel, press, billboards, and cereal boxes.

She'd lived and breathed the part of a celebrity wife, always on the go, doing whatever it took to make Logan love her as much as he loved his racing world.

Even when it had all failed, she'd still stuck in there. She'd made a commitment, and she'd faked it.

Fake it until you make it; that had been her motto.

But somewhere along the way, she'd lost herself. It seemed she always lost herself. And what made it even worse was that Logan hadn't been a bad guy, just the Wrong Guy.

So she'd escaped back to Texas once again, to lick her wounds in private, struggling to remember who she was—a woman who'd lived through some bad things and still persevered.

A woman who wouldn't lose herself again.

The steel magnolia within her had finally served Logan divorce papers. Due to his celebrity status, they'd had a prenup, of course. Without kids to complicate things, she'd willingly walked away free and clear. Still Logan had insisted on giving her a very fair settlement, which she had used every last bit of when she and her sisters had needed money for the inn.

She was now a take-no-prisoners sort of woman, and maybe also a don't-get-too-close-to-me woman. It was necessary, in order to keep her heart protected and safe.

And to keep herself pain free.

Unfortunately, she'd just broken her own rule by tangling with Ford. Problem was, when it came to him, her mind and body appeared to be at war.

Want him.

Hold him at arm's length.

Want him...

The ongoing battle was complicated by the fact that she now lived within a stone's throw of him. As she knew all too well, Ford was lethal up close, especially when he wanted something.

And he'd admitted to wanting her. Her body, anyway.

He was just watching her now, and when she said nothing, he slowly shook his head, a bittersweet smile twisting his lips. "Thanks again for the tea," he said, and when the door shut behind him Tara drew in a shaky breath and let it out slowly, struggling for her equilibrium. As always, she eventually found it, and once she had, she headed back outside to the deck.

"There you are," one of her guests said slyly. "Everything okay?"

Tara smiled. "Absolutely," she said, taking her own advice—*fake it until you make it.*

Chapter 4

*"A conclusion is the place you get to
when you're tired of thinking."*
TARA DANIELS

Two days later, Tara woke up when someone plopped down on her bed. "It's Wednesday," Maddie said, adding a bounce to make sure Tara was up.

"It's also the crack of dawn." Tara pulled her pillow back over her head and turned over. "Go away."

Maddie yanked off the pillow. "*Wednesday.*"

"Sugar, you'd best at least have coffee brewing."

Maddie reached over to the nightstand and handed her a cup.

Tara sat up and sipped, repressing the sigh that wouldn't help anyway. Maddie had decreed Wednesdays to be "Team Building Day." The three of them had to spend every Wednesday together from start to finish until they learned to get along.

It was no surprise that they didn't. They'd grown up separately, thanks to the fact that Phoebe had loved men.

A lot of them.

Tara's father was a government scientist who'd come into Phoebe's orbit and not known what hit him. After their divorce, Tara had lived with her father. Actually, her father's parents, since he'd traveled so much. Tara had spent only the occasional summer with Phoebe, before her mother had inherited the Lucky Harbor Inn, so those visits had consisted mostly of camping and/or following the Grateful Dead tour.

Maddie's father was a Hollywood set designer. He'd also taken Maddie with him when his relationship with Phoebe had gone kaput. Maddie hadn't come back for summers, so she and Tara had been virtual strangers when Phoebe had died.

Chloe had no idea who her father was and didn't seem to care. The only daughter raised by Phoebe, she had traveled around at Phoebe's desire. As a result of that wanderlust upbringing, Chloe tended not to worry about convention the way her sisters did. She didn't worry about much, actually. She lived on a whim.

Unlike Tara, who lived for convention, for order. For a plan.

When Phoebe died and left her daughters her parents' inn, not one of them had intended to stay. And yet here they sat over six months later: the steel magnolia, the mouse, and the wild child.

Having a Team-Building Wednesday.

This was their third month at it, and the days still tended to be filled with bickering, pouting, and even all-out warfare. Today, Tara guessed, would be more of the same, but for Maddie's sake she gamely rose and dressed.

First stop—the diner for brunch. Tara took grief from Jan, the woman who owned the diner. Tara's boss was fifty-something, mean as a snake unless she was taking money from a customer, and liked Tara only when Tara was behind the stovetop.

Which she wasn't at the moment.

Tara managed to get them seated with only the barest of snarls. Chloe ordered a short stack and consulted with the Magic Eight app on her iPhone, asking it if she was going to have a date anytime in the near future. Maddie ordered bacon and eggs with home fries and talked to Jax on her cell about something that was making her blush. Tara ordered oatmeal and wheat toast, and was busy calculating the balance in her checkbook. If that didn't explain their major differences right there, nothing could.

Afterward, in the already blazing sun, they walked the pier for the purpose of buying ice cream cones. In Maddie's case, they also went for getting on the Ferris wheel she'd once been so terrified of. They did that first, holding Maddie's hand. They might not see eye to eye on much, but some things could be universally shared, and ice cream and Ferris wheel rides were two of them.

Lance served them the ice cream. In his early twenties, he was small-boned enough to pass for a teenager, and thanks to the cystic fibrosis slowly ravaging his body, had a voice like he was speaking through gravel. He and Chloe were good friends, or more accurately cohorts, trouble-seekers of the highest magnitude. Lance tried to serve them for free, but Chloe refused. "We've got this," she told him firmly, then turned to Tara expectantly.

Maddie snorted.

Tara rolled her eyes and pulled out her wallet.

"I'll pay you back," Chloe said.

"You always say that," Tara said.

"Yeah? How much do I owe you?"

"One million trillion dollars."

Chloe grinned. "I'll get right on that."

Tara looked at Maddie.

"You spoil her," Maddie said with a shrug.

"Shh, don't say that," Chloe said. "She's right here."

Tara knew she wasn't exactly known for the warm, loving emotions required to spoil someone, and that she could come off as distant, even cold. This actually surprised her because she didn't *feel* distant, although she'd like to try being so sometime.

It'd be nice not to worry about things like money, or the future, or her sisters. And Tara did worry continuously, about Maddie and Chloe more than anything else—like whether Maddie was getting over her abusive ex and if Chloe would ever get over her inability to show or trust love.

Because of the these things, Tara stayed in Lucky Harbor longer than planned. Or so she told herself.

"So what's next?" Chloe asked as they walked back to the inn. "I wore my bathing suit in hopes of getting a tan."

"We're going sailing," said the Team Building Day's president.

"We went sailing last week and nearly killed each other," Chloe said.

"We went *canoeing* last week," Maddie corrected, "and

Tara nearly killed you because you tipped her over, and she'd been having a good hair day. Keep your hands to yourself and you'll survive today's Team Building Adventure."

"Hmm," Chloe said, sending a long, steady look in Tara's direction as they boarded the Cape Dory Cruiser, the sailboat that had come with the marina.

They'd also inherited kayaks, canoes, a fishing boat, and one dilapidated houseboat. Most of these equated to some modest rental income, and they were determined to wring every penny out of the place that they could.

They had to, seeing as they'd gone through money with alarming speed to get everything up and running. Maddie's savings was gone. Tara's, too. It was a small price to pay, she reminded herself, for a new lease on life. A life that was lived the way she wanted, and not for anyone else.

"Tara," Maddie said, pointing, "you're in the cockpit."

"Yes!" Chloe triumphantly pulled off her skimpy sundress, revealing an even more skimpy red bikini beneath. "Time to sun, ladies."

Tara motored them out of the marina and looked at Maddie for further instructions.

"Point the bow into the wind," Maddie said. She was the only one who knew what she was doing, having taken a few lessons from Ford.

Tara had taken lessons from Ford, too. But that had been seventeen years ago, and the lessons she'd taken had *nothing* to do with sailing.

"What?" Maddie asked, making Tara realize she was smiling at the memory.

"Nothing."

"That's more than a 'nothing' smile," Chloe noted.

Tara ignored her.

"Into the wind," Maddie repeated to Tara.

Tara looked around to figure out which way the wind was coming.

"Quickly," Maddie said. "Or you'll swamp us."

Tara didn't know exactly what that meant but it didn't sound good. The boat was lurching heavily to the right and then the left on the four-foot swells; the wind was whipping her hair from all directions so she had no idea exactly which way was "into the wind."

"West!" Maddie yelled. "To the west."

"Okay, okay," Tara said, having to laugh at the sharpness in the former mouse's voice. "To the west it is." Just as soon as she figured out which way was west exactly...

"*Left!*"

So Tara steered left.

"Pull the halyard!" Maddie called out.

Tara looked at her. "Say that again in English?"

"Hoist the sail!"

"You should add 'aye, mate' at the end of that," Chloe told Maddie, spritzing herself with suntan lotion.

Maddie stood there, feet planted wide, wind whipping at her clothes, indeed looking like a modern-day pirate. "Pull it," she commanded as Tara hustled to do her bidding. "Crank it around the winch."

Tara glanced at Chloe.

Chloe had her face tipped up to the sun, and she was smiling, the little witch. "Isn't it Chloe's turn?" Tara asked hopefully.

"Not yet," Chloe said. "I feel my asthma acting up." She gave a little *cough-cough*, then affected a wheeze. "See?"

Maddie laughed. "At least put some phlegm into it."

Chloe began to work at wheezing and ended up coughing for real.

Tara sighed and began to hoist the sail. *She* wanted to be the pirate, dictating orders, thank you very much.

"Harder," Maddie told her. "You have to do it harder."

"That sounds dirty," Chloe said.

"Unfurl the jib," Maddie said, ignoring Chloe. "Hurry." She actually made a very cute tyrant in her snug capris and a tank top, looking fit and quite in charge even as she nibbled on potato chips—

Wait a minute. Tara narrowed in on the chips. How unfair was that? "Hey, if you were a really good captain, you'd share those."

Maddie peered in the bag, probably to assess whether she had enough to share. Tara knew that Maddie believed that chips were God's gift, the second best thing on earth. They used to be Maddie's *numero uno*, but then she'd fallen in love with Jax, so sex had been moved to the top of the list.

Maddie had her priorities straight. And as she reluctantly offered Tara some chips, Tara knew it was time she got her priorities straight as well.

They sailed for an hour, with Chloe sprawled out for maximum sun coverage, her fast-acting asthma inhaler tucked into the string low at her hip. Her long red waves were corralled prettily in a ponytail sticking out the back of a baseball cap that read: DARE TO BE NAUTI, and she had huge movie-star sunglasses perched on her pert nose.

Tara looked down at herself. She hadn't dressed special for this adventure. She'd worn thin trousers and a fitted knit top that was probably better suited for a day at the office, but it was what had been clean that morning. Besides, everyone knew that it wasn't so much what you had in the bank, or even where you rested your head at night—it was what you wore and how you wore it. She turned to Maddie. "Tell me again why Chloe's just lying there looking pretty?"

"Aw, thanks, hon," Chloe said, not opening her eyes.

"Chloe's going to get up now and reverse the entire process," Maddie said. "And bring us back to the marina."

Chloe sighed but obeyed and rolled lithely to her feet.

Tara gave Chloe a very immature *ha!* smirk and took the sun-worshipping spot. It took another hour to get back, and she spent that time enjoying the feel of the boat rocking beneath her, the scent of the salty ocean air, and the warmth of the sun drying her damp clothes and skin. She listened while feeling smug and superior as Maddie turned her bossiness on Chloe for a change.

"Watch your starboard," Maddie called out when Chloe steered toward the marina as they came back in. "Starboard!"

"What the hell's *starboard*?" Chloe yelled back.

"The right side! Watch your right side! Cripes, don't you people retain *anything*?"

Chloe slid the usually easygoing Maddie a look. "Either you had too much caffeine this morning or you didn't get laid when you got up."

Maddie rolled her eyes.

"Didn't get laid," Chloe decided.

"For your information, I got up too early to get..." Maddie lowered her voice to a whisper, "*laid*. And I have no idea how that matters."

"It matters because you're much more relaxed after Jax—"

"Chloe," Tara said, not wanting her to tease Maddie, not about this. "Not *everything* revolves around sex."

"It does when you're not getting any," Chloe muttered.

"Internal editor," Tara said. "Get one."

"I don't want to hear from you. *You* could be getting plenty of the good stuff from Ford, you know that? I mean have you *seen* him look at you?"

Tara sighed. "You could start an argument in an empty house."

"Or on a boat," Chloe agreed, not insulted in the least. "And nice subject change. Why does talking about sex bother you?"

Tara shook her head. "You know that sometimes it's okay to not talk at all, right?"

Chloe smiled good-naturedly. "I do tend to miss most opportunities to shut up."

"Hey," Maddie said. "That would make a good quip for the recipe box, Tara. *Never miss an opportunity to shut up*—Chloe!" she yelped, pointing ahead. "Watch the swell—"

Too late. The five-foot swell rose up and over the nose of the boat, splashing them all.

"You're not paying attention at all," Maddie said with reproach after she'd swiped the ocean spray off her face.

"You know what?" Chloe asked, tossing up her hands. "Sailing is too stressful for me."

Maddie took over as Chloe pulled out her inhaler and took a puff.

"Who are you writing those recipe cards for anyway?" Chloe asked Tara.

"My daughter," Tara said without thinking.

"Aw." That made Maddie smile. "That's sweet. Think she'll get to read them?"

Tara shook her head. "The adoption was closed. I can't find her. She'd have to find me." She heard the wistfulness in her voice and purposely closed her mouth, not wanting to go there. She'd spent a lot of time not going there. It was her own private guilt and shame, that she'd had to give up a baby.

"While we're on the subject," Chloe said, "you ready to tell us who was the father yet?"

Tara gave her a long look. Her ex had called it her "Don't Make Me Kick Your Ass" look.

It didn't daunt Chloe. "Tell the truth," she said. "It's Anderson from the hardware store. Yeah? Because he totally has the hots for you."

"No," Tara said. "He has the hots for *Maddie*. Or he did, before she broke his heart and started dating Jax."

"Then it's Ford." Chloe nodded. "Ford's totally your Baby Daddy."

Tara froze, then carefully, purposely, forced herself to relax. "What?"

"Yeah," Chloe said, and grinned. "We've known forever, actually. I was just pulling your leg with the Anderson thing."

"Chloe," Maddie said quietly, "you're ambushing her. That wasn't in the plan."

"The plan?" Tara repeated. "There's a plan? What was it, to get me out on the water under the guise of Team Building, where you could grill me?"

"No one's grilling you," Maddie said gently. "We're your sisters. Your support system."

"And seriously," Chloe said. "You doing the whole Ignore-Ford thing was a dead giveaway anyway. *No one* ignores a man that fine."

"We're not discussing this," Tara said firmly.

Chloe sighed. "I'm telling you, if we just talked instead of being repressed all the time, we'd be less grumpy. And by 'we,' let's be clear. I mean you."

"*Not* discussing," Tara repeated.

"Sure," Chloe said. "Fine. How about your blind date tomorrow night? Can we talk about that?"

Maddie was steering the boat back into the bay with more skill than Tara had shown earlier, but Tara didn't care about that as she stared at Chloe. "How did you know about the blind date?"

"Are you kidding? This is Lucky Harbor, remember? Ethel told Carol at the post office, who told Jeanine at Jax's office, who told Sandy, who told Lucille that Ethel set you up with her grandson—the one coming through town for a short visit. So then Lucille tweeted it to Facebook."

Tara just barely resisted groaning. After serving the ladies of the Garden Society the other day, Ethel had cornered Tara to ask if Ford was courting her. Tara had choked on one of her own lemon bars, both at the old-fashioned and quaint connotation of the word "courting" and at the question itself. First of all, nothing about Ford was old-fashioned *or* quaint. Not given what he really wanted from her. Tara had firmly told Ethel no, that there hadn't been any courting—she'd kept the mutual lusting to herself—and that's when Ethel had mentioned needing a favor.

Tara had reluctantly agreed, and Ethel had laughed. "Oh, no, dear," she'd said. "You don't understand. I'm doing *you* the favor. I'm setting you up with my grandson Boyd. He's a wonderful, sweet, kind man, with a great personality."

Chloe was grinning, and Tara refused to say that she was already regretting her decision to accept a blind date. "So I'm going out to dinner. So what?"

"So if you were as smart as I thought you are, you'd be having breakfast with Ford instead."

Tara's belly tightened at the thought. "I'm sure Boyd's very nice."

"You haven't dated in how many years? Two? Three? Ten?"

Tara didn't bother to answer. Mostly because she didn't actually know.

"*Nice* isn't what you need," Chloe said. "You need—"

Maddie "accidentally" hit Chloe upside the head with a buoy. Tara ignored the following scuffle but took over the cockpit so they didn't all drown. The sails were down now so she motored them back to the docks, maybe hitting the gas a little more energetically than necessary. She ignored Maddie's squeak and Chloe's whoop and concentrated. She concentrated right into a big swell, rocking the boat hard.

"Ohmigod," Maddie gasped, lifting her head, "*you have to steer into—*"

"My bad," Tara said.

"And the—"

"I *know*," Tara said.

"Do you also know that you're a know-it-all?" Chloe asked casually, straightening up and adjusting her bikini.

When Tara just gave her a long look, Chloe shrugged. "We were just wondering."

"*We*?" Tara glanced over at Maddie, who winced.

Wheezing audibly now, Chloe pulled out her inhaler again, shook it, and took another hit. She paused to hold her breath for ten seconds, then exhaled. "I'm not supposed to wrestle," she said reproachfully to Maddie, then turned back to Tara. "And yes, *we*."

Tara swallowed a ball of unexpected hurt. "You two were discussing me being a know-it-all."

"Actually," Chloe said, "we were discussing your anal-retentiveness, your obsessive need to be right, and your all-around general crankiness."

"I'm not cranky."

Chloe laughed. "But you *are* anal and always right?"

"I'm *careful*," Tara said, lifting her chin, feeling defensive. Dammit. "And as for always being right, someone has to be." Okay, so she knew she wasn't always right but they'd been talking about her. And yes, maybe she was a little hard on them sometimes, but she was hard on everyone she cared about. She didn't see the value in letting Chloe suffer through mistakes she'd made due to the wild abandon of youth. Chloe hadn't had any guiding hand growing up with Phoebe, but Tara had at least had her father.

Which hadn't saved me from a few pretty major lapses in good judgment...

Tara shrugged that off, focusing on navigating the boat into the slip. She wanted a good relationship with her sisters, and in spite of the bickering, she knew it was happening. They were getting closer.

But the real goal here was making a go of the inn. It had to be. Distracted, she miscalculated how much to crank to the left and hit the boat slip. "Sorry," she called out as they all nearly fell to the deck. "But some assistance would be helpful!"

"You're doing fine," Maddie murmured.

"For a know-it-all, right?"

"Tara," Maddie said softly, apology heavy in her voice. "I—"

"No, it's okay." Tara shook it off. "Really. It's okay that you two discussed my personal life without me around to defend myself—"

"Hey, we do it right in front of you, too," Chloe said.

Tara shook her head and moved to follow Chloe off the boat, but ended up plowing into the back of her when Chloe stopped suddenly. "What are you—"

Chloe was staring ahead, and Tara joined her at it, even letting out a soft "oh my."

Ford stood on the deck of his racing Finn. Every single inch of him was drenched, making his board shorts and T-shirt cling to that built body as he maneuvered into his slip, his arms outstretched as he reached out to tie up the boat.

Tara had always loved his arms. They were sinewy and strong, yet capable of incredible tenderness. He gave some damn fine grade-A comfort when he put his mind to it. And his hands...they could handle rough waters or stroke her into orgasmic bliss with equal aplomb.

"You okay?" Chloe asked Tara over her shoulder without tearing her gaze off Ford.

"Yes. Why?"

"Because you just moaned." She craned her neck and eyed Tara. "And probably you should check for drool."

Tara gave her a nudge that might have been more like a push, then surreptitiously checked for drool. Then she went back to staring at Ford. Given the look of satisfaction on his face, he'd enjoyed his sail, and something pinged low in her gut because she'd seen that look on his face before: when he'd been stretched out above her, as intimately joined to her as a man could get.

She made another sound before she could stop herself, then bit her lip. Bending, she concentrated on tying up their boat, but her fingers wouldn't work. "Dammit."

Two hands appeared in her vision—big, work-roughened hands—not taking over the task, but guiding her into the correct knot. "Like this," Ford said.

"I was fixin' to do it myself."

"She can do everything by herself," Chloe told him, heavy on the irony. "Bless her heart."

Tara straightened and shot Chloe a look, and got an eye roll in return.

"Come on, Mad," Chloe said. "I think Tara needs a little time out." And then she took her itty bitty bikini-clad body toward the inn, Maddie in tow.

Once again leaving Tara with Ford.

Tara flashed a vague smile in his direction without looking directly into his eyes—the key to not melting, she'd discovered—and went to step onto the dock.

Ford slid his hand in hers to assist, not letting go of her, even after she tried to tug free. He merely tightened his grip and waited her out.

With a deep breath, she tipped her head back and met his gaze. And yep, right on cue, as she took in the two-day stubble on his square jaw, the fine laugh lines around his mesmerizing eyes and the effortlessly charming smile, she melted like a glob of butter on a stack of pancakes.

"What?" he asked.

She studied his big, wet, gorgeous self and slowly shook her head. "Why couldn't you have gone bald or gotten fat?" It really was a bee in her bonnet that he looked even better now at thirty-four than he had at seventeen. "The least you can do is burp or scratch an impolite body part, or something equally unattractive."

His brow shot up. "You want me to scratch my ass?"

"Yes," she said. "And maybe you could also pick your nose in public."

His smile came slow and sure.

"*What?*"

"You want to jump me."

God, yes. "Look, I have bigger problems than this, okay? Problems far more pressing than our being comfortable with each other now that we're living in the same town again."

Ford looked at her for a beat, then stepped into her space, crowding her up against the wall of the marina building. "I can give you something to take your mind off your other problems," he said in a silky promise.

There was no doubt in her mind.

Sensing capitulation, he pressed his mouth to the underside of her jaw. "Just say the word."

Word, she thought dizzily with a delicious shiver.

With a single stroke of his finger along her temple, he pulled back, eyes dark on hers as he waited.

Sex. Just sex. And it'd be great. But not enough. Not nearly enough. "No," she said with far more resolution than she felt.

If he was disappointed, he didn't let it show as he backed away, leaving her leaning against the wall for support, her clothes wet from his body, her body overheated to say the least.

Not a new state when it came to him.

When he was gone, Tara blew out a shaky breath and headed up to the inn. She entered the cool, fresh rooms and gave herself a minute.

"Ms. Daniels? You okay?"

Tara turned to Carlos Rodriguez, the local high school kid they'd hired for the summer to do odd jobs like moving furniture, painting, and cleaning. With his multiple visible piercings and homeboy pants that hung just a little south of civilized, they'd all been a little leery of just how good a worker he might turn out to be, but he'd done well. At seventeen, he was already six feet tall, with a lanky build that suggested he didn't get three squares a day.

Tara knew from his application and obtaining his work permit from school that he was smart but an underachiever, and possibly a bit of a troublemaker. But that's what happened when a kid had no authority figure in his life and was forced to work odd jobs to support himself, his younger siblings, and his grandma.

"I'm fine," Tara assured him.

"I did the weeding and painted the laundry room."

"Perfect. Did you eat lunch?"

"Yes."

She bit back a sigh at the lie. "I left you a sandwich in the fridge."

"Thanks, but—"

"No buts. Eat it."

He turned away so she couldn't see his face. "I'll bring it home with me."

Where he'd undoubtedly give it to his sisters or grandma. "Eat it here. I'll make you more to bring home."

He turned back and looked at her for a long beat, clearly struggling between pride and hunger. The lure of food won out, and he went into the kitchen.

Chloe came into the room from the hallway, pulling her cute little sundress on over her bikini. "Hope you're pleased with yourself," she said to Tara. "You chased Maddie away again. Little Miss Hates-Confrontations just up and vanished for friendlier waters."

"There was no confrontation."

"Are you kidding me?" Chloe said. "You're a walking confrontation."

"What are you talking about? *You're* the one who starts everything. You never know when to just keep something to yourself."

Chloe stood hands on hips, irritated. "Because sweeping things under the carpet and keeping everything deep inside would make me what, *you*? Sorry, no can do, Sis. But since you're never going to see my side of this, maybe we should just agree to disagree."

"Fine," Tara said.

"Fine. And let's not speak for a while either, at least until you can admit you're actually wrong once in a blue moon."

"I'd be happy to admit I was wrong," Tara said. "If I was."

Chloe tossed up her hands, then turned to Carlos as he came back from the kitchen, eating the sandwich. "Hey, Cutie," she said with her usual easy charm, as if she hadn't just been snarling at Tara. "What's up?"

Carlos shot her a rare smile.

Chloe had that effect on men.

"Almost done for the day unless you have anything else."

"Yes," Chloe said. "I do have something else. Maybe you can tell my sister here that no one likes a sanctimonious know-it-all."

Carlos divided a glance between them.

"Don't put him in the middle," Tara said.

"You're just worried he'll side with me." Chloe turned back to Carlos. "I'll give you a raise if you'll also tell her she's getting wrinkles from holding all her shit in."

"There's a recipe on the Facebook page for that," Carlos said, stuffing in the last bite of his sandwich.

Oh for the love of God, Tara thought, grinding her back teeth together. "She means I'm—"

"Uptight," Chloe said helpfully, laughing. "And could you also tell her that it's annoying to have to look at her lingerie that she's got constantly hanging from the shower rod?"

"Actually," Carlos said, finally looking interested, "that wouldn't annoy me one bit. Uh, which bathroom was that exactly?"

Chapter 5

"Never mess up an apology with an excuse."
CHLOE TRAEGER

A few days later, Ford was at The Love Shack, out back in the small yard hosing down the tables and chairs. He had his music on low, but no matter how low he kept it, his neighbor next door—Ted the used bookstore owner—would poke his head out and ask for it to be turned down. Ford tried to picture what the guy's house must look like and decided it was probably all Enya, cats, and houseplants.

Jax, who'd come to help, sat on top of one of the freshly cleaned tables, texting—obviously being hugely helpful.

"Working hard?" Ford asked, heavy on the sarcasm.

All hunched over so he could see his screen in the bright sun, Jax didn't answer.

"Earth to Jax."

"Hmm." Jax's dark head remained bent, his thumbs flying. "Working hard here, man."

Ford narrowed his eyes. Once upon a time, Jax had been a hotshot lawyer who wore designer suits and drove a Porsche, but these days he stuck with Levi's, tees, a beat-up old Jeep, and the laziest dog on the planet. He spent his days renovating and his nights doing Maddie, and he'd never seemed happier. Ford walked behind him to read what he was typing. " 'That's very naughty, little girl; you know what happens to naughty girls,' " Ford read out loud. "Looks like work all right."

Unrepentant, Jax grinned and hit SEND. "Hey, a relationship *is* work."

"Yeah, I bet all the sex is killing you."

"You ought to try it sometime."

"Daily sex?" Ford asked.

"A relationship, you dumb ass. It's been a while since...what was her name? That hot snowboarder you dated last winter?"

"Brandy," Ford said and felt a fond smile cross his mouth.

"Yeah. Brandy." Jax smiled. "I liked her."

"That's because she always hugged you hello and she was stacked."

"Hey, she was also very nice," Jax said. "Why did you two break up again?"

"Because her mother kept instant messaging me, asking when I was going to marry her."

"Which sent you into flight mode," Jax said. "And what about Kara, the one you actually *did* almost marry?"

"That was a long time ago. She..." Got a little fame crazy. *His* fame crazy, back during his serious racing days. "Didn't work out. And you know all this already."

"Still haven't heard a compelling reason for you to be alone," Jax said, "except that weird inability-to-commit thing you've got going."

"I do not have an inability to commit."

"Whatever, dude."

"I don't!"

"No? Then find someone to be with and let it work out for you."

"Yeah, I'll get right on that."

Jax slid his phone into his pocket and gave him a once-over. "You're in a good place, so why not?"

Ford knew damn well that his life, at least on the surface, *was* in a good place. He had everything he needed, and the ability to get things he didn't. Which was about as different from his childhood as he could get, having grown up wild and reckless and not giving a shit.

Good thing Jax and Sawyer had. Given a shit. The three adolescent best friends had stuck together like thieves, having each other's backs through thick and thin. And there'd been a lot of thin. They'd been each other's family, and still were.

But it wasn't as if Ford didn't believe in relationships. He did. In fact, he'd had his share of good ones. He just hadn't had one that had stuck.

His own fault, as Jax was not so subtly pointing out.

"How about Tara?" Jax asked.

"Huh?"

"Let me rephrase. You ever going to tell me about the thing with her?"

"What thing?"

Jax shook his head in disgust.

Fine. So they all knew there'd been a thing. A huge thing. That one long-ago summer Ford had never been able to forget. He'd been working his ass off, living on his boat so as not to put a bigger burden on his grandmother, and feeling pretty alone and shitty while he was at it. Jax had been sent off to some fancy camp by his father, and Sawyer, the third musketeer, had gone to juvie for some fairly spectacular and innovative "borrowing" of a classic Mustang that unfortunately had belonged to the chief of police at the time.

Ford had been left to his own devices, and even working his fingers to the bone at any and all odd jobs he could get hadn't kept his mind busy enough. There'd been long, hot nights alone on his boat until Tara had shown up.

With one glare of her angry, whiskey eyes, Ford had lost a piece of his heart.

He'd softened her up. She'd done things for him, too, but making him soft hadn't been one of them.

They'd burned hard and bright that summer. And when Tara had shown up on his boat in tears, pregnant, they'd had two very different knee-jerk reactions. His had been that they could make it work. They could make a family, a *real* one. He'd drop out of school and marry her.

But Tara had different ideas. She'd known that she needed to let the baby go, that she couldn't offer it any kind of life. Between the two of them, only she'd been grown up enough to see past her own grief. She'd explained to Ford that they couldn't do this, that the baby deserved more than either of them could provide.

And she'd been right. They'd done the right thing. Ford knew that. He'd always known that, but losing the baby had been hard.

Losing Tara had been even harder.

When she'd shown up in Lucky Harbor again after seventeen years, the emotions he'd capped off had easily surfaced again, shockingly so, but he hadn't worried. He'd known she was only in town to inspect the inn Phoebe had left them. He figured she'd be in and out.

But here it was, six months later, and she was *still* poking at his old wounds just by being here. He scrubbed a hand over his face. It'd taken him a long time to be okay about all that had happened, but it still haunted him when he let it. He'd done the right thing by signing away his rights to his daughter, he had. He'd done the right thing for both the baby and Tara. But there was always the regret.

Since that time, he'd done his damnedest to live his life in such a way that there were no more regrets, so that *he* called the shots. And yeah, maybe he did so to the point of being too ready to just let things go.

And people.

He shrugged. It'd all worked out fine. Or it would have, but now Tara was back in his world, and in no apparent hurry to leave.

She'd lived her life very carefully, with purpose. She was a woman who knew what she wanted. And what she didn't. Ford knew he belonged firmly in the latter category.

Worked for him. He was an unhappy memory to her. And a risk, a bad one. He got that. But defying all logic, their attraction was still strong.

"You look like you just had a Hallmark movie moment with yourself," Jax said.

Ford ignored him and turned to the gate as someone came through.

Carlos. The kid often came by looking for extra work in spite of the fact that he already worked at the inn and also bussed at the diner, on top of going to school and being head of his grandmother's household.

A situation that Ford understood all too well. "Hey. Need some hours?"

"No, I'm good," Carlos said. "I'm on at the inn today. Maddie sent me into town to get some stuff. She asked me to come by and tell you that tonight's the night."

Ford nodded. "Tell her to consider it done."

"Consider what done?" Jax asked.

"The inn's appliances were delivered today," Ford told him. "Maddie asked me to stock their kitchen tonight, as a surprise for Tara."

Jax raised a brow. "Really?" he said, his tone suggesting that he found this little tidbit fascinating.

"Like you don't know that Maddie burns water," Ford said. "And Chloe would probably booby-trap the place just to irritate Tara. So Maddie asked me to do it. It's no big deal."

"I just find it interesting that you're helping the woman that you claim to not be interested in," Jax said in his annoying, lawyerly logical voice.

Ford had *never* claimed not to be interested, and Jax knew it. He'd simply refused to talk about it.

"Maddie said to remind you that it's a surprise," Carlos said. He grimaced and shuffled his weight, looking uncomfortable now. "She said I should mention that *twice*, since you don't always take direction well."

Jax grinned proudly at this. "That's my woman."

"And she said *you're* to stay out of it," Carlos said to

Jax in apology. "She said...ah, hell." The kid pulled a piece of paper from his pocket. "You're not to poke at Ford," he read. "You're to leave him alone or else you can forget about tonight." Carlos carefully folded Maddie's note back up and didn't look at either man directly.

"That's your woman," Ford said to Jax dryly.

"Let me see that." Jax snatched the note from Carlos, unfolding it again to take a look. "Damn, she really did write that." He handed it back.

"So the inn will be empty?" Ford asked the kid.

Carlos nodded. "Maddie said she has plans with Jax— assuming he doesn't mess with you over this. Chloe's giving a yoga class at the rec center. And Tara will be out."

"Out," Ford said. "Out where?"

Carlos hesitated and went back to his notes, even turning the paper over, but apparently there was nothing there to help him.

Ford thought of all the things that "out" could mean. She could be out bossing people around at the diner. She could be out shopping for more of those fantasy-inducing, uppity clothes she favored. Hell, maybe she was out making a list on how to further stomp on his heart.

Nah, she'd already done that.

"She has a date," Carlos finally said.

"A date?" Jax looked surprised. "*Tara?*"

If things had been different, Ford might have laughed. As it was, suddenly he couldn't breathe very well. *Captain Walker to Air Traffic Control, we have a fucking problem.* "A date," he repeated.

Carlos was edging his way back to the gate. "Yeah, that's what Maddie said."

Huh. Ford should like the idea of her dragging some other guy's heart through the mud instead of his, but *Tara on a date*. Nope, he could roll it around in his head as much as he wanted, he still hated it.

Tara's blind date had made dinner reservations for them at a sushi joint in the next town over.

Probably for the best.

She'd asked Boyd to pick her up at the diner because one, she didn't want to have to go back to the inn to change after her shift, and two—and she really hated to admit this even to herself—she didn't want Ford to be at the marina and possibly see her getting picked up. She couldn't explain that one even to herself.

What she hadn't expected was for Boyd to be several inches shorter than her, fifty pounds heavier, and dressed in a suit. "Do you eat here for free?" Boyd asked. "Because we could stay here tonight if that's the case."

"Wow," Jan whispered as Tara walked by her perpetually grumpy boss. "He's a catch."

Tara ignored her.

"Do you have flats?" Boyd asked. "Because looking up at you makes my neck hurt. No offense."

Perfect. Because now they were going to have to go back to the inn after all, so she could change into flats.

It wasn't as if she was an Amazon, she thought to herself as they walked the pier to Boyd's car. Most men seemed to be okay with her height. Sure, once in a while she wished she was shorter so she could actually feel... petite. Protected.

Just right.

64 Jill Shalvis

But the truth was that only one man had ever made her feel that way.

"I just really hate having a neck ache," Boyd said.

He hated a neck ache, and she hated a headache, which she could feel coming on. This did not bode well for the evening ahead. For a moment, she looked past the Ferris wheel, eyeing the way the pier jutted from the beach into the ocean almost as far as she could see, and wished she was...

Sailing.

Ridiculous. She got into Boyd's car. He kept his eyes on the road as he drove slowly toward the inn. Slowly, as in a-herd-of-turtles-stampeding-through-peanut-butter slowly. The guy didn't pass a single indent in the road that didn't require a nearly complete stop. When they finally pulled up before the inn, Tara checked for gray hair while Boyd took a good look at the place.

Tara looked, too. She was so damn proud of what she and her sisters had done here. It'd been a long haul but the beach inn looked warm and welcoming, and she couldn't wait to see it filled with guests.

"Are you going to paint it?" Boyd asked.

"Yes." In fact, the painters were due tomorrow. She'd been waiting for a week. If they didn't show, she was going to get out a paintbrush and do it herself.

"Because it really needs to be painted if you want to make any money."

"We're aware," Tara said as mildly as she could. "Thanks. I'll change my shoes and be right back."

"No, offense," he said, getting out of the car with her. "But in my experience, letting a date out of my sight never works out well for me."

Surprise. And if he said "no offense" one more time tonight, *living* wasn't going to work out well for him.

Boyd smiled grimly. "I don't think I make the best first impression."

"Maybe if you didn't require them to be shorter than you, that would help," Tara said.

He nodded. "That's good advice."

They walked up the steps to the inn. "Hey," Boyd said. "You could cook for us here; I wouldn't mind. Grandma said you were an amazing chef. What do you suppose you could whip up?"

A major attitude, that's what she could whip up. Bless his heart. And to make it worse, she was craving comfort food for some reason, hankering for hot fried chicken and cold potato salad like nobody's business. Which proved that while you could take the girl out of the south, you couldn't really take the south out of the girl. "I haven't stocked the kitchen yet," she said. Not to mention that she'd just spent the past eight hours on her feet cooking at the diner. "Our appliances were just delivered. I haven't even unpacked the dishes."

"Oh. That's too bad." He followed her inside, right on her heels, taking the whole not-letting-her-out-of-his-sight thing very seriously. As she moved through the bottom level on the brand new wood floors, Tara drew in a deep, satisfied breath at the scent of fresh paint and polished wood. More pride filled her, as well as something more, that sense of . . .

Home.

She was still basking in the surprise of that sensation

when she realized someone was rattling around in the kitchen.

The place was empty tonight, or was supposed to be, but there was a light beneath the double kitchen doors and from the other side she heard the low, unbearably familiar voice that she'd have recognized anywhere.

"Oh, fuck, yeah." Ford, speaking low and husky. "That's the way, baby. Just like that."

Boyd blinked at Tara. "Uh, that sounds a little like someone's . . . *you know*."

Yeah. She did know.

"That's right, nice and deep," came Ford's voice. "Right up the center."

Tara turned back to Boyd to tell him to wait and bumped right into him. "*Stay*," she said firmly, and pushed open the door to face her sexy-as-hell intruder doing God-knew-what in her kitchen.

Chapter 6

"Never miss a good chance to shut up."
Tara Daniels

When Tara stepped into the kitchen, she found exactly what she'd expected. Ford: bartender, sailor, town cut-up, and overall bane of her existence.

What she didn't expect was for him to be working.

He had his back to her and was gazing into the open cabinets, a canister of sugar in his hand as he considered where to place it.

"Ford," she said with what she felt was remarkable calm.

No reaction. He kept doing his thing, which appeared to be stocking her shelves. She waited until he set the canister next to the salt and pepper. Good decision, she thought approvingly, but what the hell? "Okay, listen," she said, hands on hips. "You're in *my* place and—"

"*Yes!*" he yelled suddenly, startling her. "That's the way, baby. Go-go-go, *take it all the way*!" He accompanied this with an innately male, testosterone-fueled fist pump, turning just enough that Tara could see a cocky grin cross his face.

Catching sight of her, he kept grinning as he pulled out an earphone. "Mariners," he said. "Top of the ninth. Bases loaded. *Sweet* game."

"Baseball." Not sex on her countertops.

Ford arched a brow. "Yeah, baseball. What did you think?"

"Nothing. I don't know."

He flashed another grin, and this one was pure badass. It went well with the perfectly fitted and professionally distressed jeans sitting low on his hips and snug across his very nice ass. He wore battered cross trainers and a black T-shirt that managed to emphasize the strength and build of his wide shoulders and broad chest. And a certain naughty look in his eyes.

"Anyone ever tell you that your pretty, Southern belle accent thickens when you lie?" he asked.

"No. What in Sam Hill are you doing here, Ford?"

He smiled. "And also when you're pissy."

"I'm not pissy!"

His eyes cut to the doors behind her as they cracked open to reveal Boyd peeking his head in.

Tara gritted her teeth and introduced them. The two men shook hands while Boyd sized up the much taller Ford. "It's the heels," Boyd said.

Ford cocked his head. "Excuse me?"

"The reason I'm so short is that she's in heels."

"Of course," Ford said after a full beat. "It's the heels." He looked at Tara, face bland.

She did her best not to squirm.

"Listen, Tina—" Boyd started. "We should really get going—"

"Tara," she said.

"Tara." He nodded. "Sorry. Anyway, we really need to get a move on if we're going to make the early bird special."

Right. Except she couldn't do it. She just couldn't. She wanted something fried, in her damn heels, with someone who knew her damn name. "I think it's best if we make it for another night." Like, say, never.

Boyd blinked, slow as an owl. "Is it because you have a headache? Because I have Advil in the car for when my dates get a headache."

"Yes, it's because of a headache," Tara said, very carefully not looking at Ford. "A massive headache. But it needs more than Advil. I'm sorry, Boyd."

He sighed. "It's okay. I got further with you than any of my other dates lately. So that's something, right?"

Ford raised a brow in Tara's direction. She sent him a glare and walked Boyd out. When she came back into the kitchen, Ford was waiting for her, clearly amused.

"You used me to dump your date," he said.

" 'Dumped' is . . . harsh," she said.

"And accurate."

"And accurate," she agreed and sighed. "He had bad breath."

"Well then."

He was laughing at her, the bastard. "This isn't funny, Ford. I really needed a date."

"That's not what I would have guessed."

"And what does that mean?"

"It means," he said, pulling a frying pan and some oil out of her cabinets like he was right at home. "That I remember how you get when you're uptight and anxious. I also remember the only thing that relaxed you."

Tara had a flash to a certain long ago night on the docks, after a fight with her mother that had left her shaky and alone. Ford had found her, and in shockingly little time, had her forgetting her troubles.

Naked therapy, Ford style.

It'd worked. Tara felt heat flood her face. "Yes, well, sex isn't on the table."

He gestured to the pan. "I was talking about fried chicken, but your idea has merits, too. Come here, Tara."

Said the spider to the fly. "I don't think so."

Ford smiled and pulled a package of chicken from the refrigerator. He located the seasonings and bread crumbs he wanted, heated the pan, and poured her a glass of wine.

Tara looked around, trying to put two and two together as to why the bane of her existence was trespassing on her territory. "I just don't understand why you're here."

"I'm surprising you." Ford poured another wine for himself, looking comfortable in his own skin as he got to work cooking for her, occasionally drinking from the glass in his big hand. He fried the chicken with the easy flicks of an experienced wrist, flashing her a look that did something funny to her stomach.

And south of her stomach.

She told herself to ignore the attraction that she didn't want, but her hormones had their own agenda. Forcing herself to tear her eyes off him, she took in the kitchen, and how it felt to use it for the first time. It felt good, she realized. Really good. And there was something else. With Ford in it, the room seemed cozy, intimate.

And damn if he wasn't taking up too much of it.

The air had begun to smell like heaven, and Tara could hear the sizzle and pop of the oil. Her mouth watered. "So about this surprising me thing."

"Hush," he said, and before she could hurt him for that, he nudged her wine glass to her lips. "Just stand there and give your brain a couple of minutes off. Five minutes, Tara. Better yet, sit." He gently pushed her onto a barstool. "Take a deep breath." He waited until she did. "Good," he said. "Now let it out, slowly. Repeat a few times."

She glared at him, but continued to breathe. Slow. In and out. She drank. Breathed some more. And damn if after five minutes she didn't feel a whole hell of a lot better about the evening. "It's the wine," she said.

He refilled her glass and handed her a plate loaded with fried chicken. "It's also the company."

Tara laughed at his cockiness and took a bite of his chicken. And then moaned. "Lord almighty."

He smiled. "Yeah?"

"Oh yeah. This is amazing." She pointed at him. "Which you already know and which doesn't get you off the hook. Okay, so one more time, slowly and precisely— why were *you* putting my spices away?"

"Because your sisters asked me to. They asked because you're a control freak who'll bitch the air blue if they get left on the counter."

"I am not a—" She broke off and drew in a deep,

relaxing breath. She was. She really was a complete and utter control freak. Another deep breath. Another sip of wine.

His eyes were laughing at her, which she ignored because he was back to unloading her spices. "You can't put the basil and cumin so close to the stove," she said. "They'll go bad."

"They need to be in easy reach, and if this place sees anything close to the kind of business I think it will, the spices won't last long enough to go bad."

She stood up and moved close to reach out and stop him, accidentally brushing against his big body. That was so supremely annoying—seriously, could he be any sexier?—that she forgot to apologize. In fact, she might have given him a little tiny shove to get out of her way.

He held his ground, refusing to budge.

"*Everything* goes bad," she murmured, trying to reach the basil. She couldn't have it next to the cumin—yuck.

"Not everything," he said, and shifted to come up right behind her, crowding her.

Of their own accord, her eyes drifted closed and her body quivered. Because no matter how much time had passed, every part of her remembered every part of him. Gripping the countertop in front of her, she bowed her head and choked out his name as his long arms came around her.

But instead of touching her, he grabbed the basil for her without even stretching, the tall, gorgeous bastard, and set it down in front of her.

"The poppy seeds will start to smell disgusting if they're not in the fridge," she said.

Lowering his head, he sniffed at her neck.

"Not me," she said with a low, helpless laugh. "The poppy seeds."

"You're right. Because you smell amazing. You always did."

Oh, God. Her knees actually wobbled at that. "I smell like fried chicken."

"Mh-mmm. Finger lickin' good."

Her fingers turned white on the counter. "Why did my sisters pick you to do this?"

"Because I offered to. Jax offered, too, but he's kitchen-challenged, so they wouldn't let him."

"I didn't ask for help."

"No kidding." He turned Tara to face him, his expression amused. "You'd choke on your own tongue before you asked for help. This was to be a surprise for you, Tara. A fully stocked kitchen, ready to go."

That Maddie and Chloe had even wanted to do this for her touched Tara more than she could have imagined.

"Oh, and I brought you my crepe pan." Ford gestured toward the island counter. "Maddie said you'd wanted to make crepes but that you didn't have a good pan for it."

She glanced at it, then let out a low breath. A Le Creuset. She pushed past him to run a reverent finger over the beautiful pan and nearly moaned. "It's beautiful," she whispered.

He let her drool over it for a moment before speaking again. "As for why it's *me* specifically doing the stocking…" He shrugged. "I know what I'm doing."

Yes, this was true. Ford always knew exactly what he was doing.

"I was just startled to see you in here is all," she said. "Given that we . . . that I—"

"Hate me," he said mildly.

A knot formed in her throat and couldn't be swallowed away. "I don't hate you, Ford. I never hated you."

He was quiet a moment, just watching her. The earlier spark in his eyes was gone. "They trusted me to do this for you," he said simply. "Just as, once upon a time, you trusted me, too." With that, he slid his earphones back in and dismissed her, going back to unpacking.

She stared at his broad shoulders, the stiff back, and realized she wasn't the only one with some residual resentment issues. Something sank low in her gut at that, possibly a big serving of humble pie. Dammit. She was a lot of things, but a complete bitch wasn't one of them. With a sigh, she came up behind him. "Ford."

Not answering, he opened another cabinet and studied the space.

Ducking beneath his outstretched arms, she stepped in between him and the counter and turned to face him.

He looked down at her, and she found herself holding her breath. Unintentional as it'd been, now she was standing within the circle of his arms, and more memories slammed into her.

Good, warm, fun, sexy memories . . .

Even with the wedged heels that Boyd had resented, she only came up to Ford's chin. When he'd been seventeen, he'd been this tall, but he'd been much rangier from not having enough to eat, and also from working two, sometimes three jobs in a day. That had been before he'd gotten onto the sailing circuit and made a decent living in endorsements. Though looking at him now, one would never know money was no longer an issue. The man might drive her crazy, but he didn't have a pretentious bone in his perfect body.

And the body...goodness. He'd filled it out, with solid muscle and a double dose of testosterone. There was also a level of confidence, an air that said he'd listen to whatever anyone had to say but that he wouldn't necessarily give two shits about it. She met his gaze and drew a shaky breath.

He didn't move. His eyes were dark and unfathomable, his body relaxed and at ease. He was waiting for her to speak, or maybe, better yet, to go away. "Thank you for doing this," she said.

"You're welcome." His voice was lower now, and slightly rough as well, leaving her with the oddest and most inexplicable urge to reach up and put her hand on his face to soothe him.

She'd done that for him, once upon a time. She'd been there to listen, to ease his aches, to touch him when he needed.

He'd done the same for her.

They'd healed each other.

And now there was a huge gaping hole between them, and she had no idea how to cross it.

Or if she even wanted to.

No, that was a lie. A part of her wanted to cross it. Badly. But before she could go there, he turned away, going back to stocking her cabinets. Which he was doing simply because her sisters had asked him.

They couldn't have found anyone better equipped

for the job. Ford had always cooked. Hell, he ran a bar and grill for fun. He, better than anyone else she knew, understood what a kitchen needed and how it should be organized. She watched as he picked up a twenty-pound bag of flour as if it were nothing and set it on the counter to open it.

He had her pretty flour container next to it, ready to be filled, and she moved in. "Here, let me."

"I've got it."

"I'm here, Ford. You might as well make the best of it. I'm not going to just stand around and watch you do all the work."

When he didn't stop his movements, she gave him a little hip nudge and reached for the bag.

"Fine." Raising his hands in surrender, he backed up, just as she ripped the bag open with slightly too much force. Flour exploded out of the bag. After a few stunned beats, she blinked rapidly to clear her eyes, and looked at herself. *Covered* in flour. She lifted her head and eyed Ford, who was wisely fighting his smile. "You did this on purpose," she said.

"No, that was all you."

She attempted to shake herself off. "Better?"

He ran a hand over his mouth, probably to hide his smile. "Yes."

"You're lying," she said, eyes narrowed.

"Yes."

Okay, that was it. She stalked toward him.

Laughing out loud now, Ford straightened. "Whatever you're planning to do," he warned. "Don't."

"Oh, Sugar." Didn't he know better than to tell her

what to do by now? "*Watch me*." She backed him up
against the counter and held him there—plastering herself to him from chest to belly to thigh...and everything
in between—on a one-woman mission to cover him in
flour, too. "Gotcha," she said triumphantly as she rubbed
up against him. "Now you're just as big a mess as me."

His hands were at her hips. "Is that right?" His voice
sounded different now. Lower. Rough as sandpaper.

And heat slashed right through her. "Uh-huh." She bit
her lip, realizing that her voice was different, too, and
that she was staring at his mouth.

And then she realized something else. She wasn't
breathing.

He wasn't, either.

Of their own accord, her hands slid up his chest,
wrapped around his neck, and then...oh God, and then.

Ford said her name on a rough exhale. Holding her
against the hard planes of his body, his eyes filled with
a quiet intensity, he lowered his head. "Stop me if you're
going to," he said in quiet demand, all humor gone.

Tara sucked in some air, but didn't stop him. Not when
his lips came down on hers, and not when he kissed her
until she couldn't remember her own name.

Chapter 7

♥

"Accept that some days you're the bug, and some days you're going to be the windshield."
TARA DANIELS

Dazed, Ford tightened his grip on Tara, hearing the groan that her kiss wrenched from deep in his throat. *She* was kissing *him*. He couldn't have been more surprised if she'd hauled off and decked him. But having her push him up against the counter and kiss him hard like she was…oh, yeah. *Way* better than anything that had happened all day.

All damn year.

Ah, hell. Clearly she'd finally done it, she'd driven him bat-shit crazy, but she felt so good against him. Warm and soft, willing. *Amazing.*

And aggressive.

Christ, there was nothing more irresistible than Tara on a mission. And that he was that mission made it even better.

She pulled back slightly and he smiled. "Was that supposed to be punishment?"

"Yes." Her fingers curled into his shirt. "So be quiet and take it like a man."

Ford was still smiling when she kissed him this time, but the amusement faded fast, replaced by a blinding, all-consuming need.

All too soon, she pulled back again, eyes dark, mouth wet from his. "Is there anyone in your bed?" she asked, her voice low and extremely southern.

He loved the way her accent thickened when she felt something particularly deeply. "No," he said. "There's no one in my bed." Except for her, hopefully. Soon. Because this was waaay better than pushing each other's buttons.

"Just wanted to make sure." With each word, her lips just barely grazed his, making him all the hotter. Tightening his grip on her, he whipped them around, trapping her between him and the counter. The scent of her was as intoxicating as her kiss, and when she stared at his lips and licked hers, something inside him snapped. Hauling her up against him, flour and all, he let loose the pent-up yearning and temper and ache he'd been barely reining in.

She hesitated for less than a beat before tightening her grip on him and kissing him back with a passion that nearly knocked them both to their asses. "No one's here?" he asked against her mouth.

"No one."

He had her divested of her short, lightweight sweater and was working on the buttons of her dress, thinking this was the best idea he'd ever had. No more dancing around each other. From now on, all their dancing would be done naked. Naked was good. Naked was *great*.

Tara appeared to feel the same. Her hands were everywhere, his chest, his arms, his ass, stroking and tormenting. The only sound was their heavy breathing and the sexy little murmur she let out when he cupped her breasts.

He remembered that sound. He'd dreamed about that sound. She writhed under his touch, pressing closer, like she needed to climb up his body—which he was all for, by the way. Her fingers found their way beneath his shirt, running lightly over the skin low on his abs, just above his low-riding jeans.

Ford wanted more and took it, letting his hands do the walking and talking beneath her clothes. There was no question about what they were doing now, or why. No thinking. Just feeling, and God help him, he was feeling a whole hell of a lot. Soul-deep, wrenching hunger. And need.

Nothing new when it came to Tara.

His next staggering thought, more than the feel of her hands beneath his shirt gliding downward, caught him. The last time they'd done this, they'd nearly destroyed each other.

Or at least Tara had destroyed *him*. Ford still wasn't clear on what she'd felt. She'd been good at holding back. She didn't seem to be holding back now. Her touch felt so damn good his eyes nearly rolled back in his head, and that was before she went for the button on his Levi's, banishing his ability to think. *Yeah, baby. Go there.*

She played in the loose waistband of his jeans for a minute and he groaned. He had one hand threaded through her hair. The other was cupping a breast, his thumb teasing her nipple as he deepened their kiss until they were both panting.

"Ford," she sighed when he finally released her mouth. Her lips traveled down his throat to the base of his neck, where she licked at his pulse. "Mmm," she said, then nipped him. When he jumped, he felt her smile against him.

"You think that's funny," he asked, dipping his head to return the favor, his hands sliding south, down her back to her sweet, sweet ass. He sucked at her neck and—

"Wow," Chloe said from the doorway. "Now *that's* a way to unpack a kitchen."

"I especially like the flour accents on your pretty dress, Tara," Maddie said from next to Chloe.

Ten more seconds and they wouldn't have seen the pretty dress at all. It would have been on the floor.

Tara jerked away from him, and given her pale face, she'd realized that same thing. Or maybe that was the flour. In any case, in an irresistible bout of multi-tasking, she was busy simultaneously brushing off her dress, checking her hair, and doing her best to look innocent.

"What happened to your date?" Chloe asked Tara.

"I got a headache."

Chloe's brows went up. She started to say something but Maddie covered her mouth. "Pay no attention to us," Maddie said, dragging Chloe to the door.

"If only that was possible," Tara muttered. "And what happened to going out with Jax? And the yoga class?"

Chloe shoved free from Maddie's hand. "Still happening." She looked at her watch. "We have some time yet. We just didn't realize you'd be having casting calls for Pimp My Chef...or was that *Ride* My Chef?"

"Internal editor," Maddie murmured to her, which meant nothing to Ford.

Chloe smiled.

"We were just having a little trouble with the flour," Tara said, still brushing at her dress.

"Yes, I can see that," Chloe said. "I especially like the handprints you left on Ford's butt. Nice job there."

Ford couldn't see the handprints himself but he'd sure enjoyed getting them.

"This is all your fault," Tara said. Ford assumed she was talking to him, but she was actually looking at Chloe. Good. He was off the hook.

Chloe tossed up her hands. "How is it always my fault?"

Tara turned to Ford for backup. So much for off the hook. Probably he'd have been safer in a gunfight. Chloe was looking at him, too. He shrugged vaguely and took over wiping down the countertops to avoid opening his mouth and making everything worse.

"You got Ford to unpack the kitchen?" Tara asked. "Without telling me?"

"Sort of the definition of 'surprise,'" Chloe said.

"Honey, you're looking at this all wrong," Maddie said. "This was about you. About how you're there for us, always. We wanted to be there for you for a change."

"Well, *I* voted to get you a stripper," Chloe said with a reproachful look at Maddie. "But I was vetoed."

Tara let out a short laugh. "Good call," she said to Maddie.

"We really were just trying to help."

"I know," Tara said with a sigh. "And thank you. It was sweet. I'm sorry if I overreacted."

Chloe pulled out her iPhone and hit a few keys.

"What are you doing?" Maddie asked her.

"Marking the event of Tara's apology on my calendar."

Maddie snatched the iPhone, then turned to Tara. "We're sorry, too. We should have thought that you'd want a hand in the unpacking."

"No, it was a lovely gesture and saved me from obsessing over it."

Ford did his best not to smile at that, because he knew that nothing short of the apocalypse could stop Tara from obsessing.

"And you made a good choice with Ford," Tara admitted.

Wow. But when all three women looked at him, he remained quiet, deciding that silence was the best course of action here. They were actually communicating and trying to get somewhere.

Sort of.

In any case, his purpose seemed to be as mediator of some sort, so he tried to look wise.

"Ford," Maddie said, "I have a large ficus in the back of my car. Would you mind unloading it to the deck?"

He recognized a ploy to get rid of him when he heard one, but he was game. "Sure." As he brushed past Tara, taking the time to shift closer than necessary, he pressed his mouth to her ear. "We're not finished."

When the back door shut behind him, Tara sagged against the counter, scrubbing her hands over her face. "Good Lord." She dropped her hands to her sides and found both sisters staring at her with twin expressions of amusement and avid curiosity.

Maddie cracked first with a grin.

Chloe followed.

"Fuck all y'alls," Tara said without much heat. She did like to see their smiles; she just wished it wasn't at her expense.

"Hey, we're not judging," Chloe said. "If I had that fine a man sniffing after me, I'd grab his butt, too. In fact, I'd grab a lot more than that." She rustled through her purse and pulled out a string of condoms, which she slapped on the countertop with great ceremony. "Consider this an early birthday present."

Tara's jaw dropped. "I don't need those."

"You sure about that?"

"There's no sex happening here!"

"Really? So you were just what…playing doctor, checking his tonsils, that sort of thing?"

"We are *so* not talking about this," Tara said.

"Ah, don't be like that," Chloe said. "Join me in the shallow end of the pool, why don't you. The water's warm. Give us the details. Is he as good a kisser as he looks?"

Ignoring her, Tara shifted her gaze to the window to watch Ford unload the ficus plant from Maddie's car. He moved with economical grace and ease, lifting the heavy potted plant like it weighed nothing.

"He's ever so dreamy," Chloe said, coming up next to Tara and mimicking her southern accent.

Tara slid her a look. "Thin ice, Chloe."

Chloe snorted. "Sorry. But I can't take you seriously with flour all over your face."

Dammit. Tara swiped at her cheeks.

"Are you going to tell her or what?" Chloe asked Maddie.

"Tell me what?" Tara asked.

"The reason for the ficus," Chloe said. "It was supposed to be a bouquet of balloons, but I'm trying to go green."

Tara looked at Maddie. "Translation?"

"We want you to quit the diner and make the inn a B&B," Maddie said, then smiled.

Tara stared at her. "What?"

"Yeah," Chloe said. "You cook like an angel but you make next to nothing at the diner, which is so unfair for how hard you work."

"That 'next to nothing' has kept us in food for six months," Tara said. "I can't just quit. We like to eat."

"Well maybe you can't quit *yet*," Maddie said. "But hopefully, once we open, you could. You hate working nights, so we figured you could work here instead, making big breakfasts for the guests. It would change everything. As a bed and breakfast, we'd attract more attention, and…"

"And you think that will make me want to stay," Tara said softly, "if I'm working for myself."

"Us," Chloe said. "You'd be working for *us*."

Tara raised a brow. "Says the girl who *always* has one foot out the door."

"Yes, but *my* foot comes back every time," Chloe pointed out. "And also, I'm not a girl. One of these days you're going to open your eyes and realize I've grown up."

"I'll believe that the day Sawyer stops bringing you home from whatever misadventure you've gotten into."

"One time!" Chloe huffed.

"Actually three times," Maddie corrected, then shrugged when Chloe gave her a hard stare before turning back to Tara. "But this is about you."

"Yeah," Chloe said. "Stop sidetracking, or I'll ask you about Ford and his amazing ass again. By the way, were you going to stir him up and fry him next?"

"Oh my God, please stop talking about flour, tonsils, and *especially* Ford's amazing ass!" Tara said—okay, yelled—just as Ford—naturally—walked back into the kitchen.

In the thundering silence, he met her gaze. She did her best to look cool. Not easy with flour all over her.

"Awkward silence alert," Chloe said. "Maybe you two should just go back to—" she waved her arms, "whatever it was you were doing."

Tara sent Chloe a long look.

"Right," Chloe said, smacking her own forehead. "Stop talking. You said *stop* talking."

"Okay," Maddie said brightly, grabbing Chloe. "We'd love to stay, but we can't."

"Yes, we have to go," Chloe agreed, nonchalantly nudging the string of condoms with one finger toward Tara before Maddie yanked her to the door.

And then, *finally*, they were gone.

Tara let out a breath and turned to the sink, filling a glass of water for herself. She needed a minute.

Or a hundred.

She drank and tried to unscramble her brain cells.

Not Ford. He was leaning on the same counter that he'd pressed her against, looking relaxed and calm and very sure of himself as he eyed the string of condoms lying incongruously on the counter in front of her.

She looked at them too, and suddenly the temperature in the room shot up.

So did her body's temperature. "Ignore those," she told him.

Ford slid her a look that ratcheted the tension up even more. "Can you?"

Lord knew, she was trying. Outside the night was gorgeous, and inside there was this man, also gorgeous. She shook her head and closed her eyes. "How is it that we still feel the pull?"

Ford stepped into her, letting her feel *exactly* how much he still felt it.

"I mean, it shouldn't still be here," Tara whispered against his throat as his arms came around her. "I shouldn't..."

Ache for you...

"Some things just are," he said softly against her hair. "Day turns to night. The ocean tide drifts in and out. And I want you, Tara. Damn you, but I do. I always have."

Chapter 8

"Remember, a closed mouth can't attract a foot."
TARA DANIELS

Tara wanted Ford, too. More than she'd ever wanted anyone. The wanting was in the air around them. It was in his eyes and beating in time with her pounding heart. Maybe she couldn't have her happy ending with him, but surely she could have this.

Ford's mouth left hers to skim along her jaw to her ear. His hands were equally busy, molding her body through the thin, flowing cotton of her sundress. "Say it," he murmured, flicking her earlobe with his tongue.

Tara clutched at him. "I want you too." So much. *Too* much. "Should we—"

"Yes," he said.

She stared up at him. "You don't even know what I was going to say."

"Yes to anything."

"Are you crazy? You can't give me that kind of power. What if I wanted to tie you up and—"

"Still yes," he said and dipped his head to kiss his way down her throat.

She let out a low laugh and slid her hands up his arms, humming in pleasure at the feel of his biceps, hard beneath her fingers.

Nudging her dress off her shoulder, he continued to nibble on her. "You taste good, Tara. So damn good. You always did."

He was at her collarbone now, and her brain cells were shutting down one at a time, making it a struggle to think. "What if this makes things worse?"

His soft laugh huffed against her skin. "You've barely spoken to me the entire six months you've been in town. How can it get worse?"

Good point. "But—"

"Tara." His fingers were on the zipper low on her back. "Stop thinking."

Right. Good idea. "Stopping thinking right now." She paused. "So we're going to..."

"Yes." Ford had been very intent on her zipper but now he lifted his head, and his eyes looked both amused and aroused. "On one condition."

"Wait—" Tara shook her head, which was ineffective at clearing the haze of lust. "What? You don't get to have conditions."

"Just one."

She thought about pushing him away, but then she'd be left in this...this *state*. "What? What is it?"

"You can't go back to ignoring me."

"I don't—"

He put a finger on her lips to hold in the pretty lie. "Yes or no, Tara."

Dammit. "*Yes*."

"Yes what?"

She gaped at him. "You want me to repeat it like an oath?"

"Yes," he said very seriously.

Tara stared at him, into his stubborn green eyes. He stared right back. "*Fine*," she expelled, caving like a cheap suitcase. "I won't go back to ignoring you. Which was never about you, by the way."

Ford arched a brow and she rolled her eyes. "Okay, maybe a little. But it wasn't your fault, Ford. I want you to know that. Really. It was me, and my own...issues."

"You about over those issues?" he asked as he slid his hands down her back to cup her bottom, grinding her against a most impressive erection.

"I'm not sure," she said breathlessly, "but I'm working on them."

"Good."

"So we're done talking?"

"Christ, I hope so," he said fervently, eyes dark and hot when she grabbed the condoms from the counter. When she tucked them into the front pocket of his 501s, he went still, then sucked in a breath as her fingers brushed against the hard ridge of him through the denim.

She wanted more, much more. Taking his hand, she led him out of the inn and across the yard to the small owner's cottage where she lived with her sisters. This had been rebuilt as well. The rooms were no longer 1980s checkered blue and white, but now the same earth tones as the inn.

Home.

There was no sign of her sisters, but after earlier, Tara locked her bedroom door anyway. This room was a pretty pale green, and she'd put fluffy white bedding and a pile of pillows on the queen-sized bed. Her own little corner of heaven. She purposely left the light off, thinking that would be the wisest course of action. Much as she wanted to see Ford's glorious body, she was afraid to look too deeply into his fathomless eyes, knowing that if she did she might drown in them and never come up.

There was also the fact that the last time he'd seen her body, she'd been seventeen. She wasn't certain the years had been as kind to her as they obviously had been to him.

But Ford didn't get the memo about the light. He hit the switch, and a warm glow flooded the room.

Tara hit it again, and everything went blessedly dark.

"*On*," he said firmly, and once more the room lit up.

She opened her mouth to argue, but unceremoniously found herself pinned to the wall by a hard-muscled furnace with wandering hands.

"You still have flour everywhere," Ford whispered in her ear, right before he took the lobe between his lips and sucked. "We need the light to find it all."

Huh. This reasoning could be applied to him as well, and she could get on board with seeing his body up close and personal. To get started, she shoved his shirt up his abs. Happy to help, he tugged it over his head in one economical motion. Almost before it hit the floor, her dress did the same, pooling around her ankles. Before she could bend to pick it up, Ford slid his thigh between her legs and pressed in. He kissed her breast through the lace of her bra, and her brain went into total meltdown. She was kissing whatever part of his delicious body she could reach—his jaw, his throat, the corded muscles of his neck—when she couldn't resist taking a little bite of him.

He hissed in a breath, and she murmured an apology.

"No. Do it again."

Tara obliged, making him groan as she rocked helplessly against the thigh he had between hers, the sensation of him so hard against her making her dizzy. He tugged the straps of her bra to her elbows and trapped her arms at her sides, and then concentrated on driving her crazy. "Ford, my hands—"

"Mmm," rumbled from deep in his throat as his thumbs ran back and forth over her very interested nipples. "Missed this," he said, grinding his hips to hers. "Missed you." He kissed her, then he gave her a gentle but decided push onto the bed. Following her down, he trailed kisses across her jaw and down her neck—and slowly divested her of her bra and panties. When his tongue darted out and made direct contact with her nipple, she gasped, the sound turning into a moan as he sucked her into his mouth. Then he dragged hot, openmouthed kisses along the undersides of her breasts, sending chills up her spine.

"What?" he whispered when she went still.

"You..." Tara had an image of him making love to her all those years ago, how he'd taken the time to learn how to pleasure her. She'd always loved having the undersides of her breasts kissed.

And he'd remembered. He remembered after all this time how she preferred to be touched.

"I what, Tara?"

"You remember me."

"Vividly."

Tara sat up and helped him shove his Levi's off. His skin was warm, and he engulfed her senses, making her sigh into his next kiss. She sighed again when he rolled her beneath him, kissing and nipping his way down her body until he was at the apex of her thighs. Holding them open with his big hands, he smiled. "My favorite part," he said, and then dipped his head and proved it.

He proved it until she was helplessly shuddering and panting for air. "In me," she whispered, pulling him up. "Right now."

She was rewarded with a full-wattage smile as he tore open a condom, rolled it on, and slowly slid inside her, their twin gasps of pleasure echoing around them.

"God, Tara." His voice was so low as to be nearly inaudible. "It's been so long." He pulled out slightly, then flexed his hips and thrust back in. "So good."

The sensation of being filled by him stole her breath. She tried to rock her hips against him but his body was like steel and he had his own pace—which was set to drive-her-out-of-her-mind slow. There was no rushing him. Ever. She knew this about him but still her hands roamed over his smooth, muscular body, urging, coaxing, demanding. When that didn't work, she tugged him down and bit his lower lip.

With a growl low in his throat, he finally set an ago-nizingly measured rhythm, his hips moving in a delicious circle, making her moan with every thrust. But he didn't speed up, even when her fingernails dug into his back and she whispered a desperate "please," arching up and bend-ing her legs, angling him deeper within her.

"Oh, Christ." He dipped his head to kiss her. "Christ, that's good."

"Then go faster!"

"Not yet."

"Dammit—"

"Let go for me, Tara." He cupped her face. "Let some-one else have the control for a little bit."

No, she wasn't good at that. "But—"

"No buts." Ford tangled his fingers in her hair and made sure she shut up by kissing her thoroughly, his tongue sliding against hers.

Probably if anyone else had tried this, they'd have ended up walking funny tomorrow, but when Ford kissed her, she always lost track of her senses, not to mention the time and place. Every. Single. Time. She lost track of *everything* as he moved within her, bringing it all to a slow build that started low in her body and spread.

It took all she had to keep her eyes open and on his. Normally, she needed to close her eyes to concentrate, but with Ford, concentration wasn't necessary. He took her where she needed to go with seemingly no effort at all, and she didn't want to miss a single second of it. Even when her eyes were beginning to flutter shut on their own, she forced them open, unwilling to tear her gaze off his face, not wanting to miss the pure pleasure etched on his features.

Pleasure she was giving him. It was seductive, erotic, and she was burning with need, her entire body throbbing with it.

"Tara," he said, voice rough and thick with desire. "Now."

With nothing more than the demand, he sent her skittering right over the edge. A low, keening cry tore from her throat that she couldn't have held back to save her own life.

She'd given him control after all, she thought dazedly. And as she burst, pulsing hard around him, he pressed himself deeper, then deeper still, coming with a raw, rough, very male sound of gratification as he followed her over.

Ford was still buried deep inside Tara's gorgeous body when they heard the front door of the cottage open and then shut.

"Tara?" a male voice called out, one that had Tara jerking beneath Ford.

"No," she whispered, then shoved Ford off of her and sat up, the sheet clutched to her chest, her eyes wide and horrified. "It can't be."

"Who is it?" Ford asked, frowning.

"Tara? You here?"

Galvanized into action, Tara leapt out of the bed and started yanking on her clothes. "Give me a minute!" she yelled. "I'm coming."

"Yeah, you did," Ford murmured. He had the nail marks on his ass to prove it. "Who's out there, Tara?"

She shoved her feet back into her heels, then did a double take as she realized Ford was still lying in bed. *Naked*. "Oh my God. *Get dressed!*"

She was attempting to work her hair back into submission as he rose and pulled her against him, stilling her frenetic movements. "Talk to me."

"It's Logan," she choked out and shoved at him.

He held on. "Logan," he said, searching his memory banks. "Logan, the ex?"

"Yes. Wait—" She stilled in the act of getting back into her dress. "You know him?"

"Only that he likes to be plastered all over the papers and magazines. And once upon a time, you were plastered there with him." He caught her arm before she could run off. This had been supposedly just sex—but that didn't mean he was happy to find her ex-husband sniffing around. And actually, he was distinctly *un*happy about that. "Why is he here?"

"I don't know." Tara clapped her hands to her face. "And you're still naked."

"Yes, and less than three minutes ago you were enjoying that very fact," he said grimly. "You don't know what he wants?"

She dropped her head to his chest. "No idea."

Ford wrapped his hand around the bulk of her silky hair and gently tugged until she was looking at him. "You asked who was in my bed. Maybe I should have asked who's in yours."

"No one's been in mine! For two years!" She closed her eyes. "*Two years*, Ford."

He stroked a finger over her jaw. "You were overdue," he murmured. Okay, so she and Logan weren't still having sex. That was good. Not that he should care one way or the other. "Why so long?"

"Because I couldn't find anyone I wanted to be with," she said a little defensively. "And now there are *two* men, and one of them is naked and smells like me, and—"

He kissed her, long and deep. Crazy. Stupid. And Christ, so fucking good.

"—and *tastes* like me," she whispered with a moan when they broke apart. "Oh my God, Ford."

Since she looked so adorably miserable and confused, and sounded so panicked to boot—all a rarity for her—Ford let out a breath and stroked a hand down her hair. "I can fix the naked part. You're on your own for the rest, unless you want help encouraging him to get the hell out."

"What? *No.*"

Ouch. But a good reminder of what this was. And what it wasn't.

"Ford. I can't do this with you," she whispered.

"Do what?"

"*This.* It didn't work back then, and it won't work now."

Yes, he knew that. So he had no idea why he backed her to the wall and kissed her again, hard and ravishing, until she was clutching at him. It might have been a stupid, macho, asshole thing to do, but that she looked so dazed when he pulled back helped a lot. "I don't think we're done," he said with a calm he didn't come close to feeling.

"We have to be." She chewed on her lower lip. "I'm working."

"Everyone works, Tara."

"On myself," she blurted out, hurriedly, with a quick

glance at the door, anxiety level clearly high. "When we were together last time, I was young, and I didn't know—I didn't know how to be in a relationship. I was bad at it, at giving myself."

"And with Logan? Were you bad at giving yourself then too?"

"No." She stared up at him, leveling him with those whiskey eyes. "With him, I did the opposite. I gave too much. I gave everything. Don't you see? I have to figure it all out so I don't just repeat my mistakes."

"So that's what you're working on?" he asked. "Figuring out how to give yourself and not lose yourself at the same time?"

"Yes!"

Ah, hell. Out of all the things she could have said, this was the one that got to him, and he stroked a hand over her jaw. "How's that going?"

"Right now? Not so well, actually."

"Tara—"

But she backed up and shook her head sharply. She didn't want his help, or his sympathy. Fair enough. He didn't want to get tangled up in this again anyway.

At least not outside of the bedroom.

"*Tara*?" Logan called from down the hall.

Ford tensed.

Tara closed her eyes. "Just a minute, Logan!"

"Remember my condition," Ford said softly.

"Don't ignore you."

"That's right. And another."

"Ford—" She started to pull away but he grabbed her.

"Don't pull what you did last time," he said. "The running away thing."

"We were seventeen and stupid."

"I'll give you the stupid part."

Her mouth tightened. "I didn't exactly just run off."

"Bullshit." He risked her temper by pulling her in close. He couldn't help himself.

Her breath caught in panic. "Ford! I mean it, I can't do this with you. The first time nearly killed me. Let's just learn from our mistakes, and cut our losses now."

Yeah. Excellent plan. Cut their losses. It made perfect sense, especially given that the last time Tara was here in Lucky Harbor things didn't exactly work out for her—in no small part thanks to him. Chances were good that she'd get the hell out of Dodge sooner than later anyway. And that was okay. He knew she deserved a hell of a lot more than to be stuck in a place with nothing but bad memories.

Of which he was one. The biggest baddest memory she had, no doubt. He pulled on his clothes and without another word gave her what she wanted, what he told himself he wanted as well. He walked out the door and down the hallway, nodding as he came upon the man he recognized from the racing world.

Logan Perrish was just shy of six feet, dark-haired and dark-eyed. He was in more than decent shape and looked designer ready for a cover shoot. A good match for the elegant, sophisticated Tara, which made Ford want to shove the guy's ass out the door.

Logan looked at Ford, then purposely switched his gaze to where Ford had come from, obviously the bedroom. "Are you...a guest?" he asked. "I didn't think that the inn was open yet."

Ford opened his mouth to answer, but Tara, coming from the bedroom as well, beat him to it.

"It's actually going to be a B&B," she said. "But no, he's not a guest. And neither are you. You can't just show up. Did you even knock before you broke in?" She wore her now-wrinkled dress, no shoes. There was a definite glow about her, one Ford took some pride in since he'd put it there.

"Yes, I knocked," Logan said. "You didn't answer." He was staring at Ford. "I didn't realize you'd have company. I was going to wait for you to get home."

Ford stared back.

Tara let out a sound that was part disbelief and part irritation. Ford recognized the irritation since he tended to bring that out in her a lot.

"You didn't realize I'd have company," she repeated slowly. "Even though it's been...what, *months* since we last talked?"

"We always go that long." Logan looked confused. "Is something wrong?"

"No," Tara said. "I'm only having flashbacks to why our marriage failed."

Logan jerked his head in Ford's direction. "Who is he?"

The guy who just did your ex-wife, asshole, Ford thought. Maybe he didn't have a future with Tara, but it would appear he wasn't a big enough man to want her to have a future with Logan, either.

Tara looked at Ford and opened her mouth. Then

closed it again. Clearly she had no idea how to explain him. "Ford Walker," she finally said. "Ford, Logan."

Logan held out his hand. "I'm Tara's husband."

"*Ex*-husband." Tara smacked Logan in the chest. "What's the matter with you? And why are you here again?"

"I missed you."

Tara shocked Ford by bursting out laughing. "Come on," she finally said, still smiling. "Truth."

Logan returned the smile with good grace and some chagrin. "I did miss you." He stepped close, but Tara put up a hand and took a step back from him.

"Logan, when I left you, it took you a month to even realize I was gone. A month, Logan. So what's this really about?"

Logan looked at Ford.

Then Tara looked at Ford, too. Clearly the public forum portion of the evening was over.

Fuck it. If she didn't want to kick her ex-husband to the curb, it was none of his business, and he headed to the door.

Chapter 9

*"Today is the last day of some of your life.
Don't waste it."*
TARA DANIELS

Tara heard the door shut behind Ford as he left and felt a quick stab of pain in her chest. What would it take for him to fight for her, she wondered. For him to take a stand and stick?

More than sex, apparently. But secretly she'd hoped for *exactly* that, for something, anything, to show her that this was more than just a good time in the sack, that...

That they *deserved* another shot.

"New boyfriend?" Logan asked.

She nearly snapped out a sarcastic answer, but as he'd asked quietly and utterly without judgment, she found herself being honest. "More like an old one," she told him. It felt so odd to see him, fit and rangy and beautiful as ever. She waited for the inevitable heart pang at just the sight of him, but all she felt was the ache for what had once been.

And what hadn't been.

"You once told you me that you'd only had one serious boyfriend before me," he said. "From when you were young."

"Yes."

Logan's eyes widened. "And that's him? That's the one you...?"

She grimaced. Logan knew about the baby. He'd been the only one she'd ever told, because she hadn't wanted that kind of secret between them after they'd married. "Yes."

"Are you together now?" Logan asked.

"No." But as soon as the word left her mouth, she wished it back—she and Ford *weren't* together, so why the little stab of regret and the uncomfortable feeling that somehow she'd just been disloyal? "I don't really know," she corrected.

"Okay," Logan said, nodding to himself. "Unexpected detour."

She shook her head, baffled by his presence here, so far from his world. "Why aren't you off somewhere racing for fortune and fame?"

"I'm taking a season off."

This made no sense. Racing was everything to Logan. Everything. Plus, it was difficult if not downright impossible to just "take a season off." There were contractual obligations to owners and sponsors to deal with, pit crews and garage staff to keep on the books. "How can you just..."

Logan shoved the sleeve of his shirt back, revealing his arm. And the brace on it. "That last crash caused some serious ligament damage. I'm facing a couple of surgeries, which means I'm a liability right now on the course. They've hired a replacement for me. Indefinitely."

"Oh, Logan," Tara breathed, knowing how much racing meant to him, and what *not* racing meant, too.

"It's okay," he said. "I don't mind the time off."

"Why?"

"Because the racing world cost me something I miss. You, Tara. It cost me you."

Tara stared at him. There'd been a time when she'd have given anything to hear him say that: her so-called career, her right arm, anything. But things were different now. *She* was different now. "Logan—"

He shook his head. "Don't say anything. Just think about it. Think about me, okay?"

She let out a low laugh and sank to the couch, stunned. "It took me two years to get over you. I can't just make all that happened between us vanish with a snap of my fingers."

"I know, and there's no rush," Logan assured her. "I'm going to be here all summer, so—"

"All summer? What do you mean, all summer?"

He grinned. "To win you back, of course." He knelt down in front of her and flashed the grin that had once been panty-melting. "No decisions now, okay? Like I said, we have all summer."

Oh, God. "You can't just hang around all summer."

"Why not?"

"Because..." She had no idea. "What will you do with yourself?"

He leaned in and kissed her cheek. "I'll figure it out,"

he said. She kept him from moving in closer with a hand to his chest. "And," he went on, looking amused at her boundaries, "it's a busy time for you with the opening of the inn. I can help."

The man had two personal assistants to do his every bidding. He didn't do his own laundry, cooking, housekeeping, accounting...anything. "How exactly can you help?"

"Hey, I'm new and improved." He shot her his most charming smile. "You don't know this about me yet, but you'll see."

"Logan—"

"No rush, Tara. I'm a patient guy."

And then, like Ford, he vanished into the night.

The next morning was damp and foggy. Tara got up at the crack of dawn to walk. Probably she should run, but she hated to run. Her carefully constructed life was going to hell in a handbasket, and she was already planning on inhaling crap food by the bundle. She needed to burn some calories as a preventative measure or she'd be forced to switch to loose sweats in no time.

Tara walked into town and down the length of the pier, waving at Lance, who was hosing down the area out front of his ice cream shop.

Turning around at the end of the pier, she walked back. She could have gone straight to the cottage and had a nice shower but she decided to walk through the marina to burn a few extra calories.

Or because Ford was out there on the dock.

She was drawn to him like a damn magnet. He was

surrounded by sailing boat parts, with a tool in one hand, a part in the other, and a look of concentration on his face.

When he caught sight of her, the corners of that amazing, fantasy-inducing mouth of his quirked. Only a few hours ago, he'd been buried deep inside her, their bodies slick with sweat, their breath mingling, moving in tandem. Just in the remembering, the air around them changed, and she was swamped with more memories.

And longing...

Their gazes caught and held though neither of them spoke. Her nerves fluttered. So did a few other body parts.

"You okay?" he finally asked.

It wasn't a filler question. Last night had been emotional, and he had a look of genuine concern on his face. It conflicted with the picture she had in her head of him walking out the door without a backward glance. "I'm fine."

"Logan gone?" he asked.

"Not exactly."

His jaw tightened, and he took a moment to answer. "What then, exactly?"

"He's staying for the summer." When he locked gazes with her, she lifted her hands. "Not my idea."

He said nothing to this but his silence spoke volumes.

"So is this going to be uncomfortable now?" she asked.

He cocked his head. "Does it feel uncomfortable?"

"I'm not sure yet."

He sighed, muttered something to himself that sounded like "don't do it, man," then wrapped an arm around her waist. He snugged the lower half of his body to hers, rocking against her. "How about now?"

"No, uncomfortable is not the word I'd use," she managed. "Ford." Helpless against the pull of the attraction, not to mention his easy, sexy charm, she gripped his shirt in two fists and dropped her forehead to his chest.

He stroked his hand down her hair, a movement of affection and gentle possession, and she pressed even closer. *Not again*, her brain told her body. *You are not going to have him again.* But her brain wasn't in charge because she glanced over his shoulder at the sailboat, which had a bedroom below deck.

And a bed.

Ford followed her gaze and let out a low laugh. "Okay, but only if you ask nice."

"Not funny," she said and pushed away from him. "Besides, I'm all sweaty, and you're all dirty."

"Then we're already halfway to where I'd like to be."

"Stop it."

"Hey, you're the one who came out of your way to see me."

That was true, which didn't make it any less irritating that somehow he always knew what she was thinking. "I'm going to take a shower." A cold one.

"You want help with that?"

"No!"

"You want me bad," Ford called after her as she walked away.

Yes, she did. Quite badly, in fact. What woman could

help wanting him in her bed? The problem was that Ford didn't tend to exert much energy on things that were difficult. And Tara was just about as difficult as they came. Which meant she needed to resist him and all his gorgeousness because she already knew the ending to their story.

A few nights later, Ford was at The Love Shack serving drinks. The place was busy, which usually gave him a surge of satisfaction. He loved being here, hearing the chatter and the laughter, knowing that he brought everyone together. He'd learned a long time ago to make a family and a home wherever he could. This was both.

The walls of The Love Shack were a deep, sinful bordello red, lined with antique mining tools that he and Jax had collected over the years on various adventures. Lanterns hung from the exposed-beam ceilings and lit up the scarred bench-style tables and the bar itself, which was made of a series of old wooden doors attached end to end.

If Ford wasn't on a boat with the wind hitting his face as he flew over the water at dizzying speeds, then he was at his happiest here.

It was a simple lifestyle, but when it came right down to it, he was a simple guy. Growing up poorer than dirt had ensured that. So had being loved and protected by his grandma to the best of her abilities as they'd worked their asses off. She'd always said that someday it would pay off and she'd get to retire to Palm Springs.

It gave Ford great satisfaction that he'd been able to give that to her, that right this minute she was probably on the deck of the Palm Springs home he'd bought her, sipping iced tea and watching the mountains. It was her favorite pastime after cooking for him on the rare occasions he made it down there to visit, that is. She'd marvel at his height and build every single time he walked in her door, as if she couldn't quite believe he'd grown up from that scrawny, undersized kid he'd once been.

Ford couldn't blame her. He'd managed to live through his teens, and then his twenties in spite of himself, and was now working on his thirties and being a grownup. On accepting his mistakes and living with no regrets, though his biggest regret was heavy on his mind lately.

Tara.

"Earth to Ford." Sawyer Thompson waved a hand in Ford's face. "You with us? Or do you need a moment alone?"

"Thought tonight was your night off." Sawyer was big and broad as a mountain, and could be as intimidating as hell—unless you'd grown up with him and knew that he wouldn't watch any Disney/Pixar flick because they made him cry like a chick. Ford poured him a Coke—Sawyer's standard order when he was on duty.

"Got called in." Sawyer's smile faded. "Unexpected trouble out at Horn Crest."

"Hang gliders again?" Last time, the hang gliders had turned out to be Chloe, Lance, and Tucker, and they'd been arrested for trespassing when they'd landed in Mrs. Azalea's prized field of rhododendrons. Lance was on a mission to accumulate as many crazy adventures as he could before his cystic fibrosis caught up with him, and Chloe and Lance's brother Tucker were dedicated to assisting him in his stupidity.

For some reason, this drove Sawyer insane.

Ford was just glad to see that it ran in the family, the unique ability of the three sisters to drive men right over the edge of sanity.

"Not hang gliders this time," Sawyer said, sounding relieved. Chloe was well-liked in town, and every time she ran into trouble and Sawyer had to deal with it, *he* got the backlash.

Ford knew that Sawyer liked order. *Calm* order. Which meant that Sawyer and Chloe were oil and water. But like oil and water, they ended up together a lot. Karma was a bitch with a good sense of humor.

"It was a group of teenagers," Sawyer said. "Brought them home to their parents and caught hell from one of the mothers. She told me I'd be a better use of her tax money if I was out catching *real* bad guys." With a sigh, he sank to a stool and accepted the Coke. "And what are you doing here? I thought you were going to do that race in the Gulf this weekend."

Ford shrugged. "Maybe next time."

Sawyer lifted a brow. "You losing your edge?"

"What? No."

"What then? Over the hill already at thirty-four?"

"Shut up. You're the one who threw your back out playing foosball last month."

Sawyer scowled. "Hey, that was an amazing play. Genius even."

"So was your having to spend the rest of the week-end on the couch whining, and then desk duty for a full week."

"So?" Sawyer said. "It got me some great bedside treatment from the women."

Ford snorted. "What women?"

"Hey, I have women."

"Women on porn sites don't count."

"You're being an asshole," Sawyer said mildly. "Another sign of age. Should I tell Ciera to save you a spot in the retirement home? And get you a prescription for Viagra?"

Ciera was Ford's sister, a nurse who worked at a senior center in Seattle. "You're older than me," Ford reminded him.

"By two months, which is offset by the fact that I'm better looking. I'm also not picking a fight just to be an asshole."

Ford blew out a breath. "I'm not racing because I didn't feel like traveling."

"And?"

"And Jax is too nice to our regulars, and I needed to stick around to keep him in line."

"And?"

"And..." Shit. He had nothing.

"Admit it," Sawyer said. "You're not going anywhere because Tara's ex-husband has shown up, and you don't want to lose your place."

Ford shoved his fingers through his hair. "Yeah."

Lucille sidled up to the bar. She was in her pink sweats with her crazy white hair looking like a Q-tip. Her rheumy blue eyes landed on Ford. "A vodka on the rocks." She tapped the bar. "So how's it going with the Steel Magnolia?"

Ford handed her the drink. "What?"

"Don't play stupid, honey. It doesn't suit you."

"Actually, it does," Sawyer said helpfully.

Ford took away his soda.

"Hey."

"Tara," Lucille said to Ford. "I'm talking about Tara." She tossed back the vodka like someone who'd been doing it for a gazillion years. "Her ex is here. He's a real live celebrity, you know."

Ford sighed. He knew.

Lucille nudged him. "He's got the edge on you, boy."

Ford began to wish he didn't have a thing against drinking while serving. "We're not discussing this, Lucille."

"Well, maybe you're not, but everyone else is. You need to look sharp. *Sharp*." She reached over the bar and jabbed him in the gut with her bony finger. "Are you listening?"

"Yeah, I'm listening." Ford rubbed his belly. "And *ouch*."

"*Sharp*, I tell you!"

Like he didn't know that. Like that hadn't always been the problem, that he wasn't exactly up to Tara's standards. Something that had been slammed home to him anew now that he'd actually met Logan and seen the slick, polished ex up close. Not only that, he'd sensed a still-obvious chemistry between Logan and Tara.

Sawyer was taking all this in with his usual quiet calm. "What makes everyone think our boy here is interested in the girl?" he asked Lucille.

She cackled and slapped down her empty shot glass, indicating she wanted another. "Oh, he's interested."

Sawyer looked at Ford, studying him thoughtfully.

After a beat, a slight smile curved his lips. "Yeah, I think you're right."

"Thanks, man," Ford said.

Lucille smacked Ford upside the head.

"Okay," he said. "Stop that!"

"You need to stop. Stop messing around. It's time to get serious now, Ford. For once in your life."

What made this all worse was that in a way she was right. Ford knew what people saw when they looked at him—a guy who'd never had a serious commitment in his life, except maybe to sailing. And other than Tara and that long-ago summer, he'd never really been with a woman with whom he'd truly been friends as well as lovers. In his mind, the two were separate things. His life went day to day. His sailing. The bar. Friends. Sure he was good to his grandma but she didn't require anything much from him. Money was easy to give once you had it.

The truth was for the past six months now, he'd been...restless. Unsettled. Unhappy.

Six months. Since the day Tara had come back to Lucky Harbor. Which was especially stupid because neither of them wanted to go down that road again.

And yet there was something undeniable between them, something far more than what had happened in her bed. Something that made him itchy to both run like hell and go after her at the same time.

The door of the bar opened and in strolled...*shit*.

Logan Perrish.

He was dressed more for a hot nightclub than a small-town bar, and looking pretty damn expensive while he was at it. Ford wanted to hate him on principle but the guy stopped to sign an autograph for anyone who wanted one. Hard to hate a guy like that. When Logan got to the bar, he was clearly surprised at the sight of Ford. "Hey. You're a bartender?"

"Yep. A drink?"

"Sure." Logan scanned the list of beers available on the blackboard behind Ford. "I've heard about something called a ... Ginger Goddess?"

From the next barstool, Sawyer grimaced. "You've gotta be within fifty feet of a swimming pool in order to drink a fruity, girlie-ass drink like that. Otherwise, they revoke your guy card."

Logan smiled, unconcerned. He looked at Ford. "So you make them or what?"

"Yeah." Ford made them. For women. Sawyer was right; it was a complete pussy drink.

Logan laughed at his expression. "I know, I know. But if it has the name of a soda pop or any sort of female connotation, I'm hooked."

Ford went back to hating as he picked out a kiwi, a pear, and a cocktail shaker, and got to work. On a damn Ginger Goddess.

"Well, if it isn't the famous Logan Perrish," Lucille said in her craggy voice.

"Hello," Logan said with an easy smile. "You a racing fan, darlin'?"

She simpered. "Oh, yes." She pushed her napkin toward him. "Autograph?"

Ford shot her a level are-you-kidding-me look over his shoulder, but she just grinned at him before turning back to Logan. "And isn't it something to have you here in Lucky Harbor? Nice finish in Talladega. Sorry about the subsequent crash." She touched his brace. "I hope it's not too painful."

"I'm healing up just fine," Logan assured her, turning to include the two women who came up on his other side. They held out their napkins for him to sign as well, which he did with a flourish.

Ford added ginger, vodka, and ice to the shaker, catching Sawyer's eye.

Sawyer was back to smirking.

With a scowl, Ford strained Logan's drink into a flute, then topped it with sparkling wine.

By now Logan had half the bar circling him like he was the best thing since sliced bread, and he'd turned away from the bar, completely surrounded by fans.

"A real live celebrity," Sawyer noted to Ford. "People can't resist that."

Ford could. "I don't see what's so great about him," he muttered. "In his last eighteen starts, he's never so much as led a lap. And he dresses like he believes his own press."

"I think you missed your dose of Midol today."

"And what the fuck," Ford went on. "Driving isn't even a damn sport."

Sawyer was cracking up now. "Really?"

"Really what?"

"You're going to finally make a move for the woman you've been mooning over for what, six months now, because her ex-husband is in town? Lame, man."

"Who said I was making a move?"

"You're gearing up, I can tell," Sawyer said.

"You can not."

"I've been watching you make your moves since middle school. You haven't changed your technique much."

"Whatever." Ford slammed around a few shot glasses to look busy. "And technically, I made my move *before* Logan got here." He felt someone pat his hand and looked down at Lucille.

"Don't you worry, honey," she said in a stage whisper the people in Seattle could have heard. "We're going to help you get the girl."

"We?"

She gestured to four women that looked even older than she, all in an assortment of bright lipstick and blue hair. "We're going to tip the scales in your favor," she said. "But it'd really help if you'd ever been on TV for winning a race."

"I have!" Ford pinched the bridge of his nose. "Listen to me, Lucille. No meddling. Do you hear me?"

But Lucille had already turned to her posse. "It won't be easy, girls," she was saying to them. "But we can do it. For Ford, right?"

"For Ford," they all repeated.

Sawyer was grinning, the asshole.

"Okay, that's it," Ford said to Lucille, pointing at her. "I'm cutting you off."

"Hush, dear," she said with a dismissive wave. "We're working here. And while you're standing there looking pretty, we're going to need a pitcher of margaritas."

Jesus.

Ford was halfway through that task when Logan sauntered back up to the bar for another drink.

"Don't tell me," Ford said. "Another Ginger Goddess."

"Nah." Logan grinned. "I just wanted to see if you knew how to make a sissy drink. It was good though. Thanks."

Sawyer, still sprawled back in his chair, laughed.

Okay, that was it. Ford was cutting *everyone* off, the fuckers.

Lucille asked Logan for his autograph again.

"Didn't I already give you one, darlin'?" Logan asked.

"Yes, but that was for eBay." Lucille patted his arm and pointed to Ford. "Have you met our own local celebrity?"

Logan looked at Ford. "Yes, but I didn't know he was a celebrity."

Ford waited for someone to announce his two American Cup wins or maybe the ISAF Rolex World Sailor of the Year award. Or hey, how about either of his gold medals?

"Yes, sirree," Lucille said proudly. "Ford here makes the best margaritas on the West Coast."

Sawyer choked and indicated he needed water. Ford ignored him.

"And oh!" Lucille added. "He's real good on a boat, too."

Ford was sure that he could feel a blood vessel bursting behind his left eye. He took a deep, calming breath. It didn't help, but it wasn't worth the breath to point out that he'd also once been featured in *Sports Illustrated*.

Sawyer continued to cough, and Ford hoped he swallowed his tongue.

Lucille waved her glass around as she spoke. "Why,

just the other day Ford was working on Lucky Harbor Inn's rentals for them. Such a good boy."

Logan grinned. "That's nice."

"Oh, our Ford is *quite* the catch," Lucille went on, and her blue-haired posse all nodded sagely. "Tara thinks so, too, seeing as she pulled him into her meeting the other day and made him take off his shirt for the ladies."

Now it was Ford's turn to choke. "Okay, that's *not* what happened. I—"

"Don't be shy, dear. You look good without your shirt." Lucille glanced at Logan. "Though I'm sure you look good without yours as well. In fact, maybe we could have a contest right here."

Jesus.

Lucille's posse all sat up straighter and nodded their blue-haired perms.

Logan laughed, but he looked Ford over for a long beat.

Ford looked right back. In Logan's eyes, he saw the light of challenge. No, they weren't going to have a shirt-off contest, but they *were* competing.

Game on.

Chapter 10

*"Life isn't about finding yourself,
it's about creating yourself."*
TARA DANIELS

Tara spent the next few days organizing and then reorganizing the inn's kitchen.

They were going to open as a B&B.

Maddie had handled the paperwork for the license and inspection required, Chloe was working up ideas for special baskets for guests that could be ordered if they wanted meals on the go, and Tara was working on menu planning, recipes, and the additional supplies needed.

It could actually come together and work.

Tara could hardly believe it, both that she'd agreed and that the more time passed, the more she liked the idea. It was exhilarating to finally do something she'd always wanted—cooking for a living in her own kitchen.

It was terrifying as well, because the opportunity for an epic failure had never been greater. It wasn't as if she had a great track record succeeding at...well, anything.

But there was always a first time. This was what she told herself. It gave her hope. With the phones starting to ring and bookings coming in, and with Chloe still coming and going and Maddie feeling in over her head, they'd put out an ad for another part-time employee. They already had interviews set up with a few high school students hopefully willing to do grunt work relatively cheaply.

Plenty of the Lucky Harbor curious stopped by: Lucille toting recipes, Lance and Tucker proposing the possibility of delivering ice cream on the weekends from their shop, Sawyer to mooch coffee—the inn was on his way to work and he preferred Tara's coffee to the station's.

If nothing else, the distractions soaked up some of the terror over the upcoming opening, and took up all of Tara's available brain space, leaving none for her other problems.

Such as her man problems.

That she could even think that phrase—*man problems*—was as amazing as it was ridiculous. She never had man problems.

She never had men!

To her surprise, Logan had been serious about staying in town. He'd rented a small beach cottage a few miles up the road and had come by each day. Tara had no idea what to make of that. Her entire marriage had been about *her* chasing *him*. It felt odd, to say the least, that things were reversed.

As for Ford, he was around. He'd served her drinks the other night when she'd gone to The Love Shack with Chloe and Maddie. He'd been at the marina yesterday working on his boat.

But there'd been no one-on-one conversations between them. And given that she knew he was all too aware of Logan being in town, she got the unspoken message.

He wasn't going to press, push, or fight for her. Shock. Ford never pressed, pushed or fought. Things either came right to him, like moths to a flame, or they didn't.

Not being a moth, Tara was on her own to do as she pleased. She just wasn't exactly sure what would please her.

Okay, big fat lie. She knew what would please her, and that was one Ford Walker, served straight up. But hell if she'd go through that again....

A week after their not-so-awkward morning after, Tara headed out at the crack of dawn to return his crepe pan, which she'd used and loved. She needed to buy herself one the next time she had a couple hundred bucks lying around.

It took ten minutes to drive to his house, ten minutes she told herself she didn't have to spare. She should have given him the pan back at the marina. That would have been the logical and reasonable thing to do. Except as it applied to Ford, Tara didn't have a logical or reasonable bone in her body.

At least his house was easy enough to get to. He lived on the bluffs above the inn. As the sun rose over the mountains, casting a pink glow over the morning, she parked and headed up his walk. A small part of her secretly hoped she caught him in bed. But that really was a very small part.

The bigger part hoped he was in the shower.

She looked around and realized that she didn't see his car, which pretty much rained on the waking-him-up parade. Wondering where he was—or who he might be with so early—put a hitch in her step.

None of your business, she told herself. *None*. She blew out a breath, opened her cell phone, and called him.

"Hey," he said in his usual sex-on-a-stick voice. "Miss me?"

She ignored both that and the floaty feeling the sound of his voice put in her stomach. "I'm returning your pan," she said. "I'm on your porch." She paused, hoping he'd tell her where he was.

"Let yourself in," he said and gave her the code to unlock the door.

"Where should I leave it, in your kitchen?"

"Or on my bed," he said.

"You want the Le Creuset on your bed," she repeated, heavy on the disbelief.

"No, I want *you* on my bed. What are you wearing?"

She pulled the cell away from her ear and stared at it. "You did not just ask me that."

"Never mind," he said. "I'll just picture you how I want you."

"And how would that be?" The words popped out of her before she could stop them, fascinated in spite of herself.

"Hmm," he mused silkily. "Maybe a French maid outfit."

"That's…" She struggled a minute with why the thought turned her on. "Outdated and anti-feminist," she finally said, a little weakly. "Not to mention subservient."

"I like the subservient part," Ford mused. "A few 'yes sirs' would be nice."

"You are one seriously warped man."

"No doubt." His voice was low and sexy, and it made her forget herself, made her forget that all he wanted was her body. Especially since at the moment, she wanted his.

"I can be there in twenty minutes," he said, a smile in his voice.

"No. Don't even think about it." Tara ignored the flutter in her belly. She couldn't help it. Even when he was being a Neanderthal, he still turned her on. Sure, she'd just been fantasizing about catching him in the shower, but that had been just a fantasy. She needed to live firmly in reality. "We're done with that."

"Bet I can change your mind."

"I have no doubt," Tara said. God, she needed help. "But you're a nice guy, so you won't."

"I'm not that nice a guy."

Great. Just great. "You've been an absent guy."

He was quiet a moment. "Didn't see a need to complicate anything for you."

Like a reunion with Logan. Tara drew in a deep breath. "You ever think that sometimes complications are worth the trouble?"

"No."

Quick and easy and brutally honest. It was Ford's way. She'd have to think about that later. Right now, she punched in his front door code and listened to the lock click open. "Are you sure you don't want me to just leave the pan on the step?" she asked. "It'd be safe." In Lucky Harbor, just about everything was safe.

Except her heart, she was discovering.

"Are you afraid to step inside my lair?" Ford teased.

"Ha. And no. I'll leave it on your table."

"Ten-four." He paused. "Are you going to snoop around while you're in there?"

"No." Maybe. "What would I snoop around in?"

"I don't know. My underwear drawer?"

The last time she'd touched his underwear, he'd been wearing them. But just the thought of him in his BVDs brought a rush. "No," she said quickly.

Too quickly, because he laughed softly. "You can if you want to," he said, lowering his voice. "You can do whatever you want, Tara. Flip through my porn, eat the enchiladas I made last night from Carlos's abuelo's recipe…"

"Wait." She promptly forgot about underwear, porn, *and* jumping his bones. "Carlos gave you his abuelo's recipe? I've been asking him for it forever."

"Yes, but do you take him out on the water every week and teach him to sail? Or teach him how to pick up girls so as to achieve maximum basage?"

"Basage?"

"You know, first base, second base—"

"Ohmigod," she said. "You are such a *guy*!"

He was laughing now. "Guilty as charged."

Tara sighed. "So it's a boy's club; is that what you're saying?"

"Uh huh. And I'm glad to say that you do *not* have the right equipment to join."

"I want that recipe, Ford."

"Only men are allowed to have it. It's been handed down that way for generations."

"You're making that up."

He didn't say anything, but she could practically *hear* him smiling. "*Please*?" she asked.

"Oh, how I like the sound of that word coming from your mouth."

"*Ford.*"

"Right here, Tara." He was still using his bedroom voice. Which, as she had good reason to know, made her one hundred percent *stupid*.

"What would you do to get the recipe?" he wanted to know.

She shook her head. "I'm hanging up now."

"Okay, but if you change your mind and want to play with my underwear, text me and I'll be right there. You can play with the ones I'm wearing."

She felt herself go damp and hurriedly disconnected. She wouldn't be texting him. She wouldn't let herself go there. *Way* too big a risk when it came to him, because he wouldn't risk anything. Been there, done that.

She stepped into his big, masculine house, her heels clicking on his hardwood floor. He had a big couch and an even bigger flat screen. One wall was all windows looking out over the water. And, she realized, the marina.

Lucky Harbor Inn's marina.

She wondered if he ever stood right here and looked for her. Reminding herself that she was on a mission to drop the pan off and get out, she refused to let herself look at anything else as she headed toward his kitchen.

Except her eyes strayed to the mantel in the living room on the way and at the pictures there. There was one of Jax, Sawyer, and Ford on Ford's boat. Three hard-bodied gorgeous men, tanned and wet and mugging for the camera. She wondered who had taken the picture, and if the bikini top hanging from the mast behind them belonged to the photographer.

There was another picture of Ford with a group of guys all standing shoulder to shoulder, wearing USA track suits and holding their medals. The Olympic sailing team.

The last picture showed an older woman with two younger women, all of whom shared Ford's wide, open, mischievous smile and bright green eyes.

His grandmother and sisters.

Tara walked through an archway, past the laundry room, and into a kitchen that gave her some serious appliance envy. And Corian countertop envy. And, oh Lord, *look at his Japanese cutlery*. Just standing here was going to give her an orgasm. She set the pan on the table, forced herself to turn around, and headed back under the archway. There was a basket of clean clothes on the dryer. Drawn in by the fresh scent, she stood in the center of the laundry room and inhaled deeply.

She was pathetic.

On the top of the basket of clothes lay a T-shirt. It said LUCKY HARBOR SAILING CHAMP across the front. At one time, it'd been gray, but years of washing had softened it to nearly white. She knew this because he'd been given two of them. Ford had gotten them that long-ago summer during his first sailing race when he'd been nothing but the dock boy on a local team.

She had the other shirt. He'd given it to her all those years ago, and she'd worn it to sleep in. She'd kept it as one of her few true treasures. Unfortunately, she'd been wearing it the night of the inn fire six months ago, and it'd been destroyed. Unable to stop herself, she ran her fingers over the shirt and whoops, look at that, picked it up. Well, hey, he'd invited her to play with his underwear, and a T-shirt could be classified as underwear. She pressed her face to the soft, faded cotton and felt her knees go a little weak even though it smelled like detergent and not the man.

She wanted the shirt.

Don't do it...

But she did. She totally stole his shirt.

She drove back to the inn with it in her purse and walked straight to the marina, and then to the end of the dock.

She needed a minute.

She inhaled the wet, salty air. Sitting was a challenge in her pencil skirt and she had to kick off her heels, but once she managed, having the water lap at her feet and the sun on her face made it worth it. It meant unwanted freckles and almost dropping a Jimmy Choo knock-off into the water, but there was something about listening to the water slap up against the wood and watching the boats bob up and down on the swells that really did it for her.

It was better than dark chocolate for releasing endorphins and helping her relax.

Better than orgasms.

Okay, no. Nothing was better than orgasms, but this would have to be a close second.

She'd stolen his shirt. Good Lord, she was losing it.

Two battered cross trainers appeared in her peripheral

vision. Long legs, dark blue board shorts, and a white T-shirt came next.

And then the heart-stopping smile.

"So you didn't climb into my bed," Ford said, sitting next to her.

"How do you know I didn't just get tired of waiting for you to show up?" she asked.

His brow shot up so far it vanished into the lock of hair falling over his forehead. "Are you telling me I missed my shot?"

"Sugar, you never even had a shot."

Ford grinned and slung an arm over her shoulder, pulling her into him. He smelled delicious. Like salty air and the ocean and something woodsy too.

And male.

Very male.

"Liar," he said affectionately.

This was true. "You're in my space," Tara noted.

"That's not what you said when we—*Oomph*," he let out when she elbowed him in the gut. Unperturbed, he grinned. "Aw, don't be embarrassed that you attacked me in your kitchen."

"*What*? That night was all your fault," she told him. "You were standing there putting away spices and making me fried chicken, looking all—" Sexy. Sexy as hell. "I mean you practically force-fed me the cuteness."

"Cuteness," he repeated, testing the word out like it was a bad seed. "I'm not cute."

"Okay, true. You're far too potent for *cute*."

He cocked his head. "And you really think that us having sex was all on me?"

Her cheeks were getting hot, along with other parts of her. "I'm saying you seduced me with all the—"

"Say *'cuteness'* again," Ford warned, "and I'm going to strip you naked right here and show you exactly how *not* cute I can be. I'm going to show it to you until you scream my name."

"Okay, wait. Does anyone really scream during orgasm? I mean, you read about it all the time in books, but—"

He laughed. "Okay, so you don't scream." He leaned in close. "But your breath gets all uneven and catchy—which I love, by the way—and then you let out this sexy little purr, and—"

She elbowed him again.

"Told you I wasn't cute," he said, rubbing his ribs.

She squelched the urge to say "cute" one more time just to see if he'd follow through on his threat. She took a look around them to see if they were alone, just in case—

He laughed again, then put his lips next to her ear. "Sticking with your story, Tara?"

She shivered. "That you seduced me? Yes."

"We're even, you know." He nipped her earlobe with his teeth, making her shiver. "Since you've been seducing me since I first met you." He kissed her just below her jaw then, and along her temple, while she worked on not melting.

"W—what are you doing?"

"Seeing how far you're going to let me go."

Get a grip, she ordered herself as he got to the very corner of her mouth, and she took a big grip herself. A two-fisted one. Of *him*. She was holding him so tight that he couldn't have pulled away even if he wanted to, and given the rough sound that escaped him, he didn't want to. "We're not doing this again," she said. "You know we're not."

He sucked her bottom lip between his teeth and gave it a light tug. "I do know. I just can't remember why."

She sank her fingers into his hair. It was thick and silky and wavy, and she loved it. "Because—"

He kissed her long and hard, his hand sliding low onto her back, pulling her in closer to him.

"Ford. Ford, wait."

He smiled against her lips. "Let me guess." His mouth ghosted over hers with each word. "You have something else to say."

"Yes! You're..." She couldn't think. "Trouble. You know that? You're bad-for-me *trouble*."

"Maybe. But I'm only trouble some of the time," he said in that husky, coaxing voice that made her want to give him whatever he asked for.

"And what are you when you're not trouble?" she managed. "A Boy Scout?"

"'Fraid not. But sometimes my intentions are honorable."

"Like now?"

"No." His deep-green eyes met hers. "Right now, my intentions are definitely *not* honorable." And then he kissed her again. He kissed her until she was gripping him like she was drowning and he was her lifeline.

"Oh! Um, excuse me..."

They both turned to the young woman standing on the

dock in a cute short skirt and cotton top, shielding her eyes from the glare of the sun with her hands, her long, sun-streaked, brown hair flowing out behind her. "Hi, sorry. I'm Mia Hutchinson."

One of the Seattle high school students that had called about the ad and had an interview with Tara this morning. "Mia, hi!" Knees still knocking, Tara stood up. It was too much to hope that her little make-out session with Ford hadn't been seen, but her plan was to ignore it. *Denial, meet your queen.* "You're right on time."

Ford was on his feet as well. "I thought we set that up for this afternoon," he said to the girl.

Tara looked at him. "No, she's interviewing with me for a position at the inn."

"Actually," Ford said. "She called to interview me for an article she's writing on sailing."

"Um, yeah," Mia said with a little wince. "Actually, I contacted *both* of you. I brought my résumé." She pulled an envelope from her purse. "I didn't really have any previous work experience that applied, so I just used the résumé I made up in economics class last semester. And before you ask, no, I didn't really work for Facebook or Bill Gates. And I wasn't a personal assistant to the Mariners' manager either." She hesitated, looking younger than seventeen. "The references are real, though." She turned to Ford, apology in her gaze. "I need a job, but I made up the article thing."

"Why?" Ford asked.

"Because I wanted to meet you both in a setting where you wouldn't get all weirded out. Finding you both here was just luck, I guess."

Tara was very still, in direct opposition to the way her heart was threatening to burst right out of her chest. "You know us?"

Again, Mia dragged her teeth over her bottom lip, looking at them from mossy green eyes that exactly matched...

Ford's.

"I kinda know you," Mia said. "It's sort of a long story."

"The CliffsNotes version, then," Ford suggested mildly.

Good. Good, Tara thought. He was calm, cool, and collected. Normally that was her role, but she'd left calm a few minutes back and was quickly heading straight past cool and collected, directly to *Freaking Out*. Because looking at Mia was reminding her of a very young Ford.

If he'd been female.

With Tara's willowy build.

"I was actually really surprised to find you two...kissing," Mia said carefully. "I don't know what I expected, but it wasn't that."

"Why don't you enlighten us on what you did expect?" Ford said. "Or should I help you out with that?"

Mia cocked her head, her gaze as sharp as his. "You figured it out," she said, sounding relieved.

"Yes," he said.

Tara couldn't speak. Hell, she could hardly breathe. She reached out blindly for purchase and found Ford's hand.

"You're ours," Ford said quietly to the girl. "You're our baby."

Chapter 11

*"Always tell the truth. It eliminates the
need to remember anything."*
TARA DANIELS

Up until that moment, Ford's plans for the day had
included talking Tara into going out for a sail. And then
burning off some excess energy.

With their naked bodies.

Yeah, that would have been right at the very top of
the to-do list.

But that all changed with Mia looking at him through
his own green gaze, her expression slightly challenging
and yet braced for...hurt and rejection, he realized as
something twisted hard in his chest.

How many years had he wondered about the baby that
he and Tara had given up at birth?

Seventeen.

And how many years had he wondered if that baby
would grow up happy and whole and smart and sharp and
then...someday show up on his doorstep.

Christ, he couldn't remember ever feeling nerves like this before. Not while facing forty-foot waves threatening to tear his boat apart. Not while standing on an Olympic podium accepting a medal in the name of his country. Not ever.

Tara hadn't taken her eyes off Mia, and she was looking nervous too, her eyes misty. "You're so beautiful," she whispered.

Mia's eyes cut to her, quiet and assessing. "I look like you."

"Not as much as you look like..."

They both turned to Ford.

Having the woman he'd once loved with painful desperation, along with the daughter he'd dreamed about, both looking at him with varying degrees of emotion, was a punch in the solar plexus. Ford found he could scarcely breathe.

"Can I hug you?" Tara asked their daughter.

Mia gave a halting nod, but it was too late; they'd all seen the hesitation. Awkwardness settled over them all as Mia moved into Tara for a quick embrace. Ford was next, and he was surprised that with him Mia didn't seem awkward at all. Anxious, even eager, but not reluctant, and as he wrapped his arms around this thin, beautiful teenager that was his—Christ, *his*—he closed his eyes and breathed her in. "How did you find us?"

Mia pulled back and shifted her weight nervously, although her voice never wavered. "I thought I'd tell you *after* I got hired."

Bold. Ballsy. Probably she'd gotten a double whammy of both of those things from the gene pool, Ford thought.

"I only have seven weeks," Mia said, and Tara's hand went to her chest as if to keep her heart from leaping out.

Ford understood the panic. Hell, he felt it as his own. When Mia had been young, she'd had heart problems. A leaky valve that had required surgery. The only reason either Ford or Tara knew about it was because Tara's mother had donated a very large chunk of money to the medical bills, taking a second mortgage on the inn to get it—something that had only been discovered after Phoebe had died.

"What's the matter?" Tara asked Mia, voice thick with worry. "Your heart again?"

"No. I'm doing my senior year of high school in Spain as an exchange student, and I'll be gone for nine months."

"Oh." At this, Tara sagged in visible relief.

"So you're healthy then?" Ford asked Mia. "Everything's good?"

"Yep. I haven't had so much as a cold in years."

"That's wonderful," Tara said. "And your parents are okay with you doing this? Coming here to meet us?"

Another slight hesitation. "Well, they wanted to come with me," Mia admitted. "To be sure I'd be welcome, but I wanted to do this alone." Something came into her eyes at that. More nerves. And a dash of defensiveness.

And there was something else, too, Ford noticed. Whenever Mia spoke, she did so directly to him, not Tara. Almost as if Mia somehow resented the mother who'd given her up, but not her birth father.

Worse, given the look on Tara's face, she knew it too,

and was miserable about it. Up until now Ford had caught only glimpses of the guilt that haunted Tara, but seeing it etched so deeply on her face squeezed his heart.

"My parents know I'm applying for work," Mia told them. "They've agreed that I can drive back and forth from Seattle to Lucky Harbor. If, you know, I get the job."

Smooth, Ford thought. Also from the gene pool.

"I'll hire you," Tara said softly. "If that's what you want, to work for me."

"Really?" For a beat, the cool, tough-girl expression fell away from Mia, revealing a heartbreaking vulnerability.

"Of course," Tara said.

"But...you don't even know my real skills. Or me."

"You came all this way," Ford said quietly. "Don't lose your nerve now."

Mia turned to him, studying his face like she'd been hungry for the sight of it as he'd been for hers.

"You're hired," Tara said. "I can teach you what you need to know. And then maybe by the end of the summer, you'll be able to write a real résumé, with real experience."

"Thanks," Mia said, looking slightly softer. Younger. "And don't worry. I'm real organized and a big planner. My parents tell everyone I'm anal, and it's sorta true."

"One guess as to where you got that," Ford said.

Tara slid him a long look, making him smile.

"I think I'm more like you," Mia said, looking at Ford.

Tara looked away at the quick hurt of that, and Ford

felt unaccustomedly helpless, not sure how to breach the gap between mother and daughter.

"Excuse me, Ms. Daniels?" Carlos called from the marina office door. He was in baggy homeboy jeans and a T-shirt that advertised some surf shop in Cabo. His dark hair was in spikes today, his earrings and eyebrow piercing all black to match his untied, high-top Nikes. He'd been cleaning windows in the morning sun, and his arms and face gleamed with sweat. "You have a phone call."

Mia looked at him, and then kept looking.

"Thanks, Carlos," Tara said. "Can you take a message?"

The teen nodded, his gaze falling to Mia, meeting her outwardly curious gaze.

"Mia, this is Carlos," Tara said, introducing them. "He works for the inn part time as well."

Carlos smiled, and to Ford, the expression had *horny teenager* written all over it. A very new and entirely surprising emotion hit Ford squarely between the eyes.

Paternal protectiveness.

Which was ridiculous. Hell, when he'd been Carlos' age, he'd looked at Tara just like that. He'd also done a hell of a lot more than just look.

"I'm going to start planting those seedlings," Carlos said to Tara. "You said it was a two-person job, but everyone's busy so..."

"I could help," Mia piped up.

"No!" Tara and Ford said at the same time. Ford let out a breath. That settled it. He was going to have to kill Carlos. He glanced over at Tara and found her wearing what he imagined was a matching scowl to his.

Luckily, before either of them could do or say anything stupid, Mia's stomach growled into the silence.

"Oh, Sugar," Tara exclaimed. "You're hungry! Come on, come up to the inn. I'll get you some breakfast."

"But the planting," Mia said, still looking at Carlos.

"Maybe later," Tara said.

Much later, Ford thought. Like never.

Tara hustled them all into the kitchen. Well, except Carlos. Carlos she sent on a run into town on an errand. When he was gone, Tara sat Mia at the table and pulled ingredients out of the fridge until she had a mountain of food on the island. "What would you like? Omelets? Crepes? Pancakes? French toast? I have—"

"It doesn't matter," Mia said. She and Ford watched as Tara went to work, her hands a blur. "Anything's fine. So about you two. Are you...a two?"

"Veggie and cheese omelets?" Tara asked, looking a little desperate for a subject change. "With turkey bacon and fresh fruit?"

"Okay." Mia hesitated and then glanced at Ford. "Is she always like this?" she whispered.

Crazy? Yes. Often. "She loves to cook."

Mia nodded, glancing at the newspaper that had been left on the table. "Is this for real?"

Ford looked over her shoulder. "What?"

Mia pointed to an article on the front page and read: "It's neck and neck between two fine stallions in the race for Lucky Harbor's Beach Resort owner Tara Daniels' heart. Which sexy hunk will make it to the finish line? The NASCAR cutie Logan Perrish or our own sailing hottie, Ford Walker? This just could be a photo finish, folks. Be sure to vote in our new poll, up on Facebook now. We're looking for donations of a buck a vote. The pot goes to the pediatric cancer research center at General, so don't be shy. We all have a buck to give, right? Vote now." Mia lifted her gaze and stared at Ford and Tara. "Is this about you guys?"

Ford looked for the byline. *Lucille Oldenburg.* Nosy old bat.

Behind the stovetop, Tara had gone utterly still, her eyes horrified. "Are you kidding me?"

"Nope," Mia said. "It's all right here in black and white. Who's Logan Perrish? Cuz it also says he spent two hours of his time graciously signing autographs—and bikinis—on the beach yesterday."

Tara closed her eyes. "He's my ex-husband."

Mia turned to Ford. "You're in competition with her ex-husband? For real?"

"It's a joke." He wondered if Jax would find him a good criminal defender after he killed Lucille.

Mia glanced at the paper thoughtfully. "Do you think you're winning?" she asked Ford. "In the poll?"

"Pay no attention to that," Tara said, pointing with her spatula. "I'm not seeing either of them."

Mia looked at Ford.

Tara looked at him, too, sending him a silent plea to back her up. He refused to, on the grounds that . . . hell. He had no idea. But when he remained silent, Tara let out a noise that managed to perfectly convey what she thought of him. He was pretty sure he knew what that might be.

"So you're *not* dating each other?" Mia asked Ford.

"No," Tara said, answering for him.

"But if you're not seeing each other, why were you kissing on the dock?"

"Do you prefer Swiss, mozzarella, or American cheese in your omelet?" Tara asked a bit desperately, turning to the refrigerator again.

"I don't care." Mia was still looking at Ford. "So have you two been...*not* seeing each other all this time? The past seventeen years?"

"No," Tara said. "Yes. Wait a minute." She pressed her fingertips to her eyes. "Can you rephrase the question?"

"Until about six months ago, Tara lived in Texas," Ford told Mia. "And I lived here."

"So you two were never together?" Mia asked. "Not even when...you know. When I was conceived?"

Ford drew in a deep breath. This part was going to suck. "We were seventeen," he said.

Mia nodded. "Like me."

Yes, and he wasn't proud to say that he'd been far too experienced for his age. He'd lost his virginity two years prior, after being seduced by a sexy waitress who'd promised to rock his world. She had. For one entire glorious spring break, she'd rocked everything he had.

But Tara hadn't been experienced. At all. He had no idea how, but she'd seen something in him that had inspired her trust. "We were too young for the kind of relationship that we found ourselves in," he said carefully. *Please read between the lines and never have sex.*

Ever.

"Yeah," Mia said quietly. "I figured I was an accident. A really big one."

"No," Tara said fiercely.

"It's okay," Mia said. "The whole giving-me-up thing was a dead giveaway." She shrugged as she looked at a stricken Tara. "You needed to fix a mistake quick, so you gave me up. Easy enough."

Christ, those eyes, Ford thought. The both of them were killing him. "It wasn't easy," he said, hoping to God that Mia believed him. "And it wasn't about us giving you up to make things better for us. It was about making things right for *you*."

Tara had turned to blindly face the window, completely ignoring what she was cooking.

Ford imagined she was feeling sick over the same thing. Heartbreaking to hear that the child they'd given up was thinking that it had been an easy fix. More heartbreak that she'd felt unwanted, even for a minute.

"I think I forgot to do the dishes this morning in the cottage," Tara whispered. "I should go check."

Ford would bet his last penny that she'd done every dish in the place and he stood to go to her, but, eyes glittering, mouth grim, she shook her head.

They'd been kids when she'd gotten pregnant. Stupid kids. That was no longer the case, and yet the situation was bringing back all the emotions from that time—the fear, the stress, the anxiety.

The utter helplessness.

And that overwhelming, ever-present, life-sucking guilt. Looking at Tara, Ford saw it all. He knew that she felt that they'd done the right thing. She'd always felt that way. But any woman would still feel the pang of giving up her own flesh and blood. She'd carried Mia, had been the one to feel her wriggle and kick, to feel her every hiccup.

And then had been left with little choice but to sign her away.

"I smell something burning," Mia said, and pointed to the stovetop, which was now smoking.

Yep, something was burning all right. Ford stepped behind Tara, took the spatula out of her hand, and turned off the burner. He carried the pan, and the blackened omelet in it, to the sink, where it hissed and smoked some more when he added cold water to the mix.

"I burnt it," Tara murmured.

"Yeah," Mia said, eyeing the pan. "You killed it dead."

"I never burn anything."

"No biggie," Mia said quietly. "I wasn't that hungry anyway. Should I go?"

"No." Tara straightened, seeming to come into herself again. "Mia, my burning breakfast was an accident. Like forgetting to go to the dentist. Like running out of gas on the highway..." She paused and swallowed hard. "But having a baby, that would *never* be classified as an accident. Not by me. I want you to know that. I'm not good at this. At revisiting the past, or talking about things that—I'm not good at emotions and feelings. But I want—I *need* you to know that I never thought of you as an accident. And I want you to stay."

Mia didn't look away as a myriad of emotions crossed her face. After a long beat, she swallowed hard. "Okay. Thanks."

In the heavily weighted silence, Ford went to the refrigerator. Time for improvisation, and his eyes locked on a big, juicy-looking strawberry pie. Worked for him.

He grabbed it, carrying the tin heaped with brilliant red strawberries and dripping with glaze to the table.

"That's my Kick-Ass Strawberry Pie," Tara said, surprised.

"Yes, and now it's Kick-Ass Breakfast." Ford pointed to the chairs. "Sit."

Tara shocked him by actually following his direction. Mia followed suit, and he cut the pie into three huge thirds.

Tara choked. "I can't feed our daughter strawberry pie for breakfast."

"Why not?"

"Yeah," Mia asked. "Why not?"

"Because..." Tara appeared to search for a reason. "It's not healthy."

"It's got fruit," Mia said.

Tara looked at her. The awkwardness was still there. The air was filled with it, as well as unspoken questions and answers. But finally she nodded. Kick-Ass Breakfast it would be.

Mia gazed down at her third of the pie, her pretty hair sweeping into her eyes—which might be Ford's own green but they were guarded like Tara's.

His daughter, he repeated to himself. *God.* His daughter. She was careful. Controlled. Smart. And when she reached up and impatiently shoved her hair out of the way, he couldn't hold back the smile.

"What?" she wanted to know.

"You remind me of Tara at your age," he said. "Ready to tell us how you found us?"

"My dad helped me."

Ford couldn't help it: he flinched at the word *dad*, something he'd certainly never been to her. Tara met his gaze, and the understanding and compassion in her eyes were far too much for him to take. Getting up from the table, he poured three glasses of cold milk.

"I'd tried to find you before," Mia said, "but I couldn't. Then when Phoebe Traeger died, she left me some money." She looked at Tara. "I'm sorry about your mom."

"Thank you," Tara said quietly. "You got the money around Thanksgiving."

"Yes, and with it came a letter from her. She said she wasn't supposed to make herself known to me. That she was breaking rules and promises all over the place, but that she was dead and if people didn't like it, they could suck it. *Her* words," Mia added with a small smile. "She included your contact information in case I ever wanted it. For both of you." She paused. "I've always wanted it, but it took me a little while to find the nerve to do anything with it." She looked at Tara. "It said you lived in Texas, so I was surprised when I saw that ad to find out you were here." She paused. "I have a good life only half an hour from here. Two parents who love me very much. It should be enough." She paused. "I wanted it to be enough."

"It's natural to be curious," Tara said quietly. "It's okay to be curious."

"Yeah, well, at first I told myself I didn't care, about either of you." Mia pushed a strawberry around on the plate. "You gave me up, right? So I didn't care. I wasn't going to be curious. I refused to be, natural or not."

Tara looked devastated. Ford reached for her hand and

gave it a squeeze. "I'm glad you changed your mind," he said.

"Who says I did?"

"You're here," he pointed out. "That indicates a certain level of caring. Of curiosity."

She sagged a little. "Yeah. I always was too curious for my own good."

"And now that you're here?" he asked. "What do you want to happen?"

Mia very carefully cut a large strawberry in half with her fork. "I realize I really should know, since I came to you, but I don't. At least not exactly." She looked at Ford's hand. He was still holding Tara's fingers in his, and had been stroking his thumb across her skin, soothing her without even realizing it.

"I know I've asked this already," Mia said wryly. "But it really does seem like you two are together."

Ford understood why she thought it. But he'd told himself it was about sex. Hell, Tara had told him as well. And he'd been absolutely sure that's all there could be. It was a self-protection thing. But when he met Tara's gaze, that protection urge turned to her, as she was revealing a heartbreaking vulnerability. She'd gotten hurt the last time they'd been together, much more than he. It'd left her gun-shy, no doubt. He couldn't blame her for that. She'd been the one to face the consequences of their relationship.

"It's hard to explain," Tara said.

To say the least. Ford braced for Mia's reaction, but she was as resilient as she was smart. She merely nodded and stood up. "Can I borrow a computer?"

Tara looked confused. "Computer?"

"I want to go to Facebook and vote." Mia turned to Ford. "I'm going to vote for you. It'd be nice to have my parents together."

Tara turned to Ford. "She wants to vote for you," she said faintly.

"That's possible, right?" Mia asked. "You two getting together? You're not going to give me a line of crap about how you care about each other but it's not in the cards or something, are you?" She drew a breath. "Or how you each want to live your own lives, you have to be true to yourselves, you won't be held back anymore—" She broke off and winced. "Sorry. Wrong kitchen."

"Your parents are splitting," Ford said.

Mia nodded.

Shit. Ford found himself wanting to reach for her, but she was vibrating with a very clear don't-touch vibe, so in the end he refilled her milk. It was all he could think of, but she clutched her refilled glass and smiled at him.

"Mia," Tara breathed. "I'm so sorry."

"Yeah. Thanks." Mia got to her feet. "So...a computer?"

"Mine's in the small office behind the laundry," Tara said after a beat. "Second door to the right."

"Thanks."

When she was gone, Tara moved to the sink to stare down at the blackened mess of an omelet pan. "I burned breakfast," she murmured. "Burned it black."

Ford came up behind her. Like mother, like daughter, she was also sporting a don't-touch vibe, but he walked right through it and slid his hands to her hips. "You okay?"

Surprising him, she turned and faced him. "She's... ours."

"Yes."

"I mean, did you get a good look at her? We did that. We made her," she marveled.

"We did good." He pulled her in close.

She swallowed hard, clearly fighting tears. "We did *really* good. God, it brings me back, you know?" She dropped her forehead to his chest. "Back to that time when it was all so messed up."

"I know." He felt the same. Tara had spent the last five months of her pregnancy in Seattle. When she'd gone into labor, she hadn't wanted him there. He'd gone to the hospital anyway, though as far as he knew she'd never known he was there. He'd sat in the waiting room by himself staring at the walls, agonizing over the hell she was going through for all those hours, terrified for her.

Afterward, he'd spent more long hours just staring at their daughter through the nursery glass until they'd eventually carried her away to deliver her to her new parents.

To her new life.

"When I had her," Tara said, voice muffled against him, "it was so much harder than I thought it'd be. The pain. The worry. I kept telling myself that it would be over soon, and then when it finally was, they asked if I wanted to hold her for a minute. I had told myself no, no way could I do it and give her up, but I did. I took her." She paused, lost in the memory. "It was only for a second, but she was awake. She opened her eyes and looked right at me and I knew," she whispered. "I knew she was going to be beautiful." She pressed her lips together. "And for a minute, I didn't think I could give her up."

"Tara." Ford pressed his forehead to hers and fought with the what-ifs.

"I'd made my decision, and I was okay with it," she said, nodding as if to help convince herself. "It was just that when she looked at me...God, those eyes. She still has your eyes, Ford. And her eyes—your eyes—they've haunted me for seventeen years."

"You're shaking," he murmured.

"No, that's you."

Well, hell. It was.

"You were so good with her today," she said and sniffed. "You knew just what to say, and I...I froze."

"You did fine. It was a shock." Ford slid his fingers in her hair and tugged lightly until she lifted her face to his.

Her eyes shimmered, and she gave him a small smile that reached across the years and all the emotions, and grabbed him by the throat. As if it was the most natural thing in the world, he cupped her face and lowered his mouth to hers, just as Mia came back into the room.

After an interminable beat of silence, she said, "I don't know whether to cheer or be grossed out."

"Did you find the computer?" Tara asked, clearly trying to change the subject.

"Yes." Mia turned to Ford. "You're up in the voting so far, but not by much. Maybe you should help a few ladies across the street today if you get the chance." She grabbed her plate of pie and paused, head cocked as she studied the both of them. "Were you two really just about to kiss again?"

Tara winced. "Only a little bit."

"But you're *not* together," Mia clarified.

Tara winced again. "No."

Mia studied them both. "I don't have any siblings, do I?"

Chapter 12

*"For some unknown reason, success usually
occurs in private, while failure
occurs in full view."*
TARA DANIELS

Tara introduced Mia to her aunts, and both Maddie and
Chloe fawned all over her, loving her up. They'd all gone
to dinner, but not before Tara had called and checked in
with Mia's parents, giving Tara some peace of mind that
they were really okay with this.

With sharing their daughter.

Her daughter.

Mia had warmed up to Maddie and Chloe easily, telling them all sorts of things about herself, like how she
planned on being a lawyer because she had a talent for
arguing.

"You come by that honestly, honey," had been Maddie's response as she'd patted Tara's hand. They'd all
laughed except Mia, who hadn't looked as amused as
everyone else to hear she took after Tara.

Later, after Mia had gone home and it was just Maddie,

Chloe, and Tara sharing some wine on one of the marina docks, Tara admitted her fear—that she and Mia wouldn't connect. Maddie assured Tara that Mia had only connected with Chloe and herself so quickly because they were aunts and not a birth mother, and therefore had the benefit of not carrying any emotional baggage into the relationship.

Tara was well aware of the emotional baggage. It was currently weighing her down so that she could barely breathe. So was the bone-deep, heart-wrenching yearning for more with Mia, instead of the awkwardness, unspoken questions, and tension.

It'll happen, Maddie promised. Tara wanted that to be true more than she'd ever wanted anything.

The next day, she tried to lose herself in routine. She made a trip to the grocery store, something that usually, oddly, gave her peace, except not this time. This time she ran into Logan, and there in the ice cream aisle he introduced her to the circle of fans around him as his ex- *and* future wife. Annoyed, she corrected him and pushed her cart onward, running into several acquaintances who couldn't wait to tell her which way they'd voted on Facebook. The poll seemed to be running about 60 percent in Ford's favor, but Logan was charming the pants off Lucky Harbor and steadily gaining ground.

It was official. Her life was out of control. She had a daughter looking for a first chance, an ex-husband looking for a second chance, and Ford looking for...

She had no idea.

Shaking her head, Tara made her way back to the inn.

When she got out of the car to unload, she was surprised when Mia came out to help. "Thanks," Tara said with a heartfelt smile.

Mia returned it, though it didn't quite meet her eyes. It never seemed to when it came to Tara.

Something else to work on, Tara thought: getting her daughter to let go of seventeen years of resentment and trust her. "Mia," she said softly as they came face to face at the trunk of the car. "What can I do?"

Mia didn't pretend to misunderstand as she reached to grab bags of food. "I don't know. I just…" She shrugged. "I thought that this would be easier, that's all. That I'd instantly feel this bonded connection with you, that…" The girl sighed and shook her head. "I don't know."

"Tell me how to help," Tara said. "I *want* to help. I want the same thing you do."

Mia nodded. "I guess maybe I still have questions."

"Then ask. Anything," Tara said, and hoped that was true.

Mia hefted six bags in her thin arms. She was stronger than she looked. "Anything?"

"Yes." But Tara braced herself, hoping against hope that she'd start off light. Like maybe what was Tara's favorite color and astrological sign? They could work their way up from there.

"Was getting rid of me easy?" Mia asked.

Tara gulped. "Uh—"

"Did you think about me? Do you," Mia paused, "regret giving me up?"

So much for the light stuff first, Tara thought as her chest tightened. It hadn't been easy to give Mia up, and

Tara had thought of her baby often. But as for regret...
no. She hadn't regretted it, not at first.

That had come later.

But before she could find a way to articulate all this
without hurting her daughter, Mia's face closed, and she
took another step back. "You know what? Never mind."
Turning away, she carried the grocery bags toward the
inn's back door.

"Mia. Mia, wait."

Mia looked back, her face pinched. "My mom warned
me this might happen."

Her other mom. Her *real* mom. "Warned you what
might happen?"

"That you might not be thrilled to find your biggest mistake on your doorstep. That you might be upset
because my adoption was supposed to be a closed, con-
fidential case."

Tara stared at her, stunned. "Your mom said that?
That you were my *mistake*?"

"She didn't have to."

"Mia, that's not how I feel at all. And I'm not upset.
I—" Tara broke off, at a complete loss. She was just coming to terms with this all herself, and she didn't have a
game plan to make Mia understand. This was so important, so very important, and Tara needed time and careful
planning to make it all come out okay—

"I changed my mind, I don't want to know." Mia took
a step toward the inn. "These bags are really heavy. I
have to go in."

"*Mia.*"

But she was gone.

• • •

Weeks ago, Maddie had arranged for a "trial run" for the inn. She'd set up a raffle at the last music fest and had drawn a winner. The lucky couple's prize—one free night at the inn.

They were due to arrive in the morning.

This left Maddie running through the place like a madwoman, checking on last-minute details and barking orders at Tara. In turn, Tara was going Post-it note crazy, leaving everyone little yellow stickies everywhere and on everything, outlining what Maddie needed done. Everyone was on hand, doing their bidding without complaint.

Okay, there was complaining, but Tara ignored it and continued writing notes. Eventually she realized that Maddie was no longer barking orders, that in fact she and Jax kept vanishing for long periods of time. "Where the hell do they keep going?" she asked Chloe, exasperated.

"The attic." Chloe snatched the yellow Post-it pad from Tara's fingers. "Give me those. You're grounded." Chloe was wearing low-riding, skinny-legged Army cargos with a red tank top and her bright red Nike trainers. She'd been a surprising help and had created a large gift basket filled with her spa treatments. But she'd clearly had enough of the bossing around because she snatched the sticky note pad.

"Why the attic?" Tara asked, fingers itching to grab the pad back.

Chloe wrote something on a Post-it and slapped it to Tara's chest. Tara pulled it off and read it out loud. "They like to do it up there." She stared at Chloe. "Are you shittin' me?"

"There you go losing your *g*'s again, Miss Daisy. But no, I'm not 'shitting' you. Remember back a few months ago when you sent them to the attic to get that antique end table? They took over an hour and told you they'd taken the time to polish it?"

Tara closed her eyes. "They weren't—"

"Yep. Totally doing it."

Lord. Maddie and Jax were like a couple of freaking newlyweds with a case of nearly expired condoms. "I'm surrounded by children."

"Not exactly children," Chloe said. "More like horn-dog teenagers. Come on, admit it. You'd totally do it up there if you could."

"No, I wouldn't."

"Oh, right. That's me. *I'd* do it up there if I could. Should I pull out my phone and ask Mr. Magic Eight app if that's anywhere in your near future?" Without waiting for an answer, she did just that, then smiled at the answer.

NOT LIKELY.

Chloe slid her phone away. She'd changed her hair streaks to midnight blue. They were twisted and pulled up, holding her hair in place like a headband. "So since Maddie and Jax are taking a break—and each other—and since you don't seem to have that kind of a break in your future, I think we deserve a break of a different kind."

"Can't." Tara handed over a bucket of bathroom cleaning supplies.

Chloe frowned down at them. "Cleaning is *your* thing."

"Not today it's not."

"What's wrong with our teenage slaves?"

"Carlos is cleaning the front yard, and I'm acclimating Mia to my kitchen."

Chloe blinked. "Huh?"

"Yeah," Tara said. "In a blatant attempt to bribe her into liking me, I'm letting her bake the meet-and-greet cookies."

"Wait a minute." Chloe narrowed her eyes. "She gets to bake cookies, and I have to do toilets? I have seniority! Where's the justice in that?"

"You're completely missing the significance of my gesture. You know how important the meet-and-greet cookies are."

"How could I have forgotten?" Chloe said dryly. "What an honor you've bestowed upon her."

"Hey, she's my daughter." As the word left her mouth, Tara smiled. She couldn't help it, she liked the way it felt rolling off her tongue.

Chloe grinned unexpectedly. "You got a kick out of saying that."

"I'm just stating a fact."

"Admit it, Tara."

Tara nodded and let a small smile escape. "I like saying it." So very much.

"So she's baking cookies, huh?"

"Yes." Tara took in Chloe's smug smile. "What? What don't I know?"

"Nothing. Except that she's not baking. She's nose up against the living room window watching Carlos hose down the yard." Chloe smiled. "*Acclimating.*"

Tara sighed.

"I saw her at the diner this morning with Ford," Chloe said. "They seemed to be having a good time."

Something inside Tara warmed a little at that. For a guy who'd grown up without much direction or authority, Ford had some amazing people skills. Caring for and about others came naturally to him. Mia *would* love him instantly. But along with the warm fuzzies the image of them together gave her, she also felt a twinge of regret that she hadn't yet gotten there with Mia.

"She has his smile," Chloe said. "And his laugh."

So Mia was laughing for him. Of course she was. Ford did things like take her out to breakfast, employing his effortless charm and likability, while Tara burned breakfast and froze up when answering the simplest of questions.

And now she was jealous. Perfect. Jealous, because Ford made it easy to love him, and Tara...well, she didn't make it easy for anyone to care about her; she knew that.

"Get cranking on that bathroom. I'll be making beds."

"One," Chloe said. "You have to make *one* bed. For our two guests, who are married. Plus they're newlyweds. They probably wouldn't notice if you gave them no sheets at all. Now back to me for a minute—asthma makes me exempt from cleaning."

"I realize that your asthma is a free get-out-of-jail card for just about everything you don't want to do," Tara said. "But I bought chemical-free cleaning agents. Nothing in any of them should bother you."

"Fine. Just fine then. Call me Cinderella." Chloe blew out a breath and looked out the window, then let out a soft laugh.

"What?"

"Nothing."

Oh, it was something. Tara moved to the window. Indeed, Carlos was out there hosing down the yard.

With Mia now at his side.

Carlos was both tough and quiet, and for the most part, utterly unreadable. His clothes added to his bad-boy persona, but he showed up on time, and until today, had always worked his ass off.

At the moment, he wasn't so much working as...posturing. And although Tara had heard him utter maybe ten sentences total in the past three months, the two of them were talking nonstop.

Carlos smiled down at Mia and entirely missed the flowerbed that he was supposedly watering.

Mia was standing as close to him as she could get without sharing his too big, unlaced Nikes. She was also doing something Tara had heard about but had not yet seen firsthand.

She was laughing, a warm, genuine laugh that transformed her face.

"It's sweet," Chloe said.

"No. Not sweet." Tara shook her head. "He's a seventeen-year-old boy, and there's only one thing seventeen-year-old boys want."

Chloe laughed. "Wow, you're *such* a hypocrite."

Tara sighed and rested her forehead on the glass. "She doesn't smile like that for me."

"Of course not. She's not hoping that you're going to kiss her later, either."

Tara sighed again, and Chloe slid an arm around

her. Shocked, Tara turned her head and met her younger sister's gaze. They'd spent summers together as kids, and the past six months in each other's pockets, and yet Tara could count on one hand the number of times they'd touched each other in affection.

"It's going to be okay," Chloe assured her with a surprisingly gentle squeeze. "She's going to be okay. She's happy here."

At the unexpected comfort from the most unexpected source, Tara felt her breath leave her in a whoosh. "You sure?"

"Yes. And I get the feeling she hasn't been happy in a while. Breathe, Tara."

"I really hate it when people tell me to breathe."

"Then you should do more of it on your own."

Tara inhaled deeply, held it, then let it out. "I just wish she'd warm up to me."

"Hey, she's here, isn't she? It'll come." Chloe squeezed her again. "Let her be. For once in your life, don't direct. Just let it happen and enjoy the ride."

Tara paused and gave her the once-over. "Look at you, being all sweet."

"I know, right?" Chloe flashed a grin. "I think I'd be great at sweet, but the truth is, that's not what I'm doing."

Tara sighed. She knew that was too good to last. "Okay. What do you want?"

"To take off next week without you bitching about me leaving right before we open."

"Where're you going this time?"

"Cabo. Got a friend who works in a five-star hotel there, and they're interested in my skincare line."

"The last time you went to Cabo, you were gone for four days, dyed your hair platinum blonde, and got a nipple pierced."

Chloe winced in recollected pain. "Yeah. I'll be working so there'll be no alcohol involved this time."

"Good to know," Tara said. "You've got to be running out of parts to get pierced by now."

"Actually—"

"Don't." Tara held up a hand and grimaced. "I don't want to know." Oddly unwilling to break the rare sweet moment, she pressed her cheek to Chloe's. "Love you, you know."

Chloe hesitated a moment, then hugged her back, hard. She didn't repeat the vow of love, but then again, she never did. But perhaps in a gesture that meant even more than the words would have, Chloe took a long time to let go. Then she nodded and carefully steered Tara away from the window and the view of the teenagers. "Did you see the paper this morning? Logan and Ford are neck and neck in the townwide vote. Probably because of last night."

Tara went still. "Oh, God. What happened last night?"

"Logan was at The Love Shack again." Chloe smiled. "You had your current lover serving your ex-lover. Never thought you had it in you to catch two alpha men like that." She eyed Tara speculatively. "You must have some moves once you lose all the control issues you have going on. Or hell, maybe guys like that, I don't know. Do you boss them around in bed?"

Tara ignored that. "Logan was at the bar again?"

"Well, mostly it was Ford at the bar being accosted by

Lucille and her friends. They're on a mission to see you settled with Ford. Not that they don't think Logan is hot, but you know how they all love and adore Ford."

This was true. The whole town loved and adored Ford. Everyone did. He had effortless charm and ease, no matter what he was doing.

Or who.

"They've decided to try to sway the vote in his favor," Chloe said. "There are signs up in town and everything. The one outside the post office has Ford's high school yearbook picture. He was Class Flirt, did you know that?"

Tara stared at her. "There are *not* signs in town."

"Okay," Chloe said agreeably. "But there are."

Tara moaned. "Okay, new plan." She shoved the sheets at Chloe. "You're doing the bathrooms *and* the beds. I'm going to town to pull down the signs."

"How did your problems become my problems? And if you'd just pick one of the Hot Guys, the voting would be a moot point."

"It's not about picking one," Tara said. "Logan wants a woman who no longer exists, and Ford wants..."

But Chloe was gone. And Tara was talking to herself. Perfect. Turning, she walked directly into a brick wall that happened to be Ford's chest.

Chapter 13

"It's impossible to be both smart and in love."
Tara Daniels

Ford's hands went to Tara's hips to steady her. Dipping down a little, he met her eyes with his. "I want...what?" he asked.

Tara pushed past him and headed for the kitchen.

He followed her. Of course he followed. She was annoyed with herself for allowing it, but also a little discombobulated. Her usual state around him.

"Talk to me," he said. "I want what?"

"You tell me," she said, going for flirty because she wasn't at all sure whether or not she wanted to hear his real answer.

His eyes dilated. "I'd rather show you." He reached for her but she backed up, directly into the pantry.

He simply stepped in as well and shut the door behind them. His expression resembled that of a lion stalking its prey.

"Okay, here's the thing," Tara said, hand on his chest to hold him off. "I meant what I told you that night after we..."

He cocked a brow.

"Were together." She backed up a step and came up against the pantry door. "I told you I'm working on things. Things inside of me. And you—you distract me from those things." She poked him in the chest. "So I'm asking you to stop doing that. Stop distracting me. Yes, we slept together. Hell, we have *a lot* of chemistry, and I was out of control that night. But I have a lot going on, Ford. *We* have a lot going on, so we really need to try to ignore us. Okay? No more of this dance we have going on. We have to control ourselves."

His silence was deafening.

"Well," he finally said. "That's all *fascinating*, and informative as well. And we're going to circle back to parts of it, especially the part where you can't control yourself around me, but I was only trying to..." Slowly he reached out for her again and pulled a Post-it note from her back.

There were two words on it: Bite Me.

Tara groaned. "Chloe's idea of a joke. Can we focus here?"

"I'd rather bite you."

"Very funny. Look, I get how you might think that the natural progression would be for us to have sex again, but we can't. I can't."

"Because you're working on yourself."

So he *was* listening. "Yes. And because when I'm with you like that, I'm..." She searched for the right word.

"Multi-orgasmic?"

She closed her eyes. "You're not taking me seriously."

"On the contrary, I'm taking you very seriously."

Their gazes collided. Held. And something jumped in her stomach. His eyes were dark and solemn, belying his easy tone. He'd heard everything she'd said. He'd also heard everything she *hadn't* said. What she didn't know was if he agreed with her. "Someone's going to get their emotions in the wrong place, Ford." And by someone, she meant *her*. They had a track record. The last time she let her emotions get tangled up with his, it had been the most painful time of her life. People didn't recover from that kind of screw-up; they didn't get second chances.

"Ah," he said quietly. "*Now* we're getting somewhere." He ran a finger over her jaw. "You're afraid."

"Yes. Join me, won't you?" She gripped his shirt. "Mia—"

"Is amazing."

"Yes." Tara let out a breath. "She is. But that's what I mean. We're in danger of misplacing emotions—"

"I'm misplacing nothing." His eyes softened, and he touched her face. "Tara. It's not the same now."

Because it was just sex. She swallowed the hurt. "Look, all I need is for you to agree that we should just go back to how we were before."

"Before what?"

He knew before what. "Before we made love," she said uncomfortably, hating him for making her say it out loud.

"At least you know that that's what we did." He paused. "How much of this has to do with Logan?"

"None." She met his gaze head on. "Okay, maybe a little, but not how you think."

"Well, that makes me feel all better."

"I tried to explain this to you before," Tara said with a sigh. "I've got some issues. And so do you."

"I thought this wasn't about me."

"It's a roundabout thing," she said.

Ford paused. "Okay, help me out here. Who exactly is working on whose issues?"

"I'm working on mine." She lifted her chin. "And you should be working on yours."

"And mine are?" he asked mildly.

"Well, for one, you don't stick."

"What does that mean?"

"It means that you're laid-back, easygoing, and you like your life the same way," Tara told him. "And let's face it, you're good at just about everything. So when something's hard, or difficult, or doesn't drop into your lap, you don't tend to work at it."

Only his eyes reflected his tension. "You think things drop in my lap? That I haven't had to work hard at life?"

"No," she said, shaking her head. "I know where you came from. I know how you busted your butt to get to where you are, but sailing...face it, Ford. Sailing came easy. And Logan hasn't been the only man in my life to find his face in the papers. You've been there, too. *Cosmo* had some really interesting things to say about your bachelor life and how you live it."

"So I haven't been a monk. Jesus, Tara, I was in my twenties with too much money and women throwing themselves at me. Yeah, I enjoyed it all *way* too much, but I also eventually grew up."

"Yes, you got engaged after your gold medal to someone you met while training. You broke it off at the last minute."

Something flickered in his eyes at that. Annoyance at having to explain himself, probably. Typical male. "Because," he said, "she'd gotten caught up in the fame and fortune of the sponsorships and wanted to live in the public eye. She went nuts for the attention, and I—" He broke off and frowned. "I wanted my same old, simple life. The life I'd worked hard for."

"You took a huge contract for sponsorship and then dropped it."

He stared at her. "You *have* been reading the papers."

Truthfully, Tara had devoured every little scrap on him over the years. "Yes."

He was quiet a moment. "I wasn't feeling as competitive as I'd been, and I wanted to slow down. It didn't seem right to stick with that contract when I wasn't going to be giving them their money's worth. So yeah, maybe I haven't exactly done what was expected, but I've always done what I felt was right."

"And us?" Tara asked. "Seventeen years ago?"

His eyes hardened. "You're the one who walked away."

"Yes, but you let me."

"What? Are you kidding me?" He shoved his hands into his hair, and arms up, muscles taut, he turned in a full circle. When he faced her again, a very rare display of temper and frustration was showing on his face. "No one has ever had any luck stopping you when you have your mind set on something, Tara, and you damn well know it."

"But you never even tried." Her throat was tight with remembered pain. God, the pain. She didn't want to ever feel that scared and alone and anxious again. Yes, *she'd* been the one to walk, but she'd been so young and stupid. "You never even attempted to contact me."

She'd been okay with that in the end. Because the clean break had given her the time to get over the heartbreak without having to constantly relive it. But it was bothering her now, she realized. Deeply. She knew Ford felt very strongly about her, but she wasn't sure he felt strongly enough. Certainly not enough to want to stick for real, for the long haul. And with him, she was beginning to realize she could handle no less.

Sure, back then he'd been willing to make things work, but the promise and drive of a teenager didn't mean that it would have. And what did teenagers know about love anyway? If he'd really been right for her, wouldn't he have followed after her, or at least tried?

She knew he'd wanted to do the right thing by her, she believed that. And he was a good guy: reliable, warm, caring... but she could only go on what she knew. And she knew she hadn't been important enough to him.

She had no reason to think now would be any different.

"I remember things differently," he said quietly. "I remember that you gave up. *You* ran. I'd have gladly taken it to that happy-ever-after you were too guilt-ridden to allow yourself."

She swallowed hard against both the recrimination in

his voice and the truth of that statement. "What's done is done," she said. "And it's not just us now. There's Mia. We can't play at this anymore, Ford, not when so much is at stake. She's fragile and working through her adopted parents' split. We can't mess her up. We can't." She turned away, then changed her mind. He deserved the truth. "It's just that if by some miracle we made this work now, then..." She swallowed hard and whispered, "then maybe we really might have been able to work it out back then, too. And that *kills* me, Ford. All that pain I caused...for nothing."

Looking stunned, he stared down at her. "Tara," he said softly, regret heavy in his voice. "You can't keep punishing yourself, sabotaging your life, your own happiness for your past."

She'd never really realized it but he was right. Deep down she felt she needed to be punished for giving up Mia.

Ford was watching her, eyes solemn. "I have all those thoughts too, you know," he said. "The guilt. You're not alone in this."

She let out a breath. "How do you always know what I'm thinking?"

Running his thumb along her jaw, he let out a small smile. "It's all over your face. You made a decision back then. It was the right decision for you. Don't let it eat away at you now. It's a new chapter. Turn the page."

He was still touching her face, his other hand low on her back, holding her against him, and she fought the urge to turn her face into his palm. "So if I turn the page, then what?"

"Your choice," he said. "It always was. But know this. You're not alone. There are two of us now. Actually, there are three."

She dropped her forehead to his chest. He was big and warm and strong. Strong enough to share her burdens, at least for this moment. She shifted closer without even realizing it, then closer still. His heart was beating calm and even. His eyes were warm as he looked at her.

Into her.

She thought about how he'd said that he felt all the same things that she did, and an old, familiar closeness and tenderness welled up within her. She lifted her head and leaned back against the closed pantry door. "Ford?"

"Yeah?" He was steady and even. A rock.

Her rock.

Tired of thinking, tired of trying to keep in mind a viable reason why they needed to steer clear of each other, she followed her gut and put her lips on his. Which was when the door of the pantry suddenly opened behind her, and she spilled out, right into Logan's waiting arms.

Chapter 14

*"Generally speaking, if your mouth is moving,
you aren't learning much."*
TARA DANIELS

W hat the hell?" Logan stared down at Tara in surprise,
then lifted his head and eyed Ford.

Before Tara could budge, Chloe came into the kitchen.
She took one look at Tara—in a Logan-and-Ford sandwich—
and tossed up her hands. "I swear to God, I don't get it."
With a shake of her head, she pivoted and walked out.

Logan was still sizing up Ford.

Who was sizing up Logan right back.

Tara pushed free of both men. "This is awkward. I'm
going to go finish my work." She'd planned on going into
town, but she didn't want to go too far away. She grabbed
the vacuum cleaner and headed up the stairs. When in
doubt, vacuum. In fact, she was a vacuuming demon, well
into the second bedroom, when two arms reached around
her and turned the machine off.

Logan pulled her around to face him, a small smile on his face, his eyes serious. "Avoiding me?"

"Little bit." She blew out a breath. "Logan, why are you really here?"

"I already told you."

"You think you miss me."

"I *do* miss you," he said. "I miss you traveling with me, I miss the way you always made coffee in the mornings, and how you packed for me. I miss you taking care of me."

"Oh, Logan." She heaved out a sigh. "I'm not that woman anymore." Not even close. "And your world...it's big and shiny and exciting, and I'm...not. Lucky Harbor is not. So I don't understand."

"Don't you?" His eyes were soft as they skimmed over her features. "You're smart and funny, and you wanted to be with me for me, not for my stats or bank account. Everyone else yesses me."

"Is that what this is? You want someone who doesn't yes you?"

"See that?" he said, smiling at her raised voice. "No one ever gets mad at me. No one but you." He gave her the eyes—the Logan bedroom eyes—and in spite of herself, she sighed again.

"I really did miss you, Tara." He put his hands on her waist and his mouth to her ear. "Tell me you missed me, too."

He was familiar and comfortable, and a part of her wanted to sink into that.

Luckily, a bigger part of her wanted to smack him. "Logan, these past few years..." She'd ached for him.

She'd *wanted* him to come after her. She'd dreamed about it, much the way she once upon a time had dreamed about Ford doing the same.

But he hadn't. No one ever had.

"I'm too busy to miss you," she finally said, unwilling to reveal something so pathetic. "I'm sorry."

Logan searched her gaze, his smile fading some. "No, I deserved that. I spent way too much time being too busy for you, didn't I?" Moving further into her personal space, he gently tugged at a loose strand of her hair. His eyes were warm in that just-for-her way, the look that used to melt all her clothes off in a blink.

But that had been when she'd been Mrs. Logan Perrish, back when Tara Daniels had barely existed. She didn't want to go back to that.

"You're tired. You're overworked," he chided gently. "I called you yesterday, wanting to come help. And don't think the irony got by me. I realize it used to be *you* helping *me*. So really, it's *me* who's sorry, Tara. So damned sorry."

She pressed her fingers to her eye sockets. "I don't want you to be sorry. I got over it."

"And over me," Logan mused quietly. "I won the Sprint Cup last year."

"I know." She smiled at him. "One of your biggest dreams."

"My life's goal," he agreed. "Met by age of thirty-two. And then, when it was over, I looked around for someone to share it with, but you were gone. The best thing that had ever happened to me—gone." He cupped her face. "I want a family, Tara. With you. Maybe even a few kids—"

She choked. She hadn't yet told him about Mia showing up in Lucky Harbor. She hadn't told anyone but her sisters. She knew it would come out eventually, but she'd hoped to be in a better, stronger place with Mia first. "Logan—"

"I know. We never really talked about kids, but it's time, don't you think?"

Jesus. "No, you don't understand, I—"

"I'm going to win you back," he said softly but with steel laced beneath.

Tara sucked in a breath and tried to figure out how she felt. Flattered? Maybe. Vindicated? Definitely. A little bit heated? Well, yes, but hell, the man was gorgeous, and she wasn't dead.

But mostly she felt unease. "I'm not an upcoming race," she said. "I'm not available to be won."

"I don't see a ring on your finger."

"That's not what I meant."

"I'm not leaving town without you, Tara."

"Logan—"

He kissed her, then pressed up against her to deepen the connection, but she stepped back and put up her hand.

Eyes dark, breathing unsteadily, he let out a breath. "That got to you, right?"

It used to be he could rock her world, but she wasn't feeling rocked. Okay, maybe there'd been a mild tremor, but she hadn't been rocked. Her good parts weren't tingling. Not like when Ford kissed her. "Logan—"

"We have the entire summer," he said.

She knew exactly how big a gesture that was for him

careerwise—had it not been a forced break due to his injury. "Because you're hurt," she reminded him.

"Yes, okay, so it was good timing," he said with a wry smile. "As far as these things go."

"Logan." She shook her head. "Please. I need you to be honest."

"Fine. I was forced to take the time off to heal. Even more honestly, I needed a break." He paused. "But mostly, Tara, I need us."

If that was true, it was only because he didn't have racing at the moment. That was all. Or maybe he was bored. "There's no *us*."

Logan shot her a smile that said he disagreed and was confident that he could prove her wrong. "I have to go," he said. "I promised Chloe that if she told me where you were, I'd clean a bathroom."

While Tara sputtered, trying to picture NASCAR star Logan Perrish wielding a toilet brush, he kissed her and was gone.

Tara stared down at the vacuum. Wasn't life supposed to get simpler the older you got? She'd been really looking forward to "simple." She turned on the vacuum, then squealed for a second time when two warm arms came around her a few minutes later. "Logan, dammit, I told you *no us*!"

But she instantly realized her mistake when the arms tightened and the scent of the man came to her.

"Just me," Ford said easily, turning her to face him. "Though I do like the 'no us' thing with Logan. Stick with that." He looked her over, and some of his amusement slipped. "You okay?"

"Me? Oh sure. I mean, sure, I'm back in a town I promised to never step in again, I'm having trouble connecting with my daughter—my fault—and my ex has shown up. And you..." She closed her mouth and shook her head. Not going there. "I'm great."

"You'll connect with Mia," he said. "Just give it some time. What did Logan want?"

"To know if his kiss got to me."

Ford tensed a little. "He kissed you?"

Well, look at that. The vacuum needed to be emptied. She bent, but Ford hauled her upright again. She tilted her head up to look at him. He certainly wasn't offering the comfort that Logan had, but there was something else. Something new, something edgy and dangerous.

To her heart, anyway.

And so damn tempting. She could admit that much to herself, but not to him. She moved to go around him, but Ford backed her to the wall and held her there with his big, warm body.

"What is it with you and the caveman thing?" she asked. *And why, oh why, do I like it so much?*

"So did Logan's kiss get to you, Tara?" He took her bottom lip between his teeth and tugged before freeing her. "Did it make your knees weak?"

No, but they were weak now.

Ford turned his attention to her upper lip, nipping that too. "Did his kiss make you tremble?" He kissed her full on then, a slow, hot kiss that branded her as his before finally pulling back only enough to let her breathe. "Did it, Tara? Did he get to you?"

By this time, she was so hot that she figured she was

lucky she hadn't spontaneously combusted. Against her, Ford was humming with the same tension as she. His eyes raked down her body, sending sparks racing along every nerve ending she possessed. Then he leaned in, his mouth once again hovering over hers.

Her lips fell open as she waited breathlessly for the kiss, but instead he stepped back, and she nearly slid to the floor.

With a knowing look, he lifted her up and supported her weight with no effort at all. "Tara."

She closed her eyes, then opened them again. "No. Logan didn't get to me. You do. You always did."

His smile came slow and sinfully lethal, and she pushed at him, thinking it should be illegal to have a smile like that. "Which you already knew, damn you. It doesn't mean anything, Ford. Not without intent."

"I have plenty of intent."

No kidding. "Intent from *me*," she said. "And the only intent I have is to get to know Mia and make a wild success out of the inn this weekend. And then the next and so on, until we're making enough money that Maddie is stable here on her own."

Something came into his eyes at that. She wasn't sure what. "And then?" he said.

"And then I'll go."

Temper, she decided. *That's* what was in his eyes. A good amount of it, and frustration, too.

"You'll go where, back to Texas?" he asked. "Far away from all the strings on your heart because that's the easiest way?"

Ouch.

And true.

"Maybe," she admitted, and damn him for putting it so succinctly into words. "Which makes us one hell of a pair, doesn't it? The runner—that would be me—and the guy who..."

"Who what?" he asked, eyes narrowed.

"It's easy come, easy go for you, isn't it? Things either fall into your lap and work out, or they don't. And if they don't, you're never overly bothered much." Again she shoved clear of him.

And this time he let her go.

The next morning, Ford woke up in a rare, foul mood. Tara was right about him. He was easy come, easy go, and he didn't like what that said about him.

And then there was Tara. She was difficult and a pain in his ass, and he had no idea why he wanted her.

Except he did.

He wanted her because she saw the real him. She didn't take his shit. And she made him feel. Christ, did she make him feel. And what he felt at the moment was impatient and frustrated as hell.

Usually a sign for him to move on.

Hell if that urge didn't piss him off too, because it proved her point. Christ, he really hated that.

He didn't want to move on.

Another shock. He thought maybe he was falling for her all over again, maybe even harder than the first time. As for her, he had no idea what she was feeling. For all he knew, she was feeling everything he was—but for Logan. He hated that, too. Frustrated with her, with himself,

with every fucking thing, he did his usual morning run
and then walked to the post office to collect his mail.
Logan happened to be at the counter and Ford shook his
head. Fan-fucking-tastic, because they hadn't seen nearly
enough of each other lately.

By the looks of things, the race car driver was
attempting to reserve a mailbox for the summer and getting nowhere. "I was told it would be no problem," Logan
was saying.

This was no mystery once Ford caught sight of the
clerk. Paige Robinson had crushed on Ford all through
middle school. And again in tenth grade. They'd gone to
Homecoming together, after which Paige had pulled her
father's pilfered vodka from her purse to share. Ford had
hoped to get lucky that night, but unfortunately, Paige had
tossed back too much and thrown up on his shoes instead.

Maybe she felt she owed him now, or maybe she was
still harboring a secret crush, Ford didn't know; but for
whatever reason, she was shaking her head at Logan, saying she was very sorry but there simply wasn't an empty
post office box to be rented in Lucky Harbor.

Logan walked out of the post office looking annoyed
but resigned, and Ford watched him go, torn. *Don't do
it, man.*

Don't. Fuck. He gathered his mail and followed Logan
outside. "There's a Mailboxes-R-Us on Fourth Street,"
Ford said. "You can probably get a box there."

Instead of thanking him, Logan gave him a suspicious
look. "I don't suppose you know anything about why Jan
at the diner told me they'd run out of coffee when I tried
to get caffeine this morning. Or how it is that I was woken

up at five, six, seven, *and* eight o'clock by someone playing doorbell ditch at the cottage? Or better yet, where my rental car went?"

"Why would I know anything about any of that?"

Logan laughed low in his throat. "Maybe because while the locals are impressed with my NASCAR status, they'd do just about anything for you. Hell, Facebook is proving that."

"Facebook? Is the poll still up then?"

Logan pulled out his Blackberry and brought up the page. People's tweets were posted, and on top of that was the latest blog entry:

> *There's romance in the wind! Or at least on the docks, where Tara Daniels was seen kissing a certain sexy hometown sailor. Voting is still open but it appears Tara's running a poll of her own. And don't forget to weigh in on a side poll—should Ford ask Tara to marry him? Also, see tweets on how he should pop the question...*

Ford stared at the screen. "What the fuck?"

Logan blew out a breath. "All I know is that she's not kissing *me* on the docks." He punched 9-1-1 on his cell. "Yes, dispatch? I need to report my rental car as stolen."

Ford waited with him, somehow feeling responsible. Plus, he had a feeling Sawyer would show up.

And sure enough, his best friend arrived in less than five minutes.

Sawyer got out of his squad car in his uniform and dark mirrored sunglasses, looking his usual badass self.

At the sight of Logan and Ford standing together, he arched a brow. He was far too good to show much, but a slow smile crossed his face. "Either of you see Facebook today?"

"Yeah, yeah," Ford muttered. "Have a good laugh."

"Already did. I haven't voted on the new poll yet. I'm weighing some heavy questions. Like do guys still get down on one knee? And how much should the ring cost?"

Ford flipped him the bird.

"Verbal assault of an officer," Sawyer said. "I'd arrest you but I don't feel like doing the paperwork."

"There's a stolen rental car," Ford said. "How about you be a cop and get to that?"

"It's not stolen. It just showed up." Sawyer turned to Logan. "You parked in a no-parking zone and it got towed." He eyed Logan over the tops of his dark lenses. "The law applies even to celebrities here."

Logan sighed. "I'm going to need a ride."

Sawyer looked at Ford.

Oh, Christ. "No."

"I have to get back to work," Sawyer said.

"It's your job to take care of citizens in need," Ford pointed out.

"Unless I have a call. And I have a call."

"What, to get donuts?"

Sawyer pointed at him, miming shooting his gun. Then he got back into his squad car and drove off.

Logan looked at Ford.

"Shit." Ford shoved a hand into his pocket for his keys. "Come on."

They walked to the lot, where Logan looked at Ford's classic 1969 Camaro. "You ever race this baby?"

"I keep my racing to the water."

Logan gave him an evaluating look over the hood. "You any good?"

"Yes."

"Heard about the gold medals."

"Then you know I'm good."

Logan leaned over the roof. "How about letting me drive?"

"Maybe when hell freezes over. And get off the car, man. You lean on your car like that?"

Logan laughed. "I kill people for leaning on my car."

Ford pinched the bridge of his nose. "Where are you staying?"

"Well, I *was* at the Beachside Cottages. But when I went to the office to complain about the doorbell ditch this morning, I was unceremoniously kicked out. Something about last-minute renovations."

"They can't really do that."

"Can and did," Logan assured him. "I called Tara, and she agreed to put me up."

Oh, good. His greatest nightmare coming true. "Tara."

"Yeah," Logan said, laughter in his voice. "Guess my sabotagers didn't think that one all the way through. I'll be staying at the inn with Tara. Think she still loves to…*cook*?"

Ford knew for a fact that she did, and thinking about it, he found himself driving a little faster, a little tighter than he normally would have.

"You're trying to impress me," Logan said. "It's okay. I get that a lot."

Shit. Ford slowed down but it was too late. Logan was grinning. "Do you also get that you're an ass?" Ford asked.

Logan shrugged, completely unconcerned.

Ford concentrated on not putting the pedal to the metal. "Why are you here again?"

"I let my wife get away from me. We were good together. She traveled with me, made my life bearable, and in return, I took care of her."

Ford thought about that for a moment. If Tara had ever needed anyone, those days were long over. She'd grown up, and nothing about the new version was needy or dependent.

"And you?" Logan asked.

"Me what?" Ford slid him a look. "And be careful, because if you're about to ask about me and Tara, I'm going to kick your ass and enjoy it."

Logan snorted at the empty, hollow threat. Fan-fucking-tastic.

When Ford finally pulled up at the inn, Logan eyed him across the console. "If all you're looking for is a good time, she deserves better."

Ford was surprised he still had back teeth, what with all the grinding he'd been doing. "What I'm looking for is none of your business."

"Look, I was the guy that came along in Tara's life after you screwed her up. And she was damn tough to catch because of it. But my patience and perseverance paid off, and she married me. So man to man…." Logan gave him a tight smile. "You might *think* you have game with her now, but she isn't a game. Move onto someone else, Ford."

"Get out."

Logan did just that, then leaned in the window. "I've heard a lot about you, you know. Hard not to; you're the only thing anyone around here wants to talk about. You're the Good Time Guy, not the Keeper Guy. That's how I know I'm going to be the last one standing. And I think you know it, too."

Ford watched him walk away. It was true that all he and Tara had in common was a mutual desire, which they'd supposedly fulfilled. And Mia, of course.

Except...

Christ, the *except.* He watched Logan vanish inside the inn, thinking about how much more than desire this was. How he wasn't feeling much like just a Good Time Guy.

He was feeling like the Confused Guy, one who wanted so much more than he ever had before.

Tara and Maddie were up at the crack of dawn, standing on the docks watching as, from the very far corner of the bay, Logan seemed to be struggling with the houseboat.

"Does he look like he's okay?" Tara asked, peering through the binoculars she'd found in the marina building.

"He has the two-way," Maddie said. "He'd call for help if he needed it, right?"

"No, he wouldn't. He's a guy. He'll call for help when he's dead."

The houseboat had come with the inn and marina as a part of their inheritance. Since this had happened in the dead of winter six months ago, they'd never had an earlier opportunity to use the boat.

But when Logan had called yesterday needing a place to stay, Tara had grabbed her sisters and cleaned the thing out, and placed Logan in it.

Better than having him underfoot at the inn.

Chloe came up behind them. "Hey, thought we were doing yoga this morning."

"I get enough exercise just pushing my luck," Tara said, still watching the houseboat through the binoculars. Logan was on the deck, messing with something in the open maintenance closet. She considered calling him, but probably it was his plan to look helpless so she'd go out there. He used to do that with all the kitchen appliances when they were married.

"Did anyone look through yesterday's mail yet?" Chloe asked. "I'm waiting for a few checks to come through for the classes I gave in Tucson last month."

"No checks, only bills," Maddie said.

Chloe sighed. "The bills always travel faster than the checks. Why is that?"

Neither Tara nor Maddie had an answer for that. Tara was still looking at the houseboat. Huh. Logan did seem to be genuinely concerned about something.

"Tell me again why he couldn't just rent one of our rooms?" Maddie asked, shielding her eyes from the early morning sun. "The rooms that we actually *want* to rent out? He's a paying customer."

"That would have put him too close."

Maddie glanced at her. "If you don't want him here, why don't you ask him to leave?"

"Because he said he wasn't leaving until he won me back."

"Is that even possible?"

The "no" was on the tip of her tongue, but she was having some trouble getting it out. She had no intention of starting anything up with Logan. None. But he'd been her only family for several years, during a time when she didn't have a lot of others in her life, and he'd stuck with her until she hadn't been able to make it work anymore. There were still emotional ties.

"And what about Ford?" Maddie asked.

"What about him?"

"Is he the reason Logan doesn't have a shot? And don't lie. I've seen the way you look at him. It's how I look at junk food."

"We are *way* too busy to discuss this," Tara said. "We have guests—"

"Who have been out sightseeing in the area and are no trouble at all." Maddie took in the heavy South in Tara's voice and smiled. "You do realize that you don't scare either me or Chloe anymore with that tone, right?"

"Like I ever scared you."

Maddie's smile turned into a grin. "You know what you should do with Ford?"

Tara gave her a droll look. "Drag him up to the attic like you do Jax?"

Maddie blushed. "Hey, we go up there to—"

"I'll pay you fifty bucks not to finish that sentence," Tara said fervently.

From behind them came the sound of a soda can being popped open, and they all whirled around.

Ford stood on the deck of his Beneteau, drink in one hand and a bag of chips in the other. Breakfast of champions. He wore a WeatherTech T-shirt, board shorts, and a backward baseball cap with his hair curling out from beneath. Looking better than anyone should this early, he toasted them with his soda, his eyes never leaving Tara's. "Morning."

Maddie gasped. Only she wasn't looking at Ford, but out at the water. "Do you think Logan's all right?"

"He's always all right," Tara said. "Why?"

"Because he's waving at us."

Ford looked out on the water, then swore as he set his soda aside and leaped forward to start the engine on the Beneteau.

"What are you doing?" Tara asked.

"Saving the bastard." He paused and looked at her hopefully. "Unless it's okay with you if he dies?"

"*What*?"

"He's sinking."

Tara looked. Ford was right. Logan was definitely sinking.

"Oh my God," Maddie whispered, horrified. "I rented him that boat. Does that make me a murderer?"

Tara's heart clutched. "He's not dead yet."

"Hurry," Maddie called to Ford. "I can't be the one who killed Tara's ex! I look terrible in orange!"

Tara tried to remember if Logan was good in the water. He could drive like the best of the best, but she had no idea about swimming. She grabbed the two-way radio from Maddie's hip. "Logan, why aren't you wearing protection?"

The radio crackled, and then came Logan's voice. "I have 'protection' in my bag," he said. "But much as I don't want to say this, darlin', now's not the time to be asking if I'm carrying condoms. I have problems."

"A life vest, Logan! I'm asking where's your life vest!"

"Oh," he said. "I knew that."

Maddie was yelling at Ford. "Faster! I voted for you, and I want you to win, but not this way, not by killing the ex-husband!"

Tara shook her head in disbelief. "You voted for him? I told you and Chloe not to vote. None of us were going to vote!"

"Actually, this is pretty funny, if you think about it," Chloe said as Ford sped toward Logan.

Tara gaped at her. "What could possibly be funny about any of this?"

"How about the fact that your two men seem to be spending more time with each other than with you?"

Chapter 15

"Experience is what you get when you didn't know what you wanted."
TARA DANIELS

By noon, the houseboat had been towed back to the marina, where it was determined that the bilge pump had failed. Logan was perfectly safe although slightly disgruntled, and settled back at his original beach cottage after a phone call to the owners from Tara.

The weekend guests were no trouble at all. Chloe had been right. They were in their mid-thirties, on their honeymoon, and hadn't noticed a thing about the inn. All they wanted was their bed.

Maddie was set to handle the afternoon and evening, with both Chloe and Mia for backup if needed. Tara had a shift at the diner, and she was running late. Keys in hand, she came running out of the cottage and nearly toppled over Mia, who sat on the top step.

Holding the recipe box.

"Hey, Sugar." Tara pulled up short. "Where did you get that?"

"From Chloe." Mia opened the box and pulled out the first card, on which Tara had written *For My Daughter.* "She thought I'd like to see it."

Tara was going to be late for work if she stopped but she knew it didn't matter. Talking to Mia was worth being bitched at by Jan—and Jan *would* bitch. Eyeing the wooden step, Tara bit back a sigh. Hiking up her pencil skirt to mid-thigh, she gingerly sat.

Mia pulled her lips in, trying to hide her smile, reminding Tara that in the girl's eyes, she was not only old but also probably embarrassing.

"The porch swing would have been more dignified," Tara told her.

"I like it right here. I can see the world sail by."

That was true. From here, there was a lovely view of the marina and any ships sailing past it. "Are you interested in sailing?" Tara asked her. "Because it just so happens, you're closely related to an expert."

Mia smiled. "I know. And yeah, I'm interested. Ford said he'd take me real soon." She pulled out a card and showed it to Tara. "Never miss a good opportunity to shut up?"

Tara sagged a little and let out a huff of laughter. "It fit at the moment."

"Chloe?"

Tara looked at Mia and found the girl still smiling, and felt the helpless curve of her own mouth. "Yes. She has a way, doesn't she?"

"Yeah." Mia looked down at the box and was quiet a minute. Normal for her, not normal for Tara. She had to bite her tongue to keep it from running away with her good sense, to keep from filling the silence. And damn, it was hard to do, but when Mia finally spoke, it was worth the torturous wait.

"You thought of me," she said.

Tara let out a low laugh. "A little."

Mia lifted her gaze from the box and met Tara's.

"A lot more than a little," Tara said very softly.

Her daughter's eyes warmed, those beautiful eyes that made Tara think of Ford every single time she looked into them. She wanted nothing more than to have Mia keep looking at her like that, but she had to tell her all of it. "I want you to know the truth, Mia. I need you to know the truth. I *don't* regret giving you up."

Mia went still. "Oh."

"I loved you," Tara said, and put her hand to her chest to absolve the ache she felt there at the memory of that sweet, sweet baby looking up at her. "Oh God, how I loved you, from the moment I first felt what I thought was a butterfly on my shirt and turned out to be you kicking. But I wasn't capable of the kind of love you needed." Tara paused, her throat tight. "Even in all my teenage selfishness, I knew you deserved more. You deserved everything I couldn't provide. So *that's* why I don't regret it, Mia. Because in giving you up, you had a childhood that I couldn't have given you."

Mia ran her fingers over the grooves in the wood of the recipe box, her silence killing Tara. "And something else I don't regret." Tara reached for Mia's hand. "Having you here this summer. I wouldn't have missed this for anything, getting to know you."

Mia's fingers slowly tightened on hers. "Even if it means facing your biggest mistake?"

"Oh, Mia." Tara risked all and slowly slid an arm around her beautiful, smart, reluctant daughter. "I meant what I said about that. You were never a mistake. You were meant to be, and I'm so very, *very* glad you're here."

"Really?"

"Really."

After a beat of thinking about that, Mia laid her head on Tara's shoulder, and Tara's heart swelled to bursting. They sat there quietly a few more minutes, Tara ignoring the occasional and insistent vibration of her phone. She knew it was Jan; she could *feel* the temper coming across the airwaves, but Tara didn't want to get up.

"I'm glad I'm here, too," Mia said.

Tara smiled. "It's been fun giving you the good jobs and making Chloe clean the bathrooms."

Mia's mouth quirked. Ford could do that, too, project an emotion with next to no movement. From within Tara's pocket, her cell went off yet again, but Mia was looking at her, something clearly on her mind, so Tara didn't move.

"I've just been trying to imagine it," Mia finally said. "Me, right now, having a baby at my age. It's... incomprehensible. The trauma. The utter responsibility of it all."

Tara laughed without much humor. "Don't forget the abject terror."

"Were your parents awful about it?"

"My dad, yes." Tara could still hear the bitter disappointment in his voice over the phone line. It'd taken him days to return her tearful message from wherever he'd been traveling for work. "But your grandma, she was surprisingly supportive."

"Why surprisingly?"

"We didn't see each other often. Just sometimes in the summers. But she didn't judge or yell. She didn't try to make me feel bad. She just found me a special high school to attend in Seattle, and she was there when I needed her. She came for your birth. And she was there for you later too, when—"

"When I got sick." Mia nodded. "My parents told me. She helped pay the medical bills."

"I didn't know it at the time," Tara admitted. "I never heard anything about it until she died. But I snooped through her papers and read about your condition. You had a problem with a heart valve."

"It was...*misbehaving*." Mia put finger quotes around the word. "That's what my parents called it. I had surgery, and now my heart's perfect. That's what my cardiologist said. *Perfect*."

"It must have been so scary for you."

She shrugged. "My parents kept buying me presents, and they took me to Disneyland afterward."

The resilience of youth...

"How about Ford? How did he handle the news of you getting pregnant?" Mia asked.

"Better than me. He was..." Strong. Steady. Calm. Looking back, Tara knew he must have been freaking out every bit as much as she was, but he'd never shown it. "Amazing."

"And you're not together why?" Mia asked, smiling

when Tara sighed. "Sorry, couldn't resist asking again." She pulled out another index card. "The quickest way to double your money is to fold it in half and put it back in your pocket." Mia laughed again, and the knot in Tara's chest, the one that had been there since the girl had first shown up in Lucky Harbor, loosened. God. God, her baby was so beautiful. "This is nice," Tara said. "I like being with you like this."

Mia stared down at the box. "I'm sorry I said you were rigid and uncompromising and stubborn."

Tara blinked. "You never called me those things."

"Oh, right. Well, I thought them." Mia winced. "I'm sorry."

"It's okay. I *am* those things, and more."

"You're also smart, and pretty, and you care," Mia said quietly. "You're, like, all calm and collected, and you have this don't-mess-with-me vibe, but you also care about everyone in your orbit. Even people who drive you crazy."

Tara laughed a little, shocked. And touched. Unbearably touched that her daughter appeared to know her so well. "How do you know that?"

"Chloe told me. She said she drives you crazy and you're still there for her, no matter what. That's her favorite part about you, and mine too."

Tara's heart throbbed painfully. In a good way. "You know what my favorite part is?"

Mia shook her head.

"You."

Her daughter's eyes got misty as she smiled, and Tara had to fight for control as well. She reached for Mia, and then they were hugging just as Tara's cell phone vibrated yet again. Mia sniffed and pulled back. "Somebody really wants to get a hold of you."

"It's my boss." Tara swiped beneath her eyes. "Mascara?"

"Still okay," Mia assured her. "You need the waterproof kind, though. And a nicer boss, like I have."

Tara laughed and got to her feet, brushing off her butt and hoping she wasn't wrinkled. "Come to the diner after you finish here, and I'll make you dinner."

"Can I bring someone?"

Carlos, Tara thought, which was something else that had been keeping her up at night—the idea of the teens moving too fast. Already, they were inseparable. "Honey, about Carlos," she started slowly. "He's" —*A horny teenage boy?*— "too old for you."

"He's my age."

"Well then, he's too..." Hell. He was too nothing. He was a great kid. But no boy was going to be good enough, she knew that already.

"Actually," Mia said. "I meant Ford. Do you have any objections to him? Because he likes to watch you cook. He told me."

Tara paused, struggling to change gears. "He did? What else did he tell you about me?"

"That he *loves* to see you and me together."

Aw. *Dammit*. There went her heart again, squeezing hard.

This question was accompanied by a certain look in her daughter's eyes, a speculative gaze that had Tara narrowing hers. "Sugar, you're not up to anything sneaky, are you?"

"Like?" Mia asked innocently.

Oh, Lord. "Like trying to get Ford and me together?"

"Hey, I didn't start the poll."

"Mia."

Mia was suddenly looking much younger than her seventeen years. "Would it be so awful?"

"I just don't want to disappoint you," Tara said. "Because Ford and I, we're not—"

"I know, I know. You've mentioned this a time or a hundred." Mia's attention was suddenly diverted by something behind Tara. "You'd better go. You don't want to be late to the diner."

Tara turned to look behind her at whatever had caught Mia's eyes and saw Carlos, walking across the yard toward the marina building.

"So have a good shift," Mia said, getting to her feet. "See you later."

"Mia—"

But Mia was already halfway to Carlos, and back to looking very much seventeen.

Much later that night, Tara awoke to someone trying to chainsaw their way into the cottage. She sat straight up and realized it was just her sister snoring.

From the next bedroom over.

Tara looked at the clock—midnight. *Great.* She slipped out of bed and down the hall to Chloe's room. "Turn over."

Chloe muttered something in her sleep that sounded like "a little to the left, Paco."

"Chloe!" Tara said, louder.

Chloe rolled over and blessed silence reigned.

With a sigh, Tara went back to bed and started to drift off. She got halfway to a dream that involved her naked and being worshipped by Ford's very talented tongue before Chloe began sawing logs again. Tara looked at the clock.

Midnight plus two minutes.

Hell. Sleep was out of the question, and anyway now she was hungry. She must have been channeling her sister Maddie because suddenly she wanted some chips. *Needed* some chips, quite desperately, as a matter of fact. Only problem, there were none in the cottage; she'd removed them for Maddie's sake. The only place she knew to get chips was in town.

Or...on Ford's boat.

Was it breaking and entering to board a man's boat and steal food? No doubt. But hell, she'd already stolen his shirt. In fact, she was wearing it right now, so what was one more act of pilfering?

Her stomach growled, and making her decision, she rolled out of bed once more. At the door, she realized she needed shoes, and slipped into the only ones she had out—her wedge sandals. She gave a brief thought to how she must look in Ford's shirt, panties, and the heeled wedges. Ready for a "Girls Gone Wild" video.

No one else will see you at this hour, she assured herself. The boat was only fifty yards across the driveway. She ran in the heels, skirting around the marina building and onto the dock, by some miracle not twisting an ankle or breaking her neck.

The night was noisy. No wind, but there was an owl

hooting softly somewhere on the bluffs, and the answering cry of its mate. Crickets sang, and the water, stirred by the moon's pull, pulsed against the dock, slapping up hard against the wood.

In Houston, Tara had slept in a fourth-floor condo. City lights had slashed through her windows, blotting out the moon's glow, and there'd been no noise except for the drone of the air conditioning just about 24/7. Six months ago, when she'd first arrived in Lucky Harbor—bitchy, resentful, and unhappy—she'd hated the sound of nature at night. It'd kept her up, and she'd lay in bed for hours, mind racing. But somehow, over the months, she'd come to accept the noises. Even welcome them.

They soothed her now, as did the utter darkness of the night itself. There were no city lights here, nothing to mute the glorious stars. She would stay outside and enjoy the night but she wasn't exactly dressed for it. And those chips were calling her name. She did have a bad moment boarding the boat in the wedges, and pictured falling into the water between the boat and the dock and being found with Ford's T-shirt up around her ears.

Once she managed to board, she headed below deck, and as hoped found a bag of chips on the counter in the tiny galley. She downed her first mouthful, and her hand was loaded with her second when the light came on. Blinking in the sudden brightness, she turned and faced...

Ford.

He took in the fact that her mouth was full, her fingers loaded with more chips, and began to smile. By the time he eyed her undoubtably bedhead hair, bare legs, and heels, it was a full-blown grin. "Nice," he said.

"This isn't what it looks like."

"No?" He wore sweatpants low on his hips and nothing else. His hair was rumpled in that sexy way that guys' hair get when they've been sleeping. He leaned back against the opposite counter and slid his hands into his pockets. Relaxed. Watchful.

Amused.

Damn him.

"So what do you think it looks like?" he wanted to know.

Like she was a crazy chick so on the verge of losing it that she'd broken and entered and stolen his chips. "Uh..."

His eyes had locked in on her shirt. "You're either chilly or very happy to see me—is that my shirt?"

Crap. She looked down and crossed her arms over herself, which made the shirt rise up higher on her thighs, possibly exposing her pink lace panties.

This momentarily diverted his attention downward. His smile went naughty and the air around them heated to scorching.

Yeah, definitely she'd exposed her underwear.

"That *is*," he said. "That's my shirt."

She didn't really want to talk about the shirt. "I couldn't sleep. I got hungry and figured you had chips."

"So you committed felony B&E," he said, nodding. "Good plan. Except for the getting caught part. Were you going to sleep in my bed, too, Goldilocks?"

The way he said *bed* brought vivid memories of all the mind-blowing, amazing things he'd done to her in a bed. And *out* of a bed... "No," she said. "That would be rude."

He laughed softly. "Are you still working on your issues?"

"Yes," she said primly. "You?"

"I'm a work in progress, babe." He slid her a bad boy smile. "Still hungry?"

Oh boy. "Yes," she whispered.

He crooked a finger at her. "Come here, Goldilocks."

"That would be...a really bad idea."

"I can make it so bad it's good."

Gah. "You've *got* to stop that."

"Stop what?" he asked.

Looking hot, she thought. Talking naughty.

Breathing.

As she turned to face the counter and set down the bag of chips, she grabbed a bottle of water and washed down the crumbs. She knew by the tingling at the base of her neck that Ford was right behind her now. Then he was so close that she could feel his body heat seeping through the shirt to her skin. She could have moved away, but the truth was, she was exactly where she wanted to be.

"Okay," she said shakily. "Here's the thing. I'm... still attracted to you." Her breath shuddered out when he nudged her hair aside and brushed his lips along the nape of her neck. She locked her knees. Had to, in order to keep standing. "But I don't want to sleep with you again."

"And yet here you are," he murmured against her skin. "On my boat. In the middle of the night."

"Yeah. That looks bad," Tara admitted. "But really, it was all about the chips."

"And my shirt." He ran a finger down her spine, stopping far below the line of decency, making her breath catch in the sudden silence. "How is it that you have it?" he asked, his hand on her ass.

She fought against the urge to thrust her bottom into his palm.

Or better yet, his crotch.

"Tara."

She squeezed her eyes shut. "I stole it. The day I returned your crepe pan."

"Look at me."

No. No, thank you very much.

His hands settled on her hips and he turned her to face him. "Not that I don't like the sight of you in the shirt," he said. "Because I do. Very much. But you've been keeping your distance, and I've been trying to respect that. But you came to me tonight, so all bets are off. Tell me why you're in my shirt."

She nibbled on her lower lip. She didn't have an answer. At least, not one she wanted to give him. "You gave me one just like it when you first got them."

"I remember. I just didn't realize you did as well."

"Yes, well, I do. And I loved it," she told him. "And I lost it in the fire. I really missed it. So when I saw yours..." She closed her eyes. "Hell, Ford. I can't explain it. I lost my head and stole your damn shirt. There. You happy?"

"Hmm," he said noncommittally. "The fire was six months ago." He was still gripping her hips, his hands beneath the hem of the shirt now and his thumbs scraping lightly up and down on her bared belly, making her muscles quiver. "You had it all that time?"

"It was comfortable."

He smiled at that. "Comfortable. You kept a shirt for seventeen years because it was comfortable."

"Yes."

"Liar. Such a beautiful liar." Leaning in, he kissed her.

Soft.

A warm-up round.

She knew just how potent the next round would be, so she put her hand to his chest, not quite sure if she was stopping him or making sure he couldn't stop.

In the silence, her stomach growled, and he grinned. "I stand corrected. You really *are* hungry." Turning to the small refrigerator, he pulled out tortillas, grated cheese, and salsa.

"What are you doing?"

"Making you a quesadilla. I'd grill it, but I can't do that in here."

She watched as he stroked a spoonful of salsa onto the tortilla, then layered grated cheese over it. There was something about the way his hands moved, his concentration, the obvious ease that he felt in his kitchen, that got to her.

And he did get to her, in a big way.

He waited until she'd eaten the entire quesadilla to take the plate from her and then lifted her up to the counter. Eyes on hers, he stepped in between her thighs.

"I didn't come here for this," she whispered as he slowly lifted his shirt from her and peeled it off over her head.

"Your nose is going to start growing, Pinocchio," he said, resting his hands on her waist.

"You didn't eat anything," she said inanely.

"Wasn't hungry for a quesadilla."

"What are you hungry for?"

His eyes were so heated that she felt her bones melt away. "Guess," he said, and slid his hands up her thighs. He hooked his thumb in her panties and inched them down. Then he dropped to his knees and proceeded to show her.

Over and over again.

Chapter 16

"Things are always funnier when they're happening to someone else."
TARA DANIELS

Tara stood alone in the inn's kitchen in rare blessed silence. She was trying not to think about how many times Ford had taken her—and she him—last night before he'd walked her back to her bed at dawn.

Or how much he was coming to mean to her. Along with Mia. And her sisters. And Lucky Harbor...

It was all those strings that Ford had pointed out, tangling around her heart.

Damn strings. She didn't want them. She wanted to be able to protect her heart as needed, and that was getting damn hard to do. At least with Ford, she knew what she was getting. A good time. Okay, a *really* good time. She'd meant for it to be nothing more but it was...

Chloe came into the room just as Tara was staring blindly into the refrigerator. "Hungry?"

"No," Tara said. "Trying to decide between juice or the vodka."

Chloe laughed. "Always the vodka. It's fewer calories. But I've never actually considered vodka and OJ to be mutually exclusive. Go ahead, splurge, have both."

"Hmm," Tara said and pulled out the eggs.

"You're probably starving from burning all those calories having wild animal sex last night, right?"

Tara nearly dropped the eggs before turning to stare at Chloe. "What?"

"Well, you came in at dawn with crazy hair and a ridiculously wide smile for someone who hates early mornings." Chloe shrugged. "I figured it had to be sex. And given that it was Ford, I also figured it had to be a pretty fantastic night. It *was* Ford, right?"

"Oh my God," Tara said. "*Yes.*"

Chloe grinned at the confession.

"Stop that," Tara said. "We're not talking about this."

"Pretty please? It's so much better than what I have to talk to you about."

Tara opened her mouth to respond to that but Sawyer came in the back door with his usual long-legged stride. It faltered only slightly when he locked gazes with Chloe, whom he wasn't used to seeing in the kitchen when he made his early morning coffee run.

Tara pulled out a to-go mug from a stack that she kept just for him and filled it up.

Chloe watched the process, including Sawyer's quiet but grateful thank you, although she didn't say a word until he was gone. "Why do you let him steal your coffee?"

"Because he's a good man with a crappy job, that you

make all the more difficult for him, by the way. I feel like I owe him."

Chloe rolled her eyes. "Back to you, missy, and you're just-got-laid expression. You should try to lose that. You know, for the children."

Tara attempted to catch sight of herself in the steel door of the refrigerator. Damn, Chloe was right. She was glowing.

"Oh, and I borrowed your laptop this morning," Chloe said casually, gathering strawberries, yogurt, and the blender.

"Don't tell me you were looking at porn again," Tara said. "You froze my computer last time you opened that *See Channing Tatum Naked* attachment."

"Hey, anyone would have clicked on that, and it was a total hoax. I never even got to see him naked. And no, I didn't do any of that today. I was just getting my mail. Oh, and I accidentally clicked on your Firefox history."

"So?"

"So I happen to know you went to Facebook, created an account, and voted for Ford."

Tara went still. "Did not."

"Okay. But you did."

Tara crossed her arms. "I'll have you know that there's not a single Tara Daniels on Facebook," she said with confidence.

Chloe looked amused. "And you know this how, *Tallulah Danielson*? Tallulah? Danielson? Seriously? Because Jesus, if you ever find yourself with the need to go deep undercover again, I'm begging you, ask for help. And never consider a job with the FBI."

Well, hell. This was embarrassing. Worse, she couldn't come up with an excuse. Not a single one.

Oh! Temporary insanity. That would work. Or avoidance, Tara decided, and turned away from a grinning Chloe, only to come face to face with the man himself.

Ford. Who was also grinning. "Bless your heart, Tallulah," he said.

Chloe laughed and walked across the room to hug him. "If you weren't so totally hung up on her," she told him, "I'd claim you for myself."

Ford hugged her back. "It's true. I'm totally hung up on her."

Aw. And *dammit*, he really had to stop doing that, Tara thought, watching them, her heart going all mushy. It was all those little things that added up, like making her a quesadilla in the middle of the night, or the way he looked at her, like maybe she was a better sight than say his first cup of coffee in the morning. Or, in the case of how he was looking at her right now, like she was greatly amusing him. "You might have told me he was standing there," Tara said to Chloe.

"I might have."

Tara shook her head and looked at Ford. "I meant to vote for Logan. I hit the wrong button."

Ford burst out laughing. He wore a T-shirt and Levi's that were faded into a buttery softness and doing some nice things for his bod. He had a day of scruff on him and looked so utterly delectable that she found herself just staring.

He looked right back, that small smile still hovering at the corners of his mouth.

Chloe cleared her throat. "Well. This is cute and

all…" She looked at Tara. "But I actually do really need to talk to you. Got a few?"

"Actually, not until later and neither do you. The guests are going to want breakfast."

"This is a quick thing," Chloe said, "but an important one."

Oh hell. It was something big, Tara could see it in Chloe's eyes. "Don't tell me you got arrested again, because I'm pretty sure Sawyer's going to throw away the key on you this time—"

"No. Jeez," Chloe said, tossing up her hands. "A girl gets arrested one time—"

"*Three* times."

Chloe sighed. "This is about *you*."

"What about me?"

Chloe glanced uneasily at Ford, who clearly wasn't budging, then sighed and pulled a white plastic stick from her pocket. "I was in the downstairs bathroom setting up a basket full of lotions and soaps, cleaning up, emptying the trash, that sort of thing."

"I emptied the trash just this morning," Tara said.

"I know," Chloe said. "I saw you. Which means you were the last one in there. So I figured you'd want me to give this to you so no one else could come to the wrong conclusion."

Tara looked down at the thing in Chloe's hands in shock. "That's a pregnancy test stick."

"A negative one," Chloe said. "Probably a relief for you guys, right?"

Tara nearly went into heart failure. "What are you talking about? It's not mine."

Ford's face was utterly blank as he stared at the stick. After a beat, he lifted his head and met Tara's gaze, his eyes completely shuttered.

Because he knew what she did. They'd used a condom. Every time. It was an unspoken, very serious thing with them, and they both knew it. So undoubtedly his mind was now leaping to the next possibility, that she'd slept with...Logan?

"It's not mine," Tara said again and grabbed Chloe by the arm. "Excuse us a minute?" she said to Ford, then without waiting for an answer, yanked Chloe into the pantry and slammed the door.

"Yeah," Chloe said, looking around at the small but cozy space. "I can see why you pull Ford in here whenever you can. It screams 'do me.'" She tested a shelf. "Does this hold?"

"Chloe, *how could you*?" Tara demanded in a harsh whisper.

"I don't know. I guess I'd hop up right here, and then he'd stand between my legs and—"

"I meant how could you give this to me in front of Ford? My God, that was the most irresponsible, rude, grossly negligent sisterly thing you've ever done, and you've done a lot!"

Chloe paused a moment, clearly startled by Tara's fury, as if she sincerely, honestly hadn't given anyone else's feelings a thought. As always, though, she rebounded with an excuse for herself. "Hey, if you're close enough to need a pregnancy test with him, then he's close enough to go through the worry with you. For the second time."

"It's not mine!"

"Well, it's not mine," Chloe said emphatically. "I haven't had sex all damn year. Not since that hot Cuban guy in Miami, which landed me in the ER. A bit of a post-coital downer, I should add."

"Oh my God," Tara said. "It's Mia's."

"What?"

"The pregnancy test! It's Mia's."

Chloe contemplated this, then let out a slow breath. "Oh boy."

Tara gritted her teeth. "I'm going to kill Carlos—"

"It's not Mia's. It's mine."

Tara and Chloe looked at each other, and then at the door, which had spoken to them. Chloe pulled it open and there stood Maddie.

And Mia.

They stood side by side, Maddie looking sheepish. "I thought I wrapped it up so no one would see it," she said.

Tara stuck her head out into the kitchen and looked around for Ford.

"He left," Maddie told her.

Mia still hadn't said a word. She stood staring at Tara with barely veiled resentment. "You thought the stick was mine."

Tara opened her mouth but Mia shook her head and took a step back. "I have to go," she said and moved to the door.

"Mia, please." Tara rushed to her. "Wait—"

Mia whirled back, her eyes swimming. "You thought it was mine," she repeated. "You think I'm having sex and being stupid enough to do it without protection. You think I'd compound that stupidity by taking a pregnancy test here and then leave the stick where it could be found." She winced and shot Maddie a look. "No offense."

Maddie sighed. "None taken."

"Mia," Tara said, and heard the emotion in her own voice. "I'm sorry. It was a knee-jerk reaction, and I'm sorry."

Some of the tension drained from Mia's shoulders, but not all, as she nodded.

"So you're not having sex?" Chloe asked her.

"No!" Mia said, hugging herself. "Jeez!"

"Good," Chloe said. "Because I really didn't want to be the only one not getting any." She turned to Maddie. "And you. You really thought you might be pregnant?"

Maddie nodded, backed to a chair, and dropped into it. She confiscated Chloe's coffee and sipped. Making a face, she added three heaping spoonfuls of sugar and then sipped again and nodded.

"So since you're not preggers, you're what, going for diabetes?" Chloe asked.

Tara gave Chloe a dark look that had Chloe miming zipping up her lips and throwing away the key. Tara still wanted to strangle her, but even more than that, she wanted to go find Ford and make sure they were okay. Or as okay as they could be when they were...

Hell. She had no idea what it was they were doing exactly, except spending a lot of time making each other moan the other's name. In any case, she needed to see him, needed to make sure he knew it really wasn't her. Unfortunately, Maddie appeared to be half an inch from meltdown so Tara pulled a chair up in front of her.

"Jax wants to get married," Maddie whispered without

prompting, then let out a shuddering breath, as if a huge weight had been lifted off her shoulders.

"And?" Chloe asked.

"And I think that's just the pregnancy scare talking." Maddie lifted huge eyes to her sisters. "I don't want to get married just because of that."

"It's more," Tara said. "He loves you."

"And I love him. But I don't need the piece of paper."

"How about the diamond?" Chloe asked. "Don't you need the diamond?"

"No. Well, maybe." Maddie let out a watery laugh. "But we haven't been together all that long, really."

"Six months," Tara said.

"Yes, and we're committed," Maddie agreed. "And that's enough for me. Shouldn't that be enough?"

"Are you trying to convince you, or us?" Chloe asked. "Because I'm still on the diamond thing. It'd be pretty hard to turn down a big, fat diamond. And then you get a big party, a cool trip, and use of his credit card." At Tara's slight shake of her head, Chloe rolled her eyes. "And fine. More importantly, you're wild about him. I know you are. He makes you smile. And he thinks your OCD is cute." She smirked at Tara, like *see*? I can so be supportive.

"I'm not OCD," Maddie said. "Exactly. And I *am* crazy wild about him. Maybe if I *had* been pregnant…"

"You're just lucky the pregnancy scare happened now," Tara said, extremely aware of Mia soaking up this sisterly exchange. "At a good age with a guy who loves you as much as Jax does." She met Chloe's sharp gaze. "What?"

"You say that like you don't have one of the greatest guys we know wanting *you*."

"Want is not love," Tara said.

Chloe rolled her eyes again.

"If you don't stop doing that," Tara said. "I'm going to pop them in a jar and roll them for you."

"And here I always thought that you were the brightest crayon in the box."

Tara felt her eyes narrow. "And what does that mean?"

"Hey," Chloe said, lifting her hands. "If you don't get it, I'm not going to explain it to you. But his name starts with an F and ends with an O-R-D, and *hello*, he's as head over heels for you as Jax is for Maddie."

Tara stared uncomfortably at Mia, who was nodding. "Okay," Tara said. "It's true, we might have married all those years ago, but seventeen-year-olds shouldn't marry."

"Maybe not," Chloe said. "But Ford's all grown up now, and a pretty damn fine man if you ask me. He's financially stable, hot as hell—sorry, Mia—and would probably die before he hurt you. So what's the hold-up?"

"I've asked the same thing," Mia said. "Minus the hot part, because *ew*."

Tara sagged. "Me. Okay? The hold-up is me. The last time I was with him…" She glanced at Mia. "I didn't handle things well."

"You were a kid," Maddie said and smiled at Mia. "No offense."

"None taken," Mia said politely.

"What a cynic you turned out to be," Chloe chided Tara. "Not believing in the power of love."

"Says the woman who can't even *say* I love you," Tara shot back.

Chloe clammed up, face closed now. "This isn't about me."

Mia looked outside as Carlos pulled in, her entire demeanor perking right up. "I gotta go," she said, and vanished out the door.

Tara sighed, then turned to Maddie. "Back to you."

"I'd rather not get back to me."

"Tough," Tara said. "Because I've had enough of me. Are we happy or sad the test was negative?"

"Aw," Maddie murmured, her eyes going suspiciously damp. "You said *we*."

"Hey, *you* said we were a *we*," Tara reminded her. "About six months ago, when you pretty much demanded we all stick together and act like sisters, remember?"

"Yeah," Chloe said, adding her two cents. "That's true, Mad. You were all about the *we*. Hardcore *we*, actually."

"Since when do either of you listen to me?" Maddie asked.

"Since you made us all hug and kiss and take the blood oath," Tara said, then found herself being squeezed nearly to death by Maddie, who'd pulled her and Chloe in close.

"I love you guys," Maddie whispered.

Tara sighed. "I love you too."

Chloe merely endured the hug and the sentiment.

Maddie pulled back and, still holding their hands, sniffed. "I'm sorry about this. When I didn't get my period on time, I panicked. It's silly. I love Jax so much. And we've talked about getting married, about doing the whole wedding and dress and cake—"

"And dancing," Chloe added. "If you're going to make a production out of it, let's have dancing."

Maddie laughed. "Yeah. And dancing."

"So...panic over?" Tara asked her.

"Yeah." Maddie rubbed her chest. "I mean none of us exactly had the typical childhood. And Jax didn't either. I couldn't picture—I just couldn't imagine being a parent, I don't know how. *We* don't know how."

"You're the warmest, sweetest, kindest person I know," Tara said. "And Jax is smart and sharp as hell. What you don't know, you'll figure out. You'll make great parents."

"Oh," Maddie said, "that's so sweet." And she sniffed again. "But I really just want to be alone with him for a while first. Is that selfish?"

"Hell, no," Chloe said. "If I was going out with Jax, I'd want to be alone with him all the time. Day and night. Naked—"

Tara slid an arm around Chloe and covered her mouth. Chloe freed herself with a laugh. "So if you're done panicking now," she said to Maddie, "maybe you can explain how it is you might have gotten pregnant. Thought you were on the pill."

Maddie winced. "Yes, but apparently they're not effective when you're on antibiotics. Remember last month when I got bronchitis?"

"You were having sex with bronchitis?" Chloe asked. "You weren't supposed to tax yourself."

Maddie bit her lower lip and blushed. "I didn't tax myself. Jax did all the work."

Chloe sighed in jealousy. "Bitch."

"So," Tara said, squeezing Maddie's hand. "Let's recap. Panic is over, and we've established you're madly in love." Which would mean she could go talk to Ford now...

"I'll be better when I get my period," Maddie said. "I've been so distracted. I mean, I ordered full sheets instead of queen-sized for the guests' rooms. I tried to put diesel in my car instead of regular gas. And let's not forget *not* checking the bilge pump on the houseboat and nearly killing Logan."

"Eh," Chloe said with a playful shrug. "He's an ex. Not such a loss."

"*Chloe!*" Tara exclaimed.

Maddie laughed, then clapped a hand over her mouth. "Sorry. But admit it; that was a little funny. And we need to get breakfast going."

"Yes," Tara agreed. "But first I have to go face a man about a pregnancy scare, thank you very much." She sent Chloe a long look.

"My fault," Chloe said, raising her hand. "*I'll* make breakfast."

"*No*," Maddie and Tara said at the same time.

"Hey, I can totally do this. I *want* to do this."

Tara stared at her, then nodded. "Okay, but I'll be back if you need me." With that, she went searching for Ford, but though his car was out front, he wasn't anywhere in the inn.

Or the marina building.

And then she discovered that his Finn was gone. He'd headed out on the water. She boarded his Beneteau and sat on the hull, stretching her long legs out in front of her to catch the rays of the early sun, hoping it would warm her while she waited. Dropping her head back, she closed her eyes and tried to relax. Between the near sinking of the houseboat, the emotional talk with Mia the night before, getting even more emotional—and naked—with Ford, then Maddie's pregnancy scare, she was plum done in, all before eight in the morning.

She must have drifted off because the next thing she knew, the boat was shifting as someone stepped onboard. She didn't look. She didn't need to. She recognized the buzz along her nerves.

Ford didn't speak, and neither did she. Not when he motored them out of the marina, and not when he took them out of the bay as well, to a secluded area offshore. He dropped anchor and sat beside her, mirroring her pose so that he was sprawled out, face tipped up, the sun gilding his features.

Because she needed to see him for this, she sat up, reached over and pulled off his sunglasses.

He lifted his head and looked at her.

"The pregnancy test really wasn't mine," she said. "I'd have come to you."

His eyes met hers. "Or Logan."

"You really think I'd sleep with both of you?"

He hesitated. "If it were any other guy, I'd say hell no. But there's this little voice inside my head that keeps reminding me that you have strong ties to him. And you were married. I really hate that little fucking voice."

"Logan and I have been apart nearly two years now."

"And we've been apart seventeen."

"I'm thinking the amount of time isn't what matters," she said.

Ford was quiet a moment. "You know, back inside,

for just a minute when I saw that stick, a bunch of things hit me."

"Yes. Abject terror."

"And confusion," he said. "And maybe...excitement." His eyes met hers. "I never regretted Mia. Not for a minute. I only regretted what happened to us."

Her chest squeezed. "I hate that I hurt you."

Again he was quiet. "I feel something for you, Tara," he finally said. "You feel it, too. I see it in your eyes when you look at me. I feel it in your touch when you let me in close."

She let out a breath and watched the water. "Yes."

He tugged her onto his lap and stroked a thumb along her jaw, waiting until she opened her eyes.

"I feel it," she said, giving him the words. "And I feel it for only you. Whatever 'it' is. But—"

"No buts," he said. "That sentence was perfect without any buts." He slid his hands beneath her skirt and cupped the cheeks of her bottom in his big hands, yanking her in even closer, letting her feel what this position was doing for him. Kissing his way along her jaw to her ear, he made her shiver in anticipation.

"Here," he said. "Now. With me."

The words weren't spoken with a question mark at the end, but he *was* asking.

"Here," she agreed, cupping his face. "Now. With you. Only you..."

With an agreeing growl rumbling in his throat, he pushed up her sweater and down the cups of her bra, baring her breasts to him. "You drive me crazy," he said against her skin. "*Crazy.*"

"Ditto," she gasped, then again when he slid his hand between her thighs. She fisted her hands in his hair and cried out, rubbing against him, needing the friction, needing him inside her with a wild abandon and desperation she couldn't control.

"I think about you day and night." His voice was raw. "And Jesus, the image of you in my T-shirt and those heels, that's going to be fueling my fantasies for a good long time."

"How about doing it on your boat while anchored just off shore in the light of day?" she asked breathlessly. "Is that fantasy worthy?"

His eyes darkened. "Oh Christ, yeah." He pulled off her sweater and yanked her body flush to his, raining open-mouthed kisses down her throat to her breasts. He flicked a nipple with his tongue, causing them both to groan when it pebbled in his mouth. He was pushing up her skirt when she freed him from his jeans. "Please tell me you have a condom," she murmured when he slipped beneath her panties and unerringly touched her so that she writhed for more.

He pulled out a little packet that nearly made her weep for joy. "Now," she said. "You promised now."

Good as his word, he guided her down onto him, inch by glorious inch. "God, Tara. When I'm inside you, I feel like I'm home."

Before she could recover from the beautiful but shocking words, he roughly covered her mouth with his, and gripping her hips hard, gave a slow grind that had her gasping for more. Then he rolled them, reversing their positions. With the warm sun overhead and the pull and thrust of the ocean tide rocking them, Ford moved inside her, taking her to a place no one else ever had. It was the most erotic thing she'd ever experienced, and afterward, they lay side by side, hands entwined, staring up at the clear blue sky as they struggled to catch their breath.

Eventually, Tara rose to dress, and Ford did the same. In comfortable silence, they sailed back to the marina. After Ford had tied up at the dock, he turned to her.

She looked at him, his last few words still in her head. *I feel like I'm home.* "Ford?"

"Yeah?"

"Me too."

Chapter 17

*"A person who's willing to meet you
halfway is usually, conveniently,
a poor judge of distance."*
TARA DANIEL

Tara walked into the kitchen and found Chloe sitting on the countertop, mixing up something that smelled delicious.

"A new exfoliating face scrub," she explained. "Melon-flavored. The bonus is that it tastes delicious."

Tara tried not to panic. "I thought you were making breakfast."

"We are." Mia came into the kitchen from the dining room carrying a huge casserole dish. "I made Good Morning Sunshine Casserole," she said, looking adorable in fresh—and tiny—denim shorts and a stretchy tee. "Not strawberry pie, though I was tempted. It's a casserole with some leftover ham, Tater Tots, and cheese, all mixed together." She looked very proud of herself. "It's already been served and cleaned up."

Tara stared at this creature who was her own flesh and blood and felt her own pride bubble over. "Wow."

"I know. Cute *and* talented," Mia said.

Carlos came into the room from the back door. Mia turned a smile on him. The poor guy took one look at her mile-long legs in her short shorts, and walked smack into the island.

Chloe shot Tara a smirk.

Tara ignored her in favor of taking a good look at the teens, and didn't like what she saw, because she was seeing a whole hell of a lot of heat. "Busy day," she said to Carlos as he attempted to recover. "We need to hose down the front porch, water the flowers, and fix the flickering lights on the dock in case guests want to walk along there at night."

"On it," he said, and vanished back outside.

"I'll help," Mia said and followed him out.

Tara waited until the door shut behind them. "Those two are—"

"Having sex," Chloe said helpfully.

"She said they weren't."

"Okay, but probably I should add some condoms to the baskets I just put out in the bathrooms."

Tara choked, and Chloe patted her shoulder. "They're seventeen, babe. That's like ninety-nine percent hormones, as I'm sure you remember."

Tara felt her gut clench. "I'm going to have to fire him."

"Are you going to fire every boy that looks at her?"

"That or kill them," Tara said, only half joking.

That night Ford ended up behind the bar at The Love Shack. Earlier he and Sawyer had gone out for a long sail, something that had never once in his life failed to soothe him. They'd had clear blue skies filtered only by a few scattered clouds. Winds had come out of the northwest with knots at twelve to fourteen, which actually was "holy shit" weather on a sailboat. Just the way he usually liked it. It'd taken every ounce of concentration just to stay on the water and not ten feet under. Sawyer had bitched about it the whole time.

The sail should have cleared Ford's mind. It hadn't. He just kept thinking. About his life, and what he was doing with it. About Mia. About Tara... And Christ, he was tired of thinking. Tired of his life being in flux.

And when had *that* happened? He'd thought he had things set up. He had money in the bank, and a job running the bar when he felt like working. He wanted for nothing.

Okay, that wasn't quite true.

He wanted something new, something he'd never really wanted before—a relationship. In the past, any attempt at one had been rough to maintain while sailing eight months out of twelve. Hell, just seeing his own sisters and grandmother had been challenging, although now that he was no longer racing so much, his sisters managed to invade his life on a fairly regular basis.

Which meant that these days, a relationship could actually work.

Slightly terrifying.

Sawyer strolled into the bar after his shift. "Since you saved Logan's ass, you're now ahead in the polls by eighty percent."

Lucky Harbor's gossip train was the little engine

that could. Nothing slowed it down—not real news, not decency, and certainly not the truth.

The door to the bar opened again, and in came Logan, not looking any happier than Ford. "Fucking perfect," Ford muttered to Sawyer.

Logan headed straight for the bar. "You cheated," he said to Ford. "I'll take a beer and keep 'em coming."

Ford served him. "What do you mean, I cheated?"

"A kid? You came up with a kid?"

Ford was surprised at this. "You didn't know about Mia?"

"I knew that you'd had a baby. I didn't know that baby had grown up and then shown up."

Ford had been wondering how much Logan and Tara talked, if at all. Not much if it'd taken him this many days to learn about Mia. This fact made him feel marginally better.

"I can't compete with that," Logan said and took a long pull of his beer before turning to Sawyer. "How the hell do I compete with that?"

Sawyer shrugged. "You were married to her."

Ford slid Sawyer a look, and Sawyer shrugged again. "He asked."

"Yeah," Logan said, finding solace in Sawyer's words. "You're right. We were *married*. She used to call me her superhero." He looked at Ford to make sure he was listening. "I was her Superman, her Green Hornet, her Flash Gordon, all rolled into one."

On Logan's other side, a group of women with a pitcher of something pink and frothy were blatantly eavesdropping. One of them was Sandy, town clerk and city manager. Sandy was pretty in a no-nonsense way and never lacked for male companionship, though she'd been ignoring men in general since last year when she'd gotten two-timed by some asshole in Seattle. She was eyeing Logan like maybe she'd finally gotten over it.

"Looks like you're in trouble, Ford," Sandy said. "He's got you with the superhero thing."

"Do you even have to be in good shape to drive a race car?" someone asked.

It was Paige, from the post office. Ford could have kissed her.

"Hey, it takes more core body strength to control a car than a boat," Logan said in his defense. "And I'm completely fit. Look." He raised his shirt to show his abs.

The women all hooted and hollered. "Nice eight pack!" Amy said. She was a waitress at the diner, and tonight she was also Sandy's fearless wingman. In her late twenties, she was tall and leggy and blonde, and in possession of a smile that said she was not only tough as hell, but up for dealing with whatever came her way. "Your turn, Ford," she said with a grin.

This produced even *more* ear-splitting woo-hoos. Ford looked at Sawyer, who raised his beer in a go-for-it toast.

Oh hell, no. "We've had this conversation," Ford told whoever was listening, which was exactly *no one*. "I'm not going to show you my stomach."

This only made them all yell louder.

Logan grinned. "You're afraid of the competition. It's okay; no worries."

Goddammit. Ford wasn't afraid of shit. So he lifted his shirt.

The crowd went crazy.

Sawyer shook his head.

Ford sighed.

"Nice," Amy said. "I declare a tie."

Sandy was on the fence. "I don't know. I think we need more examples."

At this, Amy grinned wider and turned to Ford and Logan. "You heard her, boys—whip 'em out. Sandy, you gotta tape measure?"

Ford, who'd just taken a drink from his Coke, choked. Sawyer smacked him on the back, hard.

"Worth a shot," Amy said with a shrug.

Sandy smiled and nudged her shoulder to Logan's. "Never mind the poll, Logan. Besides, Tara's not the only woman in town. You know that, right?"

He sent her a slow smile. "She's not?"

"Nope." Sandy scooted a little closer to him. "And you can be my superhero any time."

At two a.m., Tara was still lying in bed, gazing at the clock. In a few hours, she needed to be wide awake and making breakfast for their guests' last day, but she couldn't relax enough to sleep.

And this time, it had nothing to do with Chloe's snoring, because Chloe wasn't even home yet. She'd gone out with Lance and friends, and they were God knew where, doing God knew what.

Maddie was at Jax's, safe and sound. One worry off Tara's plate, but she had plenty more. She'd caught Mia and Carlos in the marina building earlier. She wasn't sure exactly what she'd interrupted since they'd leapt away from each other faster than she could blink, but the guilt on their faces had been disturbing.

Short of firing one of them or locking Mia in a chastity belt, what could she do without looking like a first-class hypocrite of the highest order?

And then there was Ford. A small part of her wanted to be cuddled up with him right now. Okay, a big part. She fluffed her pillow and once again tried to fall asleep. It didn't happen. She started wondering if the bills had gotten sent out, and if she had gas in her car, and whether or not she had fresh peaches for tomorrow's pie. And where was Chloe, dammit? Rolling out of bed, she picked up her cell phone. "You'd better be okay," she said to Chloe's voice mail, then hung up and padded into the bathroom, where she took a hot bath. Thirty minutes later, warm and toasty, she climbed back into bed to try again.

Her heart tripped when she saw her cell phone, blinking multiple missed calls on the nightstand. The last time that had happened in the middle of the night, Chloe had been arrested with Lance for staging a sit-in at one of the Washington logging companies up on Rascal Pass. "Be okay," she whispered to Chloe as she accessed her messages, her pulse pounding. "Please be okay so I can kill you myself."

The first message was indeed from her sister. "I'm fine," came Chloe's voice. "I'm alive and playing paintball at an all-night venue—don't wait up. And Jesus, stop worrying, I'm a big girl."

"Oh sure," Tara muttered to no one. "I'll just stop worrying. Cuz it's that easy."

The next message surprised Tara into dropping her irritation.

"Tara," came Ford's voice, not quite sounding like his usual laid-back self. "Yeah, so I thought you should know that I don't think I'm a bad idea. I mean I *can* be bad, but I can be good, too. I can do good things…lots of very good *bad* things…" His voice was all low and husky, and combined with the words, had heat slashing through Tara's stomach. "But," he went on with deliberate slowness. "I don't think I can be your superhero."

At that, she pulled the phone away from her ear to stare at it. Superhero? Where had *that* come from? In the background, she could hear loud music and lots of laughter. Probably The Love Shack.

"I'm maybe, possibly a little drunk," he said, and shock reverberated through Tara. Ford wasn't a drinker. His biological father had been, and one of his stepfathers, and it'd turned him off of alcohol. Plus, for as easygoing as he was, he liked his control.

A lot.

"So this superhero thing," he went on. "All the skills I have, you've already seen. I'm guessing I do okay in the body department, because you seem to like it well enough. After all, just a few nights ago you were licking my—"

At this point, there seemed to be a scuttle with the phone, and Tara could hear Sawyer in the background saying "just hang up, man, or I'll do it for you and consider it a public service."

"Back off," came Ford's voice, and then there was another tussle. "Some people have no fuckin' manners," he said, slurring slightly. "I want you to know that if I *could* be your superhero, I totally would. But there's no way my ass is gonna wear a pair of tights, not even for you." He paused thoughtfully. "I could do sex slave, though. That seems like a fair trade, right?"

Tara laughed and covered her mouth in utter surprise. The man was clearly drunk and uncharacteristically out of control, and yet he could still make her laugh. And if the truth was known, in the bedroom Ford had *never* failed to command anything less than her full attention. Which meant he had it backward. *She* was a slave to *him*. To his hands, his mouth...

"What I'm trying to say is that I'll always be there for you, Tara. You need someone to help you, I'm your guy. You need a couple or three orgasms? I'm your personal toy. You need to let off some steam, someone to yell at, I'll be your doormat. Wait. Skip that. I'm not a good doormat— Hey," he said to someone else. "Back the fuck off—"

Click.

Tara was looking at her phone when the last message came on. "Goddammit. Logan's still here, and he stole my phone. *Fucker.* He had his shot with you and blew it." His voice lowered again. "He doesn't see you like I do, Tara. All in charge and bossy and sexy as hell with it. He wants you barefoot and pregnant. Nothing wrong with that, but you're more. So much more..."

Tara felt her throat tighten as the message ended. He did see her. The real her. She took a minute to gather her thoughts, then decided she couldn't possibly *not* call him.

He picked up just before it would have gone to voice mail. "Hey," he said, sounding rougher than he had in his messages. "It's late. You okay?"

"I was going to ask you the same thing, Sailor."

"I'm good," he said. "But I could be better."

"Need a ride?" she asked.

There was a beat of surprise. "You'd do that?"

"Yes," she said without hesitating.

"Would you do it for Logan?"

She closed her eyes and decided to give him the truth. "Not without killing him first."

"But you wouldn't kill me?"

"Maybe just maim or dismember."

"Bloodthirsty," Ford said, sounding cheered by the thought.

"Yeah." She hesitated. "Ford, about Logan."

"Is this the part where you tell me you and I have been nothing but a mistake?"

"No. It's the part where I tell you that Logan's not a factor between us."

Another beat of surprise. "Okay, keep talking."

She let out a huff of laughter. "He never was, you know."

"But you still care about him."

"Very much," she agreed. "But I'm not in the same place I was when I was with him. So what's with the superhero thing? Because you should know, no one's ever been my superhero, Ford. I've never wanted one."

"Okay, *now* would be a really great time for a but. Like, 'I've never wanted anyone to be my hero, Ford, but now that I'm back in Lucky Harbor *you* can be my hero, anytime.'"

Tara laughed and lay back in her bed, wondering at the need to have him here with her right now, chasing away the shadows. "I scare most guys, you know."

"Not me." Ford's voice softened. "I like how tough you are. Tough on the outside, and soft and creamy on the inside."

Again she laughed. "That sounds vaguely obscene."

"Really? Cuz I was going for *overtly* obscene."

"Do you need a ride or not?"

"Nah. Sawyer's got me."

"Oh, God. He arrested you?"

"Hey, I'm not *that* drunk."

"Yes, he is," came Sawyer's voice.

She smiled. "This is unlike you."

"I know. Logan drank me under the table. Fucker."

"Logan's with you too?"

"Was."

There was something in his voice now, something he was holding back. Probably Logan had found female companionship in the bar and Ford was trying to protect Tara's feelings, which wasn't necessary.

She knew Logan. She knew that although he *thought* he loved her, at least the woman she'd once been, above all else Logan loved his career and the lifestyle that went with it. Pretty women were drawn to him. She'd be shocked if he'd managed to sit in the bar tonight *without* garnering female attention. He hadn't cheated during their marriage, but it'd definitely been rough on her ego knowing how easy it would have been for him to cheat if he'd wanted to. She'd traveled with him for a while because of it, but the grueling schedule, plus being in the way and feeling so damn alone even while surrounded by his entourage had nearly done her in. Plus, what did it say about her marriage that she'd felt as if she needed to babysit him?

"So," Ford said. "About that sex slave thing—"

She rolled her eyes. "Say good-night, Ford."

"'Night, Ford."

She closed her phone, not knowing whether to laugh again or simply be touched.

Both, she decided, and shook her head, a smile breaking through. He made her laugh, always. Just as he made her *feel*.

Always.

Her heart knew that but her brain resisted. Her brain was capable of accessing memories and calculating odds and wasn't ready to believe that this could work. But this time at least she fell right to sleep and slept the rest of the night.

Chapter 18

*"Don't take life too seriously or you
won't get out alive."*
TARA DANIELS

Tara woke up at the crack of dawn, disconcerted to find
Chloe still wasn't back. She got up and showered then
came face-to-face with her baby sister tiptoeing into the
cottage, covered in red, blue, and yellow paint. "Are you
okay?"

"Yes. Barely."

Tara looked Chloe over, marveling at the mess. "You
look like a cross between a rainbow and a combat survi-
vor. What—"

"Don't ask." Chloe dropped her clothes on the spot
and padded naked to the shower. "There's a delivery for
you on the porch."

Tara opened the front door. Sitting on the top step was
a vase of beautiful wildflowers, obviously picked, not
purchased, with a piece of paper that simply read *Tara*.

They were beautiful. The question was, who were

they from? Neither Logan nor Ford were exactly the go-out-and-pick-wildflowers type. Tara carried the flowers across the yard to the inn's kitchen, set them on the counter, and mixed up a batch of muffins. She was back to staring at the flowers when Maddie came in the back door with an armload of fresh flowers of her own and stared at Tara's.

"Hey," she complained, pointing to Tara's surprise gift. "I thought I told you I'd get the flowers."

"I didn't buy these."

Maddie eyed the pretty wildflowers. "Logan? Ford?"

Tara shrugged.

"We should all have two men after us," Maddie said on a dreamy sigh.

"I'm not with two men."

"I would be," Chloe said, coming into the kitchen. She was back to her own color. Mostly. "Except probably after having both men naked and at my mercy, the ensuing asthma attack would kill me."

There was a momentary silence as the three of them contemplated both Ford and Logan naked at the same time.

"Is it hot in here?" Maddie asked after a minute, fanning her face. "It feels hot in here."

Chloe pulled out her inhaler and took a hit. "So who are they from? Logan?"

Tara touched the flowers. "Logan would've sent red roses from some fancy floral shop."

"Maybe they're from Ford," Mia said as she arrived for the day. She tucked her keys and purse into the broom closet. She was in capris and a spaghetti-strapped tank top, looking cool and collected. Tara gazed at her and felt a stab of envy. *She* used to be cool and collected.

Until she'd come here. "Flowers aren't really Ford's style," she said.

"Yes, but you said you two weren't together," Mia said.

"That's true."

"So then how do you know what his style is?" Mia asked.

Chloe smiled. "I like you, niece. I like you a lot."

Mia grinned at her, and Tara sighed. "Don't encourage her," she told Chloe, arranging a pile of muffins into a basket. On second thought, she grabbed a thermos and poured it full of milk as well.

"Where are you going?" Maddie asked.

"To find my Secret Santa." Tara grabbed the basket and flowers. "Hold down the fort; I'll be back in a minute to make breakfast."

"If you're back in a minute, then you're not doing it right," Chloe called after her.

Tara heard Chloe yelp, probably from Maddie smacking her upside the head.

Ford hadn't gotten to bed until three a.m. Sawyer had dumped him at the marina instead of driving him all the way up the hill to his house, then pocketed Ford's keys to both the boat and his car.

"Don't do anything stupid," Sawyer had said, then paused, clearly considering confiscating Ford's cell phone as well.

Luckily Ford had seen that coming and wisely shoved it down the front of his jeans.

With a sound of disgust, Sawyer had left.

Don't do anything stupid. Ford had repeated that carefully to himself several times. Did that include walking up to the cottage and sneaking into Tara's bedroom to make her pant and moan his name as he buried himself deep inside her?

Cuz he'd totally do it.

If he wasn't half certain he'd drown himself getting off the boat. It took all of five seconds to drift off to sleep, only to wake some time later with his head pounding like a jackhammer. Dawn was streaking across the sky, and he was sprawled across the mattress.

With someone sitting at the foot of his bed.

Ford kept very still, eyes closed. "Make it count," he warned whoever it was.

"I can do that."

Craning his neck in surprise, he risked eyeballs popping out of his head to open his eyes.

His daughter was sitting there holding a steaming mug of coffee, which she offered to him.

"Bless you," he whispered in gratitude. With a groan, he rolled over, then managed to sit up to take it.

Mia waited until he sipped. "Alcohol is bad for you, you know," she said. "Kills brain cells. And sperm cells."

He sucked in a very hot gulp of coffee and promptly choked, burning his tongue.

"Sorry." Mia met his gaze, her own bright and intense. "It's just that I don't want to rule out the possibility of a brother or sister someday. You know, when you and Tara get it together and figure yourselves out."

Just looking at her made his heart hurt, this precious

kid who—by some lucky twist of fate—he'd fathered. "Honey," he said carefully. "You do realize that things don't always happen all clean and pretty and neat like that in real life, right? Because Tara and I—"

"It could happen." She rose to her feet, eyes and mouth stubborn. He recognized the expression and knew he couldn't blame this one all on Tara.

"Oh, and FYI," she said, heading to the door. "Tara liked the flowers you delivered."

He blinked. "She...I—*What*?"

But Mia was gone.

Ford flopped back on the bed and closed his eyes. When he opened them again, the sun was a little higher in the sky, and there was a different woman sitting on his bed.

Tara let herself onto Ford's boat and made her way below deck. The boat was clean and fairly neat, if one discounted the empty pizza box on the counter and the pile of clothes on the floor by the bed.

Clearly Ford had stripped before climbing into it, which gave her a little shiver as she studied his big, very still body. He was sprawled facedown and spread-eagle across the mattress, wearing only a pair of black knit boxers and all that testosterone—which never failed to make her weak in the knees. His arms spanned the entire bed, as did his legs. And then there was the smooth, sinewy expanse of back and bitable ass...

Controlling herself, she sat at his side, watching as he began to stir. With a groan, he rolled to his back, his hands going to his head as if he needed to hold it onto his shoulders.

"Oh, Christ," he said, his voice all morning raspy. He cracked open one bleary eye, looking like a hot, adorable mess. "Shoot me in the head. I'm begging you."

"I've got something better." She lifted the basket of banana and honey nut muffins.

He closed his eyes and inhaled. "You smell like heaven."

"It's the food."

He didn't move a muscle. "Aren't you busy working?"

"Mia and Maddie are handling the inn for a few minutes. I thought maybe you might need me."

He was quiet for a long moment. "I've never been all that good at needing someone."

She nodded. She understood.

"But for you," he said. "I could try."

Her heart squeezed.

"But maybe later," he said, wincing and rubbing his head. "Because right now I'm busy dying. Do you think you could put down the anchor? The world's spinning."

Tara laughed softly and shifted closer, giving in to the urge to run her fingers over his forehead, smoothing back his hair, making him sigh in pleasure. "Why did you drink so much?" she murmured. "It's not like you."

He muttered something about trying to prove he could be Superman if he wanted to and how no one should dance on a bar while drunk because it was a long fall down.

She laughed again and went to pull away but he caught her hand and held it to his cheek. "You feel so nice and cool." He sighed, eyes still closed. "No idea how I got so lucky to get you both here this morning, but I'm grateful."

Very carefully, he sat up and reached for the basket, but Tara held it back.

"Both?" she asked.

"Our daughter showed up with coffee." His arms were longer than hers so he managed to snatch a muffin. "As well as the news that I brought you flowers."

That was so unexpected—a part of her had secretly hoped it'd been him—that she couldn't control her surprised reaction.

Ford's smile faded. "And," he said slowly, "you thought they were from me."

"No." She shook her head, then nodded. "Okay, maybe a little."

"Fuck." He grimaced and reached for her hand. "I'm sorry, Tara. But honestly, I was far too impaired for a gesture like that."

Tara shrugged. "It's okay. I mean they're not really your style anyway. I knew that. Now if it'd been pizza and beer on the porch..."

He arched a brow. "Are you saying I'm not romantic?"

"It's not your strong suit, no."

He bit into the muffin. "What is my strong suit?"

She thought about how he could make her purr with a single touch, have her writhing in three minutes flat if he put his mind to it, and blushed.

He smiled. "Come here."

"I don't think so."

"Don't trust me?"

"Don't trust *me*."

That made him chuckle, and he finished his muffin. "What are these again? They're amazing."

"They're honey banana, to calm the stomach. The honey also builds up sugar levels, and the bananas are rich in the important stuff: electrolytes, magnesium, and potassium, which you severely depleted with your alcohol intake." She opened the thermos and handed it to him. "And milk. To rehydrate."

"You always name your masterpieces. What are these muffins called?"

She squirmed a little. He knew her well, too well. She'd indeed named the muffins, but she didn't want to tell him. It was too embarrassing. Not to mention revealing.

"Come on," he coaxed.

She sucked in a breath and said it fast. "You'reMy HoneyBunMuffins."

A sole brow shot up. "One more time."

"You're My Honey Bun Muffins." She pointed at him. "And if you laugh, that's the end of our friendship. Or whatever this thing between us is."

Ford grinned. "Aw. I'm your honey bun."

"Stop it." She shoved a napkin at him. "And you're getting crumbs in the bed."

"Don't you mean, 'you're getting crumbs in the bed, *honey bun*'?"

"Okay, that's it. Give me back the muffins." Tara reached for them but Ford laughed and held them out of her reach, leaning back so that she fell on top of him.

Smooth, she thought, scrambling off his hard, warm, perfect body. He was pretty damn smooth as he proceeded to inhale three more muffins and down the milk while she watched. And so...male. Logan had always been a gym rat, his body toned from a rigorous routine of weights and cardio. Ford didn't do the whole gym thing. No, his body was honed to a mouthwatering tightness by running and sailing, and it worked for him.

It worked for her, too. "Are we going to talk about the phone messages?" she asked when he finally stopped eating, looking much better for it.

He winced. "I was really hoping that part of last night was a dream."

She laughed and shook her head. "Nope."

"Can we pretend it was?"

"So you don't want to be my sex slave?"

Ford's expression went hopeful as his gaze flew to hers, then turned crestfallen when she gave him an *are-you-kidding-me* look. "That's just mean, teasing a man when he's down."

"You're not down," Tara said. "You're never down."

"And here I thought you were so observant." He rolled off the bed.

"Where are you going?"

He dropped his boxers to the floor.

"You're naked!"

"Yes, that's usually how I like to shower," he said and walked the finest ass she'd ever seen right out of the bedroom.

Chapter 19

*"If it's going to be two against one, make
sure you aren't the one."*
TARA DANIELS

Back at the inn, Tara cooked up a big breakfast. Then
she made bread and put together a slow-cooking soup
for later. After that, she cleaned the kitchen, opening the
back door to sweep out the crumbs.

When she turned around, Logan was standing there,
watching her, eyes bloodshot and red-rimmed with
exhaustion.

"Wow," she said. "You look like crap."

His smile was grim. "You make a bedside visit to Ford
with hangover muffins, and you tell me I look like crap.
Where's the justice in that? And before you ask how I know,
it's on Facebook. Lucille reported seeing you board his boat
with the muffins. She tweeted it, too, and loaded a pic."

Tara stared at him. "She did not."

"Did."

Tara shook her head to clear it but that didn't help.

Neither did the sneaking suspicion coming to her. "So what, you came here to hopefully get caught on camera as well?"

Guilt flashed across his pretty-boy face, but he accompanied it with a charming smile. "Didn't think it could hurt."

She glared at him, then realized that beneath that do-me smile was undeniable misery, and she felt her heart constrict. "Oh, Logan," she said softly, coming around the island to push him gently into a chair.

"Ah, shit," he said, staying where she'd put him. "The *nice* Tara. I'm getting dumped, right?"

"I already dumped you." She made him some green mint tea, his favorite. "And this isn't me being nice," she said, handing him a mug. "It's mercy. It'll help your headache, but what would help even more is not trying to drink other people under the table."

"I didn't try. I *succeeded*. And it wasn't just any other people. It was your boyfriend."

"Ford's not my boyfriend."

"Uh huh."

"Okay," Tara said. "I want you to try something new—*listening* to me for once." She sat in front of him and took his hand in hers. "I'm not looking for a husband. That's over."

"But I'm not done fighting for you."

"I'm not a prize, Logan."

His smile softened. "Yes, you are."

Aw. Dammit, he really had his moments. "I don't want to hurt you," she said, "but you need to know that everything I've told you before still stands. I'm not coming back to you, Logan. We're not going to make this work, you and me."

He looked at her for a long moment. "I'm not ready to concede yet, Tara."

"Logan—"

"Look, I'm enjoying this town. I've been making friends with people who don't bow down to me or want anything from me."

"What you're enjoying is the chase," she said. "And being talked about every day."

"Okay," he admitted. "That too."

Shaking her head, Tara rose. "Go home, Logan. Go back to your life."

"I've never quit anything, you know that." He rose too and snagged her hand, pulling her back around to face him. "And I'm not going to quit this. Not even for you."

He was looking at her just as she'd always dreamed he might, warm and soft and open, and all she could think was *too little, too late*. "Logan—"

"No." He set his finger over her lips. "God, not the pity. Smack me around, tell me I'm an ass, anything but the pity eyes." He paused. "I will, however, take a pity f—*oomph*," he said when she elbowed him in the gut. "Damn, woman."

"Go," she said. Relieved to feel suddenly guilt-free, she shoved him out of her kitchen.

The inn's first real guests arrived as scheduled. A middle-aged couple on a West Coast road trip from San Diego to Vancouver, stopping at a different B&B every night.

Maddie and Tara checked them in together, and Chloe gave them a gift basket full of her natural products. The wife fingered through the items, cooing at the bath salts, the herbal teas, the...

"Massage oil?" the woman asked, lifting the bottle. She had to slip her glasses on to read the label. "Edible strawberry massage oil," she said out loud. "Perfect for that special someone. Put it on your—Oh my."

Mia gaped.

Maddie covered Mia's eyes.

Tara looked at Chloe in horror.

Chloe laughed and reached for the oil. "Whoops, I was wondering where that went. Here, try this instead." And she quickly replaced the oil with body lotion.

"Oh," the woman said, sounding greatly disappointed. "Could I maybe have both?"

"Well, sure." Chloe handed back over the oil. "Enjoy."

The woman glanced at her husband and grinned. "We will."

When the couple was safely upstairs in their room, Maddie and Tara rounded on Chloe, who held up her hands in surrender. "Okay, that was my bad," she admitted.

"You think?" Tara asked.

Mia giggled. A real, honest-to-god genuine giggle, and then Maddie snorted. She slapped her hands over her mouth, but it was too late, and the sound of it sent Mia into a new fit of laughter. Chloe promptly lost the battle as well.

"It isn't funny," Tara protested. "They're going to be up there doing...things." But her daughter was still cracking up, and Tara felt the helpless smile tug at the corners of her own mouth at the sound of it, and the next thing she knew, they'd all slid down the wall to the floor, laughing like loons.

Together.

That night, with everyone tucked into bed all safe and sound, Tara sneaked out to sit on the marina docks. She was staring up at the night sky when she felt a tingle race down her spine. "Ford," she said quietly.

His long legs appeared at her side. Then he crouched down on the balls of his feet to meet her gaze. "The guests?"

"In and settled." She felt herself smile. "They like us, I think."

"There's not much not to like." He had two beers dangling from the fingers of one hand and a pizza box in the other. "It's not flowers," he said, handing her one of the beers.

Throat tight, she accepted it, their fingers brushing together. "I don't need flowers."

"Do you need pizza?"

No. The calories would warrant a damn run in the morning, and she hated to run. But there was this gorgeous man hunkered before her, looking like everything she could ever want. "Actually," she said. "I need pizza more than I need my next breath."

Ford sat next to her, and they ate in comfortable silence. When they were done, he picked up the bottles and the empty box and disposed of them inside the marina building. He came back and again sat close enough that their arms and thighs touched. Around them, the insects hummed. The water slapped up against the dock.

Comfort sounds. "It's a beautiful night," Tara said softly.

"Yes," he said, and she could feel him looking at her. He ran a finger over the strap of her lightweight, gauzy sundress, following the line over her collarbone.

Her nipples hardened. "You're not looking at the night," she pointed out.

"No." Ford kept his fingers on her, stroking lightly back and forth until her thighs pressed together. In her high-heeled sandals, her toes curled a little bit. His gaze toured her body, ending at said toes, and a small smile curved his mouth. He knew exactly what he did to her. "Heard about the massage oil incident," he said.

"Oh my god. Facebook?"

"Yeah. Look at it this way: people will be lining up to book a room now."

She groaned, and he laughed. "It's not that bad," he said. "And it's got to be better than having everyone think you're constipated."

"I was never constipated! And can you never bring that up again, please? *Ever*?"

He grinned, and something warm slid through all her good spots. She pointed at him. "Don't you look at me like that, like you want..." Like he wanted to eat her up. *Whole*.

His soft laugh scraped at her erogenous zones. "Want me to tell you?"

"No!"

From somewhere far off, maybe the pier, maybe Lucille's place down the road, came music. Something slow, melodic, achingly beautiful and just a little bit haunting.

Ford rose with the fluid grace that only the totally physically fit with good knees could accomplish and tugged Tara to her feet as well.

"What?" she asked, sucking in a breath when he pulled her in against him, gently rocking them to the music.

"Are we slow dancing?" she murmured as they moved together.

"Yeah. We're slow dancing."

And she'd accused him of not being romantic. He was warm up against her and strong. He had one big hand low on her back, nearly on her butt, leaving her with the urge to wriggle until his fingers slid lower.

"Keep squirming," he murmured in her ear, still moving them to the beat of the music, "and I'll tell you what I want."

"What do you want?" she asked, unable to stop herself.

He put his mouth to her ear and told her. In graphic detail.

And she promptly, and purposely, squirmed some more.

Ford laughed, then kissed her just beneath her ear. And then touched his tongue to the same spot. When she shivered, he did it again as his hand stroked up and down her back. It was soothing, and also arousing, as it was when he slid a hand down and cupped her. She moaned, and he let out a rough sound of his own at the feel of her. "I can't stop touching you. I think about it all damn day and all damn night, touching you, having you touch me back."

She felt herself completely melt in his arms. The music came to an end, and they stopped swaying. It seemed the most natural thing in the world to tilt her head up and meet him halfway for a kiss.

"Dammit," she said when he lifted his head.

"That's a new reaction to a kiss," he said.

"I mean this is…romantic." She gave him an annoyed look. "And you have some serious moves, too. Good ones."

"Yeah?" His eyes were dark. Intense. "Well then, here's some more." And he covered her mouth with his.

All thinking ceased. It was as if someone switched her brain to OFF, then opened the floodgates for desire. It hummed through her body, making her nerve endings twitch and tingle. A sound escaped her throat, horrifying in its neediness, but she didn't care. She simply pressed herself closer to him, desperately, hungrily seeking more.

More, more, more…

He pulled her in and turned her, pressing her back against a wood pylon, freeing up his hands for other things. Tara wrapped her arms around him, beneath his shirt and up the bare, sleek skin of his back, and then down to his butt.

Which she squeezed.

She couldn't help it. It was a very squeezable butt.

Ford ran his thumb across her nipple while his mouth did something decadent to her neck. She could feel him hard and ready, and she rubbed shamelessly against him, soaking up the feel of him, his scent. She opened her mouth to speak but he nibbled her bottom lip and then kissed her again, making her moan.

"Tell me this is leading back to one of our beds," he said a little hoarsely when they broke apart for air. "I don't care whose."

Everything inside her wanted to say *oh yes, please.* "And then what?" she asked, holding her breath.

"And then I'm going to get you naked, and make you a very, very happy woman. All night long."

That sounded good, but she knew herself well enough to know that by morning, she'd be left fighting the emotions that being with him like this brought. She'd be all that much closer to the point of no return, at least for her heart. Ford was an amazing guy, a good guy. Maybe even The Guy for her—but not just for a night. Or were they past that now? She'd lost their place, she wasn't sure, and more than that, she was afraid. Still so very afraid that this was out of her reach. "And then...?"

"And then all day long," he murmured against her skin, running his hands over her body. "And then all night long again."

Yes. Yes, she knew he could do just that. And she also knew he was missing what she was getting at. That maybe he was missing it on purpose. "Ford, wait."

He didn't. He was, in fact, very busy trailing wet, open-mouthed kisses along her throat, silencing any protest she might have made.

And for a minute, she let him. She couldn't help it. He kissed like heaven on earth, and before she knew it *she* was kissing him. When they were breathless, he cupped her face in his hands, letting his lips brush her temple, her jaw. Then he dipped his tongue into the hollow at the base of her throat, and she felt a shiver wrack her entire body. Her fingers were in his hair now, and she couldn't let go. "Ford? And then what?"

He lifted his head. There was no mistaking the hunger and desire on his beautiful face, or the confusion as he gave one short shake of his head. "What is it?" he asked. "What do you want to hear? Tell me."

No. She didn't want to have to do that. "Never mind. Just quick, kiss me and shut me up."

He did without question, and this time she had to lock her knees. Because it was too late to protect herself, far too late to worry about if she deserved to fall for him because she already had.

Again.

Oh, God. Just the thought left her wobbly. This was going to require a lot of obsessing, and maybe some more chips. Certainly a bottle of wine, and in all likelihood her sisters as well. Not for their wisdom, but to smack her upside the head for even secretly yearning for this.

For him.

For keeps.

"I'm sorry. I have to go," she whispered, still plastered to him like a second skin.

"What?"

She grimaced at herself for being a coward. "Early morning."

Something in her voice must have alerted him to the impending meltdown because he let her pull away, not stopping her when she straightened her dress, or when she left him on the dock.

He let her go without a word; without asking anything of her.

And wasn't that the entire problem in a nutshell? *He let her go.*

He always let her go.

Chapter 20

♥

"Remember, you're unique. And so is everyone else."
TARA DANIELS

The next morning, their guests left before dawn. The woman assured Tara that everything had been great, and then asked for a sample of the oil to go.

Tara put Mia to work sweeping the wood floors, which seemed to gather dust faster than a fat dog could gather fleas. "Careful not to stir it all up into the air," Tara told her. "It irritates Chloe's throat, and she'll need to use her inhaler."

"It's sweet that you worry about her," Mia said.

Tara laughed. She, Chloe, and Maddie were just about anything *but* sweet. No, scratch that, because Maddie was sweet. Tara and Chloe? Not so much.

Mia disappeared upstairs to sweep the hallway, and Tara met with Maddie in the marina office to go over paperwork. Chloe was allergic to paperwork more than dust, so she was outside in the sun, on a yoga mat in the downward-facing-dog position. By the time Tara returned to the inn Mia was nowhere to be seen, although her broom was leaning against a wall in the upstairs hallway.

"Shh!" This came from behind the bathroom door. "She'll hear."

Mia's voice, followed by Carlos's soft laugh, and a second more emphatic "*Shh*" from Mia.

Dammit. Dammit, Tara thought. They were in there messing around. Now see, *this* was why animals ate their young. Ready to rumble, she whipped open the door and blinked.

Her daughter and Carlos sat on the countertop, separated by the sink. Mia had a laptop on her thighs, the screen facing Carlos, who was cracking up. At the sight of her, he sobered and got to his feet. "Ms. Daniels."

Weak with relief that they weren't having sex, Tara leaned back against the door, then realized they were staring at her. "You're not working," she said.

"Well, not *exactly*," Mia said. "But it is about the inn." She turned the laptop in Tara's direction.

"Mia—" Carlos tried to block the view. "Not a good idea—"

"She's going to find out sooner or later, and it might as well be from us." Mia revealed the screen. Facebook, of course, the bane of Tara's existence. She'd been forewarned by Logan, but it was another thing entirely to see it herself.

The picture was grainy and blurry, probably from a cell phone, but it was clear enough. Tara, climbing onto Ford's boat with her basket of muffins, followed by the line:

A secret rendezvous between a certain sexy sailing champion and a very beautiful innkeeper. Guess a certain poll is null and void.

There was another pic of Ford and Tara standing on the marina dock. The shot was incredibly revealing and intimate, Ford trapping Tara against a pylon, his mouth devouring hers. Tara's hands were fisted in his shirt, and he had one hand tangled in her hair, the other tightly wrapped around her back.

Guess this leaves superstar NASCAR driver Logan Perrish out in the cold. No worries, Logan, we're running a new poll starting today. Log in and give us choices for The Bachelor, Lucky Harbor Style. Single ladies, sign up to date sexy Logan now!

Tara stared at the screen in horror. "Did you—"

"No," Mia said quickly. "I didn't take either pic. Neither of us did. You have a spy. I was about to post a comment that people need to mind their own stinking business and leave you to yours."

Tara smiled grimly. "You don't know the locals here very well yet. Minding their own business isn't a strong suit."

Carlos turned to the door. "I should go. I got something to do…"

When he'd vanished, Tara raised a brow at Mia, who shrugged. "He's the tough guy at his school. But you scare him."

"I've never scared him."

"You do. He's worried you're going to kill him."

Tara paused. "Has he given me a reason to kill him?"

"It's more that he thinks you can read minds, and that you'll kill him for what's on his. Boys are kind of obvious that way, you know?"

Yes, Tara knew. She just didn't like that Mia knew.

"You won't kill him, right?" Mia asked.

Tara sighed. "Do you like him that much?"

"Yes. I love him," her daughter said without hesitation.

"Love? Mia, it's only been—"

"I know what I feel," her daughter said with the conviction of a seventeen-year-old. She shut the laptop and leaned back against the counter. "Remember when you said you'd answer any question I might have? Does that still stand?"

Oh boy. "Ask," Tara said bravely.

"I've been wondering why you lost contact with Ford after you had me. You two loved each other, and yet by all accounts, you just walked away."

Tara drew in a long breath. "I went back home. To Texas. It's pretty far from Lucky Harbor."

"Yes, but there are phones. Computers. The U.S. mail service. And your mom lived here."

"Phoebe didn't live here, not yet. She was only visiting that summer, and…and well, Ford and I had only met that summer, and we each had our lives." Lame excuses. And Mia deserved better. "Part of it was that I wasn't nearly as mature as you."

"You didn't want to keep in contact?" Mia asked. "You didn't like him anymore?"

"Mia, it wasn't that simple, and we were just kids."

"You could have come back here instead of going to Texas."

"No, because Phoebe didn't stick here, either. But even if she had, I wasn't used to living in a small town. It was different."

"Good different?"

No. Tara had felt claustrophobic and smothered, but she didn't want to say that. "I was used to more. And I wanted to go to school in Texas, to Texas A&M."

"A big college," Mia murmured.

"Yes, and..." Tara trailed off, at a loss on how to make it sound logical when the truth was it hadn't been logical at all. Her reactions had been of sheer emotion. "Honestly, I was just trying to keep it together, and not doing all that great a job." Tara took Mia's hand. "But I'd like to think I've done a lot of growing up since then. If I could go back now, I'd—"

What?

What would she do differently? She wasn't sure.

"You can't go back," Mia said quietly. "Even I know that much. You can't ever go back."

Wasn't that the truth.

With a sigh, Mia turned to the door. Tara followed, just happening to glance down at the trash can.

At the empty condom wrapper right on top.

She stared at it, then slowly looked up at Mia. Who was also looking at the empty condom wrapper, chewing on her lower lip and looking guilty as hell.

"Maddie's," Tara said hopefully.

Mia gnawed on her lip some more and slowly shook her head. "No. Not Maddie's."

"But you said you weren't having sex," Tara said with what she felt was remarkable calm.

"No, I said I wasn't having *unprotected* sex."

"God." Tara pressed her fingers to her eyes. "Mia..."

"Do you want me to go?"

"No! I want..." She dropped her hands from her face and met Mia's shuttered gaze. "I want you to be able to tell me the truth."

"Really? You wanted me to tell you I *was* having sex with Carlos?" Mia asked with disbelief, winding up to a defensive stance.

"Yes!"

Mia shook her head. "Did you tell your parents when you were having sex with Ford?"

Tara staggered back and leaned against the counter. No. No, she hadn't told anyone what she'd shared with Ford. It'd been for them alone. "I'm failing you," she whispered. "This is all my fault, somehow."

Mia sighed. "No, it's not. It has nothing to do with you. And you're acting like I'm too young or something."

"You *are* too young."

"Because you weren't doing the exact same thing when you were my age?"

Tara opened her mouth, then shut it, at a complete loss. "Mia, having sex is a huge emotional commitment, and I don't think *any* seventeen-year-old can possibly be ready for it."

"Yes, well, I need to make my own mistakes," Mia said. "Not yours. Mine. And for this to work, you're going to have to let me."

"Mia—"

But she was gone.

• • •

Tara needed a sister bad. Chloe was off God knew where doing God knew what, but Tara found Maddie at Jax's house on the bluff. They sat outside on his deck, and while he barbecued, Tara filled Maddie in on how she'd screwed up with Mia. "*Epic* failure," she said as Maddie poured them both wine. "And the worst part of all is that I practically hand-delivered Carlos right into her lap. I de-virginized my own daughter!"

"You don't know that Carlos was her first."

Tara went still as she absorbed that, then groaned and covered her eyes. "Okay, not helping."

"Look," Maddie said finally. "Seventeen is nothing but one big pleasure button, from head to toe. You know that. And Mia and Carlos care deeply for each other. You know that too. At least she's with someone who thinks the sun rises and sets on her. He'll make it good for her, Tara."

Tara groaned again.

"What, you'd rather she be with someone who doesn't care about her needs?"

"I'd rather she be with no one at all!" Tara said. "At least not until she's thirty-five, or I'm dead. Whichever comes last. And can we not talk about her having sex?" She winced. "Let's concentrate on getting her to like me."

"She does." Maddie sipped from her glass, her gaze slipping to Jax where he stood at the grill about twenty feet away, turning over the chicken. "Remember how you felt when I wanted you and Chloe to stay with me here in Lucky Harbor, and all you wanted to do was run like hell?"

"Yes." It'd been a tough time for all of them, facing the rush of fresh memories from simply setting foot inside Lucky Harbor. But Maddie had been searching for a place to belong, and at the inn, she'd found it. With Jax, she'd found it. Tara had been thrilled for her sister.

And resigned to sticking around longer than she'd wanted in order to protect their investment—the inn—and to make sure her sisters were okay. Tara had stuck until it hadn't been an obligation. Until it'd somehow become natural to live here.

"Chloe and I won you over with our charm, and that charm is hereditary." Maddie said on a smile. "You'll charm Mia too, you'll see."

"I gave her up at birth," Tara said. "I let someone else raise her. I don't think charm can help me with her."

"You had valid reasons," Maddie reminded her gently. "And Mia knows that. Honey, she came looking for you. Give her some time to put it all together and understand. It's time to stop grieving over what you lost out on and live for the now."

Jax came up behind Maddie and set down a plate of grilled veggies that looked mouthwatering. He squeezed Maddie's shoulder, then leaned in for a quick nuzzle and kiss. "Okay?" he asked.

Just looking at the two of them together had Tara's heart sighing. They were so meant for each other. That they were together was because Maddie had done what she'd just told Tara—she'd taken her *now*.

"We're good," Maddie told Jax. He smiled at her, stole a long swallow of her wine, sneaked another kiss, and ambled back to man his station at the barbecue. Maddie watched him go with a dreamy sigh on her lips. "I love his ass," she said.

Tara laughed out loud, causing Jax to turn and eye them curiously. Maddie waved at him, and Tara murmured, "You'd better snag him up, Mad. Because a good ass is *muy importante*."

Maddie grinned broadly as she blew Jax a kiss. "There's other reasons I want to marry him too, you know."

Tara lifted a brow. "Listen to you, saying the *M* word so freely now."

"He's the one," Maddie said simply. "The only one."

Tara nodded and sipped her wine, and envied the conviction that was all over Maddie's face.

The next morning Ford took Mia out for a long sail. He'd discovered that his daughter liked early mornings, as he did, so they left just before the crack of dawn and caught the sunrise. He taught her how to motor away from the marina and then point the bow into the wind, how to work the mainsail with the halyard and crank it around the winch when she needed to, in order to get it hoisted. He had her unfurl and furl the jib and pull it out with the sheets, and now she stood in the cockpit, hands on the wheel, the sail billowing in front of her, the wind whipping her hair from her face, looking happy and carefree.

Just watching her reminded Ford of a young Tara and warmed a place inside him that he hadn't even realized was cold.

She caught his eye. "What?"

Smiling, he shook his head. "I'm just sitting here thinking how glad I am that you came looking for answers."

"I don't have them all yet," she said.

He loved her bluntness and hoped growing up didn't beat that out of her. "All you have to do is ask."

Mia steered into the wind like a pro, her face thoughtful. Then she suddenly ducked as they hit a swell. The spray hit Ford right in the face, making her laugh out loud, a beautiful sound.

"You're a quick learner," he said, swiping his face with his shirt. "Jax still can't pull that off."

She grinned with pride. "Tara said you were the best of the best."

"She did?"

"Yeah." She nudged him with her shoulder. "She likes you."

Ford laughed, but Mia didn't. She just looked at him earnestly. "I have a couple of questions now," she said.

"Okay. Shoot."

"The first one might seem intrusive."

"Ask."

"Do I have any genetic diseases to look forward to?"

"No. Well, unless you count orneriness," he said. "My grandma's ninety and ornery as hell." He smiled thinking about her. He'd have to fly her up before the summer was over so she could meet Mia. "She'll love you, though. What else?"

"Are you afraid of anything?"

"No."

She rolled her eyes. "That's a typical boy answer. Everyone's afraid of *something*. Spiders? Snakes? Heights?"

"Actually," he said, "frogs."

She stared at him. "Shut up."

"No, it's true, and it's all Sawyer's fault. We were ten. We'd told his dad we were staying at my place, and my grandma that we were staying at his, and then we went camping."

"By yourselves?"

"Yeah. That night he loaded my sleeping bag with frogs. When I got in, they crawled all over me. Slimy suckers." He shuddered. "To this day I can't stand them."

She was smiling, but then her smile faded, and she studied him in that careful way that she'd inherited from Tara. "Are you really not afraid of *anything* else?"

He felt his own amusement drain as well. She was being serious, and she deserved for him to be as well. "Actually, there is one thing."

Her gaze searched his. "What?"

"I was afraid I'd never get to meet you."

Her eyes shone brilliantly, those beautiful, heart-breaking eyes. "Lucky for you I found you then," she whispered.

"Lucky for me," he repeated softly.

Since Mia was scheduled to work at noon, eventually they headed back to the marina. Ford had her reverse their original process with the mainsail and jib, then motor back into the marina and dock. He stood over her as she tied up, but she had no problems, and pride burst from his chest. She was a natural.

Tara came out of the marina office, a few files in her hands. When she saw the two of them standing on the dock, she stopped short.

She looked tired and stressed, and Ford knew she had good reason. She'd been working at the inn and the diner, and working two jobs was stressful for anybody. And here he stood with Mia, the two of them clearly back from a sail, looking carefree, like they didn't have a responsibility in the world.

For years, Ford had purposely cultivated that perception. After the way he'd grown up, he liked living low-key and easygoing. No stresses, no worries. He enjoyed not caring too much about anything. You could care about whatever you wanted: your family, your next meal, whatever, and it didn't amount to squat if you didn't have the means to obtain it.

He realized that having a daughter in his life should have been a threat to that lifestyle, or at the very least disturbed him. But it didn't. And he also didn't feel the same terror that he knew Tara felt about getting involved in Mia's life. In fact, he relished it, because here was a kid who needed them. In return, he needed her, too.

They belonged to each other by blood. No one could take that away.

"Nice day for a sail," Tara said.

Mia grinned as she hopped off the boat. "Yep. You two should go out."

"Oh," Tara said, backing up a step. "I can't. We're really busy, and—"

"Chloe and Maddie are at the inn, right?" Mia asked, giving Ford a sly look.

Oh shit, Ford thought, Look at her go.

"And I'm betting you already have dinner on," Mia said to Tara. "Yeah?"

"Berry Sweet Turkey and Cranberry Quiche," Tara admitted.

"See?" Mia nudged Tara toward the boat, giving Ford go-for-it eyes over Tara's shoulder.

His daughter, the smart, beautiful master schemer.

"Everything's handled," she was saying to Tara, "so go, and I don't want to see you back here for at *least* an hour, young lady. You hear me?"

Ford had to bite back his smile. Oh, yeah. They were being horribly manipulated by a girl half their age. "Come on," he said to Tara, taking her hand. "Let's do this. Let's go for a quick sail."

"But you just went."

"I could go all day long. And besides, like Mia said, it's perfect out there. An hour, Tara. Let's take an hour."

"I have things to do."

"You always do." He slowly but firmly reeled her in. "Chicken?" he asked softly, pressing his mouth to her ear.

"Of course not."

"One hour," he repeated, then propelled her on board with an arm around her waist.

Mia was beaming. "Gotta run," she said and ran like hell up to the inn.

Tara craned her neck to watch her go. "That girl's going to make a great lawyer."

"No doubt."

Tara turned back and met Ford's gaze, hers troubled. "I'm worried that we're leading her on, setting her up for disappointment."

"You need to stop worrying about things you can't

control. In fact, stop thinking altogether. For the next hour, your only job is to live in the moment. In the moment of a gorgeous day and..." He smiled. "Not such bad company."

She hesitated, and he gently tugged on a strand of her hair. "What's the matter? Still don't trust yourself with me?"

When she winced, telling him that was exactly what it was, he laughed. "An hour, Tara. That's all. How much trouble can we get into in one hour?"

She gave him a look of blatant disbelief. "Are you kidding me?"

Ford smiled the most innocent smile in his repertoire. She didn't buy it, but she nodded. "Okay," she said, poking him in the chest. "But no monkey business."

"Define monkey business."

"No nakedness."

"Well, damn," he said. "There goes the strip tease I had planned." He gestured for her to step ahead of him into the cockpit, but she hesitated and gave him a speculative once-over.

"Are you good at it?" she asked.

"Sailing?"

"No." She laughed. A glorious sound. "*Stripping.*"

He felt his grin split his face. "Actually, I'm a master."

She waggled a brow, and he laughed. "Tara Daniels, are you flirting with me?"

"No!" She turned and busied herself with the halyard. "Ignore me."

"Now there's one thing I've never mastered."

Chapter 21

*"You've grown up if you have learned
to laugh—at yourself."*
TARA DANIELS

Ten minutes later, Ford had them flying across the swells. The sun was at their backs, the wind in their faces, and Tara couldn't have held back her grin if she tried.

"Mmm," Ford said. "Love that look on you." He pulled her in between the steering wheel and his big body, easily holding her steady.

She cuddled up to him. "Okay, but remember, *no* monkey business," she said. "Just sailing."

"Just sailing." His hands urged hers to the wheel, freeing his up to go to her hips as he rubbed his jaw to hers, then kissed her neck. "It's good to see you smiling. And I'm seeing it more and more. I'm thinking Lucky Harbor agrees with you."

Tara was afraid that was true.

"Admit it," he said, running his hands up and down her body, just barely grazing the sides of her breasts.

She ached for more. "Admit what?" she asked faintly.

"That you're right where you want to be." He slowed them down and turned her to face him. "Here in Lucky Harbor."

"I stayed because my sisters needed me," she said. "The inn needed me."

"Maybe, but we both know that neither of those things would have held you here in the past."

Meaning, of course, that in the past, she'd considered only her own needs. Tara absorbed the truth of that for a moment and let out a breath. She could leave it or she could be honest. "I wanted to stay," she admitted.

Ford pulled off her sunglasses. His eyes were intense, and she imagined hers were the same. "Why?" he asked.

Again she could leave it, or give him the truth. "Because my life had fallen apart, and I really had nothing to go back to."

"And?"

"And..." Dammit. "Because I like being a part of a unit. I *like* being with my sisters, even when we fight."

A very small smile played at the corners of his mouth. "And?"

She stared at him, feeling a little...exposed. "Isn't this getting a little deep for you?"

"Deep?"

"Yes. Drawing me out, asking all of life's burning questions. Not your usual M.O. when we're alone like this."

Ford looked into her face for what felt like a very long time, not saying anything. "I need you to do something for me," he finally said.

She shook her head. "Oh, no. I already told you, no monkey business."

She expected a smile at that, but instead there was a spark of very rare temper in his eyes. "Don't paint all men with the same brush as your ex-husband or your father," he said.

"They're both good men," she reminded him.

"Yes, but also by the very nature of their lives, selfish, even neglectful."

"It was their jobs," she said, defending them. "They both traveled and were gone all the time because of their jobs."

"It's about choices. I'm different, Tara. And you need to remember that. Maybe even take a chance on it sometime. A real chance."

Her heart was suddenly in her throat. "We've tried that."

"We should try again."

Oh, God. She wanted to. "You wouldn't know what hit you," she whispered.

The corners of his mouth curved slightly. "I never do when it comes to you."

"I need to be getting back."

"It's been fifteen minutes. You owe me forty-five more. I'd think after working as hard as you have, you'd enjoy this."

She watched as he adjusted their direction slightly so they glided easily through the swells. "I'm used to hard work."

"And not so used to fun," he said.

"No." Tara eyed the horizon, clear and wide open.

Gorgeous. "But you're right, I am enjoying this. It'll fill my fun quota for the whole week."

Ford slid an arm around her and pulled her in close, brushing his mouth to her temple. "I bet we could come up with something even better for you."

"Like old times?"

"If you like."

She tipped up her head and met his gaze, seeing both the heat and the teasing there, and felt her stomach quiver. "I'm not that same girl," she warned him. "The one who used to live her days just to be with you and have fun every night."

"I know. You grew up. Became a smart, amazing woman. But you're still just going through the motions, not allowing for enough fun."

"*No* monkey business," she reminded him, her voice far too unsteady to convince herself, much less him, dammit.

Ford just smiled. "What if you're the one to start it?"

"I won't be," she said with far more confidence than she felt.

He was still looking amused, and she couldn't blame him. She had a history of being very weak where he was concerned. Very weak. And then there was watching him handle the boat, looking quite in charge and at ease as he did so. He stood legs apart, braced for the wind whipping at him. The sun gilded his tanned skin, reflected off his sunglasses. He wore a USA T-shirt and navy blue board shorts just past his knees, which clung to his every line and muscle as he moved with such innate grace that it was hard to believe that he was so big.

"Sheet it in?" he asked.

She was proud to be able to lean over and pull the sail in tight. She was halfway there when a swell hit and leveled her with a wall of water, leaving her dripping from hair to toes and gasping for breath.

Ford grinned. "You're supposed to duck."

Tara narrowed her eyes. "Do you have any idea how long it took me this morning to have a good hair day?" She squeezed the water from it, but it was too late. The frizzies were upon her, she could tell. "I mean *you* get to wash, shake, and go, and come out perfect while you're at it. But look at me."

They both looked at her. Her blouse was thin and wet, and working like a second skin now. Ford had been smiling during her little tirade, complete with hand waving. The corners of his mouth had twitched into the promise of an amused smile, but that was replaced by something darker and hungrier now as he set the controls and stalked toward her.

"Oh, no you don't." She backed up a step and pointed at him. "You stay right there. Or—"

Ford kept coming. "Or what?"

"Things'll happen," she said, slapping a hand to his chest. "Naked things. Really great naked things, but *no*." She shook her head. *Be strong.* "I've gotten it out of my system, Ford. I mean it."

He reached for her. She tried to step back but she had nowhere to go. "Okay, well, maybe not *all* the way out of my system," she admitted, "But we have this little chemistry problem—it's not anyone's fault. We just have to stay strong. *Ford!*" she gasped when he caught her up against his warm, hard body.

His rich laugh washed over her and felt like a touch, a kiss. "Stop," she said weakly. "You're getting me all worked up."

He dipped his head and rubbed his jaw to hers. "I love it when you get all worked up. Your eyes flash, and you say what you're really thinking."

"You're all wet now. You realize that?"

"Mmm, I think that's you." He rocked his body to hers. "Tell me just how wet you are. Slowly. In great detail."

"You're impossible."

"Incorrigible, too," he said. "And like you said, wet. Maybe I should strip."

Oh, yes. "*No!*" But she slid her arms around his neck. "What is it with you and stripping?" She snuggled into him. Lord, she was so damn weak. "How much time is left?"

He tossed his head back and laughed. "Thirty minutes."

She blew out a breath. "Probably I only need ten to fifteen."

He was still grinning. "Is this you starting it?"

She looked into his eyes. God, she missed this. The fun. The teasing. The laughing. Talking...

Him. "If I say yes, are you going to hold it against me?"

"Yes," Ford assured her. "I'm going to hold *it* against you for every single one of those minutes we have left." He dropped anchor and pulled her below deck, nudging her along toward his bed.

As if Tara needed nudging. She was practically running. She hit the mattress and rolled to her back, watching as Ford slowly peeled his wet shirt over his head. He untied his board shorts and let them slide off his hips to join the shirt on the floor.

She heard herself moan as she took him in, one glorious inch at a time, and there were a *lot* of glorious inches.

"I love your uptight, prissy clothes." That said, he stripped her right out of them until she was in just her peach lace bikini panties. He dropped to his knees beside the mattress and shot her a bad-boy smile. He gripped her ankles in each hand and leaned in to kiss her calf before slowly working his way up.

She was writhing by the time he got to her inner thighs.

He hooked his thumbs in the lace at her hips and slid it down her legs, stroking a thumb over what he'd revealed. "Pretty," he said silkily, then lowered his head and worked his usual magic. And, as it turned out, she didn't need fifteen minutes. She only needed five.

"In me," Tara demanded when she could breathe again. She sat up, trying to pull him over her.

But he wouldn't be budged.

Or rushed.

"Shh," he said, not sinking into her. Dammit. Instead, he put a hand to her chest and pushed her back down on the bed. Before she could work up her temper over that, his tongue had stroked her wet flesh again. "Ohmigod," she whispered. Her hands were fisted in his hair, and she didn't care. She thought about tugging him up to be face-to-face with her but he was doing something so amazing with that talented mouth that she held him to her, dying. "I need. God, Ford, I need..."

"Anything," he promised her, but he didn't mean it, the evil, *evil* man, because he was holding her right on the very edge, giving her everything then pulling back, teasing her until she was a panting, begging, squirming wreck, all but screaming his name.

"Ford, dammit!"

That didn't work.

"I don't get mad. I get even," she warned, and whether it was the implied threat or a decision to have mercy on her, Ford gave in. She came again long and hard and was barely back to planet Earth when he grabbed a condom from a drawer by the bed. In a blink, he was covered and sliding home, filling her completely.

"Jesus," he said, his voice low and raw, head bowed close to hers. "Every time. You slay me every fucking time." He pushed inside her again, and then again, making her clutch at him and cry out.

He went still. "Too much?"

"Just right." She dug her fingers into his butt. "And if you don't start moving, I'm going to hurt you, I swear it."

Laughing softly under his strained breath, he kissed her. He slipped an arm beneath her back to better angle her, but she was done letting him be in charge. Done letting him drag out all these raw, earthy, terrifying emotions. It was *her* turn to run the show, and silently thanking Chloe for all the yoga classes that had strengthened her core, she rolled over to claim the top.

He groaned as she straddled his hips, keeping him sheathed inside. And then groaned again when she started a grind that had her eyes drifting shut from the sheer pleasure of the friction.

"Tara, God. God, that's good."

So damn good.

She laced her fingers through his and pulled his arms above his head. Time for some of his own medicine. Leaning over him, she traced his bottom lip with her tongue.

"Mmm," he said, and took immediate control of the kiss, mating his tongue with hers, torturing her with every stroke.

She retaliated by rotating her hips, taking him deeper, and was rewarded when he breathed her name raggedly. She met each of his movements with a thrust of her own, until it became a struggle to remain in control. She could feel the flutter low in her gut, feel the heat starting at her toes and working its way north.

Definitely losing it…

As if he knew her body better than she did, Ford slipped his hands out of hers and grabbed her hips, forcing a rhythm that made both them quiver. Startled at the rawness, the utter rightness, she lifted her head and stared at him.

He met her gaze. In fact, he never looked away as they rode each other to climax. She burst first, falling forward onto his chest, panting for air as he followed her over.

"Good Christ," he muttered sometime later. His eyes were closed as he caught his breath, his entire body relaxed except for the hand he had clamped possessively on her ass. "We're going to kill each other."

A distinct possibility.

She buried her face against his neck. "Okay, now I really have to go," she said, but didn't move. Couldn't.

He pressed his mouth to her temple. "We do have a few minutes left..." His fingers dipped between her thighs.

Her entire body quivered, but she shook her head.

With a sigh, he sat up, lightly smacking her butt as he rolled off the bed and strolled casually to the tiny bathroom.

She found herself just sitting there watching him. Finally she shook herself and stood up, wrapping the sheet around her. Her clothes were scattered across the place.

"What's with the modesty now?"

She turned in time to watch him walk—bare ass nekked—across the room toward her. "I'm...cold," she said and made him laugh softly.

"Tara, I've seen every inch of you. Hell, I've kissed every inch of you. You don't need to hide it."

"Yes, but it's *really* light out."

He grinned and tugged the sheet from her. "I like it that way."

She fought to stay covered. "Well of course you do; you're perfect."

His eyes softened as he won the battle and tossed the sheet behind him. "So are you."

Chapter 22

♥

*"Death is hereditary. Make sure you enjoy
each day before it catches you."*
TARA DANIELS

Tara was walking up from the marina just as Chloe
pulled in on her Vespa. "Look at you," Chloe said, pulling off her helmet. "Glowing again."

Tara ignored that as she opened the door to the cottage, then promptly froze.

Maddie was sitting on their small couch in the living
room, staring openmouthed at Jax, tears running down
her cheeks.

Jax was on his knees at her side, holding her hand.

"Oh, God," Tara said, hand to her chest. "What's happened, what's wrong?"

Chloe came up beside Tara, took in the sight, and
immediately slid her hand into Tara's. Tara squeezed it
reassuringly, even as her heart landed in her stomach. Not
a single one of them were up for another crisis.

Jax dropped his forehead to Maddie's knee. His shoulders were shaking, and Tara stopped breathing.

"Tell us," Chloe whispered, gripping Tara's fingers hard enough to crack them. "Maybe we can help—"

Jax made a sound. Not of sorrow, Tara noted, and narrowed her eyes.

He was laughing.

When he lifted his face and met Maddie's gaze, his own softened, and he stroked her cheek, wiping away her tears. "I should have known we'd do this by committee. Should we consult the Magic Eight app or take a vote?"

Maddie laughed through her tears. "Oh, no, it's too late for that—I already said yes." She lifted her hand.

Which was weighted down by a sparkling diamond.

"Oh!" Chloe cried and jumped up and down. "I vote yes too, and that's majority. Majority rules!"

"Like I would have voted no," Tara said as she and Chloe stepped forward to hug Maddie. "Sorry we interrupted."

"Actually," Maddie said. "We were done with the proposal. We were just going to..." She blushed. "Negotiate some terms."

"For?"

Maddie and Jax smiled at each other, and their looks were so heated that Tara felt like her eyebrows went up in smoke.

"Aw." Chloe grinned. "You were totally going to do it, right there on the couch." She grabbed Tara and dragged her back to the front door. "Just pretend we never showed up. Carry on."

"We can't now," Maddie said, laughing. "You'll know."

"Yes," Chloe said. "And also, we're never going to

sit on that couch again, but don't let that stop you, Ms. Attack-Her-Boyfriend-in-the-Attic."

"Hey," Maddie said, still beet red. "What about Tara in the pantry with her two men?"

Tara sighed. "*Not* a true story," she said to an avidly listening Jax. "Logan and I haven't been together like that in over two years."

Chloe grinned at Maddie. "Notice she didn't deny having Ford 'like that.' She's totally doing him. I mean look at her. Hello, she's *still* glowing. Sex is so great for the skin. Wish I could come up with a skincare formula that gives that same glow. I'd make bank."

Maddie studied Tara's face and grinned, too. "Oh yeah, she's *definitely* doing Ford."

Jax looked pained. "Okay, you've *got* to stop saying that. Bad visual."

Maddie laughed and hugged him close. "Here, baby, let me give you another one to replace it with." She whispered something in his ear and then gently but firmly kicked her sisters out of the cottage, locking the door behind them.

That afternoon, Ford was behind the bar finishing up his monthly inventory. Jax usually helped, but he didn't show up until after it was finished. "Thanks for the help," Ford grumbled, then took in the wide, goofy-ass grin on Jax's face. "What?"

"You'll see," Jax said cryptically, and vanished into the back to do some paperwork.

The place was filling up when Maddie came in wearing a goofy grin that matched Jax's.

"Only one man I know who can put that smile on your face," Ford said.

Maddie laughed, something that had once upon a time been very rare. "Or potato chips."

Ford grinned at her. "What'll it be, Beautiful?"

"Oh, I don't know..." She set her hand down on the bar and nearly blinded him with a diamond.

"Jesus, you need sunglasses to look at that thing." And although he'd already seen the ring—Jax had shown him yesterday—Ford hugged her tight, then lifted her hand and smiled. "Hard to say no to a ring like that."

"Maybe it's just plain hard to say no to me." Jax came in from the back carrying a tray of clean glasses. He took one look at Maddie flashing the ring and smiled from ear to ear. He set down the glasses and hopped over the bar to yank her into his arms. "Hey, wife."

"Not yet, I'm not," she said, laughing as she shifted into him. "You have to get me down the aisle first."

"It's going to happen." Jax lowered his lips to her ear, whispered something that made her blush, then kissed her.

And kissed her.

"Get a room," Ford said and nudged them out of his way, their mouths still fused.

They vanished a few minutes later, and Ford figured that he'd be lucky if Jax surfaced sometime tomorrow. It wasn't a problem; neither he nor Jax was scheduled to actually tend bar tonight. But since Sawyer had a date too, Ford was left on his own with no plans ahead of him. In the old days, he'd have found himself some trouble.

Or a woman.

Neither appealed. So he got in his car and drove, and found himself at the inn. Carlos was in the yard, hosing out a big pot burned black.

"What happened?" Ford asked.

"Tara burnt the stew."

This was so odd that it took a moment to process. "She did?"

"Earlier. She said she was distracted. And now she's added pissed to the list." Carlos looked around to make sure they were alone. "If you don't have to go in there, maybe you shouldn't. No offense, but you tend to make things worse."

Ford had a feeling he'd already made it worse, that maybe she'd burned the stew when they'd been out on the water. "Does she need dinner for the guests? I can go pick something up."

"No, she's whipping up some fancy burgers right now. She's putting some really stinky cheese and seasonings in with the meat and calling them gourmet. She told me if I wrinkled my nose one more time she was going to rearrange it for me." Carlos let out a rare smile because, as they both knew, Tara could barely reach his nose. "Mia's helping her."

When the kid said Mia's name, a special quality came into his voice that Ford recognized all too well. Carlos was completely and helplessly wrapped around his daughter's pinkie.

They walked into the kitchen together, smelling the burned stew before they crossed the threshold. There was a fan going, and two candles, but they weren't helping yet. The room itself looked like an explosion in *Hell's*

Kitchen. The counters were cluttered with cooking utensils and ingredients, and a temperamental Tara stood at the stove, spatula in hand. When she caught sight of Ford, her eyes narrowed and her grip on the spatula tightened as if she was fighting the urge to smack him with it. "You," she said.

"Me," he agreed lightly. A few hours ago, she'd been naked and panting his name. Now she was back to the Steel Magnolia.

"Sugar," Tara said in a voice that was pure Pissed-Off South. "You need to go far, far away."

A few weeks ago, he'd have taken that to mean she didn't want to see his face within a six-hundred-mile radius. Now he knew the truth. He distracted her. He could live with that. "Came to see if I can help."

"I think I know how to make burgers," she said smoothly. "But bless your heart."

In other words, fuck off and die.

Carlos gave him a look like "told you so." He turned to Mia and the two of them exchanged a glance that wasn't all that hard to interpret for anyone who'd ever once been a horny teenager.

"So...I have to run into town to get the mail and fill up the propane tank," Carlos said casually.

"Oh! I'll help," Mia said quickly.

Amateurs. "No," Ford said at the same time as Tara.

Carlos let out a breath and left through the back door. Mia shot Tara a look of perfected teenage annoyance and grabbed the two vases of flowers she's just arranged, leaving through the double doors to display them in the front rooms.

When she was gone, Tara shook her head. "Why don't they tell you that raising a teenager is like trying to nail Jell-O to a freaking tree?"

Ford laughed softly. "Probably because the entire race would die out."

"He looks at her," she fretted. "A lot. He looks at her like..."

Risking his neck, Ford came up behind her and slid his arms around her. "Like I look at you?" he asked against her ear, enjoying the way she shivered before she shoved him away.

"Stop that," she said.

"That's not what you were saying earlier. You were saying 'Oh, Ford. Harder, Ford—'" His sentence ended in an *oomph* when she elbowed him in the gut.

"I have far more important things to do than relive our little..." Apparently she couldn't come up with a satisfactory word for what they'd done because she closed her mouth and inhaled sharply through her nose. "We have a bigger problem."

"I wouldn't classify anything that happened between us today as a problem," Ford said and kissed her jaw.

She pushed at him again, her mood clearly changed by the talk of the teenagers. "We have a mission, Ford. It's called *Keep the Daughter Fully Dressed*."

He grimaced.

"No, I mean it. That boy takes his job around here very seriously, and I greatly appreciate that. But there's something else he takes very seriously and that's our daughter. Do you hear me?"

"Honey, right now *everyone* can hear you."

Tara shook her head. "It's not happening, Ford. Not on my watch." She pointed at him again. "Or yours."

He arched a brow. "You don't see the irony in all this?"

"Of course I see the irony! I don't give a hoot about the irony!"

Ford very carefully relieved her of her weapon—the spatula—and once again wrapped his arms around her so she couldn't get violent. Holding her tight against him, he pressed his face into her hair. He couldn't help himself. "Even if someone had given a shit about keeping us separated, it wouldn't have helped. We'd have found a way."

"Maybe not."

"We'd have found a way," he repeated. "I was very determined."

Tara sighed. "Smartass."

"You like my ass."

"Yes," she agreed. "That's true, though it's not even your best part—Oh *crap*!" She sniffed, then sniffed again and whipped around to the stovetop. "Christ on a stick, *I did it again*! I burned another meal!" Shoving free, she flipped off the burners and stared in horror at the blackened burgers.

They could hear running footsteps, and then the door flew open. "Fire! Fire, *fire*!" Chloe shrieked, inhaler in one hand, fire extinguisher in the other. When she saw the burned burgers, she stopped and sagged in relief. "Jesus! Jesus Christ, I thought we were burning the place down again!"

Tara sank to a chair in utter disbelief. "I never burn things. And yet I've burned the last three meals I tried to make." She lifted a shocked gaze to both of them. "What's wrong with me?"

Neither Ford nor Chloe was stupid enough to answer that question. Ford poured Tara a fairly large glass of wine and turned to the refrigerator. In less than three minutes, he had the flame going again and was slathering butter on Tara's freshly made bread and slicing cheddar cheese for grilled cheese sandwiches.

"I can't serve plain old grilled cheese," Tara protested, downing her wine.

"It's not plain old grilled cheese," he said. "It's Jax's Chillax Grilled Cheese. It's the only thing the doofus could make until he was twenty-four. Damn good recipe, though."

"You're fixin' this for me," she said.

"Trying."

"You have a habit of doing that, helping me." There was something new in her eyes, something Ford couldn't quite put his finger on but hoped like hell meant that she was finally beginning to see him.

All of him.

Chapter 23

> *"Love is when someone puts you on a pedestal*
> *and yet when you fall, they're there*
> *to catch you anyway."*
> TARA DANIELS

The summer shifted into high gear, complete with tourist surge and the long, hot, lazy days that were followed by long, hot, lazy nights.

Every Wednesday night, the town hosted Music on the Pier, and Ford always ran a booth for The Love Shack. He'd hired Carlos for help with the setup, and as Ford arrived, he expected that the kid would be working hard.

Instead, Ford found him working hard on swallowing Mia's tongue.

When neither of them noticed Ford's approach—they were pretty busy after all—he cleared his throat.

Nothing. He did it again, putting some major irritation into the sound, and the two teenagers finally jumped apart.

"Hey," Mia said, breathless, swiping a hand over her wet mouth. "We were just..."

Ford raised a brow, curious as to how she was going to finish that sentence. Instead, she fell silent. "Checking each other's tonsils?" he asked her.

Mia grimaced, and Carlos slid his hand into hers. A show of comfort and solidarity, and though his shoulders were a little hunched, he stood his ground right next to her. Ford stared at him, and though Carlos definitely squirmed, he held the eye contact.

"It's my fault," Mia said quickly. "Not his."

"No," Carlos said. "It's mine. Sir."

Ford scrubbed a hand over his face. Sir. Christ, if that didn't make him feel old.

Mia stepped in front of Carlos. Or tried to, but the kid wouldn't let her. "I can kiss who I want," she said with soft steel reminiscent of Tara.

Ford looked into her earnest, sweet face. Seventeen had never looked so young. "Mia—"

"I mean, I know you're my father, but I already have a dad."

Intimidation went out the window. So did the wind in his sails. "Yes, I know."

Mia stared up at him with those bigger-than-life eyes, the ones that haunted him with what-ifs. "And Carlos is a good guy," she said, glancing up at the kid still holding her hand, smiling at him.

Carlos didn't return the expression, but his eyes never left her face.

Ford let out a breath. "I know that, too."

"And so am I," she said. "I'm a good kid."

"My own personal miracle," Ford said with feeling.

Mia hesitated, as if she hadn't been prepared for him

to be so agreeable. "So you can trust me to live my life. You know that too, right? As well as letting me make my own mistakes?"

"Yes, but that doesn't make it any easier for me. Mia..." Ford searched for the right words. "Do you have any idea how many times I hoped I'd get to meet you? Get to know you?"

"No."

"Every day. Every single day."

Her eyes softened. "Yeah?"

"Yeah."

Her eyes filled, and she finally let go of Carlos's hand. She stepped into Ford, wrapped her arms around his waist, and hugged him. "So it's okay with you if after I get back from Spain, I still show up every once in a while?"

Ford tugged on a loose strand of her beautiful hair. "If you didn't, I'd come to you."

Mia's soggy smile warmed the far corners of his heart.

"I still want to kiss your employee," she said.

Carlos winced. Mia smiled brilliantly at the teen, and his mouth quirked as if he couldn't help but love her.

Ford knew the feeling.

"I have to go," Mia said. "I promised Tara I'd find her at five." She went up on tiptoe to kiss Ford's cheek, looking him straight in the eyes. "Promise you're not going to do anything stupidly dad-like, okay?" she whispered. "No scaring off my boyfriend?"

Carlos winced again, probably thinking of his tough-guy rep and how easily she crushed it. Still, the kid said nothing as the two of them watched Mia dance off. Only when she was out of sight did Carlos turn his head and look at Ford warily.

"You got anything to say?" Ford asked.

"Would it help?"

"No. Get set up. We're expecting a crowd tonight."

Carlos hesitated, still braced for a father's wrath. "That's it?"

Ford wasn't exactly prepared for this, although he should have been. He'd gone from having no kid to having a hormonal teenager, and he felt a little off kilter. "For now, I need you to work, but stand by later to possibly have your ass kicked."

Carlos hopped to work so fast that Ford's head swam.

The businesses on the pier were making a brisk living today. Tara was out there somewhere with her sisters promoting the inn.

Ford could imagine her in her heels, all elegant and sophisticated and put together, the opposite of how she was when she was writhing beneath him. He thought about that for a few minutes and realized he was no better than Carlos.

The late afternoon was sizzling. The ocean was clear and azure blue, dotted with whitecaps from the light breeze as the sun slowly worked its way down the horizon. Behind him, Carlos was still rushing to set up, sliding the occasional wary glance Ford's way. "*What?*" Ford finally asked.

"Are you going to fire me? Cuz I'd really rather have that ass kicking. Sir."

"Call me 'sir' again and I will."

"So we're okay?"

"Hell, no. You had your hands on my daughter. I want to tell you that if you so much as think about touching her again, I'm going to make sure they never find your body."

Carlos paled a little, and Ford let out another breath. "But I can't do that, either."

The kid nodded. Yeah, he could really get behind Ford not doing that. "Why?"

"Because Mia'd be pissed at me, and I just got her in my life. And because I was seventeen once and incredibly stupid and selfish. Far more than you, actually." Ford paused. "Look, I realize you're just having a summer fling here but Mia—"

"No."

Ford arched a brow at the seriousness and vehemence of that single syllable. "No?"

"No, I'm not just having a summer fling."

"So where do you see this thing going? Because you know she's leaving for Spain when the summer's over. For a whole year. That's a lifetime for a guy your age. I don't want her hurt."

"I'm not going to hurt her. I love her."

Ford looked into Carlos' dark eyes. Whatever a seventeen-year-old could possibly know about love, Carlos meant it. Shit. "Okay, new game plan. If you touch her—"

"They'll never find my body?"

"Just don't. Don't touch her at all. Ever." Ford sighed. "Someday you're going to have a daughter and then you'll understand."

"Actually, I understand now. And what about Ms. Daniels?"

"What about her?"

"Maybe I'm not forty-four or whatever," Carlos said. "But she's a real nice lady. What about *her* getting hurt?"

Ford was so surprised that words nearly failed him. "*Thirty*-four. And I don't intend to hurt Tara. Ever."

"So..."

"I'm in this," Ford said, "to the end."

Carlos looked shocked.

But not as shocked as Ford himself was. He scratched his jaw. "Huh. I didn't see that one coming."

Carlos shook his head. "Does anyone?"

Tara was once again peddling muffins. Mia had started off doing it, but she'd wanted to wander around, so here Tara was. "Double the Pleasure Blueberry Muffins," she said, handing them out, not slowing down enough to engage in conversation until someone came up behind her and grabbed her with two strong arms, snagging a muffin in each hand.

Logan.

He bit into a muffin. "Mmm, damn you're good. Hey, I have some photographers coming in tomorrow from *People*. I made the Hottest 100 List. Your bartender ever do that?"

She shot him a look, and he laughed. "You know, I even miss your Don't-Make-Me-Kick-Your-Ass expression. Anyway, *People*'s bringing a few models in bikinis to drape themselves over a prop car to pose with me. Thought maybe you'd want to take their place."

"Oh, I would," Tara said drolly. "Except hell hasn't frozen over."

He grinned. "Okay, I guess I'll have to make do with the models then."

"Yeah, I bet that's going to be real tough."

Logan tugged on her hair. "I'm still holding out hope for me, Tara. For us."

But the "me" had come before the "us," and it always would. Logan was a good guy, just not the right good guy for her. She knew that. On some level, she'd always known that. "Logan—"

"Hold that thought, darlin'. My fan club's calling."

She watched as he stepped away to be engulfed by a group of women that included Sandy and Cindy.

With a helpless laugh, Tara turned and found Chloe standing there.

"Want a reprieve?" Chloe asked, reaching for the basket of muffins.

"Yes," Tara said. "But what's wrong with this picture, you offering to help?"

Chloe ignored that and handed out a few muffins with a welcoming smile that Tara couldn't have pulled off to save her life.

Sawyer came walking through the crowd. He was in uniform, talking on his cell when Chloe purposely stepped into his path. "Muffin, officer?"

He stopped and looked down at her, and Tara held her breath. These two hadn't exactly seen eye to eye on... anything. Sawyer was six-foot-three and more than a little intimidating, but the petite Chloe just smiled sweetly up at him as if she hadn't been a thorn in his side since she'd first come to town. "They're Double the Pleasure Blueberry Muffins. Take two and quadruple your pleasure. *Officer*."

He never looked away from Chloe's face. "You make them?"

She laughed. "Why? You afraid?"

"Depends. Answer the question."

"Ah," Chloe said. "You think I poisoned them."

"Maybe just the ones you saved for me."

Chloe slowly eyed him from head to toe and back again. "It'd be a sacrilege."

Tara almost choked.

Sawyer didn't react, other than to slowly remove his sunglasses. "What are you up to?"

She reached over and plucked an invisible piece of lint from his pec. "If I have to tell you," she murmured, "I've gotten rusty."

Sawyer's gaze locked on hers. From five feet away, Tara felt the blast of heat between them, and it nearly knocked her back a step. She had no idea why Chloe was playing with him, why she was jerking his chain, and she had even less of an idea why Sawyer put up with it. But there was a shocking amount of tension there that she hadn't noticed before.

Sexual tension.

Sawyer's radio squawked. Eyes still on Chloe, he didn't move.

"You have to go," Chloe said lightly, as if nothing had happened. She handed him a few muffins. "Stay safe now, you hear?"

Sawyer looked at her for a long beat, clearly perplexed and suspicious of her unexpected niceness, poor guy. "You," he finally said, putting his sunglasses back on, "are a menace."

Chloe smiled and nodded. "Yes. Yes, I am. Don't you forget it now. Buh-bye." She slid her arm in Tara's and steered her away.

"What was *that*?" Tara whispered.

"Me giving away a few muffins."

"I meant the messing with the poor guy's head."

Chloe lifted a shoulder. "It's a give-and-take situation."

Tara slid her a glance. "Meaning?"

"Meaning maybe his head isn't the only one being messed with." Not explaining that cryptic statement, she continued to hand out muffins.

"Chloe—"

"I don't want to talk about it."

"Then can we talk about why you're helping me?" Tara asked.

"What, a sister can't help another sister?"

"Yes, if she wants something."

"Well, I don't," Chloe said, sounding hurt.

Crap. "Okay, that was rude," Tara admitted. "I'm sorry."

Chloe grinned. "Wow, Maddie's right. You *are* a lot more mellow now that you're boinking Ford. I hadn't really noticed. I do want something. I want tonight off to go rock climbing, if you'll wake me in the morning. I'm giving a big spa day tomorrow at the Seattle Four Seasons." She smiled at the guy coming up to her side and handed him a muffin. It was Tucker, Lance's twin.

"We're leaving in half an hour," he said.

"Are we going to get arrested again?" Chloe asked hopefully.

Tucker laughed. "No. This time we really do have

permission to be on the Butte. I'm going to go get the gear ready, while Lance works the booth. Jamie and Todd are coming too."

Tara held back her negative comment. She adored Lance and Tucker, but not Jamie's cousin Todd. When he was around, bad things tended to happen.

"Well, then," Chloe said, unconcerned, "I should help." She looked at Tara, who nodded, then handed back the basket and headed off.

"Be careful," Tara said and knew that, of course, she wouldn't be. She looked down at the basket, feeling alone. Both of her sisters had other people in their lives. Tara had neglected to achieve that for herself. An oversight on her part. She'd been so busy trying to make the inn a success, and making sure not to lose herself this time, that she hadn't managed to cultivate many friends here.

Okay, that wasn't quite true. She'd made plenty of time for one person in particular—too much time.

Ford, of course. It always came back to Ford.

She realized that while thinking of him, she'd walked up to his booth. She shouldn't have been surprised, since with him and only him, she seemed to know exactly who she was.

And who she wasn't.

Jax was behind the bar though, not Ford, and she told herself it was silly to be disappointed.

"What'll it be?" Jax asked with a friendly smile.

"Oh, I..." She hadn't come for a drink. She'd come for a peek at the man she couldn't stop thinking about. She looked casually around.

Jax raised a brow. "Want a hint?"

Tara felt a tingle at the back of her neck and closed her eyes. "He's right behind me, isn't he?"

"Yep."

With a sigh, she turned around to face Ford. He was looking comfortable and relaxed in a Mariners' baseball cap, cargos, and a T-shirt that said SAIL FAST, LIVE SLOW.

He shot her a slow smile that spread warmth to parts of her that didn't need warming. "Hey," she said casually. Wow, look at her all composed. Tranquil. "Well"—she backed away—"I hope you get a good crowd tonight."

Not fooled, he stepped in her path. "Going somewhere?"

"I'm working."

"Really? Because it seemed like maybe you were looking for me."

Dammit. "Why would I do that?"

He gave that soft laugh, the one that always made her quiver. "Because you want me bad."

God. She looked around to make sure Jax couldn't hear them, but he'd turned his back and was setting up. "I already had you," she whispered.

"Yes," Ford said. "Hence the bad part. Walk with me." Without waiting for her to refuse him, he took the basket out of her hands and set it behind the bar. With a hand low on her back, he directed her through the throng of people, with the sounds of the music and laughter all around them. The Ferris wheel was slowly revolving, going round and round.

Like her life.

"You know that Carlos thinks he loves Mia."

"Yes. But they're too young for love."

Ford's mouth curved slightly. "That thought would have pissed you off at seventeen."

True. Tara rubbed her temples. "Okay, I'm going to take heart in the fact that they seem to be smarter than we were. Her adoptive parents did a good job of raising her."

"Yeah."

They were both silent as they passed the Ferris wheel, and Tara knew that they were each thinking, thank God that Mia's parents *had* done such an obviously amazing job. Tara was grateful to them, so damn grateful. "And did you know that Sawyer and Chloe are circling each other like two caged tigers?"

"That's actually just Sawyer who's the caged tiger. Chloe's in the center of the ring with the whip, toying with him."

"I'm sorry."

Ford shook his head. "Sawyer's a big boy."

They slowed in front of the ice cream parlor, which was having a tasting party. Lance stood behind the counter offering samples of everything they had. "What'll it be?" he asked them.

Tara pointed to the double fudge chocolate, which melted in her mouth.

"If you liked that, try this one." Lance handed over another tiny spoon. "It's Belgian dark chocolate."

"Oh Lord." She moaned as she swallowed the heavenly taste. "How about that one, what's that?" she asked, pointing to another chocolatey-looking concoction.

"Chocolate E. For ecstasy. Careful with it," Lance warned with a wink at Ford. "They call it pure sin."

Tara tested it and moaned again. She'd never had anything so delicious in her life.

"Want a cone with that?" Lance asked.

Indecision. They were all so amazing that she had no idea how she was going to pick. "Wait, I didn't taste the chocolate butter toffee," she murmured, and Lance patiently offered her another tiny spoon.

She was in mid-heavenly sigh when she felt Ford shift close behind her, his mouth brushing her ear. "Moan through one more sample," he warned in a thick husky whisper, "and I'm dragging you to the closest dark corner on the pier. And Tara?" His breath was warm against her skin, making her shiver. "By the time I'm done with you, you won't remember your own name."

She couldn't remember her own name now. "That's a pretty outrageous threat," she managed.

"Yes, and if you're very lucky, I'll wait until we're alone to carry through on it."

She turned to face him just as he reached past her to accept his own tiny spoon sample from Lance. Eyes on hers, Ford licked at it slowly.

Tara's thighs quivered.

"Order your ice cream," he told her, and took another lick.

Later she couldn't remember what she ordered. All she remembered was Ford holding her hand on the walk back through the crowd, with need and hunger and desire pounding through her veins instead of blood.

By silent agreement, they headed directly to his car.

He drove them to the marina and to his boat. Still silent, they boarded.

The moon was nothing but a narrow sliver on the water, lapping quietly at the boat as they turned to each other.

Chapter 24

*"For every action, there is an equal and
opposite criticism. Ignore it."*
TARA DANIELS

There was only the faintest glow of a quarter moon on
the water. The night had a hushed quiet to it—with the
exception of Tara's heavy breathing and low moans.

Ford's favorite sounds of all time.

They lay on his bed. As Tara thrashed beneath his
hands, he slowly drew her to the very edge of sanity,
watching, enthralled, as she began to come undone.

She wasn't alone in that.

Always when with her, he was completely undone,
stripped down to raw, bare soul. From her first day back
in Lucky Harbor, it'd been exactly as he remembered, and
something he'd never forgotten in all these years.

His gaze wandered down her gorgeous body, long
and curvy, and spread out across his bed for his viewing
pleasure, and he actually ached.

She opened her eyes. "You're looking at me like..."

"Like you looked at the ice cream earlier?" he asked with a smile. "Yeah, I am. I'm hungry for you, Tara."

Stretching out, she lifted her arms above her head, giving him silent permission to taste whatever he wanted. Something he'd been wanting to do for days—eat her up from head to toe and then back again, until she came for him. Again and again. He started at her throat, tasting every single inch of her, nibbling certain interesting spots, stopping to tease whenever she gasped or wriggled. "So sweet," he murmured against her skin. "You're so damn sweet." By the time he got to her belly button, she was fisting the sheets at her side and murmuring his name in a chant, a prayer, a warning to hurry the hell up.

It made him laugh. "Just lay there and take it, Tara." *Take me*... "Give me the control. I'll get you where you want to go, I promise."

"I—Ohmigod," she managed when he drew her into his mouth and gently sucked, his hands sliding beneath her sexy ass to hold her still. "Don't stop," she demanded.

Still trying to be in the driver's seat. "Please," he corrected. "Don't stop, *please*..."

She slid her fingers into his hair, tightening them to an almost painful grip, holding him to her, making him laugh again. "Say it," he demanded.

"Don't stop, *please*," she ground out, doing her best to make him bald.

"See?" he murmured. "Sweet as hell." And he didn't stop. Not until she begged him to.

Nicely.

• • •

Afterward, Tara fell asleep curled into Ford's side, one hand tucked beneath her chin, the other across his chest.

He lay there, relaxed and boneless, listening to her breathe, not wanting to move. Not wanting her to stir and remember that she was trying to hold back from him. Because then she'd get up, get dressed, and walk away.

She was good at that.

And he was good at letting her.

He had no one but himself to blame for that. Bad genes, bad childhood—all excuses and he knew it. And they no longer cut it.

Tara's coming back to Lucky Harbor had been circumstance. Her staying in town even more so. No one would argue that their connection wasn't still there, possibly even deeper than before, but she was holding back, and he couldn't blame her.

She'd been burned.

He knew that. He got it. Hell, he'd even been one of the ones to burn her. Up until now, he'd been willing to give her all the time she needed, because the truth was that he'd needed time, too. Time to deal with some of his own past mistakes. Time to understand that he was in this for the long haul.

Because she made him. She made him laugh. She made him feel. She made him think. She made him happy.

She made him...everything.

And with that everything, she also made him vulnerable. Bone-deep, scary-as-shit vulnerable. Just as gun-shy as she was.

Christ, he really hated that about himself.

With a sleepy sigh, Tara stirred and untangled herself.

"Don't," he said.

She lifted her head in surprise. "Don't what?"

He drew a deep breath. "Don't go. Stay the night."

She smiled softly, and he knew by the light in her eyes that his words meant something to her, said something important. A step in the right direction, that light said, and he smiled back.

But she still climbed out of the bed. "I can't stay tonight. I have to go check on the inn." She slipped back into her dress and bent over the bed to kiss him. "'Night, Ford." Then she was gone, her heels clicking on the deck as she walked away in tune to the only other sound Ford could hear—the roaring of his own racing heart.

Okay, so she'd left a little abruptly, but she'd kissed him first. A step in the right direction, he told himself again, and there, alone in the dark, smiled.

The next morning Tara rose and showered, determined to make their guests the most outstanding breakfast they'd ever had. She would burn nothing. First, though, she went to wake Chloe as Chloe had requested—but her bed was empty. Tara hadn't heard her come in after rock climbing, but most likely she was already in the inn kitchen making a mess.

Resigned, Tara walked to the inn, let herself into the kitchen, and prepared to be annoyed.

But the kitchen was empty. Huh. Tara called Chloe's cell, but it went right to voice mail. She tried Maddie next.

"'Lo?" came Maddie's sleepy voice. "Who's dead?"

"Is Chloe with you at Jax's?" Tara asked.

"It'd be a bit crowded here in his bed if she was. Why?"

"I don't think she came home last night."

"From rock climbing? *Crap*." Sounding more awake now, Maddie asked the question already on Tara's mind. "You suppose she's in jail again?"

"Anyone's guess."

"I'll be there in fifteen."

"No," Tara said. "You took the late shift here last night. I'll handle this."

"Honey, I was coming in anyway to help you serve breakfast. Give me fifteen."

"Okay," Tara said, grateful to have someone to worry with. "Thanks. You want to call Sawyer or should I?"

"Call Sawyer what?" Sawyer asked, coming in the back door, filling the kitchen with his big build. He was in his uniform and looking very fine as he went straight to the coffee pot.

Tara handed him one of the to-go mugs.

"Thanks." The very corners of his mouth tipped in a barely-there, bad-boy smile as he leaned back against the counter, the mug in hand. "Tell me what?" he repeated.

Tara thought about not going there with him. After all, typically when Chloe got herself in some sort of trouble, poor Sawyer was the one forced to deal with it.

But if Tara didn't tell him and something had happened to her sister...She sighed. "Chloe didn't make it home last night."

He didn't so much as blink, and yet there was a new

stillness about him that told her he wasn't happy to hear this. "And she was supposed to?"

"Yes."

"Was she with the group of rock climbers out on the Butte?"

"Possibly," Tara said warily. "Why?"

"Because I arrested one of them this morning."

Oh, God. "Who was it, and for what?"

"Todd Fitzgerald. Public intoxication."

Todd. Of course. Tara sighed, and Sawyer pushed away from the counter. "I'll make some calls."

She knew he meant he'd call the station, the hospital...the morgue. But before he got to the door, Chloe came in—hair wild, face flushed, wearing yesterday's clothes and carrying her shoes.

Sawyer looked at her impassively.

"Don't start," she said and brushed past him. Limping.

He eyed her body carefully. "You okay?"

She turned to face him. "I'm always okay."

There was a long, awkward beat between the two of them. There always was. Tara had no idea what to make of it or how to help.

"Don't you have sheriff-type stuff to do?" Chloe asked him.

Sawyer gave a short shake of his head, one that clearly said *fuck it* before he moved toward the door. Tara gave Chloe a recriminating *you-are-so-rude* look, and Chloe rolled her eyes. "Sawyer," she said with reluctant apology.

He pulled open the door. "Glad you're home safe."

"We were at the Butte," Chloe said to his broad, tense back. "We ran out of gas and had to wait until daylight to catch a ride."

He looked at her. "It's illegal to party out there."

"We ran out of gas," she repeated.

"Did you lose your cell phone too?"

Chloe sighed dramatically. "I forgot mine at home, okay? And Lance doesn't carry one."

Sawyer locked eyes with hers. "Were you with Todd?"

"For a while."

"He had a phone."

"How do you know?" she asked.

"Because it's now residing in his personal possessions baggie for when he bails himself out after he sobers up."

"You arrested him? Seriously?"

Sawyer was unapologetic and unmoved. "He staggered into the convenience store at five this morning, knocked over three displays, and urinated on the magazine stand." He shook his head. "And you and Lance have a serious death wish, you know that? What if he'd had a medical problem out there?"

"He needed to do this, Sawyer. It isn't my place to babysit him and tell him what he can and can't do."

"Jesus, Chloe, his cystic fibrosis isn't a fucking summer cold!"

"And you think he doesn't know that?"

"And what about you?" he asked. "Does the inhaler always do the job? I don't think so. You can't tell me you've never had to make a trip to the ER because of an asthma attack while climbing."

"*Nothing happened*," Chloe said. "So I don't get it. Why are you so pissed?"

"I'm not pissed." His face was impassive. The cop face. "That would imply that there were feelings between us."

Chloe stared at him for a long beat. "My mistake then," she finally said.

Sawyer stared at her right back, then swore beneath his breath and left without another word. When the door shut behind him with quiet fury, Chloe let out a breath.

"Gee," Tara said in the silence. "No tension there."

"Don't you start too." Chloe headed directly for the refrigerator and some leftover Not Yo Mama's Apple Pie.

"Was it just you, Tucker, Lance, and Todd up there?" Tara asked.

"No. Lance brought a bunch of friends, and one thing led to another."

So Sawyer was right. It *had* been a party. "I thought you can't have sex without landing yourself in the hospital."

"No one had sex. Or at least I didn't." Chloe sighed. "Bunch of stupid boys in this town."

"Sawyer isn't stupid."

"And he's not a boy, either."

Tara watched as Chloe shoveled away the pie like she hadn't eaten in a week. "What is he, then?"

"Hell, Tara, do I need to give you the birds and the bees talk? Why can't you get the deets off the Internet like all the other kids these days?"

When Tara laughed, Chloe relaxed slightly. "I really don't want to talk about it," she said.

"A common theme amongst us sisters," Tara said.

"What's this?" Chloe asked. "Regret? From the most private sister of them all?" Without waiting for an answer, she took her plate to the sink and headed to the door. "I'm out."

When Tara was alone, she sighed. "Yeah. I'd definitely call it regret." Shaking it off, she began pulling out all the ingredients she needed for the Good Morning Sunshine Casserole, which she'd adapted from Mia's recipe. She was grating cheese when the back door and the door leading to the hallway opened at the same time.

Logan came in one, and Ford the other.

Immediately, the testosterone level shot up and hit maximum velocity in two point zero seconds as both men stared at each other over Tara's head.

"Well, if it isn't the drinking buddies," Tara said dryly. "Should I break out the mimosas, boys?"

"I just came by to help," Logan said. "Since you keep burning meals and all."

"How are you going to help?" Ford asked. "You actually cook?"

"Well, no, but I give real good help," Logan said with a charming smile in Tara's direction.

"*I* cook," Ford said.

Logan's eyes narrowed, and Tara felt yet another competition coming on. She'd heard about the abs of steel contest at The Love Shack. Part of her still couldn't believe it, and the other part of her wished she'd seen it herself.

"Okay, you know what?" She dropped an empty bag into Logan's hands and gave his leanly muscled, warm body a push out the back door. "I need some apples. Go pick me some, would you?"

Ford, looking big and bad and very cocky, leaned back against the counter with a smile.

"Oh, no." Tara shoved him out after Logan. "You too. And play nice." She shut the door on them both, threw the casserole into the oven, and turned and met Mia's amused glance.

"I showed up to make sure you didn't have any trouble," the teen said.

"Well, the trouble part is taken care of. Other than that, everything's the same old status quo. My life is pretty boring."

"Yeah." Mia laughed. "Okay, let's work on *not* burning breakfast today."

"I swear I'm a good cook," Tara said, needing to be good at *something* in her daughter's eyes. She walked Mia through the steps to make dough for fresh bread. "This won't take long to bake and then we can—" Tara broke off as she got a good look out the window. "Oh, for the love of God."

Logan and Ford had each shimmied up a tree—Logan with the help of a stepladder—and were making piles of apples. Big piles.

More than she needed for the next month.

Not that they were doing it for *her.* Nope, they were competing again.

Mia joined her at the window and raised a single brow—yet another talent she'd inherited from her father. Together they watched the guys pick apples.

"And you think your life is boring," Mia murmured.

• • •

"You're sleeping with her." Logan repeated this grimly to Ford from somewhere inside his apple tree. With his arm injury, he'd been slower to climb up.

Ford, having the free use of both arms, hadn't needed a ladder to climb the adjacent tree. "This is not news," he told Logan. "You read Facebook."

"Christ. I should just kill you. Or me. It'd be less painful to be dead."

"You're not in any real pain," Ford said in disgust. "It's just your fucking ego. You hate to lose."

"Said the pot to the kettle," Logan muttered.

Okay, that might be true, but this was more than about winning for Ford. It was about Tara, a woman he couldn't live without. He pulled himself up to the next branch and dropped another three perfect apples. He glanced down. Yep, his pile was bigger than Logan's. Even as he thought so with deep satisfaction, an apple whizzed by his ear, so close it disturbed his hair. "Hey—"

Logan flashed a grim smile and chucked another one. Ford saw this one coming and ducked again, and slipped. "Shit—"

That's all he got out before he lost his grip, his temper, and his balance all at once.

And fell out of the tree.

Chapter 25

> *"Families are like fudge—mostly sweet*
> *with a few nuts."*
> TARA DANIELS

When Ford opened his eyes, he was flat on his back staring up at the sky.

"Jesus H. Christ," came a horrified, disembodied voice from the next tree over. "What, you can't hold on to a branch?"

"You beaned me in the forehead," Ford said. "With an apple."

"And you call yourself an athlete." Logan was hauling ass out of his tree as fast as he could with one arm in a brace, swearing colorfully as he went.

Ford prayed he'd fall, too, but it didn't happen. Fucking karma.

"I didn't even hit you that hard," Logan was muttering. "You weren't supposed to fall like a fucking pussy!"

"Nice," Ford said, very carefully *not* moving. "Calling me names when I'm down."

"Hey, you're the one who's always going on and on about me not being an athlete."

That was true. He had no excuse.

Okay, he did.

Jealousy. "All I'm saying is that a race car driver isn't necessarily as fit as say, a sailor—"

"Jesus, would you give it up already? And why are you just lying there? Tell me you're not hurt. You're going to fucking milk this, aren't you? You're going to get laid out of this deal, I just know it. How bad are you hurt?"

Ford let out a breath. "I'm putting all my energy into *not* figuring that out."

Logan swore again and hit the ground.

"I'm surprised to see you move so fast," Ford said. "For someone who sits on his ass for a living."

"I don't—Goddammit, *shut up*." Logan dropped to Ford's side to look him over, his eyes widening on Ford's legs. "Fuck."

"No. Don't tell me." He already knew. He could feel the fire from his toes to his groin. And not a little baby-ass fire either, but a to-the-bone burning that made him want to scream. But because he *wasn't* a pussy, as Logan had accused, he refused to make a sound. Sweating, however, was allowed. He was doing a lot of sweating. And possibly going to throw up, too.

Then came a buzzing that told him this was it. His life was fading before his very eyes—

"*Bees!*" Logan jumped up and started leaping around, running in circles, flapping his arms.

"It's just the gunk from the bruised apples," Ford told

him. "Ignore them and, gee, I don't know, *help the guy you knocked out of the tree.*"

But Logan kept doing the bee dance, and it was actually kind of fun to watch. "Man, if you'd just stand still—"

"I'm allergic!" Logan yelled.

"You're kidding me, right?"

"Fuck! Ow!" Logan slapped at his collarbone. "I'm hit, I'm hit!"

Ford wanted to ask Logan who was the pussy now, but that seemed kind of asshole-ish. And then there was the fact that Ford was suddenly feeling weird, sort of woozy...

There were running footsteps, feet pounding the ground toward him. Ford closed his eyes as the pain began to burn a path to his brain. Yeah, he was definitely going to throw up.

"Ford," Tara breathed. "Oh my God. Your leg."

He felt her drop to her knees and had the vague thought that he wished she was going into that position for a different reason altogether.

"Is he dead?"

This from Chloe, and Ford huffed out a laugh. "Not yet," he assured her.

Tara whipped out her cell phone, punched in 9-1-1, and glared at Chloe.

"What?" Chloe asked innocently. "Look, some sisters help you move, but a *real* sister helps you move bodies." She patted Ford's shoulder. "Glad it's not necessary, Big Guy."

"Me too," he muttered.

"Help," came a whisper.

Everyone looked over at Logan. He was sitting on the ground, hands clasped around his throat. His face was sweaty and beet red.

"Logan, not now," Tara said. "Ford's hurt."

"I was...stung by a bee," he rasped out and fell over.

Tara gasped and abandoned Ford, crawling over to Logan. "He's allergic!"

Great, Ford thought. Fucking great. Even while passed out, Logan could upstage him.

The ambulance came. Tara burned breakfast again. And within thirty minutes someone had already updated Facebook with:

Tara nearly kills both of her men!

Mia saved the day, coming up with pancakes that she'd learned to make in Home Ec class. She served the guests with Maddie's help while Tara rode in the ambulance with both Ford and Logan.

An hour and a half later, Tara was sitting in the hospital waiting room with Mia on one side, Chloe on the other. Maddie had taken over inn detail.

They hadn't had any news on either Logan or Ford, and Tara felt herself losing it. "What's taking so long?" she asked for the tenth time.

Chloe sat calmly reading *Cosmo*. She turned the page, eyed the very good-looking, half-naked guy there, and hummed her approval. "Maybe they're surgically removing their *In Love with Tara* gene."

Tara narrowed her eyes. "What does that mean?"

"It means I *still* don't get it. How is it that you have those two guys falling for you? You're grumpy and bossy and demanding and anal—not to mention slightly obsessive compulsive." She paused. "No offense."

Tara looked over at a quiet Mia. "Still glad you found your parents?"

A smile curved her lips. "I have my moments."

Chloe laughed. "I really, really like you."

Tara elbowed her, then turned to Mia again. "Thanks for your help in the kitchen during the fiasco."

"No problem. I've been wondering something."

Oh God. Another question, Tara thought.

"Amy, the waitress at the diner, told me you never burned anything over there. Ever."

"That's true," Tara said over Chloe's snort.

"Why is that?" Mia asked.

"I have no idea."

Finally, a doctor came out to talk to them. Logan had been treated for his severe allergic reaction to the bee sting and was going to be fine. Ford had a broken leg and had been drugged up to have it set. He was loopy, but would also be fine—in six to eight weeks.

Mia went in to see Ford first. While she did, Tara called the B&B and checked in. According to Maddie, their guests were fine and out for the day. Two more people had checked in but all was well.

Taking a deep breath, Tara walked down the hall, stopping to buy two balloons. Both the men in her life had acted like children today; so she figured what the hell.

Logan's room came first. He was sitting up in his bed, flirting with a pretty nurse who was hovering over him taking his pulse. "I've always wanted to meet a real-life NASCAR driver," she was saying.

Tara rolled her eyes and knocked on the jamb. "Am I interrupting?"

The look on the nurse's face said yes, she was absolutely interrupting, but she was professional enough to shake her head. "I just have to get the doctor to sign his forms and then he can be released." With one last little longing glance in Logan's direction, the woman was gone.

Logan smiled at the balloons. "For me?"

"One of them." Tara handed it over and kissed his cheek. "You're an idiot."

"Gee, thanks."

"But I love you anyway."

"Yeah." His smiled faded. "But you're not *in* love with me."

Tara sat at his hip and looked him in the eyes. "And you are, Logan? In love with me? *Truth*," she said when he opened his mouth. "Are you in love with me, the me I am right now?"

"Well not *right* now," he said, brooding. "Right now you're kinda mean."

"How about the me who has a life now separate from yours? The me who's now involved in her sisters' lives, the me who can no longer drop everything and travel the world to be your greatest cheerleader without a care to her own life? *That* me, Logan. Are you in love with *that* me?"

Logan looked at her for a long beat, then expelled a breath. "I don't know that you."

"No, you don't." Tara reached for his hand. "Which means you can't love me."

He was quiet a minute. "I didn't expect us to turn out this way," he finally said. He brought their joined hands up to his mouth and brushed his lips across her knuckles. "I do see what you love about Lucky Harbor, though. It's a cool place."

It wasn't the place. Tara knew that now. It was the people in it, and the relationships she'd made here. It was...home.

"So if you're not coming back to me," he said after a while, "what are your plans?"

"I'm moving on."

"Moving on while staying in Lucky Harbor?"

"Yes," she said, admitting her newfound realization. "I'm staying."

"With Ford?"

"I don't know," Tara said honestly.

Logan laughed, and in it was a wistfulness and vulnerability she hadn't expected. "*I* know," he said softly.

Chapter 26

*"Never do anything that you don't want
to have to explain to 9-1-1 personnel."*
TARA DANIELS

Tara left Logan's hospital room and went looking for
her next most pressing problem. When she heard Mia's
voice, she slowed her pace. Peeking in the door, she found
Mia sitting in a chair by Ford's bed.

All she could see of Ford was a set of long legs, one casted.
Still standing out of sight behind the curtain, Tara smiled in
spite of herself. They were playing cards. Blackjack.

"Hit me," Ford said.

Mia dealt him a card.

"Hit me," he said.

Mia obliged again.

"Hit me."

"Um," Mia said hesitantly. "You have thirty-six."

Ford blinked blearily at his cards. "You sure?"

"Wow." Mia giggled. "They must have given you
some good stuff, huh, Dad?"

Ford went still and stared her. "Did you just—"

"Yeah," Mia said softly. "Weird?"

"Yes." He smiled at her dopily. "The absolutely *best* kind of weird. You should probably ask me all my secrets now. I'm mush *and* high. I'll sing like a canary."

Mia grinned. "What kind of secrets do you have?"

"Deep, dark ones."

"Like?"

"Like how I watch *Hell's Kitchen*. Shh," he said, bringing a finger to his lips and nearly taking out an eye. "And I change the locks at the bar just to mess with Jax's head. Oh, and I push Tara's buttons cuz I like it when she gets all pissy."

Mia laughed. "You really *are* high. Make me understand why you two aren't a thing again?"

"Me and Jax? He's engaged to someone else now, so..."

"You know I mean Tara," she said, still laughing.

Ford looked at his cards as if they might hold the answer.

"Come on, it's not that tough a question."

"Yes, it is. And didn't I tell you all this already?"

"No, actually," Mia said. "You never have. Tara did. Well, kind of. But not you."

Standing in the doorway, still half-hidden behind the privacy curtain, Tara covered her mouth with her fingers to avoid interrupting them.

"It's complicated," Ford finally said. "But that's also a bullshit answer, and I've always promised myself if I ever got the chance to know you, I wouldn't bullshit you."

He'd thought about this, Tara realized. About getting

to know Mia, being with her. He'd thought about it, and he'd wanted it.

It was to her own shame that she'd tried *not* to do the same, otherwise the guilt would have killed her a long time ago.

"I'm glad, cuz I have a highly sensitive bullshit meter," Mia said.

A half-smile curved Ford's mouth as he reached for the teen's hand. "You get that from Tara, you know. You get a lot from her. Your inner strength, your determination, your brains. All your best parts actually, they come from her, not me."

Tara pressed her free hand over her aching heart.

"So would you finally just tell me?" Mia asked softly. "Will you tell me about you two, how it was back then? You know, since you're high and all."

Ford let out a long breath. "I was bad news for her, Mia."

Tara's breath caught. Out of all the things she expected him to say, that hadn't been on the list.

"Did *she* tell you that?" Mia asked. "That you were bad for her?"

He hadn't been, Tara thought with a lump in her throat. He'd been wonderful. Exactly what she'd needed. She'd been inexperienced, but he hadn't taken advantage of her. And the truth was, she'd wanted him as badly as he'd wanted her. When she'd gotten pregnant, he'd felt guilty as hell.

It hadn't been his fault. Not all of it, anyway. There'd been *two* of them in his bed, and once he'd taught her how good their bodies could feel together, it'd been all she'd wanted to do with him.

"No," Ford said. "She never said that."

"Probably because she didn't see it that way," Mia said.

Ford shrugged, and hands still over her mouth and heart, Tara shook her head. She hadn't seen him as bad for her. Ever. She'd seen past his roughness, the tough exterior, to the caring, warm boy beneath.

"It wasn't going to happen," Ford said. "Us. I couldn't have taken care of her any more than I could have taken care of you, no matter how much I wanted to. Truth is, she was made for better things than being stuck with me in this small town that she hated."

"What about love?" Mia asked. "If you loved each other—"

"We were seventeen," Ford said gently. "We didn't know real love."

Mia made a sound that said she disagreed. Vehemently. But still out of view, Tara nodded in understanding. Maybe she would have said they'd been at least a *little* in love, but she wouldn't judge him. She was the last person to judge.

"Okay," Mia said. "So Tara left, and you... what? You just let her go?"

She sounded so disappointed, and Ford laughed softly without mirth. "God, you really did get so much from her." He paused. "Yeah, I let her go. She wasn't happy with me over that. It took nearly six months of her being back in Lucky Harbor before she'd even talk to me."

"She was mad at you for letting her walk away?"

"Oh, yeah. And I deserved that."

"But you did it out of love!" the romantic Mia said dramatically. "You thought she deserved better."

"It wasn't all altruistic," he admitted. "I've tended to

go the easy route. And Tara doesn't know the meaning of
the word easy."

He sounded...proud, Tara thought. Proud of her.

"And what about now?" Mia wanted to know. "Now
that you're both older and together in the same place, it
might end differently. Right?"

The ache deepened, spreading through Tara's entire
chest as a nurse brushed past her and in the room. "Okay,
Mr. Walker," she called out. "You've been cleared and
released. You're free to go if you have someone to help
you home."

Tara stepped into the room as well, and raised her
hand. "That would be me."

Ford's eyes locked with hers. "Sawyer could—"

"It was my tree," she said, oddly loath to let anyone
else help him. "It's the least I can do."

Ford took up the entire backseat of Tara's car with his
stretched-out leg, leaving the front seat for Logan, which
he gleefully took.

Sawyer picked up Mia and Chloe. He offered to take
Ford as well, but Tara was still unwilling to part with him
and used the excuse that he was already loaded in her car.
She got behind the wheel, and nervous with both Ford
and Logan watching her, took the first turn a little rough,
nearly dumping Ford to the floor.

Logan smirked and eyed Ford in the rearview mirror.
"Got to lean into the turns, Mariner Man. Learn to use
your body."

Ford gritted his teeth. "I know how to use my body
just fine."

"So do I. Tell him, Tara."

Tara glared at Logan. "Don't you make me stop this car. Because I totally will."

Unrepentant, Logan shrugged. Tara went out of her way to drop him off first. When she pulled up to his rented beach cottage, he slumped in the seat. "Hey. Why do *I* have to go home first?"

"Because you're the one most likely to be strangled," she said. "By me."

At that, Ford stopped scowling in the backseat and sat up a little straighter.

"Fine," Logan said. "But I need you to walk me in."

"Why?"

"Maybe I'm dizzy from the meds."

"Cortisone makes you dizzy?"

He lifted his chin. "Yes, for your information, it does. I feel a little sick, too. I almost died, you know."

Tara sighed, threw the car into park, and looked into the rearview mirror at Ford. "Wait here."

"Right," he muttered. "Because I might leap out of the car and make a run for it."

Logan smiled evilly.

Ford flipped him off.

"Let's go," Tara said tightly to her ex. "Behave," she said to Ford.

His expression told her that she shouldn't count on it. She walked Logan up the porch. Sandy was there waiting for him, looking cute and perky.

"Oh, you poor baby!" she said, rising to her feet and moving to Logan's side. "I heard all about it. Are you okay?"

Of course, Logan played it up. "Well, it was touch and go there for a while." He shuddered. "But I'm going to make it."

Sandy fussed all over him. "Let me help you inside."

"Good idea," Logan said, setting his head on her shoulder. "Nearly dying from anaphylactic shock is exhausting."

Tara rolled her eyes so hard that they nearly popped right out of her head.

Paying Tara no attention, Sandy slipped her arm around Logan. "Are you really okay now? What can I do for you? Anything, just name it."

"Oh, darlin', that's so sweet, but really, don't worry about little ol' me."

"Don't be silly," Sandy exclaimed. "You need some serious TLC."

"Maybe you're right," Logan murmured, leaning into her some more, sighing in pleasure.

Tara shook her head. "I assume you're in good hands," she said dryly.

"Yes." This from Sandy. "I'll take care of him from here."

Tara got back in her car and glanced at Ford. "To your house or boat?"

"House," he said morosely, jaw dark with the day's growth, eyes hooded. "I can't maneuver enough to get around on the boat."

Fifteen minutes later, Tara got patient number two settled on his couch, his leg elevated on the coffee table. His crutches, water, snacks, and the remote were all within reach. She'd also given him two pain pills.

He looked miserable, and she melted. "How bad are you hurting?"

He didn't answer. Shifting behind him, she began to rub the knots out of his shoulders. "Better?"

He gave a little grunt of affirmation so she kept at it until the knots loosened and he finally relaxed. "Thanks," he said gruffly.

She didn't want to take her hands off all his gorgeous muscles but she had limits, and jumping his bones when he was on drugs and hurting was one of them.

Probably.

"You'll get used to the crutches," she said, hoping that it was true. "But until you do, we'll all take shifts here to make sure you have what you need."

"I have what I need." He grabbed her hand when she tried to move away. "My own private nurse."

She laughed. "I was a nurse once for Halloween, but you should know, I'm not all that good at it in real life."

"I bet you made a really hot nurse." His eyes went a little glossy as he thought about it. "You and a short short, little white uniform, with white lacy thigh-highs and a devastatingly tiny thong. Or no thong. Yeah, no thong at all."

"You've given this some thought," she said, amused. And also a little turned on to be the center of his fantasies.

"I have a very active imagination." He looked at her, no humor in his face when he said, "Something became clear to me today when I thought I was going to die."

"Ford, you fell out of a tree and broke your leg. You were never going to die."

"Could have," he insisted.

"Did I give you too many of the happy pills?" she asked, checking the bottle. "Maybe the hospital meant for me to wait until morning to dose you again." Shaking her head, she took a long pull from his soda.

He smiled. "I love you, you know. Probably, you should just marry me."

Tara inhaled soda up her nose and choked for air as she wheezed and gaped at him.

"You okay?"

"I will be," she managed through a raw throat. "When the shooting pains down my left arm go away." She drew in a ragged breath. "What did you just say to me?"

"I want to do it right this time with you," he said. "I want to get married. No more stupid Facebook, no more Logan, no more what-are-we-doing-with-each-other shit, and no more bad endings. Just you and me, and a piece of paper to make it official."

She stared at him some more, then picked up the pills again. "Okay, seriously. *What did I give you*?"

With a deceptive laziness, Ford snagged her hand and tugged her on top of him.

"Careful," she gasped. "Your leg—"

"Is fine. Since you aren't in the mood to discuss getting married, there's something else you can do."

"What?"

"Kiss it and make it better."

He was crazy. *She* was crazy. "Ford—"

"*Please*, Nurse Daniels?"

She let out a breath, then cupped his face. It was lined with exhaustion and drawn with pain. He was beautiful.

She leaned in and kissed him softly on first one rough cheek, and then went for the other; but he turned his head and caught his mouth with hers, kissing her hard and deep.

"Better?" she asked breathlessly a long moment later.

"No," he said very solemnly. "More."

"Ford, about..." The marriage proposal. Had he meant to say it? Did he even remember saying it? She looked into his eyes and had no idea how to bring it back up. "When you—"

From within her purse, her cell phone rang with insistence.

"Maybe Logan's gotten stung again," Ford said hopefully as Tara dug the phone out.

"Hey," Chloe said when Tara answered. "Our guests want to know if they could pay you to make them a dinner basket to go. They want to watch the sun set somewhere with a picnic."

Tara was standing between the couch and the coffee table, her legs bumping into Ford's uncasted one. "Uh..." She nearly jumped out of her skin when a big, warm hand slid up the back of her calf. "Sure. But—"

Ford's warm, determined fingers headed north and her brain stuttered.

"They want wine, too," Chloe said. "Do we have what you need for them?"

Ford palmed Tara's ass. Squeezed.

"Um..." she said, closing her eyes when Ford groaned softly at the feel of her.

"I know it's a bad time," Chloe told her sympathetically. "And that you have your hands full."

Actually, it was *Ford* who had his hands full. He slipped beneath her panties now, and she trembled as she smacked at his wayward hand.

The wayward hand was not deterred.

"Hang up," Ford said.

"*Shh.*"

"Hey." Chloe sounded insulted. "I'm just passing the information on here."

"No, not you." Tara bit her lip to hold back her gasp when Ford slid his uncasted leg between hers, forcing her feet into a wider stance. "Oh, God."

"What the hell are you doing?" Chloe asked suspiciously. "You sound like you're running a marathon."

"I'll make the dinner," Tara managed. "Anything else?"

"Yes, lots else," Ford whispered. "Hang up first."

"Well," Clueless Chloe said in her ear, "I get the feeling that this is going to be one of those meaningful Hallmark moments for our guests, so I thought we could also do up a really nice basket with some of my—"

Ford nipped the back of Tara's thigh to get her attention.

He had it.

She gave him a push to the chest to slow him down, but he was a man on a mission. A quick tug, and her panties hit the floor.

He was nothing if not resourceful.

"Your leg," she hissed, then bit back her moan when he lightly stroked right over ground zero.

"Not going to use my leg," he said.

Good grief.

"...*Hellllooooo*?" Chloe said. "When will you be back?" There was something new in her voice now. Definitely still suspicion, but with a big dose of humor now, too. "After you've taken care of Ford?"

"Yes. *No.* I have to go," Tara said, desperate to get off the phone before she got off in Ford's hands. He already had her halfway there. "I'll be there to get the dinner together."

"Okay, but fair warning—Maddie's going to be coming by there with some stuff for Ford so he can manage better on his own. Jax is with her."

"'Kay, gotta go." Tara dropped the phone and tried to remember why this was a bad idea.

She couldn't come up with one reason. "Maddie's going to come."

"No, I called Jax when you were in the kitchen and told him I was fine." His voice was thick with arousal. "But you. You're going to come, Tara. You're going to come hard."

"Ford. We can't...*you* can't..." She shook her head, hoping he'd see reason.

But he was most unhelpful in that regard. He'd produced a condom from God knew where and tugged her down to straddle him. He was wearing basketball shorts that Sawyer had brought for him at the hospital, which meant easy access. With a single thrust of his hips, he drove into her, pushing her to sweet ecstasy. He murmured something in her ear, something soft and sexy, but she couldn't hear it over the roaring of her own blood as he hurled her toward climax.

"Careful of your leg," she gasped.

"It's not my leg you should be worried about."

Oh boy. He was right. As she flew over the edge, her heart and soul shattering in tandem, she heard herself cry out his name. And the very last thing on her mind was his leg.

Chapter 27

*"It's frustrating when you know all the answers,
but nobody bothers to ask you the questions."*
TARA DANIELS

Touching Tara kept the leg pain from hitting the circuits
in Ford's brain. There was only room for one sensation at
a time, and his hunger for her won out.

That worked for him. *She* worked for him. He couldn't
get enough. He had no idea how it was that he was lucky
enough to have her with him here, but since he'd made a
lifelong habit of not questioning things, he just accepted
it. Accepted that she'd once again worked her way into
his heart and made herself right at home.

For good this time. He knew that much.

They were still both breathing unsteadily, sweaty and
tangled. He stroked a hand down her back, and she practically purred. He could hear his phone vibrating from
the pocket of his shorts, but with his hands full of warm,
sated woman, he couldn't give a shit.

"Are you okay?" Tara murmured.

"I just came so hard my eyes rolled back in my head. I'm so okay I can't believe it."

"I meant your leg." She slipped out of his arms. "But good to know where you're at."

"And where's that?"

"Mellow from the great sex," she said, looking around for her clothes. "Or maybe it's the drugs."

"No, pretty sure it's you," he said mildly. "And I hate to disagree with a very gorgeous, very naked lady, but that was more than sex."

Someone knocked at the door. Tara clutched her dress to her chest and peeked stealthily out the window. "*Sawyer*," she hissed, bending over for her underwear, giving Ford a world-class view.

"So," he said, getting hard again. "I guess the question is—how much more than sex was that?"

She stopped in the act of buttoning her dress. "What?"

"If you ask me, I'd say it was *way* more than just sex. But 'way' probably isn't an apt descriptive adjective."

Tara stared at him. "And maybe our definitions of 'way' are different."

"Dilemma," he agreed. "Maybe you should just tell me in your own words."

"Now? With Sawyer at the door?"

"That'd be great," he said with relief, pulling up the basketball shorts and adjusting himself since round two was apparently not in the cards. Fucking Sawyer.

"I'm going to need more time than we have available," Tara said.

"Really? You couldn't just say 'it's a fucking boatload more than just sex, Ford, thanks for asking'?"

She shoved her feet into her heels. "Did you hit your head when you fell?"

He caught her with his crutch and reeled her down to the couch next to him, ignoring Sawyer's next knock. "Stop waiting for me to let you walk away."

She eyed him speculatively. "What should I do instead?"

Fair question, he supposed. "How about we give each other everything we can, and not blame each other for what we can't?"

"That didn't work out for us before."

"Because you left without looking back," he pointed out.

"I had a problem, if you'll remember. I was pregnant."

"*We* had a problem," he said.

Sawyer knocked again, less politely this time. "Ignore him," Ford said.

"I don't run anymore," Tara said quietly. "I stay and fight."

"Well, good. Because—"

The front door opened, and Sawyer stood there looking pissed off. "Okay. When you're alive," he told Ford, "you pick up your damn phone and answer your damn door." He took in the two of them squared off on the couch, nose to nose, with Ford half dressed and Tara looking uncharacteristically mussed up. "Need a moment?"

"No," Tara said.

"Yes," Ford said, holding firm to Tara so she couldn't bail, because if he had to chase her he was going to lose and that would be embarrassing.

Without a word, Sawyer vanished into the kitchen,

and they heard him foraging around in the cupboards, no doubt planning on eating Ford out of house and home.

Ford looked at Tara. "Stay and fight then," he said. "For us."

She looked at him with a mixture of anxiety and hope. "While giving everything I can and not blaming you for what I can't?" she asked softly.

"That's right." He liked the look on her face, the one that said she was tempted.

"I like to analyze things," she warned him. "Obsess. Think too much."

"No," he said straightfaced. "Not you."

"I'm serious."

He smiled. "Yes, I know. Look, I'm sure I'll give you *plenty* to analyze and obsess over. Let's start now. I have certain parts that need analyzing and obsessing."

"Sawyer's in the kitchen!" she hissed.

"He won't listen." Ford yawned, fighting against the sudden weight of his eyelids. "Or he'll pretend not to, at least."

"Your meds are making you sleepy." She sounded concerned.

"No they're not." Yes, they were. But he didn't care. He wanted her again. And then again. Maybe she'd do all the work this time, just this once. He'd owe her. He was good for it.

"Ford, I listened to what you told Mia at the hospital."

"I know. I saw your heels beneath the curtain. So you know that I like to change the locks on Jax."

"And that you think you were bad news for me. Or that I was made for better things than being stuck with you in a town I hated." Her voice shook. "I never felt that way, Ford. Ever." She shook her head. "You were very important to me. You were my best friend. I just didn't know how to be *your* best friend. I didn't know how to give myself. I didn't learn that for a long time. When I got married to Logan, I *still* didn't know, and I went the other way and gave too much. I'm only now learning the happy medium."

Tenderness filled him. "I know," he said gently. "And you've seemed happier lately than I've ever seen you."

"Yes. That's because of you."

"Me?"

Tara smiled. "You." She kissed him, then hopped up, pulling her hair into some complicated twist. "I have to go. Our guests at the inn need me to get a picnic dinner together." Turning back to him, she was all put together again—cool and calm and gorgeous.

His.

He hoped.

"Ford?"

"Hmm?" he said, or he thought he did. He felt her come closer and smiled. "You smell good."

"I love you," she whispered.

Emotion burst through him, and he closed his eyes for a second to absorb it. He could hear her moving around as if she was at home. He liked that. A lot. Liked watching her. But then he realized he wasn't watching her; he was looking at the backs of his eyelids.

Huh. By the time he forced his eyes open, he was alone. "Tara?"

"Not exactly. But I can put on a Southern accent and get all pissy and bossy if you want."

Sawyer.

Ford looked around. He was still on the couch. Sawyer was leaning back in a chair eating chips and watching TV, his boots on the arm of the couch near Ford's face.

Ford shoved them. "What happened?"

"You needed a time-out," Sawyer said.

"Tara?"

"Gone." Sawyer cocked his head. "You're not firing on all cylinders."

No shit. Tara was gone, and Ford wasn't sure if he'd really heard what he wanted to hear—what he'd wanted to hear for a very long time—or if he'd just dreamed it. "Did she say . . . ?"

"Say what?"

I love you . . . "Nothing. Forget it."

"She totally fondled you when she kissed you good-bye. You don't remember?"

"No."

Sawyer shrugged and lifted the bag to pour the last of the crumbs straight into his mouth. "Your loss. A woman like that fondles me, I remember."

Tara headed back to the inn. Although it felt as if she'd been gone all day, it had only been four hours from start to finish since she'd looked out the kitchen window in time to see Ford fall from the tree.

She never wanted to feel her heart hit her toes like that again. The run out to him had seemed to take forever, and then seeing his leg, his pain, had nearly killed her.

She thought of how she'd just left him, sated and relaxed and feeling no pain, and felt a little better. Inside the inn, she found Chloe in the sunroom, giving their guests facials. For a minute, Tara stood in the doorway watching her baby sister work, appearing both surprisingly professional and yet so sweet. Chloe had everyone laughing and smiling and completely at ease in a way that Tara could never have managed. She was still marveling over that when Chloe looked up and caught sight of her.

"Just lay back and relax now," Chloe said to their guests, and light on her feet, moved toward Tara, pushing her out into the hallway.

"Hey," Tara said. "Smells good in there."

"It's the oatmeal and honey mix in the facial. It smells delicious when it's warmed. Don't panic; I realize the inn doesn't have a license for a spa, but I'm not charging; it's a freebie. I'll make sure to have Maddie start applying for the right licenses before I ever think about charging anyone."

"I wasn't going to say that."

"Okay, what were you going to say? Let me have it. Or should I save you some time? Yes, I stole your heavy cream, but I replaced it this morning. It helps make the facial smooth."

"I don't mind," Tara said.

But Chloe was on a roll. "And yeah, okay, I ate the last of your Not Yo Mama's Apple Pie. But..." She flashed her poker-face smile. "You're getting sex, *great* sex by the look of you, so in all fairness, you don't need the pie, right? And I made brownies to replace it anyway. You can add them to your picnic dinner."

Tara felt a little dizzy with the quick subject changes, not to mention that this Chloe—a non-lazy, responsible Chloe—was a welcome surprise. "You did?"

"Okay, no. Mia made them. That girl most *definitely* inherited Ford's talent in the kitchen." Chloe waited a sly beat, just long enough for Tara to frown before laughing softly. "And yours, of course. Anyway, the husband's allergic to a lot of veggies, did you know that? So instead of veggie oil, Mia used applesauce, of all things. And the brownies came out *fantastic*. If I hadn't seen her do it with my own eyes, I'd have sworn you made them."

Tara shook her head. Definitely dizzy. "Chloe..."

"Yeah, yeah, yell at me for all of it later, okay? I've got to get back in there."

"No, Sugar. You don't understand." She reached for Chloe's hand. "I'm not mad at all. Are you kidding? You used your own spare time to do my job, you covered my ass, and you're making the inn a day spa on top of it? You're a lifesaver."

Chloe narrowed her eyes. "You take some of Ford's pain meds?"

"What? No!"

"You sure?"

"Yes! Chloe, I'm trying to say that I'm impressed. And that maybe I was too harsh when I said you never grew up. I shouldn't have said that."

Chloe arched a brow. "Well butter my butt and call me a biscuit. Did you almost—*almost*, mind you, but not quite—admit you were wrong about me?"

"Listen, I know I've been hard on you—"

"You were wrong," Chloe said flatly. "Say it."

Tara sighed. "Okay, fine. You're right. I was *wrong*."

"Wow. And you didn't even choke on it." Chloe grinned. "Now if only you'd get that stick extracted from your ass and admit that you're also over your head in the love department, we'd all be able to enjoy ourselves."

"My relationship with Mia is a work in progress."

"I meant Ford." Chloe leaned in and sniffed at her neck. "You smell like him, you know."

Tara felt the heat on her face. "You should probably get back to the guests."

With a soft, knowing laugh, Chloe headed into the sunroom. Tara blew out a breath and moved into the kitchen to get the picnic dinner together. She was planning on ham pinwheel sandwiches with brie, herbs, and nuts. She was going to call them Pigs-in-a-Wheel Delectables.

Mia came in and silently began chopping the herbs and nuts. Tara felt a little burst of pride and affection fill her. They really did work well as a team. She smiled, then felt her smile congeal when she caught a good look at Mia's face. "You've been crying."

"No." Even as Mia said it, her eyes filled. She sniffed and swiped angrily at her eyes. "I'm not crying." And then she burst into tears.

Crap. Shit. Damn. Tara very gently took the knife out of Mia's fingers as the teen babbled something in a long watery string. The only words that Tara caught were "stupid ass," "thinks he knows what's best," and "going to hunt him down."

Tara nudged the knife farther out of their way and risked both her heart and the silk of her dress by hugging Mia in close.

Mia slumped against her. "H-he said that when the s-summer's over and I go to S-Spain, we won't see each other anymore. *Ever.*"

Ah. Carlos. "Well, Spain's pretty far away and expensive to get to, but I'm sure when you're back in Seattle, you'll—"

"No, it's not the distance. He says that he'll hold me back. That I need to go and have the whole college experience. He thinks it's unrealistic to expect…he says it's easier to break clean now. Like ripping off a Band-Aid."

"And you said…"

"I said that's the *stupidest* thing I've ever heard! That he's just a big chickenshit! That if he loved me, it wouldn't matter how far away I was; we'd make it work."

Oh God, the irony, Tara thought. "Maybe he's trying to protect you. Maybe he wants to make sure you get everything you deserve out of life. And the only way he thinks he can make sure you do that is to push you away."

"Well, that's just stupid," Mia cried. "I'll get what I want out of life on my own. It's not up to him to get it for me, or to make my decisions."

Tara hugged her as the girl sobbed with the abandon of a despairing teenager. God knew Tara herself had cried buckets when she'd been this age, but then again, she'd been in a different situation.

Sort of.

She thought about Carlos trying to protect Mia and felt her heart squeeze for him. For the selflessness…

And then closed her eyes as her heart nearly stopped beating. Back in Ford's hospital room, when she'd been eavesdropping on him and Mia, all the reasons he'd given their daughter for the two of them not being together—they'd all been for Tara.

To protect *her*.

His answer was like a knife to Tara's gut. His unselfish answer. She'd accused him of letting her go because he hadn't cared enough, but that hadn't been it at all. He'd let her go, thinking she deserved better.

What was it that she'd told Mia way back when? That she'd never spent any time in a small town, that she was used to more...God. All her reasons for leaving Lucky Harbor had been about herself.

She was made for better things than being stuck with me, Ford had said.

Carlos was doing the same thing, cutting off what he wanted and yearned for in order to give Mia the life he thought she deserved. Because in his eyes, she deserved more, not realizing that he deserved it, too.

She thought of Ford and physically ached. Because what about now? They were no longer seventeen, and she could decide for herself what she wanted, what she deserved.

What they both deserved.

How about we give each other everything we can and not blame each other for what we can't, he'd said. She'd assumed he'd been talking about himself, that he didn't want her to blame him for what he couldn't give.

But he'd meant her, she realized. He wouldn't blame *her* for what she couldn't give.

Tara waited until Mia was reduced to hiccups before offering her a kitchen towel to mop her face.

"Mascara check," Mia said, lifting her raccoon eyes to Tara's. "Am I a wreck?"

Tara took back the kitchen towel and swiped beneath Mia's eyes herself. "You're beautiful."

There was a knock at the back door. Carlos stood there wearing his baggy jeans and tight T-shirt, piercings glinting, eyes hooded, holding a case of cranberry juice. "Jax sent me over with this from the bar. They got a double shipment. He thought you might get use out of them." He glanced at Mia, and his mouth went grim. "You've been crying."

"Yes," Mia said. "It's what happens when a stupid guy dumps me."

Still holding the case of juice, he grimaced in misery.

Tara pulled Carlos the rest of the way into the kitchen. "Could you load that into the pantry?" She turned to Mia. "He'll need your help."

Mia looked surprised. "But the other day you said I couldn't be alone with him in the pantry except over your dead body."

"You have three minutes," Tara told her. "And if you don't emerge exactly as you are, there *will* be a dead body—just not mine. Take it or leave it."

Mia was staring at Carlos. "Take it," she said softly.

Tara watched Carlos wait for Mia to go ahead of him before he looked back at Tara.

"There's always a way to make things work," she told him quietly. "If you want it bad enough."

He nodded and followed Mia into the pantry.

Tara looked around at the empty but chaotic kitchen and for once realized she didn't feel an ounce of the usual panic and anxiety over the mess. Instead, she felt...

Utterly at home.

She stepped out the back door and drew a deep breath

of the salty air. She bent and picked a pesky weed out of the flower bed. Then she looked at her watch. Their three minutes were up. Back inside, she moved to the pantry and knocked.

No answer. Dammit. Give teenagers an inch, and they'd take a mile. She should know; she'd taken hundreds of miles when she'd been a teen. *Thousands.* "Hey," she said, knocking harder, "I wasn't kidding about the dead body."

"It's okay, Mom."

Tara whirled around, her throat locked at the word "Mom." Mia and Carlos stood there, holding hands. "Oh," she breathed, scarcely able to talk. "You called me Mom."

"Yes. Is that okay?"

"*So* okay," Tara managed. "Did you two work it out?"

"No," Mia said softly, looking at Carlos.

He looked at her right back, not smiling, but with a world of warmth in his eyes.

"We've decided to enjoy the rest of the summer," Mia said, never taking her eyes off of him. "Take it as it comes. When I leave and then come back..." She lifted a shoulder. "We'll see."

"Sounds very grown up," Tara managed, nearly losing it at the look on Carlos's face as he watched Mia. He was doing his best to be cool. Calm. Collected. She recognized the technique.

But he was hurting, and her heart ached for him. He'd wanted to rip the Band-Aid off as much for him as he had for Mia. But he'd agreed to wait, knowing the painful sting was coming eventually. Very likely, he didn't believe in good outcomes for himself. That was okay. She had a feeling that Mia believed enough for all of them. "How about helping me out in here?" she asked them.

They chopped. Sautéed. Stirred. Tasted. By the time the food was finished, Tara was red-faced and sweaty, which she knew because Mia forced her to view her own reflection in a spoon.

Mia was grinning. "You look..."

Tara stared at herself. "Like a mess. A complete mess."

"I think you're beautiful," Mia said.

That afternoon, Tara had her first real success right there in the kitchen, both with the meal *and* her time with her daughter, and she realized it was because of love.

If she cooked with love, things came out right.

So maybe if she lived with love... same thing? With love maybe she could be a real chef, a mom, a sister, a lover.

She could be anything she wanted.

She could have anything she wanted.

God, she really could. She looked at Mia. "I have to go for a few minutes. Can you man the phone?"

"Of course. Maddie and Chloe are here, too."

Tara grabbed her keys and ran outside. She had to go to Ford, had to tell him all she'd realized, but there he was in the yard, struggling out of the passenger seat of Sawyer's truck.

Chapter 28

"You haven't lived until you've loved."
TARA DANIELS

As Ford stepped clumsily out of the truck, concern and worry choked Tara, and she ran forward.

He stopped her with a single, violent shake of his head.

"Yeah, don't bother," Sawyer said over the hood. "He gets all PMS-y if you try to help."

Tara took a good look at Ford. He was pale and sweaty, and unstable on his feet. Dammit. "You need to be inside. Off your leg."

"In a minute," he said.

"Ford, please," she said. "Just wait, let me—"

"Actually," he said. "I'm done waiting. Done doing things the easy way and letting things happen as they will."

Her heart caught. "What does that mean?"

"It means this is too important to let slip away again.

You're too important." He leaned back against the truck with a low grunt of effort, eyes dark, jaw clenched. "I love you too, Tara."

She stopped breathing, and he went still. "You did say that you love me, right? Oh, Christ, don't tell me that was the drugs."

She choked out a half-laugh, half-sob and shook her head.

He stared at her. "Okay, for the poor drugged man—is that no it wasn't the drugs, or no you didn't say it?"

She swallowed hard past the lump of emotion and gave him the words that she'd previously only managed to whisper when she'd thought he'd been sleeping. "I said it."

"Good. Because I love you, too. I think I always have. I always will." One of the crutches clattered to the ground. He started to bend for it and stopped short, going from pale to green.

"*Ford.*" Tara was at his side in two seconds, slipping an arm around him as Sawyer came around the other side.

"No," Ford said, resisting them both. "Just give me a damn minute. I think...Fuck. I think I'm going to pass out now."

"Okay, that's it," Tara said and nodded at Sawyer. "Inside. Now."

"Love it when you're bossy," Ford murmured. "Especially in bed. Can we do that again soon?"

"You don't listen to me when I boss you," she said, holding onto him.

"If you get naked, I'll try. I swear."

Sawyer looked deeply pained. "Hello, I'm right here."

When he tried to steer Ford toward the inn, Ford dug in his heels.

Or heel.

"Don't," Ford grated out. "Not yet. Sawyer—"

"Let me guess. You need a minute."

"Yeah."

"Ford, you're hurting," Tara said, and just sighed when Sawyer gave in and backed away, heading to the porch.

"My pain meds wore off," Ford announced.

"I know, which is why—"

"I need to do this, Tara. I came here to do this."

"You're trying to tell me something," she said.

"Yes. Actually, I'm trying to *ask* you something. The last time I asked, you didn't take me seriously because I was high as a kite. I'm not high as a kite this time, Tara." His eyes held pain, but also warmth and affection and love.

"I know this because I've been watching the clock," he said. "Waiting."

Before she could say a word to that, her sisters and Mia, along with Carlos, came out of the inn. So did their two guests with their picnic basket. Everyone crowded onto the porch with Sawyer.

Ford looked at them and let out one low oath.

"Oh, no," Tara said, ignoring their audience as she gripped his shirt. "No more waiting. You said so. Now ask me, dammit."

He seemed surprised that she'd managed to follow his rambling logic. "Now?"

"*Now.*"

"I ask you to marry me when we're alone, and you assume I'm out of my mind and don't respond. And now

you want me to ask you while we're being stared at by..."
He paused to look at all the people on the porch.

Everyone waved.

Shaking his head, Ford waved back. "I don't even
know some of those people but the ones I do know are
probably going to mock me for the rest of my life. And
Jesus, is Chloe videotaping this?"

Chloe had her phone aimed at them. "For Facebook,"
she called out.

Tara turned her back on them. "Just do it!"

He stared at her. "You really are the most stubborn
woman on the planet."

"Yeah, yeah, I'm working on that. *Ask me*!"

"You sure do like to tell people what to do. You know
that?"

"Yes, but to be fair, I'm good at it. Ford—"

"*And* impatient," he mused. "Interrupting me when
I'm trying to outline the reasons I love you."

She blinked. "You're...you mean you love my stubborn, bossy, interrupting self?"

"Well, I'd say you were more perversely inflexible and
mule-headed, but yeah. I also love the way you drop your
*g*s like a Southern belle, and the way you talk to yourself when you're cooking. And how you think you're so
badass cool, calm, and collected, when really, if you know
what to look for, you show everything in your eyes, and
usually you're not cool, calm, or collected at all."

Her breath caught.

"Yeah," he said softly. "I know all the secrets. I love
them, too." He pressed his mouth to her temple. "I love you,
Tara. Love me back. Marry me."

She pressed her forehead to his and felt all the little pieces of her heart knit together. "Yes," she said, and the crowd on the porch erupted into cheers.

"I did that," Mia told Maddie and Chloe proudly, pointing to Ford and Tara embracing. "I totally brought them together."

Ford grinned at her, then looked down at Tara. "I even have a ring," he said. "I've had it since right after you poured me a glass of iced tea while you were serving the Garden Biddies." He lifted a shoulder. "It was wishful thinking. It's on my boat," he said and waggled a brow.

She laughed. "Are you trying to lure me back to your place?"

"Yes. Is it working?"

She thought about it for a beat. "It'll be hard."

He lowered his voice for her ears only. "I can promise you that."

"I mean I'm no picnic, Ford."

"No," he agreed, closing his eyes when she slid her arms around his waist, brushing his lips along her jaw. "But you sure taste good."

With a sigh, Tara turned her face, pressing it against his chest. He wrapped her in his arms and held on, although to be fair, she was doing most of the supporting. "How long do you figure until you fall down?" she asked.

"Maybe ten seconds."

"Sawyer!" she yelled, without taking her eyes off of her new fiancé, who cupped her face and looked deep into his eyes.

"*Forever* this time," he said as Sawyer strode toward them.

Tara sighed blissfully. "You know what this means, right?"

"I'm done guessing," he said. "Tell me."

"It means you're mine," she said. "And I'm yours. No more walking away. We are going to get it right this time."

His smile was slow and easy, and just for her. "Well, finally."

Good Morning Sunshine Casserole

Ingredients:

1 layer of tater tots

1 layer of ham or sausage cubes
(or crumbled bacon, whatever makes
your skirt blow up)

1 layer of grated cheddar cheese
(there's no such thing as too much cheese
for breakfast)

Mix the following together and pour on top:

6 beaten eggs

1/2 tsp. salt (or more, if no one's looking)

1/2 tsp. pepper

1 tsp. dry mustard

1/2 cup of chopped onion

3 cups of milk

2 tsp. Worcestershire sauce

Add 1/2 cup melted butter over all that. Shh, don't tell…

Cook 1 hour at 350 degrees uncovered.

Chloe has always been
a little bit wild.
But she may have met her match
in Sheriff Sawyer Thompson…

Please turn this page
for a preview of

Head Over Heels

Available in December 2011.

Chapter 1

*"If at first you don't succeed, destroy all
evidence that you tried."*
CHLOE TRAEGER

It wasn't often that Chloe Traeger beat her sisters into
the kitchen in the morning, but with Tara and Maddie
currently sleeping with the town's two hottest hotties, it'd
been only a matter of time.

Okay, in the name of fairness, Chloe hadn't actually
gotten to bed yet, but that was just a technicality.

With a big yawn, she started the coffee. Then gathering what she needed, she hopped up onto the counter
to rest her tired—and throbbing—legs. The quiet in
the kitchen soothed her as she mixed her ingredients
together, and she liked it. Given how loudly she lived her
life, the silence was a nice start to the day. Especially
today, which promised to get crazy quickly. Later in the
afternoon, she'd be doing her esthetician thing. Natural
skincare products were all the rage right now, and she had
nearly created an entire line that was a surprise hit. In the

past year, Chloe had made enough of a name for herself that she was in demand with select high-end spas across the country, which booked her for their clients. Today she was going to a five-star hotel in Seattle, but first she had to work here in Lucky Harbor at the B&B that she ran with her sisters.

That very grown-up thought had Chloe shaking her head and marveling. Only a year ago, she'd been free as a bird, roaming happily from spa to spa at will, with no real ties. Then she and her sisters had inherited a dilapidated, falling-down-on-its-axis beach inn, with absolutely no knowledge of what to do with it.

Hard to believe how far they'd come. They'd renovated, turned the place into a thriving B&B, and now Chloe, Tara, and Maddie were real sisters instead of strangers. Friends, even.

Well, okay, so they were still working on the friends part, but they hadn't fought all week. Progress, right? And that Chloe had been gone for four of the past seven days working in Arizona didn't count. She looked down at the organic lavender oil she'd just "borrowed" from Tara for her homeopathic antibacterial cream and winced.

Probably Chloe could work harder on the friend thing...

Yawning again, she looked out the window. Waves pounded the rocky shore in the purple light of dawn as she stirred the softened beeswax and lanolin together with the lavender oil. When Chloe was done, she carefully poured the cream into a sterile bottle. Then, still sitting on the counter, she tugged the sweats up to her thighs and began to apply the natural antiseptic to the two long gashes on each of her calves. She was still hissing in a pained breath when the back door opened.

The man who entered practically had to duck to do so. Sheriff Sawyer Thompson was in uniform, gun at his hip, expression dialed to Dirty Harry, and just looking at him had something pinging low in her belly.

He didn't appear to have the same reaction to her, of course. Nothing rippled his implacable calm or got past that tough exterior. And Chloe had to admit, the sheriff had a hell of an exterior. At six feet three inches, he was built like a linebacker. But in a stunning defiance of physics, he had a way of moving all those mouth-watering muscles with an easy, male, fluid grace that would make a fighter jealous.

Stupid muscles, Chloe thought as something deep within her tightened again from just looking at him. In the year since she'd first come to Lucky Harbor, she and the sheriff had developed a sort of uneasy truce. She did her thing; he didn't approve. But then she didn't approve of him very much either, so that seemed fair enough. And, okay, so *one* time his disapproval had concluded with her in the back of his squad car but she'd managed to overlook that. The problem now was that somehow lately whenever they'd been in close proximity, she'd reacted with a very inconvenient . . . lust.

Not that she'd be sharing *that* information with the good sheriff. No, that'd be like letting the big bad wolf in for some cookies and milk. Quickly yanking down her sweatpants to hide her injuries, she shot him the most professional smile in her repertoire. "Sheriff," she said smoothly.

The guarded expression that he wore as purposefully as he did the gun at his hip slipped for a single beat. "Chloe."

At his tone, her smile turned genuine. She couldn't help it. She'd just achieved what few could, she'd knocked that blank expression right off his face. She knew that was because he hadn't been expecting her. It was usually Tara who made the coffee every morning, coffee so amazing that Sawyer routinely stopped by on his way to the station.

"Tara's not out of Ford's bed yet," she said.

This made him grimace. Apparently the vision of his best friend and Chloe's sister in bed didn't work for him. Or more likely, it was Chloe's bluntness that bothered him, which in turn pleased her quite a bit.

Recovering, he strode to the coffee maker, his gait oddly measured, as if he was as tired-to-the-bone as she.

The police and sheriff departments played weekly baseball games against the firefighters and paramedics, and they'd had one last night. Maybe he'd played too hard. Maybe he'd had a hot date after. Given how women drivers tried to get pulled over by him just to get face time, it was possible. After all, according to Lucky Harbor's Facebook page, phone calls to the county dispatch made by females between the ages of twenty-one and forty went up substantially whenever Sawyer was on duty.

His utility belt gleamed in the bright overhead light as he moved to the coffee pot. His uniform shirt was wrinkled in the back and damp with sweat. She was wondering about that when he turned to her, gesturing to the pot with the question in his eyes.

Heaven forbid the man waste a single word. "Help yourself," she said. "I just made it."

That made him pause. "You poison it?"

She smiled.

With a small head shake, Sawyer reached into the cupboard for the to-go mugs Tara kept there for him.

"You're feeling brave then," Chloe said.

He lifted a broad-as-a-mountain shoulder as he poured, then pointed to her own mug steaming on the counter at her side. "You're drinking it." He leaned his big frame against the counter to study her. Quiet. Speculative.

Undoubtedly, people caved when he did this, rushing to fill the silence. But silence had never bothered Chloe. No, what bothered her was the way she felt when he looked at her like that. For one thing, his eyes were mesmerizing. They were the color of melting milk chocolate when he was amused, but when he was quiet, like now, the tiny gold flecks in them sparked like fire. His hair was brown too, the sort that contained every hue under the sun and could never be replicated in a salon. At the moment, it was on the wrong side of his last cut and in a state of dishevelment, falling over his forehead in front and nearly to his collar in back. The lines in his face were drawn tight with exhaustion, and she realized that he probably hadn't been headed *in* for his shift as she'd assumed, but finishing one. Which meant that he'd been out all night too, fighting crime like a superhero.

And yet somehow, he still managed to smell good. Guy good. She didn't understand it, but everything about him reminded her that she was a woman. And that she hadn't had sex in far too long. "Seems a little early even for you," she said.

"Could say the same for you."

Something in his voice caused a little niggle of suspicion. "Got a lot of things to mix up for the day spa I'm running later."

His eyes never wavered from hers. "Or …?"

Crap. Crap, he was onto her, and nerves quivered in her belly. "Or what?" she asked casually, shifting to get down off the counter.

Sawyer moved before she could, blocking her escape.

"Romantic," she said dryly, even as her heart began to pound. His hips wedged between her legs, one hand on her thigh, the other on her opposite ankle, holding her in place. "Don't I even get breakfast first?"

"You're bleeding through your sweatpants." He shoved the sweats back up her legs to her knees, careful to avoid the wounds. His eyes fixed on the deep gashes.

She tried to pull free, but he tightened his grip on her thigh. "Hold still." He looked over the injuries, expression grim. "Explain."

"Um, I fell getting out of bed?"

He lifted his head and pinned her with his sharp gaze. "Try again, without the question mark."

"I fell hiking."

"Yeah, and I have some swamp land to sell you."

"Hey, I could be telling the truth."

"You don't hike, Chloe. It aggravates your asthma."

Actually, as it turned out, *living* aggravated her asthma.

Sawyer bent to look more closely, pushing her hand

away when she tried to block his view. "Steel," he said. "Steel fencing, I'm guessing. Probably rusted."

Her heart stopped. He knew. It seemed impossible, she'd been so careful, but *he knew*.

"You need a tetanus shot." He straightened, but didn't move from between her legs or let her go. "And a keeper," he added tightly. "Where are the dogs, Chloe?"

"I don't know what you're talking about." Except that she did. She knew because she'd spent long hours the night before with her best friend Lance, procuring the very two dogs he'd just mentioned.

AKA stealing them.

But in her defense, it had been a matter of life and death. The young pit bulls belonged to a guy named Nick Raybo, who'd planned on fighting them for sport. What Chloe and Lance had done had undoubtedly saved the dogs' lives, but also had been good-old-fashioned breaking and entering. And since B&E wasn't legal...

Sawyer waited her out, and for the record, he was good at it. As big and bad as he was, he had more patience than Job, a result no doubt of his years behind the badge and hearing every outrageous story under the sun. And like probably thousands before her, Chloe caved like a cheap suitcase. "The dogs are with Lance."

He stared at her for one stunned beat. "Jesus, Chloe."

"They were going to die!"

His expression still said one-hundred-percent cop but there was a very slight softening. "You should have called me," he said.

Maybe, she thought. "And you would have done what? They hadn't begun the fighting yet, so you couldn't have taken the dogs off the property. And they were going to fight them tonight, Sawyer." Even now it made her feel sick. "They were going to pit them against each other, to the death."

Her voice cracked a little but he didn't comment on that as he once again bent his head and studied the gouges on her legs. He'd been right about how she'd gotten them—it had happened when she'd crawled beneath the fence behind Lance as they'd made their escape. She held her breath, not knowing what he'd do. Sawyer could arrest her, certainly. But he didn't reach for his cuffs or cite her Miranda rights. "These are deep," was all he said.

She let out a breath. "They're not so bad."

"You clean them out?" He ran a long, callused finger down her calf alongside one particularly nasty gash, and she shivered. Not from pain. Maybe it was her exhaustion, or hell, maybe it was just from having him stand so close, but the stoic, tough-guy thing was really doing it for her. He was, after all, a little on edge and sweaty, and a whole lot hot and sexy, and utterly without her permission, her brain began to play a "Stern Cop And The Bad Girl" fantasy . . .

"Chloe."

She blinked. "Yeah?"

His expression a little wary now, he repeated himself. "Did you clean these out?"

"Yes, sir."

He slid her a look, and she smiled innocently, but clearly she needed to have her hormone levels checked when she got her tetanus booster because she was *way* too aware of the heat and strength of him emanating through his uniform, not to mention the matching heat washing through her. Which was especially annoying because she had a personal decree that she *never* dated uptight, unbending men, particularly ones with badges. "Also, I just mixed up some natural antibiotic cream and used it."

The back door opened again, and Chloe nearly jumped right out of her skin. Not Sawyer. Nothing ruffled him. Hell, he probably had sex without getting ruffled.

No, she thought, glancing up into his eyes. That wasn't true. Sawyer would have no qualms about getting ruffled, and a little shiver racked her body just as Maddie walked into the kitchen, followed by her fiancé, Jax.

Maddie took one look at Sawyer wedged between her sister's thighs and stopped short so fast that Jax plowed into the back of her. "What's this?" she asked, shocked. Not that Chloe could blame her, as typically she and Sawyer didn't share space well. In fact, usually when forced into close proximity, they resembled two tigers circling each other, teeth bared.

"I'm not sure what it is," Jax said, taking in the scene. "But it looks like fun." Jax was tall, lean, and on a mission as he skirted around Maddie. He poured himself a coffee and came directly toward Chloe, reaching for the drawer beneath her right thigh. "Can you move her leg?" he asked Sawyer. "I need a spoon, man."

Mouth still agog, Maddie plopped down into a chair. She waggled a finger between Chloe and Sawyer. "So you two are...?"

"No!" Chloe said and shoved at Sawyer, who still didn't budge. The two-hundred-plus lug was bent over her left calf again—it was the worst one—his hair brushing the insides of her thighs. She told herself *not* to think about how the silky strands of his hair would feel on her bare skin, but it was too late, and she shivered again.

Sawyer looked up at her sharply. "You might actually need stitches."

With a horrified gasp, Maddie hopped up to come look. Seconds later, Chloe had her sister, her sister's fiancé, and the man she didn't quite know how to categorize at all, standing far too close, staring at her injuries. She tried to close her legs but couldn't, and tossed up her hands. "They're just scratches!"

"Oh, Chloe," Maddie murmured, concern creasing her brow. "Honey, you should have called me. What happened, and where else are you hurt?"

Sawyer's gaze ran over Chloe's entire body now, as if he could see through her sweats. A very naughty part of her brain considered telling him that the scratches went further up her legs and beyond just so he'd demand a more thorough inspection.

Bad brain. Because at just the thought, her chest tightened, and she had to reach for her inhaler. Damn the stupid asthma that always kept her slightly breathless.

And sexless. "It's nothing," she said to them. "I'm fine."

"She and Lance rescued two dogs from the McCarthy place last night," Sawyer told Maddie, ratting Chloe out as he gave Jax a light shove to back off.

"I can't believe how dangerous that was, Chloe," Maddie said, worry heavy in her voice.

Guilt tugged at Chloe. She couldn't believe how much

she'd grown to care about the two strangers that were her half-sisters, or for that matter, about Lucky Harbor and the people in it. The fact that Chloe had let down her guard enough to care at all was new.

When it had been just her and her mom, the lessons had been clear: connections weren't meant to last past the overnight camping pass. Only traditionalists let themselves get trapped by things like boring relationships or full-time jobs. The special people, like Chloe and Phoebe, were destined to spread their wings and live life fully and freely.

"Raybo is crazy," Maddie said. "It could have gotten ugly." Maddie moved to get coffee.

Chloe wished Sawyer would move too, and gave him a nudge with her foot. Actually, it might have been more like a kick. Didn't matter, he was a mountain.

"It's awfully hot in here," Maddie said and opened the window.

"It's called sexual tension," Jax said with an eyebrow wriggle in Sawyer's and Chloe's direction.

Humor from the Peanut Gallery.

Sawyer sent Jax the sort of long, level look that undoubtedly had bad guys peeing in their pants, but Jax just kept grinning. "If *I* was going to make a move on a woman like that, I'd at least have bought her breakfast first."

"That's what I said," Chloe said.

Maddie plopped into Jax's lap to cuddle up to him. "You made *plenty* of moves on me before you ever bought me breakfast."

"I'm not making moves," Sawyer said.

Maddie and Jax stared pointedly at his position between Chloe's thighs.

Lifting his hands like he'd just realized he'd been touching a live wire, Sawyer backed up. "*No* moves. And I'm going to bed now. Alone."

"You know what your problem is?" Jax asked him. "You don't know how to have fun. Haven't for a long time."

"Does this..." Sawyer pointed in the general vicinity of Chloe's lower body, "look anything like *fun* to you?"

Jax choked back a snort, and even Maddie bit her lower lip to hide a smile.

"Jesus," Sawyer said. "You know what I mean."

Chloe was pretty sure he'd meant the sorry mess she'd made of her legs, as well as the risks she'd taken last night, but she said "*hey*" anyway in token protest. Because dammit, her lower half could be lots of fun.

If she ever got to use it, that is.

THE DISH

Where authors give you the inside scoop!

♥ ♥ ♥ ♥ ♥ ♥ ♥ ♥ ♥ ♥ ♥ ♥ ♥ ♥

From the desk of Roxanne St. Claire

Dear Reader,

I know it's right out of the *Romancing The Stone* opening credits, but I do usually get a little teary when writing the final scene of a book. Maybe my heart and head are fried from months of storytelling, maybe the looming deadline gets the best of me, or maybe I just adore a good Happily Ever After and can't resist writing one that tugs at my heartstrings.

But when I wrote SHIVER OF FEAR, I admit I shed some *serious* waterworks—and not just because the hero, Marc Rossi, has found true love after never believing he could again . . . and the heroine, Devyn Sterling, is finally part of a big, happy family after a lifetime of loneliness. I was emotional because I set the scene during *La Vigilia*, also known to Italian families as The Feast of the

Seven Fishes. What better place for a happy ending than around the dining room table during a meal that has deep personal meaning for me and for most members of a big Italian clan? No, I'm not Italian by descent, but my husband is "first generation"—the son of an immigrant and, therefore, deeply entrenched in some of the country's best customs. I have no doubt that the fictional blended family that peppers the pages of The Guardian Angelinos series would embrace this time-honored tradition as we do.

No one really knows the origin of the required "seven" fishes that are served on Christmas Eve in Italian families. Some say the number reflects the seven sacraments and others believe the "fishes" represent the seven hills of Rome. It doesn't matter, because most of us go way past seven that night. From the scungilli salad to the baccala amalfi and all of the salmon, swordfish, clams, scallops, shrimp, lobster, and calamari in between . . . it's a night to celebrate the gifts of the sea and the season. I rarely make it through the evening without looking around at my loved ones, blinking back a tear of gratitude, and going back for seconds on the lobster.

During an earlier scene in SHIVER OF FEAR, I used Marc's description of the evening to highlight Devyn's aching for a family and intensify her belief that she isn't destined to have that kind of love in her life. While he takes the tradition for granted, she is left to imagine the magic of that night and the warmth that comes from celebrating with food and family. Most of the story is set in Northern Ireland, where Devyn and Marc are on a hunt to find her birth mother and discover a hornet's nest of terrorist activity along with an unexpected attraction that soon blooms into love. But when it came time to give the reader the ultimate *dolce* moment—the sweet dessert of a lifetime together—it seemed natural to set that scene on a snowy Christmas Eve with the loud, laughing, loving Angelino and Rossi families gathered to celebrate.

So, I wiped a few tears when I typed "the end" of SHIVER OF FEAR and hoped that whatever traditions my readers honor and celebrate, they can relate to the atmosphere of joy that fills a home during The Feast of the Seven Fishes. If nothing else, I'll send them all out in search of good seafood!

Best,

Roxanne St. Claire

www.roxannestclaire.com

♥ ♥ ♥ ♥ ♥ ♥ ♥ ♥ ♥ ♥ ♥ ♥ ♥ ♥ ♥

From the desk of Eileen Dreyer

Dear Reader,

Marriage of Convenience. Those three words alone will convince me to buy a book. I can't think of anything I enjoy more than a romance where two people who would never have chosen each other, find themselves having to negotiate a marriage neither one wanted. So when I had the chance to write historical romance, I knew that it wouldn't be long before I wrote a Marriage of Convenience book.

NEVER A GENTLEMAN is that book. Diccan Hilliard is known among Society as *The Perfection*. Suave, smooth, sophisticated, with a taste for only the most beautiful women, he has a keen wit and rapier tongue. The fact that he is also a member of Drake's Rakes, a group of aristocrats caught up in espionage, is a well-guarded secret. That secret, though, leads to marriage vows, when he wakes to find that his enemies have left him naked in bed with Grace Fairchild, the woman known to his friends as *The Most Notorious Virgin* in Britain.

Poor Grace. As tall as a man, painfully plain with an ungainly limp, Grace has spent her life following her father around the world with the army. She has no female accomplishments, no wish to mingle in a society that has long since shunned her, and even less desire to be shackled to a man who did not choose her, especially since she has long been fascinated by him. But Grace has secrets too. The question is, will those secrets help her gain Diccan's love, or condemn her to loneliness? And will Diccan's secrets cost them not just the chance at a lasting love, but their very lives?

Do you like Marriage of Convenience books as much as I do? What draws you to them? Let me know at my website, www.eileendreyer.com.

Enjoy!

Eileen Dreyer

♥ ♥ ♥ ♥ ♥ ♥ ♥ ♥ ♥ ♥ ♥ ♥ ♥

From the desk of Jill Shalvis

Dear Reader,

Writing a romance called THE SWEETEST THING, which centers around a decidedly *not* sweet heroine, amused me. Tara Daniels is wound a little tightly and likes things her way. She's also a former southern belle who appreciates the fact that she's right. A lot.

The Sweetest Thing? Not exactly.

But her heart's in the right place, always. And, as it turns out, there's a man who melts her like butter on a hot roll. Not only that, but he can soften her in a way that she isn't sure she likes. See, Tara thinks she has it all together, but it turns out she doesn't. She doesn't know a lot about herself. About all she has is the fact that she can cook like nobody's business. Oh, how she loves to cook.

Tara was a challenge for me because—here's where I must admit it—I got a lot of her recipes from my husband. True story. I'm married to a big guy who works with his hands and is the ultimate Alpha Man—and yet he can cook. Don't try to figure him out; it'll hurt your brain, trust me.

Good Morning Sunshine Casserole is all his. Just don't tell him I "borrowed" it and am telling the world that it's my heroine's. It would just go to his head.

Happy reading and cooking!

Jill Shalvis

www.jillshalvis.com

Find out more about Forever Romance!

Visit us at
www.hachettebookgroup.com/publishing_forever.aspx

Find us on Facebook
http://www.facebook.com/ForeverRomance

Follow us on Twitter
http://twitter.com/ForeverRomance

NEW AND UPCOMING TITLES

Each month we feature our new titles
and reader favorites.

CONTESTS AND GIVEAWAYS

We give away galleys, autographed copies,
and all kinds of exclusive items.

AUTHOR INFO

You'll find bios, articles, and links to personal websites
for all your favorite authors—and so much more.

GET SOCIAL

Connect with your favorite authors, editors, and
other Forever fans, and share what's important to you.

THE BUZZ

Sign up for our monthly romance newsletter,
and be the first to read all about it.

VISIT US ONLINE

@ WWW.HACHETTEBOOKGROUP.COM.

AT THE HACHETTE BOOK GROUP WEB SITE YOU'LL FIND: